2018年度天津工业大学学位与研究生教育改革项目“文学专题研究教材建设”（编号Y20180304）

2021年度国家社科基金后期资助项目“多元视角下的古罗马作家卢奇安”（编号21FWWB027）

知库

文学与艺术

文学专题研究

牛红英 编

吉林大学出版社
·长春·

图书在版编目（CIP）数据

文学专题研究 / 牛红英编 .— 长春：吉林大学出版社，2022.10

ISBN 978-7-5768-0782-0

Ⅰ.①文… Ⅱ.①牛… Ⅲ.①世界文学—文学研究 Ⅳ.① I106

中国版本图书馆 CIP 数据核字（2022）第 192411 号

书　　名　文学专题研究
　　　　　WENXUE ZHUANTI YANJIU

作　　者　牛红英
策划编辑　李潇潇
责任编辑　刘　丹
责任校对　邹燕妮
装帧设计　中联华文
出版发行　吉林大学出版社
社　　址　长春市人民大街 4059 号
邮政编码　130021
发行电话　0431-89580028/29/21
网　　址　http://www.jlup.com.cn
电子邮箱　jldxcbs@sina.com
印　　刷　三河市华东印刷有限公司
开　　本　710mm × 1000mm　1/16
印　　张　18
字　　数　280 千字
版　　次　2023 年 1 月第 1 版
印　　次　2023 年 1 月第 1 次
书　　号　ISBN 978-7-5768-0782-0
定　　价　98.00 元

CONTENTS

Monograph One　Literature and Mythology

I　The Aeneid

(Excerpt)

Virgil (70 BC-19 BC)

translated into English by John Dryden (1631–1700)

Arms, and the man I sing, who, forc'd by fate,
And haughty Juno's unrelenting hate,
Expell'd and exil'd, left the Trojan shore.
Long labors, both by sea and land, he bore,
And in the doubtful war, before he won
The Latian realm, and built the destin'd town;
His banish'd gods restor'd to rites divine,
And settled sure succession in his line,
From whence the race of Alban fathers come,
And the long glories of majestic Rome.

O Muse! The causes and the crimes relate;
What goddess was provok'd, and whence her hate;
For what offense the Queen of Heav'n began
To persecute so brave, so just a man;

Involv'd his anxious life in endless cares,
Expos'd to wants, and hurried into wars!
Can heav'nly minds such high resentment show,
Or exercise their spite in human woe?

Against the Tiber's mouth, but far away,
An ancient town was seated on the sea;
A Tyrian colony; the people made
Stout for the war, and studious of their trade:
Carthage the name; belov'd by Juno more
Than her own Argos, or the Samian shore.
Here stood her chariot; here, if Heav'n were kind,
The seat of awful empire she design'd.
Yet she had heard an ancient rumor fly,
(Long cited by the people of the sky,)
That times to come should see the Trojan race
Her Carthage ruin, and her tow'rs deface;
Nor thus confin'd, the yoke of sov'reign sway
Should on the necks of all the nations lay.
She ponder'd this, and fear'd it was in fate;
Nor could forget the war she wag'd of late
For conqu'ring Greece against the Trojan state.
Besides, long causes working in her mind,
And secret seeds of envy, lay behind;
Deep graven in her heart the doom remain'd
Of partial Paris, and her form disdain'd;
The grace bestow'd on ravish'd Ganymed,
Electra's glories, and her injur'd bed.
Each was a cause alone; and all combin'd

To kindle vengeance in her haughty mind.
For this, far distant from the Latian coast
She drove the remnants of the Trojan host;
And sev'n long years th' unhappy wand'ring train
Were toss'd by storms, and scatter'd thro' the main.
Such time, such toil, requir'd the Roman name,
Such length of labor for so vast a frame.

Now scarce the Trojan fleet, with sails and oars,
Had left behind the fair Sicilian shores,
Ent'ring with cheerful shouts the wat'ry reign,
And plowing frothy furrows in the main;
When, lab'ring still with endless discontent,
The Queen of Heav'n did thus her fury vent:

"Then am I vanquish'd? must I yield?"said she,
"And must the Trojans reign in Italy?
So Fate will have it, and Jove adds his force;
Nor can my pow'r divert their happy course.
Could angry Pallas, with revengeful spleen,
The Grecian navy burn, and drown the men?
She, for the fault of one offending foe,
The bolts of Jove himself presum'd to throw:
With whirlwinds from beneath she toss'd the ship,
And bare expos'd the bosom of the deep;
Then, as an eagle gripes the trembling game,
The wretch, yet hissing with her father's flame,
She strongly seiz'd, and with a burning wound
Transfix'd, and naked, on a rock she bound.

But I, who walk in awful state above,
The majesty of heav'n, the sister wife of Jove,
For length of years my fruitless force employ
Against the thin remains of ruin'd Troy!
What nations now to Juno's pow'r will pray,
Or off'rings on my slighted altars lay?"

Thus rag'd the goddess; and, with fury fraught.
The restless regions of the storms she sought,
Where, in a spacious cave of living stone,
The tyrant Aeolus, from his airy throne,
With pow'r imperial curbs the struggling winds,
And sounding tempests in dark prisons binds.
This way and that th' impatient captives tend,
And, pressing for release, the mountains rend.
High in his hall th' undaunted monarch stands,
And shakes his scepter, and their rage commands;
Which did he not, their unresisted sway
Would sweep the world before them in their way;
Earth, air, and seas thro' empty space would roll,
And heav'n would fly before the driving soul.
In fear of this, the Father of the Gods
Confin'd their fury to those dark abodes,
And lock'd'em safe within, oppress'd with mountain loads;
Impos'd a king, with arbitrary sway,
To loose their fetters, or their force allay.
To whom the suppliant queen her pray'rs address'd,
And thus the tenor of her suit express'd:

"O Aeolus! For to thee the King of Heav'n
The pow'r of tempests and of winds has giv'n;
Thy force alone their fury can restrain,
And smooth the waves, or swell the troubled main-
A race of wand'ring slaves, abhorr'd by me,
With prosp'rous passage cut the Tuscan sea;
To fruitful Italy their course they steer,
And for their vanquish'd gods design new temples there.
Raise all thy winds; with night involve the skies;
Sink or disperse my fatal enemies.
Twice sev'n, the charming daughters of the main,
Around my person wait, and bear my train:
Succeed my wish, and second my design;
The fairest, Deiopeia, shall be thine,
And make thee father of a happy line."

To this the god: "'T is yours, O queen, to will
The work which duty binds me to fulfil.
These airy kingdoms, and this wide command,
Are all the presents of your bounteous hand:
Yours is my sov'reign's grace; and, as your guest,
I sit with gods at their celestial feast;
Raise tempests at your pleasure, or subdue;
Dispose of empire, which I hold from you."

He said, and hurl'd against the mountain side
His quiv'ring spear, and all the god applied.
The raging winds rush thro' the hollow wound,
And dance aloft in air, and skim along the ground;

Then, settling on the sea, the surges sweep,
Raise liquid mountains, and disclose the deep.
South, East, and West with mix'd confusion roar,
And roll the foaming billows to the shore.
The cables crack; the sailors' fearful cries
Ascend; and sable night involves the skies;
And heav'n itself is ravish'd from their eyes.
Loud peals of thunder from the poles ensue;
Then flashing fires the transient light renew;
The face of things a frightful image bears,
And present death in various forms appears.
Struck with unusual fright, the Trojan chief,
With lifted hands and eyes, invokes relief;
And, "Thrice and four times happy those," he cried,
"That under Ilian walls before their parents died!
Tydides, bravest of the Grecian train!
Why could not I by that strong arm be slain,
And lie by noble Hector on the plain,
Or great Sarpedon, in those bloody fields
Where Simois rolls the bodies and the shields
Of heroes, whose dismember'd hands yet bear
The dart aloft, and clench the pointed spear!"

Thus while the pious prince his fate bewails,
Fierce Boreas drove against his flying sails,
And rent the sheets; the raging billows rise,
And mount the tossing vessels to the skies:
Nor can the shiv'ring oars sustain the blow;
The galley gives her side, and turns her prow;

While those astern, descending down the steep,
Thro' gaping waves behold the boiling deep.
Three ships were hurried by the southern blast,
And on the secret shelves with fury cast.
Those hidden rocks th' Ausonian sailors knew:
They call'd them Altars, when they rose in view,
And show'd their spacious backs above the flood.
Three more fierce Eurus, in his angry mood,
Dash'd on the shallows of the moving sand,
And in mid ocean left them moor'd aland.
Orontes' bark, that bore the Lycian crew,
(A horrid sight!) ev'n in the hero's view,
From stem to stern by waves was overborne:
The trembling pilot, from his rudder torn,
Was headlong hurl'd; thrice round the ship was toss'd,
Then bulg'd at once, and in the deep was lost;
And here and there above the waves were seen
Arms, pictures, precious goods, and floating men.
The stoutest vessel to the storm gave way,
And suck'd thro' loosen'd planks the rushing sea.
Ilioneus was her chief: Alethes old,
Achates faithful, Abas young and bold,
Endur'd not less; their ships, with gaping seams,
Admit the deluge of the briny streams.

Meantime imperial Neptune heard the sound
Of raging billows breaking on the ground.
Displeas'd, and fearing for his wat'ry reign,
He rear'd his awful head above the main,

Serene in majesty; then roll'd his eyes
Around the space of earth, and seas, and skies.
He saw the Trojan fleet dispers'd, distress'd,
By stormy winds and wintry heav'n oppress'd.
Full well the god his sister's envy knew,
And what her aims and what her arts pursue.
He summon'd Eurus and the western blast,
And first an angry glance on both he cast;
Then thus rebuk'd: "Audacious winds! from whence
This bold attempt, this rebel insolence?
Is it for you to ravage seas and land,
Unauthoriz'd by my supreme command?
To raise such mountains on the troubled main?
Whom I- but first't is fit the billows to restrain;
And then you shall be taught obedience to my reign.
Hence! to your lord my royal mandate bear-
The realms of ocean and the fields of air
Are mine, not his. By fatal lot to me
The liquid empire fell, and trident of the sea.
His pow'r to hollow caverns is confin'd:
There let him reign, the jailer of the wind,
With hoarse commands his breathing subjects call,
And boast and bluster in his empty hall."
He spoke; and, while he spoke, he smooth'd the sea,
Dispell'd the darkness, and restor'd the day.
Cymothoe, Triton, and the sea-green train
Of beauteous nymphs, the daughters of the main,
Clear from the rocks the vessels with their hands:
The god himself with ready trident stands,

And opes the deep, and spreads the moving sands;
Then heaves them off the shoals. Where'er he guides
His finny coursers and in triumph rides,
The waves unruffle and the sea subsides.
As, when in tumults rise th' ignoble crowd,
Mad are their motions, and their tongues are loud;
And stones and brands in rattling volleys fly,
And all the rustic arms that fury can supply:
If then some grave and pious man appear,
They hush their noise, and lend a list'ning ear;
He soothes with sober words their angry mood,
And quenches their innate desire of blood:
So, when the Father of the Flood appears,
And o'er the seas his sov'reign trident rears,
Their fury falls: he skims the liquid plains,
High on his chariot, and, with loosen'd reins,
Majestic moves along, and awful peace maintains.
The weary Trojans ply their shatter'd oars
To nearest land, and make the Libyan shores.

Within a long recess there lies a bay:
An island shades it from the rolling sea,
And forms a port secure for ships to ride;
Broke by the jutting land, on either side,
In double streams the briny waters glide.
Betwixt two rows of rocks a sylvan scene
Appears above, and groves for ever green:
A grot is form'd beneath, with mossy seats,
To rest the Nereids, and exclude the heats.

Down thro' the crannies of the living walls
The crystal streams descend in murm'ring falls:
No haulsers need to bind the vessels here,
Nor bearded anchors; for no storms they fear.
Sev'n ships within this happy harbor meet,
The thin remainders of the scatter'd fleet.
The Trojans, worn with toils, and spent with woes,
Leap on the welcome land, and seek their wish'd repose.

First, good Achates, with repeated strokes
Of clashing flints, their hidden fire provokes:
Short flame succeeds; a bed of wither'd leaves
The dying sparkles in their fall receives:
Caught into life, in fiery fumes they rise,
And, fed with stronger food, invade the skies.
The Trojans, dropping wet, or stand around
The cheerful blaze, or lie along the ground:
Some dry their corn, infected with the brine,
Then grind with marbles, and prepare to dine.
Aeneas climbs the mountain's airy brow,
And takes a prospect of the seas below,
If Capys thence, or Antheus he could spy,
Or see the streamers of Caicus fly.
No vessels were in view; but, on the plain,
Three beamy stags command a lordly train
Of branching heads: the more ignoble throng
Attend their stately steps, and slowly graze along.
He stood; and, while secure they fed below,
He took the quiver and the trusty bow

Achates us'd to bear: the leaders first
He laid along, and then the vulgar pierc'd;
Nor ceas'd his arrows, till the shady plain
Sev'n mighty bodies with their blood distain.
For the sev'n ships he made an equal share,
And to the port return'd, triumphant from the war.
The jars of gen'rous wine (Acestes' gift,
When his Trinacrian shores the navy left)
He set abroach, and for the feast prepar'd,
In equal portions with the ven'son shar'd.
Thus while he dealt it round, the pious chief
With cheerful words allay'd the common grief:
"Endure, and conquer! Jove will soon dispose
To future good our past and present woes.
With me, the rocks of Scylla you have tried;
Th' inhuman Cyclops and his den defied.
What greater ills hereafter can you bear?
Resume your courage and dismiss your care,
An hour will come, with pleasure to relate
Your sorrows past, as benefits of Fate.
Thro' various hazards and events, we move
To Latium and the realms foredoom'd by Jove.
Call'd to the seat (the promise of the skies)
Where Trojan kingdoms once again may rise,
Endure the hardships of your present state;
Live, and reserve yourselves for better fate."

These words he spoke, but spoke not from his heart;
His outward smiles conceal'd his inward smart.

The jolly crew, unmindful of the past,
The quarry share, their plenteous dinner haste.
Some strip the skin; some portion out the spoil;
The limbs, yet trembling, in the caldrons boil;
Some on the fire the reeking entrails broil.
Stretch'd on the grassy turf, at ease they dine,
Restore their strength with meat, and cheer their souls with wine.
Their hunger thus appeas'd, their care attends
The doubtful fortune of their absent friends:
Alternate hopes and fears their minds possess,
Whether to deem'em dead, or in distress.
Above the rest, Aeneas mourns the fate
Of brave Orontes, and th' uncertain state
Of Gyas, Lycus, and of Amycus.
The day, but not their sorrows, ended thus.

When, from aloft, almighty Jove surveys
Earth, air, and shores, and navigable seas,
At length on Libyan realms he fix'd his eyes-
Whom, pond'ring thus on human miseries,
When Venus saw, she with a lowly look,
Not free from tears, her heav'nly sire bespoke:

"O King of Gods and Men! Whose awful hand
Disperses thunder on the seas and land,
Disposing all with absolute command;
How could my pious son thy pow'r incense?
Or what, alas! Is vanish'd Troy's offense?
Our hope of Italy not only lost,

On various seas by various tempests toss'd,
But shut from ev'ry shore, and barr'd from ev'ry coast.
You promis'd once, a progeny divine
Of Romans, rising from the Trojan line,
In after times should hold the world in awe,
And to the land and ocean give the law.
How is your doom revers'd, which eas'd my care
When Troy was ruin'd in that cruel war?
Then fates to fates I could oppose; but now,
When Fortune still pursues her former blow,
What can I hope? What worse can still succeed?
What end of labors has your will decreed?
Antenor, from the midst of Grecian hosts,
Could pass secure, and pierce th' Illyrian coasts,
Where, rolling down the steep, Timavus raves
And thro' nine channels disembogues his waves.
At length he founded Padua's happy seat,
And gave his Trojans a secure retreat;
There fix'd their arms, and there renew'd their name,
And there in quiet rules, and crown'd with fame.
But we, descended from your sacred line,
Entitled to your heav'n and rites divine,
Are banish'd earth; and, for the wrath of one,
Remov'd from Latium and the promis'd throne.
Are these our scepters? these our due rewards?
And is it thus that Jove his plighted faith regards?"

To whom the Father of th' immortal race,
Smiling with that serene indulgent face,

With which he drives the clouds and clears the skies,
First gave a holy kiss; then thus replies:

"Daughter, dismiss thy fears; to thy desire
The fates of thine are fix'd, and stand entire.
Thou shalt behold thy wish'd Lavinian walls;
And, ripe for heav'n, when fate Aeneas calls,
Then shalt thou bear him up, sublime, to me:
No councils have revers'd my firm decree.
And, lest new fears disturb thy happy state,
Know, I have search'd the mystic rolls of Fate:
Thy son (nor is th' appointed season far)
In Italy shall wage successful war,
Shall tame fierce nations in the bloody field,
And sov'reign laws impose, and cities build,
Till, after ev'ry foe subdued, the sun
Thrice thro' the signs his annual race shall run:
This is his time prefix'd. Ascanius then,
Now call'd Iulus, shall begin his reign.
He thirty rolling years the crown shall wear,
Then from Lavinium shall the seat transfer,
And, with hard labor, Alba Longa build.
The throne with his succession shall be fill'd
Three hundred circuits more: then shall be seen
Ilia the fair, a priestess and a queen,
Who, full of Mars, in time, with kindly throes,
Shall at a birth two goodly boys disclose.
The royal babes a tawny wolf shall drain:
Then Romulus his grandsire's throne shall gain,

Of martial tow'rs the founder shall become,
The people Romans call, the city Rome.
To them no bounds of empire I assign,
Nor term of years to their immortal line.
Ev'n haughty Juno, who, with endless broils,
Earth, seas, and heav'n, and Jove himself turmoils;
At length aton'd, her friendly pow'r shall join,
To cherish and advance the Trojan line.
The subject world shall Rome's dominion own,
And, prostrate, shall adore the nation of the gown.
An age is ripening in revolving fate
When Troy shall overturn the Grecian state,
And sweet revenge her conqu'ring sons shall call,
To crush the people that conspir'd her fall.
Then Caesar from the Julian stock shall rise,
Whose empire ocean, and whose fame the skies
Alone shall bound; whom, fraught with eastern spoils,
Our heav'n, the just reward of human toils,
Securely shall repay with rites divine;
And incense shall ascend before his sacred shrine.
Then dire debate and impious war shall cease,
And the stern age be soften'd into peace:
Then banish'd Faith shall once again return,
And Vestal fires in hallow'd temples burn;
And Remus with Quirinus shall sustain
The righteous laws, and fraud and force restrain.
Janus himself before his fane shall wait,
And keep the dreadful issues of his gate,
With bolts and iron bars: within remains

Imprison'd Fury, bound in brazen chains;
High on a trophy rais'd, of useless arms,
He sits, and threats the world with vain alarms."

He said, and sent Cyllenius with command
To free the ports, and ope the Punic land
To Trojan guests; lest, ignorant of fate,
The queen might force them from her town and state.
Down from the steep of heav'n Cyllenius flies,
And cleaves with all his wings the yielding skies.
Soon on the Libyan shore descends the god,
Performs his message, and displays his rod:
The surly murmurs of the people cease;
And, as the fates requir'd, they give the peace:
The queen herself suspends the rigid laws,
The Trojans pities, and protects their cause.

II Frankenstein's Creation

(Excerpt from *Frankenstein, or, The Modern Prometheus*)

Mary W. Shelley (1797–1851)

From this day natural philosophy, and particularly chemistry, in the most comprehensive sense of the term, became nearly my sole occupation. I read with ardour those works, so full of genius and discrimination, which modern inquirers have written on these subjects. I attended the lectures and cultivated the acquaintance of the men of science of the university, and I found even in M. Krempe a great deal of sound sense and real information, combined, it is true, with a repulsive physiognomy and manners, but not on that account the less valuable. In M. Waldman I found a true friend. His gentleness was never tinged by dogmatism, and his instructions were given with an air of frankness and good nature that banished every idea of pedantry. In a thousand ways he smoothed for me the path of knowledge, and made the most abstruse inquiries clear and facile to my apprehension. My application was at first fluctuating and uncertain; it gained strength as I proceeded, and soon became so ardent and eager that the stars often disappeared in the light of morning whilst I was yet engaged in my laboratory.

As I applied so closely, it may be easily conceived that my progress was rapid. My ardour was indeed the astonishment of the students, and my proficiency that of the masters. Professor Krempe often asked me, with a sly smile, how Cornelius Agrippa went on? whilst M. Waldman expressed the most heartfelt exultation in my progress. Two years passed in this manner, during which I paid no visit to Geneva, but was engaged, heart and soul, in the pursuit of some discoveries, which I hoped to make. None but those who have experienced them can conceive of the enticements of science. In other studies you go as far as others have gone before you, and there is nothing more to know; but in a scientific pursuit there is continual food for discovery and wonder. A mind of moderate capacity, which closely pursues one study, must infallibly arrive at great proficiency in that study; and I, who continually sought the attainment of one object of pursuit and was solely wrapped up in this, improved so rapidly that at the end of two years, I made some discoveries in the improvement of some chemical instruments which procured me great esteem and admiration at the university. When I had arrived at this point, and had become as well acquainted with the theory and practice of natural philosophy as depended on the lessons of any of the professors at Ingolstadt, my residence there being no longer conducive to my improvement, I thought of returning to my friends and my native town, when an incident happened that protracted my stay.

One of the phenomena which had peculiarly attracted my attention was the structure of the human frame, and, indeed, any animal endued with life. Whence, I often asked myself, did the principle of life proceed? It was a bold question, and one which has ever been considered as a mystery; yet with how many things are we upon the brink of becoming acquainted, if cowardice or carelessness did not restrain our inquiries. I revolved these circumstances in my mind, and determined thenceforth to apply myself more particularly to those branches of natural philosophy which relate to physiology. Unless I had been animated by an almost supernatural enthusiasm, my application to this study would have been irksome, and almost intolerable. To examine the causes of life, we must first have recourse to death. I became acquainted with the science of anatomy, but this was not sufficient; I must also observe the natural decay and corruption of the human body. In my education my father had taken the greatest precautions that my mind should be impressed with no supernatural horrors. I do not ever remember to have trembled at a tale of superstition, or to have feared the apparition of a spirit. Darkness had no effect upon my fancy, and a churchyard was to me merely the receptacle of bodies deprived of life, which, from being the seat of beauty and strength, had become food for the worm. Now I was led to examine the cause and progress of this decay, and forced to spend days and nights in vaults and charnel-houses. My attention was fixed upon every object the most insupportable to the delicacy of the human feelings. I saw how the fine form of man was degraded and wasted; I beheld the corruption of death succeed to the blooming cheek of life; I saw how the worm inherited the wonders of the eye and brain. I paused, examining and analysing all the minutiae of causation, as exemplified in the change from life to death, and death to life, until from the midst of this darkness a sudden light broke in upon me — a light so brilliant and wondrous, yet so simple, that while I became dizzy with the immensity of the prospect which it illustrated, I was surprised that among so many men of genius who had directed their inquiries towards the same science, that I alone should be reserved to discover so astonishing a secret.

Remember, I am not recording the vision of a madman. The sun does not more certainly shine in the heavens, than that which I now affirm is true. Some miracle might have produced it, yet the stages of the discovery were distinct and probable. After days and nights of incredible labour and fatigue, I succeeded in discovering the cause of generation and life; nay, more, I became myself capable of bestowing animation upon lifeless matter.

The astonishment which I had at first experienced on this discovery soon gave place to delight and rapture. After so much time spent in painful labour, to arrive at once at the summit of my desires was the most gratifying consummation of my toils. But this discovery was so great and overwhelming that all the steps by which I had been progressively led to it were obliterated, and I beheld only the result. What had been the study and desire of the wisest men since the creation of the world was now within my grasp. Not that, like a magic scene, it all opened upon me at once: the information I had obtained was of a nature rather to direct my endeavours so soon as I should point them towards the object of my search, than to exhibit that object already accomplished. I was like the Arabian who had been buried with the dead and found a passage to life, aided only by one glimmering and seemingly ineffectual light.

I see by your eagerness and the wonder and hope which your eyes express, my friend, that you expect to be informed of the secret with which I am acquainted; that cannot be: listen patiently until the end of my story, and you will easily perceive why I am reserved upon that subject. I will not lead you on, unguarded and ardent as I then was, to your destruction and infallible misery. Learn from me, if not by my precepts, at least by my example, how dangerous is the acquirement of knowledge and how much happier that man is who believes his native town to be the world, than he who aspires to become greater than his nature will allow.

When I found so astonishing a power placed within my hands, I hesitated a long time concerning the manner in which I should employ it. Although I possessed the capacity of bestowing animation, yet to prepare a frame for the reception of it, with all its intricacies of fibres, muscles, and veins, still remained a work of inconceivable difficulty and labour. I doubted at first whether I should attempt the creation of a being like myself, or one of simpler organisation; but my imagination was too much exalted by my first success to permit me to doubt of my ability to give life to an animal as complex and wonderful as man. The materials at present within my command hardly appeared adequate to so arduous an undertaking, but I doubted not that I should ultimately succeed. I prepared myself for a multitude of reverses; my operations might be incessantly baffled, and at last my work be imperfect, yet when I considered the improvement which every day takes place in science and mechanics, I was encouraged to hope my present attempts would at least lay the foundations of future success. Nor could I consider the magnitude and complexity of my plan as any argument of its impracticability. It was with these feelings that I began the creation of a human being. As the minuteness of the parts formed a great hindrance to my speed, I resolved, contrary to my first intention, to make the being of a gigantic stature; that is to say, about eight feet in height, and proportionably large. After having formed this determination and having spent some months in successfully collecting and arranging my materials, I began.

No one can conceive the variety of feelings which bore me onwards, like a hurricane, in the first enthusiasm of success. Life and death appeared to me ideal bounds, which I should first break through, and pour a torrent of light into our dark world. A new species would bless me as its creator and source; many happy and excellent natures would owe their being to me. No father could claim the gratitude of his child so completely as I should deserve theirs. Pursuing these reflections, I thought that if I could bestow animation upon lifeless matter, I might in process of time (although I now found it impossible) renew life where death had apparently devoted the body to corruption.

These thoughts supported my spirits, while I pursued my undertaking with unremitting ardour. My cheek had grown pale with study, and my person had become emaciated with confinement. Sometimes, on the very brink of certainty, I failed; yet still I clung to the hope which the next day or the next hour might realise. One secret which I alone possessed was the hope to which I had dedicated myself; and the moon gazed on my midnight labours, while, with unrelaxed and breathless eagerness, I pursued nature to her hiding-places. Who shall conceive the horrors of my secret toil as I dabbled among the unhallowed damps of the grave or tortured the living animal, to animate the lifeless clay? My limbs now tremble, and my eyes swim with the remembrance; but then a resistless and almost frantic impulse urged me forward; I seemed to have lost all soul or sensation but for this one pursuit. It was indeed but a passing trance, that only made me feel with renewed acuteness so soon as, the unnatural stimulus ceasing to operate, I had returned to my old habits. I collected bones from charnel-houses and disturbed, with profane fingers, the tremendous secrets of the human frame. In a solitary chamber, or rather cell, at the top of the house, and separated from all the other apartments by a gallery and staircase, I kept my workshop of filthy creation: my eye-balls were starting from their sockets in attending to the details of my employment. The dissecting room and the slaughter-house furnished many of my materials; and often did my human nature turn with loathing from my occupation, whilst, still urged on by an eagerness which perpetually increased, I brought my work near to a conclusion.

The summer months passed while I was thus engaged, heart and soul, in one pursuit. It was a most beautiful season; never did the fields bestow a more plentiful harvest, or the vines yield a more luxuriant vintage, but my eyes were insensible to the charms of nature. And the same feelings which made me neglect the scenes around me caused me also to forget those friends who were so many miles absent, and whom I had not seen for so long a time. I knew my silence disquieted them; and I well remembered the words of my father: "I know that while you are pleased with yourself, you will think of us with affection, and we shall hear regularly from you. You must pardon me if I regard any interruption in your correspondence as a proof that your other duties are equally neglected."

I knew well, therefore, what would be my father's feelings, but I could not tear my thoughts from my employment, loathsome in itself, but which had taken an irresistible hold of my imagination. I wished, as it were, to procrastinate all that related to my feelings of affection until the great object, which swallowed up every habit of my nature, should be completed.

I then thought that my father would be unjust if he ascribed my neglect to vice or faultiness on my part, but I am now convinced that he was justified in conceiving that I should not be altogether free from blame. A human being in perfection ought always to preserve a calm and peaceful mind, and never to allow passion or a transitory desire to disturb his tranquillity. I do not think that the pursuit of knowledge is an exception to this rule. If the study to which you apply yourself has a tendency to weaken your affections, and to destroy your taste for those simple pleasures in which no alloy can possibly mix, then that study is certainly unlawful, that is to say, not befitting the human mind. If this rule were always observed; if no man allowed any pursuit whatsoever to interfere with the tranquillity of his domestic affections, Greece had not been enslaved, Caesar would have spared his country; America would have been discovered more gradually; and the empires of Mexico and Peru had not been destroyed.

But I forget that I am moralising in the most interesting part of my tale; and your looks remind me to proceed. My father made no reproach in his letters, and only took notice of my silence by inquiring into my occupations more particularly than before. Winter, spring, and summer passed away during my labours; but I did not watch the blossom or the expanding leaves — sights which before always yielded me supreme delight — so deeply was I engrossed in my occupation. The leaves of that year had withered before my work drew near to a close; and now every day showed me more plainly how well I had succeeded. But my enthusiasm was checked by my anxiety, and I appeared rather like one doomed by slavery to toil in the mines, or any other unwholesome trade than an artist occupied by his favourite employment. Every night I was oppressed by a slow fever, and I became nervous to a most painful degree; the fall of a leaf startled me, and I shunned my fellow-creatures as if I had been guilty of a crime. Sometimes I grew alarmed at the wreck I perceived that I had become — the energy of my purpose alone sustained me: my labours would soon end, and I believed that exercise and amusement would then drive away incipient disease; and I promised myself both of these when my creation should be complete.

It was on a dreary night of November that I beheld the accomplishment of my toils. With an anxiety that almost amounted to agony, I collected the instruments of life around me, that I might infuse a spark of being into the lifeless thing that lay at my feet. It was already one in the morning; the rain pattered dismally against the panes, and my candle was nearly burnt out, when, by the glimmer of the half-extinguished light, I saw the dull yellow eye of the creature open; it breathed hard, and a convulsive motion agitated its limbs.

How can I describe my emotions at this catastrophe, or how delineate the wretch whom with such infinite pains and care I had endeavoured to form? His limbs were in proportion, and I had selected his features as beautiful. Beautiful! Great God! His yellow skin scarcely covered the work of muscles and arteries beneath; his hair was of a lustrous black, and flowing; his teeth of a pearly whiteness; but these luxuriances only formed a more horrid contrast with his watery eyes, that seemed almost of the same colour as the dun white sockets in which they were set, his shrivelled complexion and straight black lips.

The different accidents of life are not so changeable as the feelings of human nature. I had worked hard for nearly two years, for the sole purpose of infusing life into an inanimate body. For this I had deprived myself of rest and health. I had desired it with an ardour that far exceeded moderation; but now that I had finished, the beauty of the dream vanished, and breathless horror and disgust filled my heart. Unable to endure the aspect of the being I had created, I rushed out of the room and continued a long time traversing my bed chamber, unable to compose my mind to sleep. At length lassitude succeeded to the tumult I had before endured; and I threw myself on the bed in my clothes, endeavouring to seek a few moments of forgetfulness. But it was in vain: I slept, indeed, but I was disturbed by the wildest dreams. I thought I saw Elizabeth, in the bloom of health, walking in the streets of Ingolstadt. Delighted and surprised, I embraced her, but as I imprinted the first kiss on her lips, they became livid with the hue of death; her features appeared to change, and I thought that I held the corpse of my dead mother in my arms; a shroud enveloped her form, and I saw the grave-worms crawling in the folds of the flannel. I started from my sleep with horror; a cold dew covered my forehead, my teeth chattered, and every limb became convulsed: when, by the dim and yellow light of the moon, as it forced its way through the window shutters, I beheld the wretch — the miserable monster whom I had created. He held up the curtain of the bed and his eyes, if eyes they may be called, were fixed on me. His jaws opened, and he muttered some inarticulate sounds, while a grin wrinkled his cheeks. He might have spoken, but I did not hear; one hand was stretched out, seemingly to detain me, but I escaped and rushed downstairs. I took refuge in the courtyard belonging to the house which I inhabited; where I remained during the rest of the night, walking up and down in the greatest agitation, listening attentively, catching and fearing each sound as if it were to announce the approach of the demoniacal corpse to which I had so miserably given life.

Oh! No mortal could support the horror of that countenance. A mummy again endued with animation could not be so hideous as that wretch. I had gazed on him while unfinished; he was ugly then, but when those muscles and joints were rendered capable of motion, it became a thing such as even Dante could not have conceived.

I passed the night wretchedly. Sometimes my pulse beat so quickly and hardly that I felt the palpitation of every artery; at others, I nearly sank to the ground through languor and extreme weakness. Mingled with this horror, I felt the bitterness of disappointment; dreams that had been my food and pleasant rest for so long a space were now become a hell to me; and the change was so rapid, the overthrow so complete!

Morning, dismal and wet, at length dawned and discovered to my sleepless and aching eyes the church of Ingolstadt, its white steeple and clock, which indicated the sixth hour. The porter opened the gates of the court, which had that night been my asylum, and I issued into the streets, pacing them with quick steps, as if I sought to avoid the wretch whom I feared every turning of the street would present to my view. I did not dare return to the apartment which I inhabited, but felt impelled to hurry on, although drenched by the rain which poured from a black and comfortless sky.

I continued walking in this manner for some time, endeavouring by bodily exercise to ease the load that weighed upon my mind. I traversed the streets, without any clear conception of where I was, or what I was doing. My heart palpitated in the sickness of fear, and I hurried on with irregular steps, not daring to look about me: —

> "Like one who, on a lonely road,
> Doth walk in fear and dread,
> And, having once turned round, walks on,
> And turns no more his head;
> Because he knows a frightful fiend
> Doth close behind him tread."

Continuing thus, I came at length opposite to the inn at which the various diligences and carriages usually stopped. Here I paused, I knew not why; but I remained some minutes with my eyes fixed on a coach that was coming towards me from the other end of the street. As it drew nearer, I observed that it was the Swiss diligence; it stopped just where I was standing, and on the door being opened, I perceived Henry Clerval, who, on seeing me, instantly sprung out. "My dear Frankenstein," exclaimed he, "how glad I am to see you! How fortunate that you should be here at the very moment of my alighting!"

Nothing could equal my delight on seeing Clerval; his presence brought back to my thoughts my father, Elizabeth, and all those scenes of home so dear to my recollection. I grasped his hand, and in a moment forgot my horror and misfortune; I felt suddenly, and for the first time during many months, calm and serene joy. I welcomed my friend, therefore, in the most cordial manner, and we walked towards my college. Clerval continued talking for some time about our mutual friends, and his own good fortune in being permitted to come to Ingolstadt. "You may easily believe," said he, "how great was the difficulty to persuade my father that all necessary knowledge was not comprised in the noble art of bookkeeping; and, indeed, I believe I left him incredulous to the last, for his constant answer to my unwearied entreaties was the same as that of the Dutch schoolmaster in the *Vicar of Wakefield*: — 'I have ten thousand florins a year without Greek, I eat heartily without Greek.' But his affection for me at length overcame his dislike of learning, and he has permitted me to undertake a voyage of discovery to the land of knowledge."

"It gives me the greatest delight to see you; but tell me how you left my father, brothers, and Elizabeth."

"Very well, and very happy, only a little uneasy that they hear from you so seldom. By the by, I mean to lecture you a little upon their account myself. But, my dear Frankenstein," continued he, stopping short and gazing full in my face, "I did not before remark how very ill you appear; so thin and pale; you look as if you had been watching for several nights."

"You have guessed right; I have lately been so deeply engaged in one occupation that I have not allowed myself sufficient rest, as you see; but I hope, I sincerely hope, that all these employments are now at an end, and that I am at length free."

I trembled excessively; I could not endure to think of, and far less to allude to, the occurrences of the preceding night. I walked with a quick pace, and we soon arrived at my college. I then reflected, and the thought made me shiver, that the creature whom I had left in my apartment might still be there, alive, and walking about. I dreaded to behold this monster; but I feared still more that Henry should see him. Entreating him, therefore, to remain a few minutes at the bottom of the stairs, I darted up towards my own room. My hand was already on the lock of the door before I recollected myself. I then paused, and a cold shivering came over me. I threw the door forcibly open, as children are accustomed to do when they expect a spectre to stand in waiting for them on the other side; but nothing appeared. I stepped fearfully in: the apartment was empty, and my bedroom was also freed from its hideous guest. I could hardly believe that so great a good fortune could have befallen me, but when I became assured that my enemy had indeed fled, I clapped my hands for joy and ran down to Clerval.

We ascended into my room, and the servant presently brought breakfast; but I was unable to contain myself. It was not joy only that possessed me; I felt my flesh tingle with excess of sensitiveness, and my pulse beat rapidly. I was unable to remain for a single instant in the same place; I jumped over the chairs, clapped my hands, and laughed aloud. Clerval at first attributed my unusual spirits to joy on his arrival; but when he observed me more attentively he saw a wildness in my eyes for which he could not account; and my loud, unrestrained, heartless laughter frightened and astonished him.

"My dear Victor," cried he, "what, for God's sake, is the matter? Do not laugh in that manner. How ill you are! What is the cause of all this?"

"Do not ask me," cried I, putting my hands before my eyes for I thought I saw the dreaded spectre glide into the room; "he can tell. Oh, save me! Save me!"I imagined that the monster seized me; I struggled furiously and fell down in a fit.

Poor Clerval! What must have been his feelings? A meeting, which he anticipated with such joy, so strangely turned to bitterness. But I was not the witness of his grief, for I was lifeless, and did not recover my senses for a long, long time.

This was the commencement of a nervous fever, which confined me for several months. During all that time Henry was my only nurse. I afterwards learned that, knowing my father's advanced age, and unfitness for so long a journey, and how wretched my sickness would make Elizabeth, he spared them this grief by concealing the extent of my disorder. He knew that I could not have a more kind and attentive nurse than himself; and, firm in the hope he felt of my recovery, he did not doubt that, instead of doing harm, he performed the kindest action that he could towards them.

But I was in reality very ill; and surely nothing but the unbounded and unremitting attentions of my friend could have restored me to life. The form of the monster on whom I had bestowed existence was forever before my eyes, and I raved incessantly concerning him. Doubtless my words surprised Henry; he at first believed them to be the wanderings of my disturbed imagination, but the pertinacity with which I continually recurred to the same subject, persuaded him that my disorder indeed owed its origin to some uncommon and terrible event.

By very slow degrees, and with frequent relapses that alarmed and grieved my friend, I recovered. I remember the first time I became capable of observing outward objects with any kind of pleasure, I perceived that the fallen leaves had disappeared, and that the young buds were shooting forth from the trees that shaded my window. It was a divine spring; and the season contributed greatly to my convalescence. I felt also sentiments of joy and affection revive in my bosom; my gloom disappeared, and in a short time I became as cheerful as before I was attacked by the fatal passion.

"Dearest Clerval," exclaimed I, "how kind, how very good you are to me. This whole winter, instead of being spent in study, as you promised yourself, has been consumed in my sick room. How shall I ever repay you? I feel the greatest remorse for the disappointment of which I have been the occasion; but you will forgive me."

"You will repay me entirely if you do not discompose yourself, but get well as fast as you can; and since you appear in such good spirits, I may speak to you on one subject, may I not?"

I trembled. One subject! What could it be? Could he allude to an object on whom I dared not even think?

"Compose yourself," said Clerval, who observed my change of colour, "I will not mention it, if it agitates you; but your father and cousin would be very happy if they received a letter from you in your own handwriting. They hardly know how ill you have been, and are uneasy at your long silence."

"Is that all, my dear Henry? How could you suppose that my first thoughts would not fly towards those dear, dear friends whom I love, and who are so deserving of my love."

"If this is your present temper, my friend, you will perhaps be glad to see a letter that has been lying here some days for you; it is from your cousin, I believe."

Topics for Discussion

1. Why does the speaker (or the poet) appeal to Muse at the beginning of *Aeneid*?
2. How is the story of *Aeneid* related to the Trojan myth?
3. Interpret the myth of the founding of Rome based on *Aeneid*.
4. How does Mary W. Shelley rewrite the myths about Prometheus in her fiction?
5. In which sense can *Frankenstein* be called the *Modern Prometheus*?
6. Give more literary examples as records or rewritings of Greco-Roman myths.

Monograph Two Literature and Philosophy

I Er's Tale Told by Socrates

Plato (427 BC-347 BC)

translated by Benjamin Jowett (1817-1893)

Well, I said, I will tell you a tale; not one of the tales which Odysseus tells to the hero Alcinous, yet this too is a tale of a hero, Er the son of Armenius, a Pamphylian by birth. He was slain in battle, and ten days afterwards, when the bodies of the dead were taken up already in a state of corruption, his body was found unaffected by decay, and carried away home to be buried.

And on the twelfth day, as he was lying on the funeral pile, he returned to life and told them what he had seen in the other world. He said that when his soul left the body he went on a journey with a great company, and that they came to a mysterious place at which there were two openings in the earth; they were near together, and over against them were two other openings in the heaven above.

In the intermediate space there were judges seated, who commanded the just, after they had given judgment on them and had bound their sentences in front of them, to ascend by the heavenly way on the right hand; and in like manner the unjust were bidden by them to descend by the lower way on the left hand; these also bore the symbols of their deeds, but fastened on their backs.

He drew near, and they told him that he was to be the messenger who would carry the report of the other world to men, and they bade him hear and see all that was to be heard and seen in that place. Then he beheld and saw on one side the souls departing at either opening of heaven and earth when sentence had been given on them; and at the two other openings other souls, some ascending out of the earth dusty and worn with travel, some descending out of heaven clean and bright.

And arriving ever and anon they seemed to have come from a long journey, and they went forth with gladness into the meadow, where they encamped as at a festival; and those who knew one another embraced and conversed, the souls which came from earth curiously enquiring about the things above, and the souls which came from heaven about the things beneath.

And they told one another of what had happened by the way, those from below weeping and sorrowing at the remembrance of the things which they had endured and seen in their journey beneath the earth (now the journey lasted a thousand years), while those from above were describing heavenly delights and visions of inconceivable beauty.

The story, Glaucon, would take too long to tell; but the sum was this: — He said that for every wrong which they had done to any one they suffered tenfold; or once in a hundred years—such being reckoned to be the length of man's life, and the penalty being thus paid ten times in a thousand years. If, for example, there were any who had been the cause of many deaths, or had betrayed or enslaved cities or armies, or been guilty of any other evil behaviour, for each and all of their offences they received punishment ten times over, and the rewards of beneficence and justice and holiness were in the same proportion.

I need hardly repeat what he said concerning young children dying almost as soon as they were born. Of piety and impiety to gods and parents, and of murderers, there were retributions other and greater far which he described. He mentioned that he was present when one of the spirits asked another, "Where is Ardiaeus the Great?" (Now this Ardiaeus lived a thousand years before the time of Er: he had been the tyrant of some city of Pamphylia, and had murdered his aged father and his elder brother, and was said to have committed many other abominable crimes.)

The answer of the other spirit was: "He comes not hither and will never come. And this," said he, "was one of the dreadful sights which we ourselves witnessed. We were at the mouth of the cavern, and, having completed all our experiences, were about to reascend, when of a sudden Ardiaeus appeared and several others, most of whom were tyrants; and there were also besides the tyrants private individuals who had been great criminals: they were just, as they fancied, about to return into the upper world, but the mouth, instead of admitting them, gave a roar, whenever any of these incurable sinners or some one who had not been sufficiently punished tried to ascend; and then wild men of fiery aspect, who were standing by and heard the sound, seized and carried them off; and Ardiaeus and others they bound head and foot and hand, and threw them down and flayed them with scourges, and dragged them along the road at the side, carding them on thorns like wool, and declaring to the passers-by what were their crimes, and that they were being taken away to be cast into hell."

And of all the many terrors which they had endured, he said that there was none like the terror which each of them felt at that moment, lest they should hear the voice; and when there was silence, one by one they ascended with exceeding joy. These, said Er, were the penalties and retributions, and there were blessings as great.

Now when the spirits which were in the meadow had tarried seven days, on the eighth they were obliged to proceed on their journey, and, on the fourth day after, he said that they came to a place where they could see from above a line of light, straight as a column, extending right through the whole heaven and through the earth, in colour resembling the rainbow, only brighter and purer; another day's journey brought them to the place, and there, in the midst of the light, they saw the ends of the chains of heaven let down from above: for this light is the belt of heaven, and holds together the circle of the universe, like the under-girders of a trireme.

From these ends is extended the spindle of Necessity, on which all the revolutions turn. The shaft and hook of this spindle are made of steel, and the whorl is made partly of steel and also partly of other materials.

Now the whorl is in form like the whorl used on earth; and the description of it implied that there is one large hollow whorl which is quite scooped out, and into this is fitted another lesser one, and another, and another, and four others, making eight in all, like vessels which fit into one another; the whorls show their edges on the upper side, and on their lower side all together form one continuous whorl.

This is pierced by the spindle, which is driven home through the centre of the eighth. The first and outermost whorl has the rim broadest, and the seven inner whorls are narrower, in the following proportions — the sixth is next to the first in size, the fourth next to the sixth; then comes the eighth; the seventh is fifth, the fifth is sixth, the third is seventh, last and eighth comes the second.

The largest (of fixed stars) is spangled, and the seventh (or sun) is brightest; the eighth (or moon) coloured by the reflected light of the seventh; the second and fifth (Saturn and Mercury) are in colour like one another, and yellower than the preceding; the third (Venus) has the whitest light; the fourth (Mars) is reddish; the sixth (Jupiter) is in whiteness second.

Now the whole spindle has the same motion; but, as the whole revolves in one direction, the seven inner circles move slowly in the other, and of these the swiftest is the eighth; next in swiftness are the seventh, sixth, and fifth, which move together; third in swiftness appeared to move according to the law of this reversed motion the fourth; the third appeared fourth and the second fifth.

The spindle turns on the knees of Necessity; and on the upper surface of each circle is a siren, who goes round with them, hymning a single tone or note.

The eight together form one harmony; and round about, at equal intervals, there is another band, three in number, each sitting upon her throne: these are the Fates, daughters of Necessity, who are clothed in white robes and have chaplets upon their heads, Lachesis and Clotho and Atropos, who accompany with their voices the harmony of the sirens— Lachesis singing of the past, Clotho of the present, Atropos of the future; Clotho from time to time assisting with a touch of her right hand the revolution of the outer circle of the whorl or spindle, and Atropos with her left hand touching and guiding the inner ones, and Lachesis laying hold of either in turn, first with one hand and then with the other.

When Er and the spirits arrived, their duty was to go at once to Lachesis; but first of all there came a prophet who arranged them in order; then he took from the knees of Lachesis lots and samples of lives, and having mounted a high pulpit, spoke as follows: "Hear the word of Lachesis, the daughter of Necessity. Mortal souls, behold a new cycle of life and mortality. Your genius will not be allotted to you, but you choose your genius; and let him who draws the first lot have the first choice, and the life which he chooses shall be his destiny. Virtue is free, and as a man honours or dishonours her he will have more or less of her; the responsibility is with the chooser—God is justified."

When the Interpreter had thus spoken he scattered lots indifferently among them all, and each of them took up the lot which fell near him, all but Er himself (he was not allowed), and each as he took his lot perceived the number which he had obtained.

Then the Interpreter placed on the ground before them the samples of lives; and there were many more lives than the souls present, and they were of all sorts. There were lives of every animal and of man in every condition. And there were tyrannies among them, some lasting out the tyrant's life, others which broke off in the middle and came to an end in poverty and exile and beggary; and there were lives of famous men, some who were famous for their form and beauty as well as for their strength and success in games, or, again, for their birth and the qualities of their ancestors; and some who were the reverse of famous for the opposite qualities.

And of women likewise; there was not, however, any definite character them, because the soul, when choosing a new life, must of necessity become different. But there was every other quality, and the all mingled with one another, and also with elements of wealth and poverty, and disease and health; and there were mean states also.

And here, my dear Glaucon, is the supreme peril of our human state; and therefore the utmost care should be taken. Let each one of us leave every other kind of knowledge and seek and follow one thing only, if peradventure he may be able to learn and may find some one who will make him able to learn and discern between good and evil, and so to choose always and everywhere the better life as he has opportunity.

He should consider the bearing of all these things which have been mentioned severally and collectively upon virtue; he should know what the effect of beauty is when combined with poverty or wealth in a particular soul, and what are the good and evil consequences of noble and humble birth, of private and public station, of strength and weakness, of cleverness and dullness, and of all the natural and acquired gifts of the soul, and the operation of them when conjoined; he will then look at the nature of the soul, and from the consideration of all these qualities he will be able to determine which is the better and which is the worse; and so he will choose, giving the name of evil to the life which will make his soul more unjust, and good to the life which will make his soul more just; all else he will disregard.

For we have seen and know that this is the best choice both in life and after death. A man must take with him into the world below an adamantine faith in truth and right, that there too he may be undazzled by the desire of wealth or the other allurements of evil, lest, coming upon tyrannies and similar villainies, he do irremediable wrongs to others and suffer yet worse himself; but let him know how to choose the mean and avoid the extremes on either side, as far as possible, not only in this life but in all that which is to come. For this is the way of happiness.

And according to the report of the messenger from the other world this was what the prophet said at the time: "Even for the last comer, if he chooses wisely and will live diligently, there is appointed a happy and not undesirable existence. Let not him who chooses first be careless, and let not the last despair." And when he had spoken, he who had the first choice came forward and in a moment chose the greatest tyranny; his mind having been darkened by folly and sensuality, he had not thought out the whole matter before he chose, and did not at first sight perceive that he was fated, among other evils, to devour his own children.

But when he had time to reflect, and saw what was in the lot, he began to beat his breast and lament over his choice, forgetting the proclamation of the prophet; for, instead of throwing the blame of his misfortune on himself, he accused chance and the gods, and everything rather than himself. Now he was one of those who came from heaven, and in a former life had dwelt in a well-ordered State, but his virtue was a matter of habit only, and he had no philosophy.

And it was true of others who were similarly overtaken, that the greater number of them came from heaven and therefore they had never been schooled by trial, whereas the pilgrims who came from earth, having themselves suffered and seen others suffer, were not in a hurry to choose. And owing to this inexperience of theirs, and also because the lot was a chance, many of the souls exchanged a good destiny for an evil or an evil for a good.

For if a man had always on his arrival in this world dedicated himself from the first to sound philosophy, and had been moderately fortunate in the number of the lot, he might, as the messenger reported, be happy here, and also his journey to another life and return to this, instead of being rough and underground, would be smooth and heavenly. Most curious, he said, was the spectacle—sad and laughable and strange; for the choice of the souls was in most cases based on their experience of a previous life.

There he saw the soul which had once been Orpheus choosing the life of a swan out of enmity to the race of women, hating to be born of a woman because they had been his murderers; he beheld also the soul of Thamyras choosing the life of a nightingale; birds, on the other hand, like the swan and other musicians, wanting to be men.

The soul which obtained the twentieth lot chose the life of a lion, and this was the soul of Ajax the son of Telamon, who would not be a man, remembering the injustice which was done him in the judgment about the arms. The next was Agamemnon, who took the life of an eagle, because, like Ajax, he hated human nature by reason of his sufferings.

About the middle came the lot of Atalanta; she, seeing the great fame of an athlete, was unable to resist the temptation: and after her there followed the soul of Epeus the son of Panopeus passing into the nature of a woman cunning in the arts; and far away among the last who chose, the soul of the jester Thersites was putting on the form of a monkey.

There came also the soul of Odysseus having yet to make a choice, and his lot happened to be the last of them all. Now the recollection of former toils had disenchanted him of ambition, and he went about for a considerable time in search of the life of a private man who had no cares; he had some difficulty in finding this, which was lying about and had been neglected by everybody else; and when he saw it, he said that he would have done the had his lot been first instead of last, and that he was delighted to have it.

And not only did men pass into animals, but I must also mention that there were animals tame and wild who changed into one another and into corresponding human natures— the good into the gentle and the evil into the savage, in all sorts of combinations.

All the souls had now chosen their lives, and they went in the order of their choice to Lachesis, who sent with them the genius whom they had severally chosen, to be the guardian of their lives and the fulfiller of the choice: this genius led the souls first to Clotho, and drew them within the revolution of the spindle impelled by her hand, thus ratifying the destiny of each; and then, when they were fastened to this, carried them to Atropos, who spun the threads and made them irreversible, whence without turning round they passed beneath the throne of Necessity; and when they had all passed, they marched on in a scorching heat to the plain of Forgetfulness, which was a barren waste destitute of trees and verdure; and then towards evening they encamped by the river of Unmindfulness, whose water no vessel can hold; of this they were all obliged to drink a certain quantity, and those who were not saved by wisdom drank more than was necessary; and each one as he drank forgot all things.

Now after they had gone to rest, about the middle of the night there was a thunderstorm and earthquake, and then in an instant they were driven upwards in all manner of ways to their birth, like stars shooting. He himself was hindered from drinking the water. But in what manner or by what means he returned to the body he could not say; only, in the morning, awaking suddenly, he found himself lying on the pyre.

And thus, Glaucon, the tale has been saved and has not perished, and will save us if we are obedient to the word spoken; and we shall pass safely over the river of Forgetfulness and our soul will not be defiled. Wherefore my counsel is that we hold fast ever to the heavenly way and follow after justice and virtue always, considering that the soul is immortal and able to endure every sort of good and every sort of evil.

Thus shall we live dear to one another and to the gods, both while remaining here and when, like conquerors in the games who go round to gather gifts, we receive our reward. And it shall be well with us both in this life and in the pilgrimage of a thousand years which we have been describing.

II The Poet

Ralph Waldo Emerson (1803–1882)

A moody child and wildly wise

Pursued the game with joyful eyes,
Which chose, like meteors, their way,
And rived the dark with private ray:
They overleapt the horizon's edge,
Searched with Apollo's privilege;
Through man, and woman, and sea, and star,
Saw the dance of nature forward far;
Through worlds, and races, and terms, and times,
Saw musical order, and pairing rhymes.

Olympian bards who sung
Divine ideas below,
Which always find us young,
And always keep us so.

Those who are esteemed umpires of taste, are often persons who have acquired some knowledge of admired pictures or sculptures, and have an inclination for whatever is elegant; but if you inquire whether they are beautiful souls, and whether their own acts are like fair pictures, you learn that they are selfish and sensual. Their cultivation is local, as if you should rub a log of dry wood in one spot to produce fire, all the rest remaining cold. Their knowledge of the fine arts is some study of rules and particulars, or some limited judgment of color or form, which is exercised for amusement or for show. It is a proof of the shallowness of the doctrine of beauty, as it lies in the minds of our amateurs, that men seem to have lost the perception of the instant dependence of form upon soul. There is no doctrine of forms in our philosophy. We were put into our bodies, as fire is put into a pan, to be carried about; but there is no accurate adjustment between the spirit and the organ, much less is the latter the germination of the former. So in regard to other forms, the intellectual men do not believe in any essential dependence of the material world on thought and volition. Theologians think it a pretty air-castle to talk of the spiritual meaning of a ship or a cloud, of a city or a contract, but they prefer to come again to the solid ground of historical evidence; and even the poets are contented with a civil and conformed manner of living, and to write poems from the fancy, at a safe distance from their own experience. But the highest minds of the world have never ceased to explore the double meaning, or, shall I say, the quadruple, or the centuple, or much more manifold meaning, of every sensuous fact: Orpheus, Empedocles, Heraclitus, Plato, Plutarch, Dante, Swedenborg, and the masters of sculpture, picture, and poetry. For we are not pans and barrows, nor even porters of the fire and torch-bearers, but children of the fire, made of it, and only the same divinity transmuted, and at two or three removes, when we know least about it. And this hidden truth, that the fountains whence all this river of Time, and its creatures, floweth, are intrinsically ideal and beautiful, draws us to the consideration of the nature and functions of the Poet, or the man of Beauty, to the means and materials he uses, and to the general aspect of the art in the present time.

The breadth of the problem is great, for the poet is representative. He stands among partial men for the complete man, and apprises us not of his wealth, but of the common-wealth. The young man reveres men of genius, because, to speak truly, they are more himself than he is. They receive of the soul as he also receives, but they more. Nature enhances her beauty, to the eye of loving men, from their belief that the poet is beholding her shows at the same time. He is isolated among his contemporaries, by truth and by his art, but with this consolation in his pursuits, that they will draw all men sooner or later. For all men live by truth, and stand in need of expression. In love, in art, in avarice, in politics, in labor, in games, we study to utter our painful secret. The man is only half himself, the other half is his expression.

Notwithstanding this necessity to be published, adequate expression is rare. I know not how it is that we need an interpreter; but the great majority of men seem to be minors, who have not yet come into possession of their own, or mutes, who cannot report the conversation they have had with nature. There is no man who does not anticipate a supersensual utility in the sun, and stars, earth, and water. These stand and wait to render him a peculiar service. But there is some obstruction, or some excess of phlegm in our constitution, which does not suffer them to yield the due effect. Too feeble fall the impressions of nature on us to make us artists. Every touch should thrill. Every man should be so much an artist, that he could report in conversation what had befallen him. Yet, in our experience, the rays or appulses have sufficient force to arrive at the senses, but not enough to reach the quick, and compel the reproduction of themselves in speech. The poet is the person in whom these powers are in balance, the man without impediment, who sees and handles that which others dream of, traverses the whole scale of experience, and is representative of man, in virtue of being the largest power to receive and to impart.

For the Universe has three children, born at one time, which reappear, under different names, in every system of thought, whether they be called cause, operation, and effect; or, more poetically, Jove, Pluto, Neptune; or, theologically, the Father, the Spirit, and the Son; but which we will call here, the Knower, the Doer, and the Sayer. These stand respectively for the love of truth, for the love of good, and for the love of beauty. These three are equal. Each is that which he is essentially, so that he cannot be surmounted or analyzed, and each of these three has the power of the others latent in him, and his own patent.

The poet is the sayer, the namer, and represents beauty. He is a sovereign, and stands on the centre. For the world is not painted, or adorned, but is from the beginning beautiful; and God has not made some beautiful things, but Beauty is the creator of the universe. Therefore the poet is not any permissive potentate, but is emperor in his own right. Criticism is infested with a cant of materialism, which assumes that manual skill and activity is the first merit of all men, and disparages such as say and do not, overlooking the fact, that some men, namely, poets, are natural sayers, sent into the world to the end of expression, and confounds them with those whose province is action, but who quit it to imitate the sayers. But Homer's words are as costly and admirable to Homer, as Agamemnon's victories are to Agamemnon. The poet does not wait for the hero or the sage, but, as they act and think primarily, so he writes primarily what will and must be spoken, reckoning the others, though primaries also, yet, in respect to him, secondaries and servants; as sitters or models in the studio of a painter, or as assistants who bring building materials to an architect.

For poetry was all written before time was, and whenever we are so finely organized that we can penetrate into that region where the air is music, we hear those primal warblings, and attempt to write them down, but we lose ever and anon a word, or a verse, and substitute something of our own, and thus miswrite the poem. The men of more delicate ear write down these cadences more faithfully, and these transcripts, though imperfect, become the songs of the nations. For nature is as truly beautiful as it is good, or as it is reasonable, and must as much appear, as it must be done, or be known. Words and deeds are quite indifferent modes of the divine energy. Words are also actions, and actions are a kind of words.

The sign and credentials of the poet are, that he announces that which no man foretold. He is the true and only doctor; he knows and tells; he is the only teller of news, for he was present and privy to the appearance which he describes. He is a beholder of ideas, and an utterer of the necessary and causal. For we do not speak now of men of poetical talents, or of industry and skill in metre, but of the true poet. I took part in a conversation the other day, concerning a recent writer of lyrics, a man of subtle mind, whose head appeared to be a music-box of delicate tunes and rhythms, and whose skill, and command of language, we could not sufficiently praise. But when the question arose, whether he was not only a lyrist, but a poet, we were obliged to confess that he is plainly a contemporary, not an eternal man. He does not stand out of our low limitations, like a Chimborazo under the line, running up from the torrid base through all the climates of the globe, with belts of the herbage of every latitude on its high and mottled sides; but this genius is the landscape-garden of a modern house, adorned with fountains and statues, with well-bred men and women standing and sitting in the walks and terraces. We hear, through all the varied music, the ground-tone of conventional life. Our poets are men of talents who sing, and not the children of music. The argument is secondary, the finish of the verses is primary.

For it is not metres, but a metre-making argument, that makes a poem, — a thought so passionate and alive, that, like the spirit of a plant or an animal, it has an architecture of its own, and adorns nature with a new thing. The thought and the form are equal in the order of time, but in the order of genesis the thought is prior to the form. The poet has a new thought: he has a whole new experience to unfold; he will tell us how it was with him, and all men will be the richer in his fortune. For, the experience of each new age requires a new confession, and the world seems always waiting for its poet. I remember, when I was young, how much I was moved one morning by tidings that genius had appeared in a youth who sat near me at table. He had left his work, and gone rambling none knew whither, and had written hundreds of lines, but could not tell whether that which was in him was therein told: he could tell nothing but that all was changed, — man, beast, heaven, earth, and sea. How gladly we listened! How credulous! Society seemed to be compromised. We sat in the aurora of a sunrise which was to put out all the stars. Boston seemed to be at twice the distance it had the night before, or was much farther than that. Rome, — what was Rome? Plutarch and Shakespeare were in the yellow leaf, and Homer no more should be heard of. It is much to know that poetry has been written this very day, under this very roof, by your side. What! That wonderful spirit has not expired! These stony moments are still sparkling and animated! I had fancied that the oracles were all silent, and nature had spent her fires, and behold! All night, from every pore, these fine auroras have been streaming. Every one has some interest in the advent of the poet, and no one knows how much it may concern him. We know that the secret of the world is profound, but who or what shall be our interpreter, we know not. A mountain ramble, a new style of face, a new person, may put the key into our hands. Of course, the value of genius to us is in the veracity of its report. Talent may frolic and juggle; genius realizes and adds. Mankind, in good earnest, have availed so far in understanding themselves and their work, that the foremost watchman on the peak announces his news. It is the truest word ever spoken, and the phrase will be the fittest, most musical, and the unerring voice of the world for that time.

All that we call sacred history attests that the birth of a poet is the principal event in chronology. Man, never so often deceived, still watches for the arrival of a brother who can hold him steady to a truth, until he has made it his own. With what joy I begin to read a poem, which I confide in as an inspiration! And now my chains are to be broken; I shall mount above these clouds and opaque airs in which I live, — opaque, though they seem transparent, — and from the heaven of truth I shall see and comprehend my relations. That will reconcile me to life, and renovate nature, to see trifles animated by a tendency, and to know what I am doing. Life will no more be a noise; now I shall see men and women, and know the signs by which they may be discerned from fools and satans. This day shall be better than my birthday: then I became an animal; now I am invited into the science of the real. Such is the hope, but the fruition is postponed. Oftener it falls, that this winged man, who will carry me into the heaven, whirls me into the clouds, then leaps and frisks about with me from cloud to cloud, still affirming that he is bound heavenward; and I, being myself a novice, am slow in perceiving that he does not know the way into the heavens, and is merely bent that I should admire his skill to rise, like a fowl or a flying fish, a little way from the ground or the water; but the all-piercing, all-feeding, and ocular air of heaven, that man shall never inhabit. I tumble down again soon into my old nooks, and lead the life of exaggerations as before, and have lost my faith in the possibility of any guide who can lead me thither where I would be.

But leaving these victims of vanity, let us, with new hope, observe how nature, by worthier impulses, has ensured the poet's fidelity to his office of announcement and affirming, namely, by the beauty of things, which becomes a new, and higher beauty, when expressed. Nature offers all her creatures to him as a picture-language. Being used as a type, a second wonderful value appears in the object, far better than its old value, as the carpenter's stretched cord, if you hold your ear close enough, is musical in the breeze.

"Things more excellent than every image," says Jamblichus, "are expressed through images."Things admit of being used as symbols, because nature is a symbol, in the whole, and in every part. Every line we can draw in the sand, has expression; and there is no body without its spirit or genius. All form is an effect of character; all condition, of the quality of the life; all harmony, of health; (and for this reason, a perception of beauty should be sympathetic, or proper only to the good). The beautiful rests on the foundations of the necessary. The soul makes the body, as the wise Spenser teaches: —

> "So every spirit, as it is most pure,
> And hath in it the more of heavenly light,
> So it the fairer body doth procure
> To habit in, and it more fairly dight,
> With cheerful grace and amiable sight.
> For, of the soul, the body form doth take,
> For soul is form, and doth the body make."

Here we find ourselves, suddenly, not in a critical speculation, but in a holy place, and should go very warily and reverently. We stand before the secret of the world, there where Being passes into Appearance, and Unity into Variety.

The Universe is the externization of the soul. Wherever the life is, that bursts into appearance around it. Our science is sensual, and therefore superficial. The earth, and the heavenly bodies, physics, and chemistry, we sensually treat, as if they were self-existent; but these are the retinue of that Being we have. "The mighty heaven," said Proclus, "exhibits, in its transfigurations, clear images of the splendor of intellectual perceptions; being moved in conjunction with the unapparent periods of intellectual natures."Therefore, science always goes abreast with the just elevation of the man, keeping step with religion and metaphysics; or, the state of science is an index of our self-knowledge. Since everything in nature answers to a moral power, if any phenomenon remains brute and dark, it is that the corresponding faculty in the observer is not yet active.

No wonder, then, if these waters be so deep, that we hover over them with a religious regard. The beauty of the fable proves the importance of the sense; to the poet, and to all others; or, if you please, every man is so far a poet as to be susceptible of these enchantments of nature: for all men have the thoughts whereof the universe is the celebration. I find that the fascination resides in the symbol. Who loves nature? Who does not? Is it only poets, and men of leisure and cultivation, who live with her? No; but also hunters, farmers, grooms, and butchers, though they express their affection in their choice of life, and not in their choice of words. The writer wonders what the coachman or the hunter values in riding, in horses, and dogs. It is not superficial qualities. When you talk with him, he holds these at as slight a rate as you. His worship is sympathetic; he has no definitions, but he is commanded in nature, by the living power which he feels to be there present. No imitation, or playing of these things, would content him; he loves the earnest of the northwind, of rain, of stone, and wood, and iron. A beauty not explicable, is dearer than a beauty which we can see to the end of. It is nature the symbol, nature certifying the supernatural, body overflowed by life, which he worships, with coarse, but sincere rites.

The inwardness, and mystery, of this attachment, drives men of every class to the use of emblems. The schools of poets, and philosophers, are not more intoxicated with their symbols, than the populace with theirs. In our political parties, compute the power of badges and emblems. See the great ball which they roll from Baltimore to Bunker hill! In the political processions, Lowell goes in a loom, and Lynn in a shoe, and Salem in a ship. Witness the cider-barrel, the log-cabin, the hickory-stick, the palmetto, and all the cognizances of party. See the power of national emblems. Some stars, lilies, leopards, a crescent, a lion, an eagle, or other figure, which came into credit God knows how, on an old rag of bunting, blowing in the wind, on a fort, at the ends of the earth, shall make the blood tingle under the rudest, or the most conventional exterior. The people fancy they hate poetry, and they are all poets and mystics!

Beyond this universality of the symbolic language, we are apprised of the divineness of this superior use of things, whereby the world is a temple, whose walls are covered with emblems, pictures, and commandments of the Deity, in this, that there is no fact in nature which does not carry the whole sense of nature; and the distinctions which we make in events, and in affairs, of low and high, honest and base, disappear when nature is used as a symbol. Thought makes every thing fit for use. The vocabulary of an omniscient man would embrace words and images excluded from polite conversation. What would be base, or even obscene, to the obscene, becomes illustrious, spoken in a new connexion of thought. The piety of the Hebrew prophets purges their grossness. The circumcision is an example of the power of poetry to raise the low and offensive. Small and mean things serve as well as great symbols. The meaner the type by which a law is expressed, the more pungent it is, and the more lasting in the memories of men: just as we choose the smallest box, or case, in which any needful utensil can be carried. Bare lists of words are found suggestive, to an imaginative and excited mind; as it is related of Lord Chatham, that he was accustomed to read in *Bailey's Dictionary*, when he was preparing to speak in Parliament. The poorest experience is rich enough for all the purposes of expressing thought. Why covet a knowledge of new facts? Day and night, house and garden, a few books, a few actions, serve us as well as would all trades and all spectacles. We are far from having exhausted the significance of the few symbols we use. We can come to use them yet with a terrible simplicity. It does not need that a poem should be long. Every word was once a poem. Every new relation is a new word. Also, we use defects and deformities to a sacred purpose, so expressing our sense that the evils of the world are such only to the evil eye. In the old mythology, mythologists observe, defects are ascribed to divine natures, as lameness to Vulcan, blindness to Cupid, and the like, to signify exuberances.

For, as it is dislocation and detachment from the life of God, that makes things ugly, the poet, who re-attaches things to nature and the Whole, — reattaching even artificial things, and violations of nature, to nature, by a deeper insight, — disposes very easily of the most disagreeable facts. Readers of poetry see the factory-village, and the railway, and fancy that the poetry of the landscape is broken up by these; for these works of art are not yet consecrated in their reading; but the poet sees them fall within the great Order not less than the beehive, or the spider's geometrical web. Nature adopts them very fast into her vital circles, and the gliding train of cars she loves like her own. Besides, in a centred mind, it signifies nothing how many mechanical inventions you exhibit. Though you add millions, and never so surprising, the fact of mechanics has not gained a grain's weight. The spiritual fact remains unalterable, by many or by few particulars; as no mountain is of any appreciable height to break the curve of the sphere. A shrewd country-boy goes to the city for the first time, and the complacent citizen is not satisfied with his little wonder. It is not that he does not see all the fine houses, and know that he never saw such before, but he disposes of them as easily as the poet finds place for the railway. The chief value of the new fact, is to enhance the great and constant fact of Life, which can dwarf any and every circumstance, and to which the belt of wampum, and the commerce of America, are alike.

The world being thus put under the mind for verb and noun, the poet is he who can articulate it. For, though life is great, and fascinates, and absorbs, — and though all men are intelligent of the symbols through which it is named, — yet they cannot originally use them. We are symbols, and inhabit symbols; workman, work, and tools, words and things, birth and death, all are emblems; but we sympathize with the symbols, and, being infatuated with the economical uses of things, we do not know that they are thoughts. The poet, by an ulterior intellectual perception, gives them a power which makes their old use forgotten, and puts eyes, and a tongue, into every dumb and inanimate object. He perceives the independence of the thought on the symbol, the stability of the thought, the accidency and fugacity of the symbol. As the eyes of Lyncaeus were said to see through the earth, so the poet turns the world to glass, and shows us all things in their right series and procession. For, through that better perception, he stands one step nearer to things, and sees the flowing or metamorphosis; perceives that thought is multiform; that within the form of every creature is a force impelling it to ascend into a higher form; and, following with his eyes the life, uses the forms which express that life, and so his speech flows with the flowing of nature. All the facts of the animal economy, sex, nutriment, gestation, birth, growth, are symbols of the passage of the world into the soul of man, to suffer there a change, and reappear a new and higher fact. He uses forms according to the life, and not according to the form. This is true science. The poet alone knows astronomy, chemistry, vegetation, and animation, for he does not stop at these facts, but employs them as signs. He knows why the plain, or meadow of space, was strown with these flowers we call suns, and moons, and stars; why the great deep is adorned with animals, with men, and gods; for, in every word he speaks he rides on them as the horses of thought.

By virtue of this science the poet is the Namer, or Language-maker, naming things sometimes after their appearance, sometimes after their essence, and giving to every one its own name and not another's, thereby rejoicing the intellect, which delights in detachment or boundary. The poets made all the words, and therefore language is the archives of history, and, if we must say it, a sort of tomb of the muses. For, though the origin of most of our words is forgotten, each word was at first a stroke of genius, and obtained currency, because for the moment it symbolized the world to the first speaker and to the hearer. The etymologist finds the deadest word to have been once a brilliant picture. Language is fossil poetry. As the limestone of the continent consists of infinite masses of the shells of animalcules, so language is made up of images, or tropes, which now, in their secondary use, have long ceased to remind us of their poetic origin. But the poet names the thing because he sees it, or comes one step nearer to it than any other. This expression, or naming, is not art, but a second nature, grown out of the first, as a leaf out of a tree. What we call nature, is a certain self-regulated motion, or change; and nature does all things by her own hands, and does not leave another to baptise her, but baptises herself; and this through the metamorphosis again. I remember that a certain poet described it to me thus:

> Genius is the activity which repairs the decays of things, whether wholly or partly of a material and finite kind. Nature, through all her kingdoms, insures herself. Nobody cares for planting the poor fungus: so she shakes down from the gills of one agaric countless spores, any one of which, being preserved, transmits new billions of spores to-morrow or next day. The new agaric of this hour has a chance which the old one had not. This atom of seed is thrown into a new place, not subject to the accidents which destroyed its parent two rods off. She makes a man; and having brought him to ripe age, she will no longer run the risk of losing this wonder at a blow, but she detaches from him a new self, that the kind may be safe from accidents to which the individual is exposed. So when the soul of the poet has come to ripeness of thought, she detaches and sends away from it its poems or songs,— a fearless, sleepless, deathless progeny, which is not exposed to the accidents of the weary kingdom of time: a fearless, vivacious offspring, clad with wings (such was the virtue of the soul out of which they came), which carry them fast and far, and infix them irrecoverably into the hearts of men. These wings are the beauty of the poet's soul. The songs, thus flying immortal from their mortal parent, are pursued by clamorous flights of censures, which swarm in far greater numbers, and threaten to devour them; but these last are not winged. At the end of a very short leap they fall plump down, and rot, having received from the souls out of which they came no beautiful wings. But the melodies of the poet ascend, and leap, and pierce into the deeps of infinite time.

So far the bard taught me, using his freer speech. But nature has a higher end, in the production of new individuals, than security, namely, ascension, or the passage of the soul into higher forms. I knew, in my younger days, the sculptor who made the statue of the youth which stands in the public garden. He was, as I remember, unable to tell directly, what made him happy, or unhappy, but by wonderful indirections he could tell. He rose one day, according to his habit, before the dawn, and saw the morning break, grand as the eternity out of which it came, and, for many days after, he strove to express this tranquility, and lo! His chisel had fashioned out of marble the form of a beautiful youth, Phosphorus, whose aspect is such, that, it is said, all persons who look on it become silent. The poet also resigns himself to his mood, and that thought which agitated him is expressed, but alter idem in a manner totally new. The expression is organic, or, the new type which things themselves take when liberated. As, in the sun, objects paint their images on the retina of the eye, so they, sharing the aspiration of the whole universe, tend to paint a far more delicate copy of their essence in his mind. Like the metamorphosis of things into higher organic forms, is their change into melodies. Over everything stands its daemon, or soul, and, as the form of the thing is reflected by the eye, so the soul of the thing is reflected by a melody. The sea, the mountain-ridge, Niagara, and every flower-bed, pre-exist, or super-exist, in pre-cantations, which sail like odors in the air, and when any man goes by with an ear sufficiently fine, he overhears them, and endeavors to write down the notes, without diluting or depraving them. And herein is the legitimation of criticism, in the mind's faith, that the poems are a corrupt version of some text in nature, with which they ought to be made to tally. A rhyme in one of our sonnets should not be less pleasing than the iterated nodes of a sea-shell, or the resembling difference of a group of flowers. The pairing of the birds is an idyl, not tedious as our idyls are; a tempest is a rough ode, without falsehood or rant: a summer, with its harvest sown, reaped, and stored, is an epic song, subordinating how many admirably executed parts. Why should not the symmetry and truth that modulate these, glide into our spirits, and we participate the invention of nature?

This insight, which expresses itself by what is called Imagination, is a very high sort of seeing, which does not come by study, but by the intellect being where and what it sees, by sharing the path, or circuit of things through forms, and so making them translucid to others. The path of things is silent. Will they suffer a speaker to go with them? A spy they will not suffer; a lover, a poet, is the transcendency of their own nature,— him they will suffer. The condition of true naming, on the poet's part, is his resigning himself to the divine aura which breathes through forms, and accompanying that.

It is a secret which every intellectual man quickly learns, that, beyond the energy of his possessed and conscious intellect, he is capable of a new energy (as of an intellect doubled on itself), by abandonment to the nature of things; that, beside his privacy of power as an individual man, there is a great public power, on which he can draw, by unlocking, at all risks, his human doors, and suffering the ethereal tides to roll and circulate through him: then he is caught up into the life of the Universe, his speech is thunder, his thought is law, and his words are universally intelligible as the plants and animals. The poet knows that he speaks adequately, then, only when he speaks somewhat wildly, or, "with the flower of the mind"; not with the intellect, used as an organ, but with the intellect released from all service, and suffered to take its direction from its celestial life; or, as the ancients were wont to express themselves, not with intellect alone, but with the intellect inebriated by nectar. As the traveller who has lost his way, throws his reins on his horse's neck, and trusts to the instinct of the animal to find his road, so must we do with the divine animal who carries us through this world. For if in any manner we can stimulate this instinct, new passages are opened for us into nature, the mind flows into and through things hardest and highest, and the metamorphosis is possible.

This is the reason why bards love wine, mead, narcotics, coffee, tea, opium, the fumes of sandal-wood and tobacco, or whatever other species of animal exhilaration. All men avail themselves of such means as they can, to add this extraordinary power to their normal powers; and to this end they prize conversation, music, pictures, sculpture, dancing, theatres, travelling, war, mobs, fires, gaming, politics, or love, or sciencc, or animal intoxication, which are several coarser or finer quasi-mechanical substitutes for the true nectar, which is the ravishment of the intellect by coming nearer to the fact. These are auxiliaries to the centrifugal tendency of a man, to his passage out into free space, and they help him to escape the custody of that body in which he is pent up, and of that jail-yard of individual relations in which he is enclosed. Hence a great number of such as were professionally expressors of Beauty, as painters, poets, musicians, and actors, have been more than others wont to lead a life of pleasure and indulgence; all but the few who received the true nectar; and, as it was a spurious mode of attaining freedom, as it was an emancipation not into the heavens, but into the freedom of baser places, they were punished for that advantage they won, by a dissipation and deterioration. But never can any advantage be taken of nature by a trick. The spirit of the world, the great calm presence of the creator, comes not forth to the sorceries of opium or of wine. The sublime vision comes to the pure and simple soul in a clean and chaste body. That is not an inspiration which we owe to narcotics, but some counterfeit excitement and fury. Milton says, that the lyric poet may drink wine and live generously, but the epic poet, he who shall sing of the gods, and their descent unto men, must drink water out of a wooden bowl.

For poetry is not "Devil's wine," but God's wine. It is with this as it is with toys. We fill the hands and nurseries of our children with all manner of dolls, drums, and horses, withdrawing their eyes from the plain face and sufficing objects of nature, the sun, and moon, the animals, the water, and stones, which should be their toys. So the poet's habit of living should be set on a key so low and plain, that the common influences should delight him. His cheerfulness should be the gift of the sunlight; the air should suffice for his inspiration, and he should be tipsy with water. That spirit which suffices quiet hearts, which seems to come forth to such from every dry knoll of sere grass, from every pine-stump, and half-imbedded stone, on which the dull March sun shines, comes forth to the poor and hungry, and such as are of simple taste. If thou fill thy brain with Boston and New York, with fashion and covetousness, and wilt stimulate thy jaded senses with wine and French coffee, thou shalt find no radiance of wisdom in the lonely waste of the pinewoods.

If the imagination intoxicates the poet, it is not inactive in other men. The metamorphosis excites in the beholder an emotion of joy.

The use of symbols has a certain power of emancipation and exhilaration for all men. We seem to be touched by a wand, which makes us dance and run about happily, like children. We are like persons who come out of a cave or cellar into the open air. This is the effect on us of tropes, fables, oracles, and all poetic forms. Poets are thus liberating gods. Men have really got a new sense, and found within their world, another world, or nest of worlds; for, the metamorphosis once seen, we divine that it does not stop. I will not now consider how much this makes the charm of algebra and the mathematics, which also have their tropes, but it is felt in every definition; as, when Aristotle defines space to be an immovable vessel, in which things are contained; — or, when Plato defines a line to be a flowing point; or, figure to be a bound of solid; and many the like. What a joyful sense of freedom we have, when Vitruvius announces the old opinion of artists, that no architect can build any house well, who does not know something of anatomy. When Socrates, in Charmides, tells us that the soul is cured of its maladies by certain incantations, and that these incantations are beautiful reasons, from which temperance is generated in souls; when Plato calls the world an animal; and Timaeus affirms that the plants also are animals; or affirms a man to be a heavenly tree, growing with his root, which is his head, upward; and, as George Chapman, following him, writes, —

> "So in our tree of man, whose nervie root
> Springs in his top;"

when Orpheus speaks of hoariness as "that white flower which marks extreme old age"; when Proclus calls the universe the statue of the intellect; when Chaucer, in his praise of "Gentilesse," compares good blood in mean condition to fire, which, though carried to the darkest house betwixt this and the mount of Caucasus, will yet hold its natural office, and burn as bright as if twenty thousand men did it behold; when John saw, in the apocalypse, the ruin of the world through evil, and the stars fall from heaven, as the fig tree casteth her untimely fruit; when Aesop reports the whole catalogue of common daily relations through the masquerade of birds and beasts; — we take the cheerful hint of the immortality of our essence, and its versatile habit and escapes, as when the gypsies say, "it is in vain to hang them, they cannot die."

The poets are thus liberating gods. The ancient British bards had for the title of their order, "Those who are free throughout the world."They are free, and they make free. An imaginative book renders us much more service at first, by stimulating us through its tropes, than afterward, when we arrive at the precise sense of the author. I think nothing is of any value in books, excepting the transcendental and extraordinary. If a man is inflamed and carried away by his thought, to that degree that he forgets the authors and the public, and heeds only this one dream, which holds him like an insanity, let me read his paper, and you may have all the arguments and histories and criticism. All the value which attaches to Pythagoras, Paracelsus, Cornelius Agrippa, Cardan, Kepler, Swedenborg, Schelling, Oken, or any other who introduces questionable facts into his cosmogony, as angels, devils, magic, astrology, palmistry, mesmerism, and so on, is the certificate we have of departure from routine, and that here is a new witness. That also is the best success in conversation, the magic of liberty, which puts the world, like a ball, in our hands. How cheap even the liberty then seems; how mean to study, when an emotion communicates to the intellect the power to sap and upheave nature: how great the perspective! Nations, times, systems, enter and disappear, like threads in tapestry of large figure and many colors; dream delivers us to dream, and, while the drunkenness lasts, we will sell our bed, our philosophy, our religion, in our opulence.

There is good reason why we should prize this liberation. The fate of the poor shepherd, who, blinded and lost in the snow-storm, perishes in a drift within a few feet of his cottage door, is an emblem of the state of man. On the brink of the waters of life and truth, we are miserably dying. The inaccessibleness of every thought but that we are in, is wonderful. What if you come near to it, —you are as remote, when you are nearest, as when you are farthest. Every thought is also a prison; every heaven is also a prison. Therefore we love the poet, the inventor, who in any form, whether in an ode, or in an action, or in looks and behavior, has yielded us a new thought. He unlocks our chains, and admits us to a new scene.

This emancipation is dear to all men, and the power to impart it, as it must come from greater depth and scope of thought, is a measure of intellect. Therefore all books of the imagination endure, all which ascend to that truth, that the writer sees nature beneath him, and uses it as his exponent. Every verse or sentence, possessing this virtue, will take care of its own immortality. The religions of the world are the ejaculations of a few imaginative men.

But the quality of the imagination is to flow, and not to freeze. The poet did not stop at the color, or the form, but read their meaning; neither may he rest in this meaning, but he makes the same objects exponents of his new thought. Here is the difference betwixt the poet and the mystic, that the last nails a symbol to one sense, which was a true sense for a moment, but soon becomes old and false. For all symbols are fluxional; all language is vehicular and transitive, and is good, as ferries and horses are, for conveyance, not as farms and houses are, for homestead. Mysticism consists in the mistake of an accidental and individual symbol for an universal one. The morning-redness happens to be the favorite meteor to the eyes of Jacob Behmen, and comes to stand to him for truth and faith; and he believes should stand for the same realities to every reader. But the first reader prefers as naturally the symbol of a mother and child, or a gardener and his bulb, or a jeweller polishing a gem. Either of these, or of a myriad more, are equally good to the person to whom they are significant. Only they must be held lightly, and be very willingly translated into the equivalent terms which others use. And the mystic must be steadily told, — All that you say is just as true without the tedious use of that symbol as with it. Let us have a little algebra, instead of this trite rhetoric, — universal signs, instead of these village symbols, — and we shall both be gainers. The history of hierarchies seems to show, that all religious error consisted in making the symbol too stark and solid, and, at last, nothing but an excess of the organ of language.

Swedenborg, of all men in the recent ages, stands eminently for the translator of nature into thought. I do not know the man in history to whom things stood so uniformly for words. Before him the metamorphosis continually plays. Everything on which his eye rests, obeys the impulses of moral nature. The figs become grapes whilst he eats them. When some of his angels affirmed a truth, the laurel twig which they held blossomed in their hands. The noise which, at a distance, appeared like gnashing and thumping, on coming nearer was found to be the voice of disputants. The men, in one of his visions, seen in heavenly light, appeared like dragons, and seemed in darkness: but, to each other, they appeared as men, and, when the light from heaven shone into their cabin, they complained of the darkness, and were compelled to shut the window that they might see.

There was this perception in him, which makes the poet or seer, an object of awe and terror, namely, that the same man, or society of men, may wear one aspect to themselves and their companions, and a different aspect to higher intelligences. Certain priests, whom he describes as conversing very learnedly together, appeared to the children, who were at some distance, like dead horses: and many the like misappearances. And instantly the mind inquires, whether these fishes under the bridge, yonder oxen in the pasture, those dogs in the yard, are immutably fishes, oxen, and dogs, or only so appear to me, and perchance to themselves appear upright men; and whether I appear as a man to all eyes. The Bramins and Pythagoras propounded the same question, and if any poet has witnessed the transformation, he doubtless found it in harmony with various experiences. We have all seen changes as considerable in wheat and caterpillars. He is the poet, and shall draw us with love and terror, who sees, through the flowing vest, the firm nature, and can declare it.

I look in vain for the poet whom I describe. We do not, with sufficient plainness, or sufficient profoundness, address ourselves to life, nor dare we chaunt our own times and social circumstance. If we filled the day with bravery, we should not shrink from celebrating it. Time and nature yield us many gifts, but not yet the timely man, the new religion, the reconciler, whom all things await. Dante's praise is, that he dared to write his autobiography in colossal cipher, or into universality. We have yet had no genius in America, with tyrannous eye, which knew the value of our incomparable materials, and saw, in the barbarism and materialism of the times, another carnival of the same gods whose picture he so much admires in *Homer*; then in the middle age; then in Calvinism. Banks and tariffs, the newspaper and caucus, methodism and unitarianism, are flat and dull to dull people, but rest on the same foundations of wonder as the town of Troy, and the temple of Delphos, and are as swiftly passing away. Our logrolling, our stumps and their politics, our fisheries, our Negroes, and Indians, our boasts, and our repudiations, the wrath of rogues, and the pusillanimity of honest men, the northern trade, the southern planting, the western clearing, Oregon, and Texas, are yet unsung. Yet America is a poem in our eyes; its ample geography dazzles the imagination, and it will not wait long for metres. If I have not found that excellent combination of gifts in my countrymen which I seek, neither could I aid myself to fix the idea of the poet by reading now and then in Chalmers's collection of five centuries of English poets. These are wits, more than poets, though there have been poets among them. But when we adhere to the ideal of the poet, we have our difficulties even with Milton and Homer. Milton is too literary, and Homer too literal and historical.

But I am not wise enough for a national criticism, and must use the old largeness a little longer, to discharge my errand from the muse to the poet concerning his art.

Art is the path of the creator to his work. The paths, or methods, are ideal and eternal, though few men ever see them, not the artist himself for years, or for a lifetime, unless he come into the conditions. The painter, the sculptor, the composer, the epic rhapsodist, the orator, all partake one desire, namely, to express themselves symmetrically and abundantly, not dwarfishly and fragmentarily. They found or put themselves in certain conditions, as, the painter and sculptor before some impressive human figures; the orator, into the assembly of the people; and the others, in such scenes as each has found exciting to his intellect; and each presently feels the new desire. He hears a voice, he sees a beckoning. Then he is apprised, with wonder, what herds of daemons hem him in. He can no more rest; he says, with the old painter, "By God, it is in me, and must go forth of me."He pursues a beauty, half seen, which flies before him. The poet pours out verses in every solitude. Most of the things he says are conventional, no doubt; but by and by he says something which is original and beautiful. That charms him. He would say nothing else but such things. In our way of talking, we say, "That is yours, this is mine;"but the poet knows well that it is not his; that it is as strange and beautiful to him as to you; he would fain hear the like eloquence at length. Once having tasted this immortal ichor, he cannot have enough of it, and, as an admirable creative power exists in these intellections, it is of the last importance that these things get spoken. What a little of all we know is said! What drops of all the sea of our science are baled up! and by what accident it is that these are exposed, when so many secrets sleep in nature! Hence the necessity of speech and song; hence these throbs and heart-beatings in the orator, at the door of the assembly, to the end, namely, that thought may be ejaculated as Logos, or Word.

Doubt not, O poet, but persist. Say, "It is in me, and shall out."Stand there, baulked and dumb, stuttering and stammering, hissed and hooted, stand and strive, until, at last, rage draw out of thee that dream-power which every night shows thee is thine own; a power transcending all limit and privacy, and by virtue of which a man is the conductor of the whole river of electricity. Nothing walks, or creeps, or grows, or exists, which must not in turn arise and walk before him as exponent of his meaning. Comes he to that power, his genius is no longer exhaustible.

All the creatures, by pairs and by tribes, pour into his mind as into a Noah's ark, to come forth again to people a new world. This is like the stock of air for our respiration, or for the combustion of our fireplace, not a measure of gallons, but the entire atmosphere if wanted. And therefore the rich poets, as Homer, Chaucer, Shakespeare, and Raphael, have obviously no limits to their works, except the limits of their lifetime, and resemble a mirror carried through the street, ready to render an image of every created thing.

O poet! A new nobility is conferred in groves and pastures, and not in castles, or by the sword-blade, any longer. The conditions are hard, but equal. Thou shalt leave the world, and know the muse only. Thou shalt not know any longer the times, customs, graces, politics, or opinions of men, but shalt take all from the muse. For the time of towns is tolled from the world by funereal chimes, but in nature the universal hours are counted by succeeding tribes of animals and plants, and by growth of joy on joy. God wills also that thou abdicate a manifold and duplex life, and that thou be content that others speak for thee. Others shall be thy gentlemen, and shall represent all courtesy and worldly life for thee; others shall do the great and resounding actions also. Thou shalt lie close hid with nature, and canst not be afforded to the Capitol or the Exchange. The world is full of renunciations and apprenticeships, and this is thine: thou must pass for a fool and a churl for a long season. This is the screen and sheath in which Pan has protected his well-beloved flower, and thou shalt be known only to thine own, and they shall console thee with tenderest love. And thou shalt not be able to rehearse the names of thy friends in thy verse, for an old shame before the holy ideal. And this is the reward: that the ideal shall be real to thee, and the impressions of the actual world shall fall like summer rain, copious, but not troublesome, to thy invulnerable essence. Thou shalt have the whole land for thy park and manor, the sea for thy bath and navigation, without tax and without envy; the woods and the rivers thou shalt own; and thou shalt possess that wherein others are only tenants and boarders. Thou true land-lord! sea-lord! air-lord! Wherever snow falls, or water flows, or birds fly, wherever day and night meet in twilight, wherever the blue heaven is hung by clouds, or sown with stars, wherever are forms with transparent boundaries, wherever are outlets into celestial space, wherever is danger, and awe, and love, there is Beauty, plenteous as rain, shed for thee, and though thou shouldest walk the world over, thou shalt not be able to find a condition inopportune or ignoble.

Topics for Discussion

1. What literary strategy is adopted in Plato's/Socrates' elaboration on the immortality of the soul?
2. Is Plato's/Socrates' elaboration about the immortality of the soul a philosophical argumentation or literary imagination?
3. Could you find any intertextuality between Plato's/Socrates' tale of Er and Odysseus' trip to the underworld in Homer's *Odyssey*?
4. Could you find any philosophical idea(s) embodied in Emerson's elaboration on the poet?
5. Analyze Emerson's view about the relationship between poetry and philosophy.
6. Give more examples of intertextuality between literature and philosophy.

Monograph Three Literature and History

I The Way to Write History

Lucian of Samosata (120-180)

translated by H. W. Fowler (1858–1933)

MY DEAR PHILO,

There is a story of a curious epidemic at Abdera, just after the accession of King Lysimachus. It began with the whole population's exhibiting feverish symptoms, strongly marked and unintermittent from the very first attack. About the seventh day, the fever was relieved, in some cases by a violent flow of blood from the nose, in others by perspiration not less violent. The mental effects, however, were most ridiculous; they were all stage-struck, mouthing blank verse and ranting at the top of their voices. Their favourite recitation was the *Andromeda* of Euripides; one after another would go through the great speech of Perseus; the whole place was full of pale ghosts, who were our seventh-day tragedians vociferating,

O Love, who lord'st it over Gods and men,

and the rest of it. This continued for some time, till the coming of winter put an end to their madness with a sharp frost. I find the explanation of the form it took in this fact: Archelaus was then the great tragic actor, and in the middle of the summer, during some very hot weather, he had played the *Andromeda* there; most of them took the fever in the theatre, and convalescence was followed by a relapse—into tragedy, the Andromeda haunting their memories, and Perseus hovering, Gorgon's head in hand, before the mind's eye.

Well, to compare like with like, the majority of our educated class is now suffering from an Abderite epidemic. They are not stage-struck, indeed; that would have been a minor infatuation—to be possessed with other people's verses, not bad ones either; no; but from the beginning of the present excitements—the barbarian war, the Armenian disaster, the succession of victories—you cannot find a man but is writing history; nay, every one you meet is a Thucydides, a Herodotus, a Xenophon. The old saying must be true, and war be the father of all things, seeing what a litter of historians it has now teemed forth at a birth.

Such sights and sounds, my Philo, brought into my head that old anecdote about the Sinopean. A report that Philip was marching on the town had thrown all Corinth into a bustle; one was furbishing his arms, another wheeling stones, a third patching the wall, a fourth strengthening a battlement, every one making himself useful somehow or other. Diogenes having nothing to do—of course no one thought of giving him a job—was moved by the sight to gird up his philosopher's cloak and begin rolling his tub-dwelling energetically up and down the Craneum; an acquaintance asked, and got, the explanation: "I do not want to be thought the only idler in such a busy multitude; I am rolling my tub to be like the rest."

I too am reluctant to be the only dumb man at so vociferous a season; I do not like walking across the stage, like a "super," in gaping silence; so I decided to roll my cask as best I could. I do not intend to write a history, or attempt actual narrative; I am not courageous enough for that; have no apprehensions on my account; I realize the danger of rolling the thing over the rocks, especially if it is only a poor little jar of brittle earthenware like mine; I should very soon knock against some pebble and find myself picking up the pieces. Come, I will tell you my idea for campaigning in safety, and keeping well out of range.

Give a wide berth to all that foam and spray,

and to the anxieties which vex the historian—that I shall be wise enough to do; but I propose to give a little advice, and lay down a few principles for the benefit of those who do venture. I shall have a share in their building, if not in the dedicatory inscription; my finger-tips will at least have touched their wet mortar.

However, most of them see no need for advice here: there might as well be an art of talking, seeing, or eating; history-writing is perfectly easy, comes natural, is a universal gift; all that is necessary is the faculty of translating your thoughts into words. But the truth is—you know it without my telling, old friend—, it is not a task to be lightly undertaken, or carried through without effort; no, it needs as much care as any sort of composition whatever, if one means to create "a possession for ever," as Thucydides calls it. Well, I know I shall not get a hearing from many of them, and some will be seriously offended—especially any who have finished and produced their work; in cases where its first reception was favourable, it would be folly to expect the authors to recast or correct; has it not the stamp of finality? is it not almost a State document? Yet even they may profit by my words; we are not likely to be attacked again; we have disposed of all our enemies; but there might be a Celto-Gothic or an Indo-Bactrian war; then our friends' composition might be improved by the application of my measuring-rod—always supposing that they recognize its correctness; failing that, let them do their own mensuration with the old foot-rule; the doctor will not particularly mind, though all Abdera insists on spouting the Andromeda.

Advice has two provinces—one of choice, the other of avoidance;

let us first decide what the historian is to avoid—of what faults he must purge himself—, and then proceed to the measures he must take for putting himself on the straight high road. This will include the manner of his beginning, the order in which he should marshal his facts, the questions of proportion, of discreet silence, of full or cursory narration, of comment and connexion. Of all that, however, later on; for the present we deal with the vices to which bad writers are liable. As to those faults of diction, construction, meaning, and general amateurishness, which are common to every kind of composition, to discuss them is neither compatible with my space nor relevant to my purpose.

But there are mistakes peculiar to history; your own observation will show you just those which a constant attendance at authors' readings has impressed on me; you have only to keep your ears open at every opportunity. It will be convenient, however, to refer by the way to a few illustrations in recent histories. Here is a serious fault to begin with. It is the fashion to neglect the examination of facts, and give the space gained to eulogies of generals and commanders; those of their own side they exalt to the skies, the other side they disparage intemperately. They forget that between history and panegyric there is a great gulf fixed, barring communication; in musical phrase, the two things are a couple of octaves apart. The panegyrist has only one concern—to commend and gratify his living theme some way or other; if misrepresentation will serve his purpose, he has no objection to that. History, on the other hand, abhors the intrusion of any least scruple of falsehood; it is like the windpipe, which the doctors tell us will not tolerate a morsel of stray food.

Another thing these gentlemen seem not to know is that poetry and history offer different wares, and have their separate rules. Poetry enjoys unrestricted freedom; it has but one law—the poet's fancy. He is inspired and possessed by the Muses; if he chooses to horse his car with winged steeds, or set others a-galloping over the sea, or standing corn, none challenges his right; his Zeus, with a single cord, may haul up earth and sea, and hold them dangling together—there is no fear the cord may break, the load come tumbling down and be smashed to atoms. In a complimentary picture of Agamemnon, there is nothing against his having Zeus's head and eyes, his brother Posidon's chest, Ares's belt—in fact, the son of Atreus and Aërope will naturally be an epitome of all Divinity; Zeus or Posidon or Ares could not singly or severally provide the requisite perfections. But, if history adopts such servile arts, it is nothing but poetry without the wings; the exalted tones are missing; and imposition of other kinds without the assistance of metre is only the more easily detected. It is surely a great, a superlative weakness, this inability to distinguish history from poetry; what, bedizen history, like her sister, with tale and eulogy and their attendant exaggerations? As well take some mighty athlete with muscles of steel, rig him up with purple drapery and meretricious ornament, rouge and powder his cheeks; faugh, what an object would one make of him with such defilements!

I would not be understood to exclude eulogy from history altogether; it is to be kept to its place and used with moderation, is not to tax the reader's patience; I shall presently show, indeed, that in all such matters an eye is to be had to posterity. It is true, there is a school which makes a pretty division of history into the agreeable and the useful, and defends the introduction of panegyric on the ground that it is agreeable, and pleases the general reader. But nothing could be further from the truth. In the first place the division is quite a false one; history has only one concern and aim, and that is the useful; which again has one single source, and that is truth. The agreeable is no doubt an addition, if it is present; so is beauty to an athlete; but a Nicostratus, who is a fine fellow and proves himself a better man than either of his opponents, gets his recognition as a Heracles, however ugly his face may be; and if one opponent is the handsome Alcaeus himself—handsome enough to make Nicostratus in love with him, says the story, —that does not affect the issue. History too, if it can deal incidentally in the agreeable, will attract a multitude of lovers; but so long as it does its proper business efficiently—and that is the establishment of truth, —it may be indifferent to beauty.

It is further to be remarked, that in history sheer extravagance has not even the merit of being agreeable; and the extravagance of eulogy is doubly repulsive, as extravagance, and as eulogy; at least it is only welcome to the vulgar majority, not to that critical, that perhaps hypercritical audience, whom no slip can escape, who are all eyes like Argus, but keener than he, who test every word as a moneychanger might his coins, rejecting the false on the spot, but accepting the good and heavy and true; it is they that we should have in mind as we write history, and never heed the others, though they applaud till they crack their voices. If you neglect the critics, and indulge in the cloying sweetness of tales and eulogies and such baits, you will soon find your history a "Heracles in Lydia." No doubt you have seen some picture of him: he is Omphale's slave, dressed up in an absurd costume, his lion-skin and club transferred to her, as though she were the true Heracles, while he, in saffron robe and purple jacket, is combing wool and wincing under Omphale's slipper. A degrading spectacle it is—the dress loose and flapping open, and all that was man in him turned to woman.

The vulgar may very likely extend their favour to this; but the select (whose judgement you disregard) will get a good deal of entertainment out of your heterogeneous, disjointed, fragmentary stuff. There is nothing which has not a beauty of its own; but take it out of its proper sphere, and the misuse turns its beauty to ugliness. Eulogy, I need hardly say, may possibly please one person, the eulogized, but will disgust every one else; this is particularly so with the monstrous exaggerations which are in fashion; the authors are so intent on the patron-hunt that they cannot relinquish it without a full exhibition of servility; they have no idea of finesse, never mask their flattery, but blurt out their unconvincing bald tale anyhow.

The consequence is, they miss even their immediate end; the objects of their praise are more inclined (and quite right too) to dislike and discard them for toadies—if they are men of spirit, at any rate. Aristobulus inserted in his history an account of a single combat between Alexander and Porus, and selected this passage to read aloud to the former; he reckoned that his best chance of pleasing was to invent heroic deeds for the king, and heighten his achievements. Well, they were on board ship in the Hydaspes; Alexander took hold of the book, and tossed it overboard; "the author should have been treated the same way, by rights," he added, "for presuming to fight duels for me like that, and shoot down elephants single-handed." A very natural indignation in Alexander, of a piece with his treatment of the intrusive architect; this person offered to convert the whole of Mount Athos into a colossal statue of the king—who however decided that he was a toady, and actually gave him less employment in ordinary than before.

The fact is, there is nothing agreeable in these things, except to any one who is fool enough to enjoy commendations which the slightest inquiry will prove to be unfounded; of course there *are* ugly persons—women more especially—who ask artists to paint them as beautiful as they can; they think they will be really better-looking if the painter heightens the rose a little and distributes a good deal of the lily. There you have the origin of the present crowd of historians, intent only upon the passing day, the selfish interest, the profit which they reckon to make out of their work; execration is their desert—in the present for their undisguised clumsy flattery, in the future for the stigma which their exaggerations bring upon history in general. If any one takes some admixture of the agreeable to be an absolute necessity, let him be content with the independent beauties of style; these are agreeable without being false; but they are usually neglected now, for the better foisting upon us of irrelevant substitutes.

Passing from that point, I wish to put on record some fresh recollections of Ionian histories—supported, now I think of it, by Greek analogies also of recent date—both concerned with the war already alluded to. You may trust my report, the Graces be my witness; I would take oath to its truth, if it were polite to swear on paper. One writer started with invoking the Muses to lend a hand. What a tasteful exordium! How suited to the historic spirit! How appropriate to the style! When he had got a little way on, he compared our ruler to Achilles, and the Parthian king to Thersites; he forgot that Achilles would have done better if he had had Hector instead of Thersites to beat, if there had been a man of might fleeing in front,

But at his heels a mightier far than he.

He next proceeded to say something handsome about himself, as a fit chronicler of such brilliant deeds. As he got near his point of departure, he threw in a word for his native town of Miletus, adding that he was thus improving on Homer, who never so much as mentioned his birthplace. And he concluded his preface with a plain express promise to advance our cause and personally wage war against the barbarians, to the best of his ability. The actual history, and recital of the causes of hostilities, began with these words:—"The detestable Vologesus (whom Heaven confound!) commenced war on the following pretext."

Enough of him. Another is a keen emulator of Thucydides, and by way of close approximation to his model starts with his own name—most graceful of beginnings, redolent of Attic thyme! Look at it: "Crepereius Calpurnianus of Pompeiopolis wrote the history of the war between Parthia and Rome, how they warred one upon the other, beginning with the commencement of the war." After that exordium, what need to describe the rest—what harangues he delivers in Armenia, resuscitating our old friend the Corcyrean envoy—what a plague he inflicts on Nisibis (which would not espouse the Roman cause), lifting the whole thing bodily from Thucydides—except the Pelasgicum and the Long Walls, where the victims of the earlier plague found shelter; there the difference ends; like the other, "it began in Ethiopia, whence it descended to Egypt," and to most of the Parthian empire, where it very discreetly remained. I left him engaged in burying the poor Athenians in Nisibis, and knew quite well how he would continue after my exit. Indeed it is a pretty common belief at present that you are writing like Thucydides, if you just use his actual words, mutatis mutandis. Ah, and I almost forgot to mention one thing: this same writer gives many names of weapons and military engines in Latin—phossa for trench, pons for bridge, and so forth. Just think of the dignity of history, and the Thucydidean style—the Attic embroidered with these Latin words, like a toga relieved and picked out with the purple stripe—so harmonious!

Another puts down a bald list of events, as prosy and commonplace as a private's or a carpenter's or a sutler's diary. However, there is more sense in this poor man's performance; he flies his true colours from the first; he has cleared the ground for some educated person who knows how to deal with history. The only fault I have to find with him is that he inscribes his volumes with a solemnity rather disproportioned to the rank of their contents—"Parthian History, by Callimorphus, Surgeon of the 6th Pikemen, volume so-and-so." Ah, yes, and there is a lamentable preface, which closes with the remark that, since Asclepius is the son of Apollo, and Apollo director of the Muses and patron of all culture, it is very proper for a doctor to write history. Also, he starts in Ionic, but very soon, for no apparent reason, abandons it for every-day Greek, still keeping the Ionic es and ks and ous, but otherwise writing like ordinary people—rather too ordinary, indeed.

Perhaps I should balance him with a philosophic historian; this gentleman's name I will conceal, and merely indicate his attitude, as revealed in a recent publication at Corinth. Much had been expected of him, but not enough; starting straight off with the first sentence of the preface, he subjects his readers to a dialectic catechism, his thesis being the highly philosophic one, that no one but a philosopher should write history. Very shortly there follows a second logical process, itself followed by a third; in fact the whole preface is one mass of dialectic figures. There is flattery, indeed, ad nauseam, eulogy vulgar to the point of farce; but never without the logical trimmings; always that dialectical catechism. I confess it strikes me as a vulgarity also, hardly worthy of a philosopher with so long and white a beard, when he gives it in his preface as our ruler's special good fortune that philosophers should consent to record his actions; he had better have left us to reach that conclusion for ourselves—if at all.

Again, it would be a sinful neglect to omit the man who begins like this: —"I devise to tell of Romans and Persians"; then a little later, "For' twas Heaven's decree that the Persians should suffer evils"; and again, "One Osroes there was, whom Hellenes name Oxyroes"—and much more in that style. He corresponds, you see, to one of my previous examples; only he is a second Herodotus, and the other a second Thucydides.

There is another distinguished artist in words—again rather more Thucydidean than Thucydides—, who gives, according to his own idea, the clearest, most convincing descriptions of every town, mountain, plain, or river. I wish my bitterest foe no worse fate than the reading of them. Frigid? Caspian snows, Celtic ice, are warm in comparison. A whole book hardly suffices him for the Emperor's shield—the Gorgon on its boss, with eyes of blue and white and black, rainbow girdle, and snakes twined and knotted. Why, Vologesus's breeches or his bridle, God bless me, they take up several thousand lines apiece; the same for the look of Osroes's hair as he swims the Tigris—or what the cave was like that sheltered him, ivy and myrtle and bay clustered all together to shut out every ray of light. You observe how indispensable it all is to the history; without the scene, how could we have comprehended the action?

It is helplessness about the real essentials, or ignorance of what should be given, that makes them take refuge in word-painting—landscapes, caves, and the like; and when they do come upon a series of important matters, they are just like a slave whose master has left him his money and made him a rich man; he does not know how to put on his clothes or take his food properly; partridges or sweetbreads or hare are served; but he rushes in, and fills himself up with pea soup or salt fish, till he is fit to burst. Well, the man I spoke of gives the most unconvincing wounds and singular deaths: some one has his big toe injured, and dies on the spot; the general Priscus calls out, and seven-and-twenty of the enemy fall dead at the sound. As to the numbers killed, he actually falsifies dispatches; at Europus he slaughters 70, 236 of the enemy, while the Romans lose two, and have seven wounded! How any man of sense can tolerate such stuff, I do not know.

Here is another point quite worth mention. This writer has such a passion for unadulterated Attic, and for refining speech to the last degree of purity, that he metamorphoses the Latin names and translates them into Greek; Saturninus figures as Cronius, Fronto must be Phrontis, Titianus Titanius, with queerer transmogrifications yet. Further, on the subject of Severian's death, he accuses all other writers of a blunder in putting him to the sword; he is really to have starved himself to death, as the most painless method; the fact, however, is that it was all over in three days, whereas seven days is the regular time for starvation; are we perhaps to conceive an Osroes waiting about for Severian to complete the process, and putting off his assault till after the seventh day?

Then, Philo, how shall we class the historians who indulge in poetical phraseology? "The catapult rocked responsive," they say, "Loud thundered the breach"; or, somewhere else in this delectable history, "Thus Edessa was girdled with clash of arms, and all was din and turmoil," or, "The general pondered in his heart how to attack the wall." Only he fills up the interstices with such wretched common lower-class phrases as "The military prefect wrote His Majesty," "The troops were procuring the needful," "They got a wash and put in an appearance," and so on. It is like an actor with one foot raised on a high buskin, and the other in a slipper.

You will find others writing brilliant high-sounding prefaces of outrageous length, raising great expectations of the wonders to follow—and then comes a poor little appendix of a—history; it is like nothing in the world but a child—say the Eros you must have seen in a picture playing in an enormous mask of Heracles or a Titan; *parturient montes*, cries the audience, very naturally. That is not the way to do things; the whole should be homogeneous and uniform, and the body in proportion to the head—not a helmet of gold, a ridiculous breastplate patched up out of rags or rotten leather, shield of wicker, and pig-skin greaves. You will find plenty of historians prepared to set the Rhodian Colossus's head on the body of a dwarf; others on the contrary show us headless bodies, and plunge into the facts without exordium. These plead the example of Xenophon, who starts with "Darius and Parysatis had two children"; if they only knew it, there is such a thing as a *virtual* exordium, not realized as such by everybody; but of that hereafter.

However, any mistake in mere expression or arrangement is excusable; but when you come to fancy geography, differing from the other not by miles or leagues, but by whole days' journeys, where is the classical model for that? One writer has taken so little trouble with his facts—never met a Syrian, I suppose, nor listened to the stray information you may pick up at the barber's,—that he thus locates Europus:—"Europus lies in Mesopotamia, two days' journey from the Euphrates, and is a colony from Edessa." Not content with that, this enterprising person has in the same book taken up my native Samosata and shifted it, citadel, walls, and all, into Mesopotamia, giving it the two rivers for boundaries, and making them shave past it, all but touching the walls on either side. I suspect you would laugh at me, Philo, if I were to set about convincing you that I am neither Parthian nor Mesopotamian, as this whimsical colony-planter makes me.

By the way, he has also a very attractive tale of Severian, learnt, he assures us on oath, from one of the actual fugitives. According to this, he would not die by the sword, the rope, or poison, but contrived a death which should be tragic and impressive. He was the owner of some large goblets of the most precious glass; having made up his mind to die, he broke the largest of these, and used a splinter of it for the purpose, cutting his throat with the glass. A dagger or a lancet, good enough instruments for a manly and heroic death, he could not come at, forsooth!

Then, as Thucydides composed a funeral oration over the first victims of that old war, our author feels it incumbent on him to do the same for Severian; they all challenge Thucydides, you see, little as he can be held responsible for the Armenian troubles. So he buries Severian, and then solemnly ushers up to the grave, as Pericles's rival, one Afranius Silo, a centurion; the flood of rhetoric which follows is so copious and remarkable that it drew tears from me—ye Graces!—tears of laughter; most of all where the eloquent Afranius, drawing to a close, makes mention, with weeping and distressful moans, of all those costly dinners and toasts. But he is a very Ajax in his conclusion. He draws his sword, gallantly as an Afranius should, and in sight of all cuts his throat over the grave—and God knows it was high time for an execution, if oratory can be felony. The historian states that all the spectators admired and lauded Afranius; as for me, I was inclined to condemn him on general grounds—he had all but given a catalogue of sauces and dishes, and shed tears over the memory of departed cakes, —but his capital offence was that he had not cut the historian-tragedian's throat before he left this life himself.

I assure you, my friend, I could largely increase my list of such offenders; but one or two more will suffice, before proceeding to the second part of my undertaking, the suggestions for improvement. There are some, then, who leave alone, or deal very cursorily with, all that is great and memorable; amateurs and not artists, they have no selective faculty, and loiter over copious laboured descriptions of the veriest trifles; it is as if a visitor to Olympia, instead of examining, commending or describing to his stay-at-home friends the general greatness and beauty of the Zeus, were to be struck with the exact symmetry and polish of its footstool, or the proportions of its shoe, and give all his attention to these minor points.

For instance, I have known a man get through the battle of Europus in less than seven whole lines, and then spend twenty mortal hours on a dull and perfectly irrelevant tale about a Moorish trooper. The trooper's name was Mausacas; he wandered up the hills in search of water, and came upon some Syrian yokels getting their lunch; at first they were afraid of him, but when they found he was on the right side, they invited him to share the meal; for one of them had travelled in the Moorish country, having a brother serving in the army. Then come long stories and descriptions of how he hunted there, and saw a great herd of elephants at pasture, and was nearly eaten up by a lion, and what huge fish he had bought at Caesarea. So this quaint historian leaves the terrible carnage to go on at Europus, and lets the pursuit, the forced armistice, the settling of outposts, shift for themselves, while he lingers far into the evening watching Malchion the Syrian cheapen big mackarel at Caesarea; if night had not come all too soon, I dare say he would have dined with him when the fish was cooked. If all this had not been accurately set down in the history, what sad ignorance we should have been left in! The loss to the Romans would have been irreparable, if Mausacas the Moor had got nothing to quench his thirst, and come back fasting to camp. Yet I am wilfully omitting innumerable details of yet greater importance—the arrival of a flute-girl from the next village, the exchange of gifts (Mausacas's was a spear, Malchion's a brooch), and other incidents most essential to the battle of Europus. It is no exaggeration to say that such writers never give the rose a glance, but devote all their curiosity to the thorns on its stem.

Another entertaining person, who has never set foot outside Corinth, nor travelled as far as its harbour—not to mention seeing Syria or Armenia,—starts with words which impressed themselves on my memory:—"Seeing is believing: I therefore write what I have seen, not what I have been told." His personal observation has been so close that he describes the Parthian "Dragons" (they use this ensign as a numerical formula—a thousand men to the Dragon, I believe): they are huge live dragons, he says, breeding in Persian territory beyond Iberia; these are first fastened to great poles and hoisted up aloft, striking terror at a distance while the advance is going on; then, when the battle begins, they are released and set on the enemy; numbers of our men, it seems, were actually swallowed by them, and others strangled or crushed in their coils; of all this he was an eye-witness, taking his observations, however, from a safe perch up a tree. Thank goodness he did not come to close quarters with the brutes! We should have lost a very remarkable historian, and one who did doughty deeds in this war with his own right hand; for he had many adventures, and was wounded at Sura (in the course of a stroll from the Craneum to Lerna, apparently). All this he used to read to a Corinthian audience, which was perfectly aware that he had never so much as seen a battle-picture. Why, he did not know one weapon or engine from another; the names of manoeuvres and formations had no meaning for him; flank or front, line or column, it was all one.

Then there is a splendid fellow, who has boiled down into the compass of five hundred lines (or less, to be accurate) the whole business from beginning to end—campaigns in Armenia, in Syria, in Mesopotamia, on the Tigris, and in Media; and having done it, he calls it a history. His title very narrowly misses being longer than his book: "An account of the late campaigns of the Romans in Armenia, Mesopotamia, and Media, by Antiochianus, victor at the festival of Apollo"; he had probably won some junior flat race.

I have known one writer compile a history of the future, including the capture of Vologesus, the execution of Osroes (he is to be thrown to the lions), and, crowning all, our long-deferred triumph. In this prophetic vein, he sweeps hastily on to the end of his work; yet he finds time for the foundation in Mesopotamia of a city, greatest of the great, and fairest of the fair; he is still debating, however, whether the most appropriate name will be Victoria, Concord, or Peacetown; that is yet unsettled; we must leave the fair city unnamed for the present; but it is already thickly populated—with empty dreams and literary drivellings. He has also pledged himself to an account of coming events in India, and a circumnavigation of the Atlantic; nay, the pledge is half redeemed; the preface to the *India* is complete; the third legion, the Celtic contingent, and a small Moorish division, have crossed the Indus in full force under Cassius; our most original historian will soon be posting us up in their doings—their method of 'receiving elephants', for instance—in letters dated Muziris or Oxydracae.

These people's uneducated antics are infinite; they have no eyes for the noteworthy, nor, if they had eyes, any adequate faculty of expression; invention and fiction provide their matter, and belief in the first word that comes their style; they pride themselves on the number of books they run to, and yet more on their titles; for these again are quite absurd: —*So-and-so's so many books of Parthian victories*; *The Parthis*, book I; *The Parthis*, book II—quite a rival to the *Atthis*, eh? Another does it (I have read the book) still more neatly—'*The Parthonicy of Demetrius of Sagalassus*.' I do not wish to ridicule or make a jest of these pretty histories; I write for a practical purpose: any one who avoids these and similar errors is already well on the road to historical success; nay, he is almost there, if the logical axiom is correct, that, with incompatibles, denial of the one amounts to affirmation of the other.

Well, I may be told, *you have now a clear field*; *the thorns and brambles have all been extirpated, the debris of others' buildings has been carted of, the rough places have been made smooth*; *come, do a little construction yourself, and show that you are not only good at destroying, but capable of yourself planning a model, in which criticism itself shall find nothing to criticize.*

Well then, my perfect historian must start with two indispensable qualifications; the one is political insight, the other the faculty of expression; the first is a gift of nature, which can never be learnt; the second should have been acquired by long practice, unremitting toil, and loving study of the classics. There is nothing technical here, and no room for any advice of mine; this essay does not profess to bestow insight and acumen on those who are not endowed with them by nature; valuable, or invaluable rather, would it have been, if it could recast and modify like that, transmute lead into gold, tin into silver, magnify a Conon or Leotrophides into Titormus or Milo.

But what is the function of professional advice? Not the creation of qualities which should be already there, but the indication of their proper use. No trainer, of course, —let him be Iccus, Herodicus, Theon, or who he may—will suggest that he can take a Perdiccas and make an Olympic victor of him, fit to face Theagenes of Thasos or Polydamas of Scotussa; what he *will* tell you is that, given a constitution that will stand training, his system will considerably improve it. So with us—we are not to have every failure cast in our teeth, if we claim to have invented a system for so great and difficult a subject. We do not offer to take the first comer and make a historian of him—only to point out to any one who has natural insight and acquired literary skill certain straight roads (they may or may not be so in reality) which will bring him with less waste of time and effort to his goal.

I do not suppose you will object that the man with insight has no need of system and instruction upon the things he is ignorant of; in that case he might have played the harp or flute untaught, and in fact have been omniscient. But, as things are at present, he cannot perform in these ways untaught, though with some assistance he will learn very easily, and soon be able to get along by himself.

You now know what sort of a pupil I (like the trainer) insist upon. He must not be weak either at understanding or at making himself understood, but a man of penetration, a capable administrator—potentially, that is,—with a soldierly spirit (which does not however exclude the civil spirit), and some military experience; at the least he must have been in camp, seen troops drilled or manoeuvred, know a little about weapons and military engines, the differences between line and column, cavalry and infantry tactics (with the reasons for them), frontal and flank attacks; in a word, none of your armchair strategists relying wholly on hearsay.

But first and foremost, let him be a man of independent spirit, with nothing to fear or hope from anybody; else he will be a corrupt judge open to undue influences. If Philip's eye is knocked out at Olynthus by Aster the Amphipolite archer, it is not his business to exclaim, but just to show him as he is; he is not to think whether Alexander will be annoyed by a circumstantial account of the cruel murder of Clitus at table. If a Cleon has the ear of the assembly, and a monopoly of the tribune, he will not shrink on that account from describing him as a pestilent madman; all Athens will not stop him from dwelling on the Sicilian disaster, the capture of Demosthenes, the death of Nicias, the thirst, the foul water, and the shooting down of the drinkers. He will consider very rightly that no man of sense will blame him for recounting the effects of misfortune or folly in their entirety; he is not the author, but only the reporter of them. If a fleet is destroyed, it is not he who sinks it; if there is a rout, he is not in pursuit—unless perhaps he ought to have prayed for better things, and omitted to do so. Of course, if silence or contradiction would have put matters right, Thucydides might with a stroke of the pen have knocked down the counterwall on Epipolae, sent Hermocrates's trireme to the bottom, let daylight through the accursed Gylippus before he had done blocking the roads with wall and trench, and, finally, have cast the Syracusans into their own quarries and sent the Athenians cruising round Sicily and Italy with Alcibiades's first high hopes still on board. Alas, not Fate itself may undo the work of Fate.

The historian's one task is to tell the thing as it happened. This he cannot do, if he is Artaxerxes's physician trembling before him, or hoping to get a purple cloak, a golden chain, a horse of the Nisaean breed, in payment for his laudations. A fair historian, a Xenophon, a Thucydides, will not accept that position. He may nurse some private dislikes, but he will attach far more importance to the public good, and set the truth high above his hate; he may have his favourites, but he will not spare their errors. For history, I say again, has this and this only for its own; if a man will start upon it, he must sacrifice to no God but Truth; he must neglect all else; his sole rule and unerring guide is this—to think not of those who are listening to him now, but of the yet unborn who shall seek his converse.

Any one who is intent only upon the immediate effect may reasonably be classed among the flatterers; and History has long ago realized that flattery is as little congenial to her as the arts of personal adornment to an athlete's training. An anecdote of Alexander is to the point. "Ah, Onesicritus," said he, "how I should like to come to life again for a little while, and see how your stuff strikes people by that time; at present they have good enough reason to praise and welcome it; that is their way of angling for a share of my favour." On the same principle some people actually accept Homer's history of Achilles, full of exaggerations as it is; the one great guarantee which they recognize of his truth is the fact that his subject was not living; that leaves him no motive for lying.

There stands my model, then: fearless, incorruptible, independent, a believer in frankness and veracity; one that will call a spade, make no concession to likes and dislikes, nor spare any man for pity or respect or propriety; an impartial judge, kind to all, but too kind to none; a literary cosmopolite with neither suzerain nor king, never heeding what this or that man may think, but setting down the thing that befell.

Thucydides is our noble legislator; he marked the admiration that met Herodotus and gave the Muses' names to his nine books; and thereupon he drew the line which parts a good historian from a bad: our work is to be a possession for ever, not a bid for present reputation; we are not to seize upon the sensational, but bequeath the truth to them that come after; he applies the test of use, and defines the end which a wise historian will set before himself: it is that, should history ever repeat itself, the records of the past may give present guidance.

Such are to be my historian's principles. As for diction and style, he is not to set about his work armed to the teeth from the rhetorician's arsenal of impetuosity and incisiveness, rolling periods, close-packed arguments, and the rest; for him a serener mood. His matter should be homogeneous and compact, his vocabulary fit to be understanded of the people, for the clearest possible setting forth of his subject.

For to those marks which we set up for the historic spirit—frankness and truth—corresponds one at which the historic style should first of all aim, namely, a lucidity which leaves nothing obscure, impartially avoiding abstruse out-of-the-way expressions, and the illiberal jargon of the market; we wish the vulgar to comprehend, the cultivated to commend us. Ornament should be unobtrusive, and never smack of elaboration, if it is not to remind us of over-seasoned dishes.

The historian's spirit should not be without a touch of the poetical; it needs, like poetry, to employ impressive and exalted tones, especially when it finds itself in the midst of battle array and conflicts by land or sea; it is then that the poetic gale must blow to speed the vessel on, and help her ride the waves in majesty. But the diction is to be content with *terra firma*, rising a little to assimilate itself to the beauty and grandeur of the subject, but never startling the hearer, nor forgetting a due restraint; there is great risk at such times of its running wild and falling into poetic frenzy; and then it is that writers should hold themselves in with bit and bridle; with them as with horses an uncontrollable temper means disaster. At these times it is best for the spirit to go a-horseback, and the expression to run beside on foot, holding on to the saddle so as not to be outstripped.

As to the marshalling of your words, a moderate compromise is desirable between the harshness which results from separating what belongs together, and the jingling concatenations—one may almost call them—which are so common; one extreme is a definite vice, and the other repellent.

Facts are not to be collected at haphazard, but with careful, laborious, repeated investigation; when possible, a man should have been present and seen for himself; failing that, he should prefer the disinterested account, selecting the informants least likely to diminish or magnify from partiality. And here comes the occasion for exercising the judgment in weighing probabilities.

The material once complete, or nearly so, an abstract should be made of it, and a rough draught of the whole work put down, not yet distributed into its parts; the detailed arrangement should then be introduced, after which adornment may be added, the diction receive its colour, the phrasing and rhythm be perfected.

The historian's position should now be precisely that of Zeus in *Homer*, surveying now the Mysians', now the Thracian horsemen's land. Even so *he* will survey now his own party (telling us what we looked like to him from his post of vantage), now the Persians, and yet again both at once, if they come to blows. And when they are face to face, his eyes are not to be on one division, nor yet on one man, mounted or afoot—unless it be a Brasidas leading the forlorn hope, or a Demosthenes repelling it; his attention should be for the generals first of all; their exhortations should be recorded, the dispositions they make, and the motives and plans that prompted them. When the engagement has begun, he should give us a bird's eye view of it, show the scales oscillating, and accompany pursuers and pursued alike.

All this, however, with moderation; a subject is not to be ridden to death; no neglect of proportion, no childish engrossment, but easy transitions. He should call a halt here, while he crosses over to another set of operations which demands attention; that settled up, he can return to the first set, now ripe for him; he must pass swiftly to each in turn, keeping his different lines of advance as nearly as possible level, fly from Armenia to Media, thence swoop straight upon Iberia, and then take wing for Italy, everywhere present at the nick of time.

He has to make of his brain a mirror, unclouded, bright, and true of surface; then he will reflect events as they presented themselves to him, neither distorted, discoloured, nor variable. Historians are not writing fancy school essays; what they have to say is before them, and will get itself said somehow, being solid fact; their task is to arrange and put it into words; they have not to consider what to say, but how to say it. The historian, we may say, should be like Phidias, Praxiteles, Alcamenes, or any great sculptor. They similarly did not create the gold, silver, ivory, or other material they used; it was ready to their hands, provided by Athens, Elis, or Argos; they only made the model, sawed, polished, cemented, proportioned the ivory, and plated it with gold; that was what their art consisted in—the right arrangement of their material. The historian's business is similar—to superinduce upon events the charm of order, and set them forth in the most lucid fashion he can manage. When subsequently a hearer feels as though he were looking at what is being told him, and expresses his approval, then our historical Phidias's work has reached perfection, and received its appropriate reward.

When all is ready, a writer will sometimes start without formal preface, if there is no pressing occasion to clear away preliminaries by that means, though even then his explanation of what he is to say constitutes a virtual preface.

When a formal preface is used, one of the three objects to which a public speaker devotes his exordium may be neglected; the historian, that is, has not to bespeak goodwill—only attention and an open mind. The way to secure the reader's attention is to show that the affairs to be narrated are great in themselves, throw light on Destiny, or come home to his business and bosom; and as to the open mind, the lucidity in the body of the work, which is to secure that, will be facilitated by a preliminary view of the causes in operation and a precise summary of events.

Prefaces of this character have been employed by the best historians—by Herodotus, "to the end that what befell may not grow dim by lapse of time, seeing that it was great and wondrous, and showed forth withal Greeks vanquishing and barbarians vanquished"; and by Thucydides, "believing that that war would be great and memorable beyond any previous one; for indeed great calamities took place during its course."

After the preface, long or short in proportion to the subject, should come an easy natural transition to the narrative; for the body of the history which remains is nothing from beginning to end but a long narrative; it must therefore be graced with the narrative virtues—smooth, level, and consistent progress, neither soaring nor crawling, and the charm of lucidity—which is attained, as I remarked above, partly by the diction, and partly by the treatment of connected events. For, though all parts must be independently perfected, when the first is complete the second will be brought into essential connexion with it, and attached like one link of a chain to another; there must be no possibility of separating them; no mere bundle of parallel threads; the first is not simply to be next to the second, but part of it, their extremities intermingling.

Brevity is always desirable, and especially where matter is abundant; and the problem is less a grammatical than a substantial one; the solution, I mean, is to deal summarily with all immaterial details, and give adequate treatment to the principal events; much, indeed, is better omitted altogether. Suppose yourself giving a dinner, and extremely well provided; there is pastry, game, kickshaws without end, wild boar, hare, sweetbreads; well, you will not produce among these a pike, or a bowl of peasoup, just because they are there in the kitchen; you will dispense with such common things.

Restraint in descriptions of mountains, walls, rivers, and the like, is very important; you must not give the impression that you are making a tasteless display of word-painting, and expatiating independently while the history takes care of itself. Just a light touch—no more than meets the need of clearness,—and you should pass on, evading the snare, and denying yourself all such indulgences. You have the mighty Homer's example in such a case; poet as he is, he yet hurries past Tantalus and Ixion, Tityus and the rest of them. If Parthenius, Euphorion, or Callimachus had been in his place, how many lines do you suppose it would have taken to get the water to Tantalus's lip; how many more to set Ixion spinning? Better still, mark how Thucydides—a very sparing dealer in description—leaves the subject at once, as soon as he has given an idea (very necessary and useful, too) of an engine or a siege-operation, of the conformation of Epipolae, or the Syracusan harbour. It may occur to you that his account of the plague is long; but you must allow for the subject; then you will appreciate his brevity; *he* is hastening on; it is only that the weight of matter holds him back in spite of himself.

When it comes in your way to introduce a speech, the first requirement is that it should suit the character both of the speaker and of the occasion; the second is (once more) lucidity; but in these cases you have the counsel's right of showing your eloquence.

Not so with praise or censure; these should be sparing, cautious, avoiding hypercriticism and producing proofs, always brief, and never intrusive; historical characters are not prisoners on trial. Without these precautions you will share the ill name of Theopompus, who delights in flinging accusations broadcast, makes a business of the thing in fact, and of himself rather a public prosecutor than a historian.

It may occasionally happen that some extraordinary story has to be introduced; it should be simply narrated, without guarantee of its truth, thrown down for any one to make what he can of it; the writer takes no risks and shows no preference.

But the general principle I would have remembered—it will ever be on my lips—is this: do not write merely with an eye to the present, that those now living may commend and honour you; aim at eternity, compose for posterity, and from it ask your reward; and that reward?—that it be said of you, "This was a man indeed, free and free-spoken; flattery and servility were not in him; he was truth all through." It is a name which a man of judgement might well prefer to all the fleeting hopes of the present.

Do you know the story of the great Cnidian architect? He was the builder of that incomparable work, whether for size or beauty, the Pharus tower. Its light was to warn ships far out at sea, and save them from running on the Paraetonia, a spot so fatal to all who get among its reefs that escape is said to be hopeless. When the building was done, he inscribed on the actual masonry his own name, but covered this up with plaster, on which he then added the name of the reigning king. He knew that, as happened later, letters and plaster would fall off together, and reveal the words:

SOSTRATUS SON OF DEXIPHANES OF CNIDUS
ON BEHALF OF ALL MARINERS
TO THE SAVIOUR GODS

He looked not, it appears, to that time, nor to the space of his own little life, but to this time, and to all time, as long as his tower shall stand and his art abide.

So too should the historian write, consorting with Truth and not with flattery, looking to the future hope, not to the gratification of the flattered.

There is your measuring-line for just history. If any one be found to use it, well; I have not written in vain: if none, yet have I rolled my tub on the Craneum.

II Some Words About *War and Peace*

Leo Tolstoy (1828-1910)

translated by Louise (1855–1939) and Aylmer Maude (1858–1938)

On publishing this work, on which I have spent five years of uninterrupted and exceptionally strenuous labour under the best conditions of life, I wish to express my own view of it and thus counteract misunderstandings which might arise in the reader's mind. I do not want readers of this book to see in it, or look for, what I did not wish, or was unable, to express, and I should like to direct their attention to what I wished to say but owing to the conditions of the work could not enlarge on. Neither my time nor capacity allowed me fully to accomplish what I intended, and I now avail myself of the hospitality of a specialist periodical to state, though but briefly and incompletely, the author's view of his work for those whom it may interest.

(1) What is *War and Peace*? It is not a novel, even less is it an epic poem, and still less an historical chronicle. *War and Peace* is what the author wished and was able to express in the form in which it is expressed. Such an announcement of disregard of conventional form in an artistic production might seem presumptuous were it premeditated, and were there no precedents for it. But the history of Russian literature since the time of Pushkin not merely affords many examples of such deviation from European forms, but does not offer a single example of the contrary. From Gogol's *Dead Souls* to Dostoevsky's *House of the Dead* in the recent period of Russian literature there is not a single artistic prose work, rising at all above mediocrity, which quite fits into the form of a novel, epic, or story.

(2) *The character of the period.* When the first part of this book appeared some readers told me that this is not sufficiently defined in my work. To that reproach I make the following reply: I know what "the characteristics of the period" are that people do not find in my novel—the horrors of serfdom, the immuring of wives, the flogging of grown-up sons, Saltykova, and so on; but I do not think that these characteristics of the period as they exist in our imagination are correct, and I did not wish to reproduce them. On studying letters, diaries, and traditions, I did not find the horrors of such savagery to a greater extent than I find them now, or at any other period. In those days also people loved, envied, sought truth and virtue, and were carried away by passion; and there was the same complex mental and moral life

among the upper classes, who were in some instances even more refined than now. If we have come to believe in the perversity and coarse violence of that period, that is only because the traditions, memoirs, stories, and novels that have been handed to us, record for the most part exceptional cases of violence and brutality. To suppose that the predominant characteristic of that period was turbulence, is as unjust as it would be for a man, seeing nothing but the tops of trees beyond a hill, to conclude that there was nothing to be found in that locality but trees. That period had its own characteristics (as every epoch has), which resulted from the predominant alienation of the upper class from other classes, from the religious philosophy of the time, from peculiarities of education, from the habit of using the French language, and so forth. That is the character I tried to depict as well as I could.

(3) *The use of the French language in a Russian book.* Why in my book do Russians as well as Frenchmen sometimes speak Russian and sometimes French? The reproach that in a Russian book people speak and write French, is like the reproach of a man who, looking at a portrait, notices black spots (shadows) on it which do not exist in nature. The painter is not to blame if to some people the shadow he has put on the face of the portrait appears as a black spot non-existent in nature; he is only to blame if such shadows are put on wrongly or coarsely. Dealing with the beginning of the nineteenth century, and depicting the Russians of a certain class and Napoleon and other Frenchmen who had so direct a part in the life of that epoch, I was involuntarily carried away to an unnecessary extent by the form in which they expressed their French way of thought. And so, without denying that the shadows put on by me are probably incorrect and coarse, I would only ask those to whom it seems absurd that Napoleon should speak now Russian and now French, to realize that this seems so to them only because they, like the man looking at the portrait, notice a black spot under the nose instead of observing the face with its lights and shades.

(4) *The names of the people in the book.* Bolkonsky, Drubetskoy, Bilibin, Kuragin and others, suggest well-known Russian names. When confronting

fictitious with historical characters I felt it awkward for the ear to make a Count Rastopchin speak to a Prince Pronsky, Strelsky, or other princes or counts bearing such invented (single or hyphenated) names. Bolkonsky or Drubetskoy, though they are neither Volkonsky nor Trubetskoy, sound familiar and natural in a Russian aristocratic circle. I was unable to devise for all my characters names which did not sound false to my ear, such as Bezukhov and Rostov, and I could not find any other way to overcome this difficulty except by taking at random names quite familiar to a Russian ear and changing some of the letters in them. I should be very sorry if the similarity between the invented names and real ones should suggest to anyone that I wished to describe this or that actual person, more especially as the literary activity which consists of describing real people who exist or have existed has nothing in common with the activity I was engaged on.

M. D. Akhrosimova and Denisov are the only persons to whom I involuntarily and unreflectingly gave names closely resembling those of two particularly characteristic and charming people of the real society of that time. That was my mistake, arising from the specially typical character of those two persons, but my mistake in this matter is limited to their mere introduction, and readers will probably agree that nothing resembling the actual facts of their lives is ascribed to these characters in the novel. All the other people are entirely invented, and have for me no definite prototypes in tradition or in reality.

(5) *The divergence between my description of historical events and that given by the historians*. This was not accidental but inevitable. An historian and an artist describing an historic epoch have two quite different tasks before them. As an historian would be wrong if he tried to present an historical person in his entirety, in all the complexity of his relations with all sides of life, so the artist would fail to perform his task were he to represent the person always in his historic significance. Kutuzov did not always hold a telescope, point at the enemy, and ride a white horse. Rastopchin was not always setting fire with a torch to the Voronovsky House (which in fact he never did) and the Empress Marya Fyodorovna did not always stand in

an ermine cloak leaning her hand on the code of laws, but that is how the popular imagination pictures them.

For an historian considering the achievement of a certain aim, there are heroes; for the artist treating of man's relation to all sides of life there cannot and should not be heroes, but there should be men.

An historian is sometimes obliged by bending the truth to subordinate all the actions of an historical personage to the one idea he has ascribed to that person. The artist, on the contrary, finds the very singleness of that idea incompatible with his problem, and tries to understand and show not a certain actor but a man.

In the description of the events themselves the difference is still sharper and more essential.

The historian has to deal with the results of an event, the artist with the fact of the event. An historian in describing a battle says: "The left flank of such and such an army was advanced to attack such and such a village and drove out the enemy, but was compelled to retire; then the cavalry, which was sent to attack, overthrew..." and so on. But these words have no meaning for an artist and do not actually touch the event itself. Either from his own experience, or from letters, memoirs, and accounts, the artist realizes a certain event to himself, and very often (to take the example of a battle) the deductions the historian permits himself to make as to the activity of such and such armies prove to be the very opposite of the artist's deductions. The difference of the results arrived at is also to be explained by the sources from which the two draw their information. For the historian (to keep to the case of a battle) the chief source is found in the reports of the commanding officers and of the commander-in-chief. The artist can draw nothing from such sources; they tell him nothing and explain nothing to him. More than that: the artist turns away from them as he finds inevitable falsehood in them. To say nothing of the fact that after any battle the two sides nearly always describe it in quite contradictory ways, in every description of a battle there is a necessary lie, resulting from the need of describing in a few words the actions of thousands of men spread over several miles, and subject to most violent moral excitement under the influence of fear, shame, and death.

In descriptions of battles it is generally said that such and such armies were sent to attack such and such points, and were then ordered to retire and so on, as if assuming that discipline, which subjects tens of thousand of men to the will of one man on a parade-ground, will have the same effect where it is a question of life and death. Anyone who has been in a war knows how untrue that is, yet the reports are based on that assumption, and on them the military descriptions. Make a round of the troops immediately after a battle, or even next day or the day after before the reports have been drawn up, and ask any of the soldiers and senior and junior officers how the affair went: you will be told what all these men experienced and saw, and you will form a majestic, complex, infinitely varied, depressing and indistinct impression; and from no one—least of all from the commander-in-chief—will you learn what the whole affair was like. Two or three days later the reports begin to be handed in. Gossips begin to narrate how things happened which they did not see; finally a general report is drawn up, and on this report the general opinion of the army is formed. Everyone is glad to exchange his own doubts and questionings for this deceptive, but clear and always flattering, presentation. Question a month or two later a man who was in the battle, and you will no longer feel in this account the raw, vital material that was there before, but he will answer according to the report. Thus I was told of the battle of Borodino by many lively, clever participants in that affair. They all told me one and the same thing, and all in accord with the false accounts of Mikhailovsky-Danilievsky, Glinka, and others: even the details they mentioned were all identical, though the narrators had been several miles apart from one another.

After the fall of Sevastopol the Commander of the Artillery, Kryzhanovsky, sent me the reports of the officers of artillery from all the bastions, and asked me to draw up a report from these (more than twenty) separate accounts. I am sorry I did not take copies of them. It would have been the best example of the naive, inevitable, military falsehoods from which reports are made. I imagine that many of my comrades who drew up those reports will laugh on reading these lines, at the recollection of how they, by order of their superior, wrote what they could not know. All who have had experience of war know how capable Russians are of doing their work in a war, and how little fit they are to describe it with the boastful falsity indispensable for that purpose. Everyone knows that in our armies that duty of drawing up reports and dispatches is generally carried out by men of foreign birth.

I say all this to show the inevitability of falsehood in military descriptions which serve as material for military historians, and thus to show how unavoidable are frequent disagreements between artists and historians in their understanding of historical events. But besides this necessary error in the narration of historical events, I noticed in the histories of the epoch on which I was engaged (probably as a result of the habit of grouping events to express them briefly, and of conforming to the tragic import of those events) a special kind of high-flown diction in which the falsehood and perversion extended not merely to the occurrences but also to the interpretation and significance of them. Often when studying the two chief historical works on that epoch, Thiers and Mikhailovsky-Danilievsky, I felt perplexed that such books could have been printed and read. To say nothing of the fact that they present the same events in a most serious, significant tone, citing the sources they have drawn on, and are yet in diametrical opposition to one another, in these histories I came across such accounts that I did not know whether to laugh or to cry, remembering that these books are the chief memorials of that epoch and have had millions of readers. I will give a single example from the work of the famous historian Thiers. After telling how Napoleon brought with him forged paper rubles, he says: "*Relevant l'emploi de ces moyens par un acte de bienfaisance* digne de lui et de l'armée francaise, *il fit distribuer des secours aux incendiés. Mais les vivres étant trop précieux pour être donnés longtemps à ces étrangers, laplupart ennemis, Napoléon aima mieux leur fournir de l'argent, et il leur fit distribuer des roubles papier.*" (Original note: "Dignifying these measures by an act of charity *worthy of himself and of the French army*, he let relief be distributed to those who had been burnt out. But as food was too precious to be given for a long time to foreigners, who were for the most part enemies, Napoleon preferred to supply them with money, and had paper rubles distributed to them.")

This passage when taken by itself amazes one, I will not say by its immorality but simply by its stupidity; but in the whole book it does not surprise one, for it is quite in accord with the general high-flown pompous style, devoid of any direct meaning.

So the tasks of artist and historian are quite different, and the reader should not be surprised when my book disagrees with an historian in the descriptions of events or persons.

But an artist must not forget that the popular conception of historical persons and events is not based on fancy, but on historical documents in so far as the historians have been able to group them, and therefore, though he understands and presents them differently, the artist like the historian should be guided by historical material. *Wherever in my novel historical persons speak or act, I have invented nothing, but have used historical material of which I have accumulated a whole library during my work. I do not think it necessary to cite the titles of those books here, but could cite them at any time in proof of what I say.*

(6) *Finally, the sixth and for me most important consideration relates to the small significance that, in my conception, should be ascribed to so-called great men in historical events.*

Studying so tragic an epoch, so rich in the importance of its events, so near to our own time, and regarding which so many varied traditions survive, I arrived at the evident fact that the causes of historical events when they take place cannot be grasped by our intelligence. To say (which seems to everyone very simple) that the causes of the events of 1812 lay in Napoleon's domineering disposition and the patriotic firmness of the Emperor Alexander I, is as meaningless as to say that the causes of the fall of the Roman Empire were that a certain barbarian led his people westwards and a certain Roman emperor ruled his State badly, or that an immense hill that was being levelled toppled over because the last labourer struck it with his spade.

The cause of such an event, in which millions of people fought one another and killed half a million men, cannot be the will of one man. Just as one man could not have levelled the hill, so no single man could cause five hundred thousand to die. But what were the causes? One historian says it was the aggressive spirit of the French and the patriotism of the Russians. Others speak of the democratic element Napoleon's hordes carried abroad, and of Russia's need to form relations with Europe, and so forth. But why did millions of people begin to kill one another? Who told them to do it? It would seem that it was clear to each of them that this could not benefit any of them but would be worse for them all. Why did they do it? Endless retrospective conjectures can be made, and are made, of the causes of this senseless event, but the immense number of these explanations, and their concurrence in one purpose, only proves that the causes were innumerable and that not one of them deserves to be called the cause.

Why did millions of people kill one another when it has been known since the world began that it is physically and morally bad to do so? Because it was such an inevitable necessity that in doing it men fulfilled the elemental zoological law which bees fulfil when they kill one another in autumn, and which causes male animals to destroy one another. One can give no other reply to that terrible question.

This truth is not only evident, but is so innate in every man's consciousness that it would not be worth while proving it were there not another sentiment in man which convinces himself that he is free at each moment that he commits an action.

Taking a wide view of history we are indubitably convinced of a sempiternal law by which events occur. Looking at it from a personal point of view we are convinced of the opposite.

A man who kills another, Napoleon who orders the crossing of the Niemen, you or I handing in a petition to be admitted to the army, or lifting or lowering our arm, are all indubitably convinced that our every action is based on reasonable grounds and on our own freewill, and that it depends on us whether we do this or that. This conviction is so inherent in us and so precious to each of us, that in spite of the proofs of history and the statistics of crime (which convince us of absence of freedom in the actions of other people) we extend the consciousness of our freedom to all our actions.

The contradiction seems insoluble. When committing an act I am convinced that I do it by my own freewill, but considering that action in its connection with the general life of mankind (in its historical significance), I am convinced that this action was predestined and inevitable. Where is the error?

Psychological observations of man's capacity for retrospectively supplying a whole series of supposedly free reasons for something that has been done (as I intend to expound in more detail in another place) confirm the assumption that man's consciousness of freedom in the commission of a certain kind of action is erroneous. But the same psychological observations prove that there is another series of actions in which the consciousness of freedom is not retrospective but instantaneous and indubitable. In spite of all that the materialists may say, I can undoubtedly commit an act or refrain from it if the act relates to me alone. I have undoubtedly by my own will just lifted and lowered my arm. I can at once stop writing. You can at once stop reading. I can certainly, by my own will and free from all obstacles, transfer my thoughts to America, or to any mathematical problem I choose. Testing my freedom I can lift and forcibly lower my hand in the air. I have done so. But near me stands a child and I raise my hand above him and want to lower it with the same force onto the child. I *cannot* do this. A dog rushes at that child, and I *cannot* refrain from lifting my hand at the dog. I am on parade, and cannot help following the movement of the regiment. In action I cannot refrain from attacking with my regiment or from running when all around me run—*I cannot.* When I appear in Court as the defender of an accused person, I cannot help speaking or knowing what I am going to say. I cannot help blinking when a blow is directed at my eye.

So there are two kinds of actions: some that do and others that do not depend on my will. And the mistake causing the contradiction is due only to the fact that I wrongly transfer the consciousness of freedom (which properly accompanies every act relating to my *ego*, to the highest abstractions of my existence) to actions performed in conjunction with others and dependent on the coincidence of other wills with my own. To define the limits of freedom and dependence is very difficult and the definition of those limits forms the sole and essential problem of psychology, but observing the conditions of the manifestation of our greatest freedom and greatest dependence, we cannot but see that the more abstract and therefore the less connected with the activity of others our activity is, the more free it is; and on the contrary, the more our activity is connected with other people the less free it is.

The strongest, most indissoluble, most burdensome, and constant bond with other men is what is called power over others, which in its real meaning is only the greatest dependence on them.

Having wrongly or rightly become fully convinced of this in the course of my work, I naturally was unable—when describing the historical events of 1805, 1807 and especially of 1812 in which this law of predetermination is most prominently displayed—to attribute importance to the actions of those who thought they controlled the events, but who introduced less free human activity into them than did all the other participants. The activity of these people interested me only as an illustration of the law of predetermination which in my opinion guides history, and of that psychological law which compels a man who commits actions under the greatest compulsion to supply in his imagination a whole series of retrospective reflections to prove his freedom to himself.

Topics for Discussion

1. List some literary techniques that Lucian discovers in contemporary history writings.
2. How does Lucian distinguish literature from history?
3. What historical events are rewritten in *War and Peace*?
4. How does Tolstoy explain his artistic strategy in rewriting history?
5. "It is not a novel, even less is it an epic poem, and still less an historical chronicle."How to interpret Tolstoy's such statement about *War and Peace*?
6. Give more examples of intertextuality between literature and history.

Monograph Four Literature and Religion

I Apology for *Pilgrim's Progress*

John Bunyan (1628-1688)

When at the first I took my pen in hand
Thus for to write,
I did not understand
That I at all should make a little book
In such a mode: nay,
I had undertook
To make another, which when almost done,
Before I was aware, I this begun.

And thus it was:
I was writing of the way
And race of saints in this our gospel day,
Fell suddenly into an allegory
About their journey, and the way to glory,
In more than twenty things, which I set down.
This done, I twenty more had in my crown;
And they again began to multiply,

Like sparks that from the coals of fire do fly.
Nay, then, thought I, if that you breed so fast,
I'll put you by yourselves, lest you at last
Should prove ad infinitum, and eat out
The book that I already am about.

Well, so I did; but yet I did not think
To shew to all the world my pen and ink
In such a mode;
I only thought to make I knew not what.
Nor did I undertake
Thereby to please my neighbour — no, not I!
I did it mine own self to gratify.
Neither did I but vacant seasons spend
In this my scribble; nor did I intend
But to divert myself in doing this,
From worser thoughts, which make me do amiss.

Thus I set pen to paper with delight,
And quickly had my thoughts in black and white,
For having now my method by the end,
Still as I pulled, it came; and so I penned
It down; until it came at last to be,
For length and breadth, the size which you see.

Well, when I had thus put my ends together,
I showed them others, that I might see whether
They would condemn them, or them justify;
And some said, "Let them live"; some said, "Let them die";

Some said, "John, print it"; others said, "Not so";
Some said, "It might do good"; others said, "No."

Now was I in a strait, and did not see
Which was the best thing to be done by me:
At last I thought, "Since you are thus divided,
I print it will"; and so the case decided:
"For," thought I, "some, I see, would have it done,
Though others in that channel do not run."
To prove then who advised for the best,
Thus I thought fit to put it to the test.

I further thought: if now I did deny
Those that would have it thus to gratify,
I did not know but hinder them I might
Of that which would to them be great delight.

For those which were not for its coming forth,
I said to them, "Offend you I am loth;
Yet, since your brethren pleased with it be,
Forbear to judge, till you do further see.

If that thou will not read, let it alone;
Some love the meat; some love to pick the bone:
Yea, that I might them better moderate,
I did too with them thus expostulate:

"May I not write in such a style as this;
In such a method too; and yet not miss

My end, thy good?
Why may it not be done?
Dark clouds bring waters, when the bright bring none.
Yea, dark or bright, if they their silver drops
Cause to descend, the earth, by yielding crops
Gives praise to both, and carps not at either;
But treasures up the fruit they yield together:
Yea, so mixes both, that in her fruit
None can distinguish this from that: they suit
Her well when hungry: but if she be full,
She spews out both, and makes their blessings null.

You see the ways the fisherman doth take
To catch the fish: what devices doth he make!
Behold how he engages all his wits;
Also his snares, lines, angles, hooks, and nets:
Yet fish there be that neither hook nor line,
Nor snare, nor net, nor device, can make thine;
They must be groped for, and be tickled too,
Or they will not be caught whate'er you do.

How doth the fowler seek to catch his game
By divers means, all which one cannot name!
His gun, his nets, his lime twigs, light, and bell;
He creeps, he goes, he stands; yea, who can tell
Of all his postures? Yet there's none of these
Will make him master of what fowls he please.
Yea, he must pipe and whistle to catch this;
Yet if he does so, that bird he will miss.

If that a pearl may in a toad's head dwell,
And may be found too in an oyster shell;
If things that promise nothing do contain
What better is than gold; who will disdain
That have an inkling of it, there to look,
That they may find it? Now my little book
(Though void of all those paintings that may make
It with this or the other man to take),
Is not without those things that do excel
What do in brave, but empty notions dwell.

"Well, yet I am not fully satisfied,
That this your book will stand when soundly tried."
"Why, what's the matter?"
"It is dark.""What though?"
"But it is feigned.""What of that?"I trow
Some men by feigned words as dark as mine
Make truth to spangle, and its rays to shine."
"But they want solidness."
"Speak, man, thy mind."
"They drown'd the weak; metaphors make us blind."

Solidity, indeed, becomes the pen
Of him that writes things Divine to men;
But must I needs want solidness because
By metaphors I speak?
Were not God's laws, His gospel laws, in olden time held forth
By types, shadows, and metaphors? Yet loth

Will any sober man be to find fault
With them, lest he be found for to assault
The highest wisdom. No, he rather stoops,
And seeks to find out what by pins and loops,
By calves and sheep, by heifers and by rams,
By birds and herbs, and by the blood of lambs,
God speaks to him; and happy is he
That finds the light and grace that in them be.

Be not too forward therefore to conclude
That I want solidness — that I am rude.
All things solid in show, not solid be;
All things in parables despise not we;
Lest things most harmful lightly we receive,
And things that good are of our souls bereave.
My dark and cloudy words they do but hold
The truth, as cabinets enclose the gold.

The prophets used much by metaphors
To set forth truth; yea, whoso considers
Christ, his apostles too, shall plainly see
That truths to this day in such mantles be.

Am I afraid to say that Holy Writ,
Which for its style and phrase puts down all wit,
Is everywhere so full of all these things —
Dark figures, allegories; yet there springs
From that same book, that lustre, and those rays
Of light that turn our darkest nights todays?

Come, let my carper to his life now look,
And find there darker lines than in my book
He finds any; yea, and let him know
That in his best things there are worse lines too.
May we but stand before impartial men,
To his poor one I dare adventure ten,
That they will take my meaning in these lines
Far better than his lies in silver shrines.
Come, Truth, although in swaddling clouts, I find
Informs the judgment; rectifies the mind;
Pleases the understanding, makes the will
Submit; the memory too it doth fill
With what doth our imaginations please;
Likewise it tends our troubles to appease.

Sound words, I know, Timothy is to use,
And old wives' fables he is to refuse;
But yet grave Paul, he nowhere did forbid
The use of parables, in which lay hid
That gold, those pearls, and precious stones that were
Worth digging for, and that with greatest care.

Let me add one word more: O man of God,
Art thou offended? Dost thou wish I had
Put forth my matter in another dress?
Or that I had in things been more express?
Three things let me propound, then I submit
To those that are my betters, as is fit.

1. I find not that I am denied the use
Of this my method, so I no abuse
Put on the words, things, readers; or be rude
In handling figure or similitude
In application: but, all that I may,
Seek the advance of truth, this or that way.
Denied, did I say? Nay, I have leave —
(Examples too and that from them that have
God better pleased by their words or ways
Than any man that breathes now-a-days) —
Thus to express my mind, thus to declare
Things unto thee, that excellentest are.

2. I find that men (as high as trees) will write
Dialogue wise; yet no man doth them slight
For writing so: indeed, if they abuse
Truth, cursed be they and the craft they use
To that intent; but yet let truth be free
To make her sallies upon thee and me
Which way it pleases God: for who knows how
Better than he that taught us first to plough,
To guide our minds and pens for his design
And he makes base things usher in divine.

3. I find that Holy Writ in many places
Hath semblance with this method, where the cases
Do call for one thing to set forth another.
Use it I may then, and yet nothing smother
Truth's golden beams; nay, by this method may

Make it cast forth its rays as light as day.

And now, before I do put up my pen,
I'll show the profit of my book, and then
Commit both thee and it unto that hand
That pulls the strong down, and makes weak ones stand.

This book it chalks out before thine eyes,
The man that seeks the everlasting prize:
It shows you whence he comes, whither he goes,
What he leaves undone; also what he does:
It also shows you how he runs, and runs
Till he unto the gate of glory comes.

It shows too who set out for life amain,
As if the lasting crown they would attain:
Here also you may see the reason why
They lose their labour, and like fools do die.

This book will make a traveller of thee,
If by its counsel thou wilt ruled be;
It will direct thee to the Holy Land,
If thou wilt its directions understand:
Yea, it will make the slothful active be;
The blind also delightful things to see.

Art thou for something rare and profitable?
Wouldst thou see a truth within a fable? Art thou forgetful?
Wouldst thou remember

From New Year's day to the last of December?
Then read my fancies; they will stick like burrs
And may be, to the helpless, comforters.

This book is writ in such a dialect,
As may the minds of listless men affect:
It seems a novelty, and yet contains
Nothing but sound and honest gospel strains.

Wouldst thou divert thyself from melancholy,
Wouldst thou be pleasant, yet be far from folly?
Wouldst thou read riddles, and their explanation
Or else be drowned in thy contemplation?
Dost thou love picking meat? Or wouldst thou see
A man in the clouds, and hear him speak to thee?
Wouldst thou be in a dream, and yet not sleep?
Or wouldst thou in a moment laugh and weep?

Wouldst thou lose thyself and catch no harm?
And find thyself again without a charm?
Wouldst read thyself, and read thou know'st not what,
And yet know whether thou are blest or not,
By reading the same lines? Oh then, come hither,
And lay my book, thy head, and heart together.

II Letters from the Earth

Mark Twain (1835-1910)

The Creator sat upon the throne, thinking. Behind him stretched the illimitable continent of heaven, steeped in a glory of light and color; before him rose the black night of Space, like a wall. His mighty bulk towered rugged and mountain-like into the zenith, and His divine head blazed there like a distant sun. At His feet stood three colossal figures, diminished to extinction, almost, by contrast — archangels — their heads level with His ankle-bone.

When the Creator had finished thinking, He said, "I have thought. Behold!"

He lifted His hand, and from it burst a fountain-spray of fire, a million stupendous suns, which clove the blackness and soared, away and away and away, diminishing in magnitude and intensity as they pierced the far frontiers of Space, until at last they were but as diamond nailheads sparkling under the domed vast roof of the universe.

At the end of an hour the Grand Council was dismissed.

They left the Presence impressed and thoughtful, and retired to a private place, where they might talk with freedom. None of the three seemed to want to begin, though all wanted somebody to do it. Each was burning to discuss the great event, but would prefer not to commit himself till he should know how the others regarded it. So there was some aimless and halting conversation about matters of no consequence, and this dragged tediously along, arriving nowhere, until at last the archangel Satan gathered his courage together — of which he had a very good supply — and broke ground. He said, "We know what we are here to talk about, my lords, and we may as well put pretense aside, and begin. If this is the opinion of the Council — "

"It is, it is!"said Gabriel and Michael, gratefully interrupting.

"Very well, then, let us proceed. We have witnessed a wonderful thing; as to that, we are necessarily agreed. As to the value of it — if it has any — that is a matter which does not personally concern us. We can have as many opinions about it as we like, and that is our limit. We have no vote. I think Space was well enough, just as it was, and useful, too. Cold and dark — a restful place, now and then, after a season of the overdelicate climate and trying splendors of heaven. But these are details of no considerable moment; the new feature, the immense feature, is — what, gentlemen?"

"The invention and introduction of automatic, unsupervised, self-regulating *law* for the government of those myriads of whirling and racing suns and worlds!"

"That is it!"said Satan. "You perceive that it is a stupendous idea. Nothing approaching it has been evolved from the Master Intellect before. Law — *Automatic Law*— exact and unvarying Law— requiring no watching, no correcting, no readjusting while the eternities endure! He said those countless vast bodies would plunge through the wastes of Space ages and ages, at unimaginable speed, around stupendous orbits, yet never collide, and never lengthen nor shorten their orbital periods by so much as the hundredth part of a second in two thousand years! That is the new miracle, and the greatest of all—*Automatic Law*! And He gave it a name — the LAW OF NATURE — and said Natural Law is the LAW OF GOD -- interchangeable names for one and the same thing."

"Yes," said Michael, "and He said He would establish Natural Law— the Law of God — throughout His dominions, and its authority should be supreme and inviolable."

"Also," said Gabriel, "He said He would by and by create animals, and place them, likewise, under the authority of that Law."

"Yes," said Satan, "I heard Him, but did not understand. What *is* animals,

Gabriel?"

"Ah, how should I know? How should any of us know? It is a new word."

[*Interval of three centuries, celestial time— the equivalent of a hundred million years, earthly time. Enter a Messenger-Angel.*]

"My lords, He is making animals. Will it please you to come and see?"

They went, they saw, and were perplexed. Deeply perplexed— and the Creator noticed it, and said, "Ask. I will answer."

"Divine One," said Satan, making obeisance, "what are they for?"

"They are an experiment in Morals and Conduct. Observe them, and be instructed."

There were thousands of them. They were full of activities. Busy, all busy — mainly in persecuting each other. Satan remarked — after examining one of them through a powerful microscope: "This large beast is killing weaker animals, Divine One."

"The tiger — yes. The law of his nature is ferocity. The law of his nature is the Law of God. He cannot disobey it."

"Then in obeying it he commits no offense, Divine One?"

"No, he is blameless."

"This other creature, here, is timid, Divine One, and suffers death without resisting."

"The rabbit — yes. He is without courage. It is the law of his nature — the Law of God. He must obey it."

"Then he cannot honorably be required to go counter to his nature and resist, Divine One?"

"No. No creature can be honorably required to go counter to the law of his nature — the Law of God."

After a long time and many questions, Satan said, "The spider kills the fly, and eats it; the bird kills the spider and eats it; the wildcat kills the goose; the — well, they all kill each other. It is murder all along the line. Here are countless multitudes of creatures, and they all kill, kill, kill, they are all murderers. And they are not to blame, Divine One?"

"They are not to blame. It is the law of their nature. And always the law of nature is the Law of God. Now — observe — behold! A new creature — and the masterpiece — *Man!*"

Men, women, children, they came swarming in flocks, in droves, in millions.

"What shall you do with them, Divine One?"

"Put into each individual, in differing shades and degrees, all the various Moral Qualities, in mass, that have been distributed, a single distinguishing characteristic at a time, among the nonspeaking animal world— courage, cowardice, ferocity, gentleness, fairness, justice, cunning, treachery, magnanimity, cruelty, malice, malignity, lust, mercy, pity, purity, selfishness, sweetness, honor, love, hate, baseness, nobility, loyalty, falsity, veracity, untruthfulness— each human being shall have *all* of these in him, and they will constitute his nature. In some, there will be high and fine characteristics which will submerge the evil ones, and those will be called good men; in others the evil characteristics will have dominion, and those will be called bad men. Observe — behold — they vanish!"

"Whither are they gone, Divine One?"

"To the earth — they and all their fellow animals."

"What is the earth?"

"A small globe I made, a time, two times and a half ago. You saw it, but did not notice it in the explosion of worlds and suns that sprayed from my hand. Man is an experiment, the other animals are another experiment. Time will show whether they were worth the trouble. The exhibition is over; you may take your leave, my lords."

Several days passed by.

This stands for a long stretch of (our) time, since in heaven a day is as a thousand years.

Satan had been making admiring remarks about certain of the Creator's sparkling industries — remarks which, being read between the lines, were sarcasms.

He had made them confidentially to his safe friends the other archangels, but they had been overheard by some ordinary angels and reported at Headquarters.

He was ordered into banishment for a day—the celestial day. It was a punishment he was used to, on account of his too flexible tongue. Formerly he had been deported into Space, there being nowhither else to send him, and had flapped tediously around there in the eternal night and the Arctic chill; but now it occurred to him to push on and hunt up the earth and see how the Human-Race experiment was coming along.

By and by he wrote home — very privately — to St. Michael and St. Gabriel about it.

Satan's Letter

This is a strange place, and extraordinary place, and interesting. There is nothing resembling it at home. The people are all insane, the other animals are all insane, the earth is insane, Nature itself is insane. Man is a marvelous curiosity. When he is at his very very best he is a sort of low grade nickel-plated angel; at his worst he is unspeakable, unimaginable; and first and last and all the time he is a sarcasm. Yet he blandly and in all sincerity calls himself the "noblest work of God." This is the truth I am telling you. And this is not a new idea with him, he has talked it through all the ages, and believed it. Believed it, and found nobody among all his race to laugh at it.

Moreover— if I may put another strain upon you— he thinks he is the Creator's pet. He believes the Creator is proud of him; he even believes the Creator loves him; has a passion for him; sits up nights to admire him; yes, and watch over him and keep him out of trouble. He prays to Him, and thinks He listens. Isn't it a quaint idea? Fills his prayers with crude and bald and florid flatteries of Him, and thinks He sits and purrs over these extravagancies and enjoys them. He prays for help, and favor, and protection, every day; and does it with hopefulness and confidence, too, although no prayer of his has ever been answered. The daily affront, the daily defeat, do not discourage him, he goes on praying just the same. There is something almost fine about this perseverance. I must put one more strain upon you: he thinks he is going to heaven!

He has salaried teachers who tell him that. They also tell him there is a hell, of everlasting fire, and that he will go to it if he doesn't keep the Commandments. What are Commandments? They are a curiosity. I will tell you about them by and by.

Letter II

"I have told you nothing about man that is not true."You must pardon me if I repeat that remark now and then in these letters; I want you to take seriously the things I am telling you, and I feel that if I were in your place and you in mine, I should need that reminder from time to time, to keep my credulity from flagging.

For there is nothing about man that is not strange to an immortal. He looks at nothing as we look at it, his sense of proportion is quite different from ours, and his sense of values is so widely divergent from ours, that with all our large intellectual powers it is not likely that even the most gifted among us would ever be quite able to understand it.

For instancc, takc this sample: he has imagined a heaven, and has left entirely out of it the supremest of all his delights, the one ecstasy that stands first and foremost in the heart of every individual of his race—and of ours—sexual intercourse!

It is as if a lost and perishing person in a roasting desert should be told by a rescuer he might choose and have all longed-for things but one, and he should elect to leave out water!

His heaven is like himself: strange, interesting, astonishing, grotesque. I give you my word, it has not a single feature in it that he *actually values.* It consists — utterly and entirely— of diversions which he cares next to nothing about, here in the earth, yet is quite sure he will like them in heaven. Isn't it curious? Isn't it interesting? You must not think I am exaggerating, for it is not so. I will give you details.

Most men do not sing, most men cannot sing, most men will not stay when others are singing if it be continued more than two hours. Note that.

Only about two men in a hundred can play upon a musical instrument, and not four in a hundred have any wish to learn how. Set that down.

Many men pray, not many of them like to do it. A few pray long, the others make a short cut.

More men go to church than want to.

To forty-nine men in fifty the Sabbath Day is a dreary, dreary bore.

Of all the men in a church on a Sunday, two-thirds are tired when the service is half over, and the rest before it is finished.

The gladdest moment for all of them is when the preacher uplifts his hands for the benediction. You can hear the soft rustle of relief that sweeps the house, and you recognize that it is eloquent with gratitude.

All nations look down upon all other nations.

All nations dislike all other nations.

All white nations despise all colored nations, of whatever hue, and oppress them when they can.

White men will not associate with "niggers," nor marry them.

They will not allow them in their schools and churches.

All the world hates the Jew, and will not endure him except when he is rich.

I ask you to note all those particulars.

Further. All sane people detest noise.

All people, sane or insane, like to have variety in their life. Monotony quickly wearies them.

Every man, according to the mental equipment that has fallen to his share, exercises his intellect constantly, ceaselessly, and this exercise makes up a vast and valued and essential part of his life. The lowest intellect, like the highest, possesses a skill of some kind and takes a keen pleasure in testing it, proving it, perfecting it. The urchin who is his comrade's superior in games is as diligent and as enthusiastic in his practice as are the sculptor, the painter, the pianist, the mathematician and the rest. Not one of them could be happy if his talent were put under an interdict.

Now then, you have the facts. You know what the human race enjoys, and what it doesn't enjoy. It has invented a heaven out of its own head, all by itself: guess what it is like! In fifteen hundred eternities you couldn't do it. The ablest mind known to you or me in fifty million aeons couldn't do it. Very well, I will tell you about it.

1. First of all, I recall to your attention the extraordinary fact with which I began. To wit, that the human being, like the immortals, naturally places sexual intercourse far and away above all other joys — yet he has left it out of his heaven! The very thought of it excites him; opportunity sets him wild; in this state he will risk life, reputation, everything — even his queer heaven itself — to make good that opportunity and ride it to the overwhelming climax. From youth to middle age all men and all women prize copulation above all other pleasures combined, yet it is actually as I have said: it is not in their heaven; prayer takes its place.

They prize it thus highly; yet, like all their so-called "boons," it is a poor thing. At its very best and longest the act is brief beyond imagination — the imagination of an immortal, I mean. In the matter of repetition the man is limited — oh, quite beyond immortal conception. We who continue the act and its supremest ecstasies unbroken and without withdrawal for centuries, will never be able to understand or adequately pity the awful poverty of these people in that rich gift which, possessed as we possess it, makes all other possessions trivial and not worth the trouble of invoicing.

2. In man's heaven *everybody sings!* The man who did not sing on earth sings there; the man who could not sing on earth is able to do it there. The universal singing is not casual, not occasional, not relieved by intervals of quiet; it goes on, all day long, and every day, during a stretch of twelve hours. And *everybody stays*;

whereas in the earth the place would be empty in two hours. The singing is of hymns alone. Nay, it is of *one* hymn alone. The words are always the same, in number they are only about a dozen, there is no rhyme, there is no poetry: "Hosannah, hosannah, hosannah, Lord God of Sabaoth, 'rah! 'rah! 'rah! siss!— boom!... a-a-ah!"

3. Meantime, every person is playing on a harp — those millions and millions! — whereas not more than twenty in the thousand of them could play an instrument in the earth, or ever wanted to.

Consider the deafening hurricane of sound — millions and millions of voices screaming at once and millions and millions of harps gritting their teeth at the same time! I ask you: is it hideous, is it odious, is it horrible?

Consider further: it is a *praise* service; a service of compliment, of flattery, of adulation! Do you ask who it is that is willing to endure this strange compliment, this insane compliment; and who not only endures it, but likes it, enjoys it, requires if, *commands* it? Hold your breath!

It is God! This race's god, I mean. He sits on his throne, attended by his four and twenty elders and some other dignitaries pertaining to his court, and looks out over his miles and miles of tempestuous worshipers, and smiles, and purrs, and nods his satisfaction northward, eastward, southward; as quaint and nave a spectacle as has yet been imagined in this universe, I take it.

It is easy to see that the inventor of the heavens did not originate the idea, but copied it from the show-ceremonies of some sorry little sovereign State up in the back settlements of the Orient somewhere.

All sane white people hate noise; yet they have tranquilly accepted this kind of heaven — without thinking, without reflection, without examination — and they actually want to go to it! Profoundly devout old gray-headed men put in a large part of their time dreaming of the happy day when they will lay down the cares of this life and enter into the joys of that place. Yet you can see how unreal it is to them, and how little it takes a grip upon them as being fact, for they make no practical preparation for the great change: you never see one of them with a harp, you never hear one of them sing.

As you have seen, that singular show is a service of praise: praise by hymn, praise by prostration. It takes the place of "church." Now then, in the earth these people cannot stand much church— an hour and a quarter is the limit, and they draw the line at once a week. That is to say, Sunday. One day in seven; and even then they do not look forward to it with longing. And so — consider what their heaven provides for them: "church" that lasts forever, and a Sabbath that has no end! They quickly weary of this brief hebdomadal Sabbath here, yet they long for that eternal one; they dream of it, they talk about it, they *think* they think they are going to enjoy it — with all their simple hearts they think they think they are going to be happy in it!

It is because they do not think at all; they only think they think. Whereas they can't think; not two human beings in ten thousand have anything to think with. And as to imagination — oh, well, look at their heaven! They accept it, they approve it, they admire it. That gives you their intellectual measure.

4. The inventor of their heaven empties into it all the nations of the earth, in one common jumble. All are on an equality absolute, no one of them ranking another; they have to be "brothers"; they have to mix together, pray together, harp together, hosannah together — whites, niggers, Jews, everybody — there's no distinction. Here in the earth all nations hate each other, and every one of them hates the Jew. Yet every pious person adores that heaven and wants to get into it. He really does. And when he is in a holy rapture he thinks he thinks that if he were only there he would take all the populace to his heart, and hug, and hug, and hug!

He is a marvel — man is! I would I knew who invented him.

5. Every man in the earth possesses some share of intellect, large or small; and be it large or be it small he takes pride in it. Also his heart swells at mention of the names of the majestic intellectual chiefs of his race, and he loves the tale of their splendid achievements. For he is of their blood, and in honoring themselves they have honored him. Lo, what the mind of man can do! he cries, and calls the roll of the illustrious of all ages; and points to the imperishable literatures they have

given to the world, and the mechanical wonders they have invented, and the glories wherewith they have clothed science and the arts; and to them he uncovers as to kings, and gives to them the profoundest homage, and the sincerest, his exultant heart can furnish — thus exalting intellect above all things else in the world, and enthroning it there under the arching skies in a supremacy unapproachable. And then he contrived a heaven that hasn't a rag of intellectuality in it anywhere!

Is it odd, is it curious, is it puzzling? It is exactly as I have said, incredible as it may sound. This sincere adorer of intellect and prodigal rewarder of its mighty services here in the earth has invented a religion and a heaven which pay no compliments to intellect, offer it no distinctions, fling it no largess: in fact, never even mention it.

By this time you will have noticed that the human being's heaven has been thought out and constructed upon an absolute definite plan; and that this plan is, that it shall contain, in labored detail, each and every imaginable thing that is repulsive to a man, and not a single thing he likes!

Very well, the further we proceed the more will this curious fact be apparent.

Make a note of it: in man's heaven there are no exercises for the intellect, nothing for it to live upon. It would rot there in a year — rot and stink. Rot and stink — and at that stage become holy. A blessed thing: for only the holy can stand the joys of that bedlam.

Letter III

You have noticed that the human being is a curiosity. In times past he has had (and worn out and flung away) hundreds and hundreds of religions; today he has hundreds and hundreds of religions, and launches not fewer than three new ones every year. I could enlarge that number and still be within the facts.

One of his principle religions is called the Christian. A sketch of it will interest you. It sets forth in detail in a book containing two million words, called the Old and New Testaments. Also it has another name — The Word of God. For the Christian thinks every word of it was dictated by God — the one I have been speaking of.

It is full of interest. It has noble poetry in it; and some clever fables; and some blood-drenched history; and some good morals; and a wealth of obscenity; and upwards of a thousand lies.

This Bible is built mainly out of the fragments of older Bibles that had their day and crumbled to ruin. So it noticeably lacks in originality, necessarily. Its three or four most imposing and impressive events all happened in earlier Bibles; all its best precepts and rules of conduct came also from those Bibles; there are only two new things in it: hell, for one, and that singular heaven I have told you about.

What shall we do? If we believe, with these people, that their God invented these cruel things, we slander him; if we believe that these people invented them themselves, we slander them. It is an unpleasant dilemma in either case, for neither of these parties has done us any harm.

For the sake of tranquility, let us take a side. Let us join forces with the people and put the whole ungracious burden upon *him* — heaven, hell, Bible and all. It does not seem right, it does not seem fair; and yet when you consider that heaven, and how crushingly charged it is with everything that is repulsive to a human being, how can we believe a human being invented it? And when I come to tell you about hell, the stain will be greater still, and you will be likely to say, No, a man would not provide that place, for either himself or anybody else; he simply couldn't.

That innocent Bible tells about the Creation. Of what — the universe? Yes, the universe. In six days!

God did it. He did not call it the universe — that name is modern. His whole attention was upon this world. He constructed it in five days— and then? It took him only one day to make twenty million suns and eighty million planets!

What were they for— according to this idea? To furnish light for this little toy-world. That was his whole purpose; he had no other. One of the twenty million suns (the smallest one) was to light it in the daytime, the rest were to help one of the universe's countless moons modify the darkness of its nights.

It is quite manifest that he believed his fresh-made skies were diamond-sown with those myriads of twinkling stars the moment his first-day's sun sank below the horizon; whereas, in fact, not a single star winked in that black vault until three years and a half after that memorable week's formidable industries had been completed. Then one star appeared, all solitary and alone, and began to blink. Three years later another one appeared. The two blinked together for more than four years before a third joined them. At the end of the first hundred years there were not yet twenty-five stars twinkling in the wide wastes of those gloomy skies. At the end of a thousand years not enough stars were yet visible to make a show. At the end of a million years only half of the present array had sent their light over the telescopic frontiers, and it took another million for the rest to follow suit, as the vulgar phrase goes. There being at that time no telescope, their advent was not observed.

For three hundred years, now, the Christian astronomer has known that his Deity didn't make the stars in those tremendous six days; but the Christian astronomer does not enlarge upon that detail. Neither does the priest.

In his Book, God is eloquent in his praises of his mighty works, and calls them by the largest names he can find— thus indicating that he has a strong and just admiration of magnitudes; yet he made those millions of prodigious suns to light this wee little orb, instead of appointing this orb's little sun to dance attendance upon them. He mentions Arcturus in his book— you remember Arcturus; we went there once. It is one of the earth's night lamps!— that giant globe which is fifty thousand times as large as the earth's sun, and compares with it as a melon compares with a cathedral.

However, the Sunday school still teaches the child that Arcturus was created to help light this earth, and the child grows up and continues to believe it long after he has found out that the probabilities are against it being so.

According to the Book and its servants the universe is only six thousand years old. It is only within the last hundred years that studious, inquiring minds have found out that it is nearer a hundred million.

During the Six Days, God created man and the other animals.

He made a man and a woman and placed them in a pleasant garden, along with the other creatures. they all lived together there in harmony and contentment and blooming youth for some time; then trouble came. God had warned the man and the woman that they must not eat of the fruit of a certain tree. And he added a most strange remark: he said that if they ate of it they should surely die. Strange, for the reason that inasmuch as they had never seen a sample death they could not possibly know what he meant. Neither would he nor any other god have been able to make those ignorant children understand what was meant, without furnishing a sample. The mere word could have no meaning for them, any more than it would have for an infant of days.

Presently a serpent sought them out privately, and came to them walking upright, which was the way of serpents in those days. The serpent said the forbidden fruit would store their vacant minds with knowledge. So they ate it, which was quite natural, for man is so made that he eagerly wants to know; whereas the priest, like God, whose imitator and representative he is, has made it his business from the beginning to keep him from knowing any useful thing.

Adam and Eve ate the forbidden fruit, and at once a great light streamed into their dim heads. They had acquired knowledge. What knowledge — useful knowledge? No — merely knowledge that there was such a thing as good, and such a thing as evil, and how to do evil. they couldn't do it before. Therefore all their acts up to this time had been without stain, without blame, without offense.

But now they could do evil — and suffer for it; now they had acquired what the Church calls an invaluable possession, the Moral Sense; that sense which differentiates man from the beast and sets him above the beast. Instead of below the beast — where one would suppose his proper place would be, since he is always foul-minded and guilty and the beast always clean-minded and innocent. It is like valuing a watch that must go wrong, above a watch that can't.

The Church still prizes the Moral Sense as man's noblest asset today, although the Church knows God had a distinctly poor opinion of it and did what he could in his clumsy way to keep his happy Children of the Garden from acquiring it.

Very well, Adam and Eve now knew what evil was, and how to do it. They knew how to do various kinds of wrong things, and among them one principal one — the one God had his mind on principally. That one was the art and mystery of sexual intercourse. To them it was a magnificent discovery, and they stopped idling around and turned their entire attention to it, poor exultant young things!

In the midst of one of these celebrations they heard God walking among the bushes, which was an afternoon custom of his, and they were smitten with fright. Why? Because they were naked. They had not known it before. They had not minded it before; neither had God.

In that memorable moment immodesty was born; and some people have valued it ever since, though it would certainly puzzle them to explain why.

Adam and Eve entered the world naked and unashamed — naked and pure-minded; and no descendant of theirs has ever entered it otherwise. All have entered it naked, unashamed, and clean in mind. They have entered it modest. They had to acquire immodesty and the soiled mind; there was no other way to get it. A Christian mother's first duty is to soil her child's mind, and she does not neglect it. Her lad grows up to be a missionary, and goes to the innocent savage and to the civilized Japanese, and soils their minds. Whereupon they adopt immodesty, they conceal their bodies, they stop bathing naked together.

The convention miscalled modesty has no standard, and cannot have one, because it is opposed to nature and reason, and is therefore an artificiality and subject to anybody's whim, anybody's diseased caprice. And so, in India the refined lady covers her face and breasts and leaves her legs naked from the hips down, while the refined European lady covers her legs and exposes her face and her breasts. In lands inhabited by the innocent savage the refined European lady soon gets used to full-grown native stark-nakedness, and ceases to be offended by it. A highly cultivated French count and countess — unrelated to each other — who were marooned in their nightclothes, by shipwreck, upon an uninhabited island in the eighteenth century, were soon naked. Also ashamed — for a week. After that their nakedness did not trouble them, and they soon ceased to think about it.

You have never seen a person with clothes on. Oh, well, you haven't lost anything.

To proceed with the Biblical curiosities. Naturally you will think the threat to punish Adam and Eve for disobeying was of course not carried out, since they did not create themselves, nor their natures nor their impulses nor their weaknesses, and hence were not properly subject to anyone's commands, and not responsible to anybody for their acts. It will surprise you to know that the threat was carried out. Adam and Eve were punished, and that crime finds apologists unto this day. The sentence of death was executed.

As you perceive, the only person responsible for the couple's offense escaped; and not only escaped but became the executioner of the innocent.

In your country and mine we should have the privilege of making fun of this kind of morality, but it would be unkind to do it here. Many of these people have the reasoning faculty, but no one uses it in religious matters.

The best minds will tell you that when a man has begotten a child he is morally bound to tenderly care for it, protect it from hurt, shield it from disease, clothe it, feed it, bear with its waywardness, lay no hand upon it save in kindness and for its own good, and never in any case inflict upon it a wanton cruelty. God's treatment of his earthly children, every day and every night, is the exact opposite of all that, yet those best minds warmly justify these crimes, condone them, excuse them, and indignantly refuse to regard them as crimes at all, when *he* commits them. Your country and mine is an interesting one, but there is nothing there that is half so interesting as the human mind.

Very well, God banished Adam and Eve from the Garden, and eventually assassinated them. All for disobeying a command which he had no right to utter. But he did not stop there, as you will see. He has one code of morals for himself, and quite another for his children. He requires his children to deal justly — and gently — with offenders, and forgive them seventy-and-seven times; whereas he deals neither justly nor gently with anyone, and he did not forgive the ignorant and thoughtless first pair of juveniles even their first small offense and say, "You may go free this time, and I will give you another chance."

On the contrary! He elected to punish *their* children, all through the ages to the end of time, for a trifling offense committed by others before they were born. He is punishing them yet. In mild ways? No, in atrocious ones.

You would not suppose that this kind of Being gets many compliments. Undeceive yourself: the world calls him the All-Just, the All-Righteous, the All-Good, the All-Merciful, the All-Forgiving, the All-Truthful, the All-Loving, the Source of All Morality. These sarcasms are uttered daily, all over the world. But not as conscious sarcasms. No, they are meant seriously: they are uttered without a smile.

Topics for Discussion

1. What might have been the reason for John Bunyan's writing an apology for *Pilgrim's Progress*?
2. John Bunyan calls *Pilgrim's Progress* an allegory. Does he mean that this religious book has an artistic framework?
3. How to interpret John Bunyan's allusion to the fisherman?
4. Why does Mark Twain rewrite the biblical *Genesis* in a literary way?
5. Are the central messages in Satan's letters from the earth purely religious? Why?
6. Give more examples of intertextuality between literature and religious writings.

Monograph Five　Literature and Arts

I　Laocoon

(Excerpt)

Gotthold Ephraim Lessing (1729-1781)

translated by Robert Phillimore (1810-1885)

There are connoisseurs of antiquity who hold indeed that the Laocoon group was the work of a Greek master, but of the time of the emperors, because they believe that the Virgilian Laocoon served as the model for it. Of all the ancient learned men who have been of this opinion I will only mention Bartholomew Marliani; and of the modern, Montfaucon. Thcy found, without doubt, so remarkable an agreement between the work of art and the description of the poet that it appeared to them impossible that both should by accident have lighted upon the same circumstances, which certainly do not naturally suggest themselves. They further maintain that as to the honour attaching to the invention and first conception, the probability is much more in favour of the poet than the artist.

Only they appear to have forgotten that a third predicament is possible. For, perhaps, the poet has as little imitated the artist as the artist has the poet, but both have drawn their supply from the same ancient fountains. According to Macrobius, the works of Pisander were these ancient sources. For while the works of this Greek poet were yet extant, it was a matter of school learning, *pueris decantatum*, that the

Roman writer had not so much imitated as literally translated the whole conquest and destruction of Ilium, that is, his whole second book. If, moreover, Pisander had been Virgil's predecessor in the history of Laocoon, it was nevertheless not the custom of the Greek artists to derive their instruction from any Latin poet, and the conjecture drawn from the epoch rests on no foundation.

In the meanwhile, if I were compelled to maintain the opinion of Marliani and Montfaucon, I would offer them the following escape from the objection. The poems of Pisander are lost: how he told the story of Laocoon cannot certainly be said; but it is probable that it was narrated with the same circumstances of which we now find the traces in Greek authors. Now these do not in the least accord with the narrative of Virgil, but the Roman poet must have molten together the Greeks' traditions according to his good pleasure. The misfortune of Laocoon, as he narrates it, is his own invention. It follows that if the artists did agree in their representations with him they must have lived after his time and have worked after his model. Quintus Calaber, it is true, like Virgil, makes Laocoon manifest a suspicion of the wooden horse; but the wrath of Minerva, which on this account he draws down upon himself, is very differently, expressed by Virgil. The earth gapes under the forewarning Trojan. Terror and anxiety overtake him; burning anguish flames in his eyes; his brain is affected; he raves; he is blinded. Blind as he is, he ceases not to counsel the burning of the wooden horse, and then Minerva sends two dreadful serpents, which, however, only seize the children of Laocoon. In vain do these stretch out their hands to their father: the poor blind man cannot help them; they are torn to pieces, and the serpents disappear in the earth. To Laocoon they do no harm; and that this circumstance is not peculiar to Quintus, but must rather be taken to be generally adopted, is evident from a passage in Lycophron, where these serpents have the epithet of children-eaters. But if this incident had been generally accepted by the Greeks, Greek artists would scarcely have ventured to depart from it, and it could hardly have happened that they would have departed from it in the same manner as the Roman poet if they had not known him, and had not received an express commission to work after his model. He who wishes to defend Marliani and Montfaucon must take up this position. Virgil is the first and the only writer who makes the father as well as the children to be killed by the serpents. The sculptors do the same, though, as Greeks, they ought not to do it; it is therefore probable that they did it in imitation of Virgil. I know very well how much this probability falls short of historical certainty. But, although I do not wish to push further this conclusion from history, at least I think it may stand as an hypothesis upon which the critic may express his opinion. Be it proved or not proved that sculptors have not followed Virgil, I will assume the fact merely for the purpose of seeing how they have imitated him. I have already expressed my opinion as to the scream. Perhaps a further comparison may bring me to results not less instructive. The incident of binding the father through the coils of the devouring serpents into one knot with his two sons is unquestionably very happy, manifesting an uncommon picturesque imagination. Who invented it?—the poet, or the artist? Montfaucon is determined that it shall but be the poet; but I think that Montfaucon has not read the poet with sufficient care.

Illi agmine certo
Laocoonta petunt, et primiun parva duorum
Corpora natorum serpens amplexus uterque
Implieat, et miseros morsu depascitur artus.
Post ipsum, auxilio subeuntem et tela ferentem
Corripiunt spirisque ligant ingentibus.

The poet has described the wonderful length of the serpents. They have entwined themselves round the boys, and when the father comes to their help they seize on him (*corripiunt*). Such is their size that they are not obliged for an instant to let go the boys; there must also be a moment when they have just fallen upon the father with their heads and foremost parts, and yet hold the children fast by their hind parts, already twisted round them. This moment in the progress of the poetical picture is necessary—the poet makes us fully perceive it; but that was not the time to paint it in detail. That the old commentators were perfectly aware of this, appears probable from a passage in Donatus. How improbable it is that it would have escaped the artists to whose intelligent eye all that can be advantageously used so quickly and so clearly appears!

In the very windings of the serpents, which the poet entwines round Laocoon, he carefully avoids including the arms, in order to leave the arms fall liberty of action.

Ille simul manibus tendit divellere nodos

In this the artist must necessarily follow him. Nothing, gives more expression and life than the movement of the hands, especially in the representation of the passions; the most speaking countenance without it is insignificant. Arms fast bound to the body through the coils of the serpent would have spread coldness and death over the whole group. But we see them in the principal figure, as well as in the accessory figures, in full activity, and there most employed where for the present the pain is greatest.

But the artist found nothing except this freedom of the arms from the coils of the serpents useful to borrow from the poet. Virgil makes the serpents wind themselves in double coils round the body and the neck of Laocoon, and tower high above him with their heads.

Bis medium amplexi, bis coilo squamea circum
Terga dati, superant capite et cervicibus altis

This figure admirably fills our imagination. The noblest parts of the body are compressed even to suffocation, and the poison is carried directly into the face.

Nevertheless, the figure is not one for the artist who wishes to show the working of the poison and of the pain in the body. For, in order to make these conspicuous, the principal parts must be left as free as possible, and throughout no external pressure must operate upon them which would change and weaken the play of the suffering nerves and working muscles. The double coils of the serpents would have covered the whole body, and that agonised contraction of the lower part of the body, which is so expressive, would have remained invisible. Whatever parts of the body, above, below, or between the coils could be seen, would appear amid the pressure and the distension not to have been caused by pain within, but by weight without. The neck enclosed in such repeated folds would have entirely lost that pyramidal termination of the group which is so agreeable to the eye; and the summits of the serpents' heads stretching out of these folds into the air would have made so sudden a falling off of proportion that the shape of the whole would have been extremely repulsive. There are, nevertheless, artists who are so unintelligent as to follow servilely the poet. We recognise with horror the consequences, to take one of several instances, from a print of Frank Cleyn. The old sculptors saw with a glance that their art in this respect required an entire alteration. They transferred all the coils from the body and neck to the thighs and feet. Here the coils, without injury to the expression, could cover and bind as much as was necessary. Here arose the idea of an impeded flight and of a kind of immovability, which is very favourable to the idea produced by Art, of permanence in one and the same condition.

I know not how it has happened that the artists have passed over in complete silence this difference in the coils of the serpents which so plainly appears between the works of the artist and the description of the poet. It exalts the wisdom of the artist quite as much as other things which they all seize upon, but which they do not so much venture to praise as seek to excuse. I mean the difference as to the dress. Virgil's Laocoon is in his priestly robes, and he appears in the group with both his sons quite naked. It is said that there are persons who find a gross absurdity in representing a king's son, a priest at his sacrifice, as naked, and to these persons the connoisseurs reply in sober earnestness that it is certainly an unusually grave fault, but that the artist was constrained to commit it because his figures could have no becoming dress. Statuary, they say, cannot imitate any stuff. Thick folds have a bad effect. Of two inconveniences the least must be chosen, and it is better to run counter to the truth than to be subject to blame for the drapery. The old artists would have laughed at this reproach, but I do not know what they would have said to the answer. It is impossible to degrade Art to a lower depth than by these means. For let it be granted that sculpture can imitate stuffs of different kinds as well as painting, must Laocoon have therefore necessarily been clothed? Should we lose nothing by the adoption of this clothing? Has a garment, the work of servile hands, as much beauty as the work of eternal wisdom, the organised body? Docs it require the same capacity, —is there the same merit, — does it confer the same honour, to imitate the one as the other? Do our eyes only require to be deceived, and is it all the same to them wherewith they are deceived? With the poet a garment is no garment: it covers nothing: our imagination sees entirely through it. Let the Laocoon of Virgil either have it or have it not, his suffering is as visible in one part of his body as in the other. The forehead is bound by the priestly fillet, but is not veiled by it. Hay, this fillet hides nothing, absolutely nothing: it only strengthens the idea which we form of the misfortune of the sufferer.

Perfusus sanie vittas atroqne veneno

The priestly dignity nothing avails him. The very emblem of it, which everywhere procures for him respect and honour, is thoroughly defiled and desecrated by the poisonous saliva. But the artist must abandon this subordinate idea if the principal work is not to suffer. If he had left even this fillet to Laocoon, he would greatly have weakened the expression. The forehead would have been covered, and the forehead is the seat of expression. As in the matter of screaming he sacrificed expression to beauty, so here he sacrifices what is conventional to expression. With the ancients what is conventional was considered a very small thing. They felt that the highest end of their art led them entirely to dispense with it. Beauty is their highest end. Necessity invented clothes. What has Art to do with necessity? I grant that there is a kind of beauty in apparel, but what is it when put in competition with the human form? And shall he who can attain the greater be content with the less? I much fear that the most perfect painter of dress shows by this very dexterity in what he is really wanting.

My supposition that the artists have imitated the poet in no way depreciates the former. Rather does their wisdom in this imitation appear in the very best light. They follow the poet without allowing themselves to be in the slightest particular corrupted by him. They have a model, but as to the mode of transferring this model from one art to the other they have ample scope to think for themselves; and the original ideas which they manifest in their departures from the model demonstrate that they are as great in their Art as he in his.

Now, I will reverse this supposition: the poet shall have imitated the artists. There are learned men who maintain this proposition as a truth. I do not know that they have any historical grounds for so doing; but finding this work of Art overwhelmingly beautiful, they cannot persuade themselves that it belongs to a later epoch. It must belong to that time when Art was in its most perfect bloom, because it deserves to belong to it.

It has been shown that, however excellent Virgil's picture may be, nevertheless there are several features in it of which the artist could not avail himself. This proposition is also subject to limitations.

That a good poetical painting must make a really good picture, and that the poet has painted well only so far as the artist can follow him in all his details. We are disposed to take for granted this limitation, before we see it confirmed by examples. Simply from a consideration of the wider sphere of Poetry, of the unbounded field of our imagination, of the immateriality of its images, which can stand side by side in the greatest multitude and multi-formity, without the one concealing or injuring the other, just as the things themselves, or the natural signs of them, in the narrow limits of space or time, would stand.

If, however, the less cannot contain the greater, the less can be contained in the greater, or I will put it thus: although not every trait which the painting poet uses can produce as good an effect on canvas or in marble, yet perhaps every trait of the artist may produce as good an effect in the work of the poet? Certainly; for that which we discover to be beautiful in a work of art is not discovered by our eye, but by the force of our imagination, through the eye. The same form may, moreover, be excited in our imagination by arbitrary or by natural signs, and, each time, the same pleasure, though not in the same degree, will arise.

All this being granted, I must confess that, to me, the proposition that Virgil has imitated the artist appears much more unintelligible than the opposite proposition. If the artist followed the poet I can give a reason and can account for all his deviations from him. He must deviate from him if the very traits of the poet would have caused improprieties in his work which they do not produce in that of the poet. But why must the poet deviate? If he had copied the group faithfully in all its parts, would he not have delivered to us an excellent picture? I quite understand how his fancy working for himself could bring him to this or that trait: but the causes why his judgment was obliged to change the traits of beauty before his eyes into these other traits are by no means apparent to me.

It seems to me that if Virgil had had the group for his model, he would hardly have so far restrained himself as to have left us to conjecture that all the three bodies were entwined in one knot. They would have been placed in too lively a representation before his eyes, and he would have found the effect resulting from them too excellent not to have given them a more conspicuous place in his description. I have said that it was not then the moment to paint in detail this entwining. No; but one single word more would have produced, perhaps, a very marked effect even in the shadow in which the poet was obliged to leave it. What the artist would, without this word, have revealed, the poet, if he had seen it in the work of the artist, would not have left without this word.

The artist had the most urgent reasons for not allowing the anguish of Laocoon to burst forth into a scream. If, however, the poet had had before him so affecting a combination of pain and beauty in the work of art, what could have so irresistibly compelled him to leave altogether unexpressed the idea of manly demeanour and magnanimous patience, which arises out of this combination of pain and beauty, and to shock us at once with the ghastly screaming of his Laocoon? Richardson says: "Virgil's Laocoon must scream because the poet does not wish so much to excite pity for him as horror and dismay in the Trojans." I will grant, although Richardson does not seem to have considered it, that the poet does not make the description in his own proper person, but causes Aeneas to make it, and to make it in the presence of Dido, whose sympathy Aeneas was eager to take by storm. But it is not the scream which so much surprises me as the want of all gradation up to this scream to which the work of the artist would naturally have led the poet, if he had, as has been assumed, taken it for his model. Richardson remarks: "The history of Laocoon is intended only to lead up to a pathetic description of the final destruction of the city; the poet, therefore, did not intend to make Laocoon too interesting, in order not to dissipate, through the misfortune of one individual citizen, the attention which this last night of horrors ought to concentrate upon itself." But this is arbitrarily to consider the matter from the one moment of a painter's view, from which it ought not to be considered at all. The misfortune of Laocoon and the destruction of the city are not intended by the poet to be two pictures, one next to the other; they do not both together make one whole, so that our eye may or ought to overlook both at the same moment; and on no other hypothesis would it be desirable that our glance should rather light upon Laocoon than upon the burning city. Both descriptions follow one upon the other, and I do not see what advantage accrues to the one which follows, from the fact that the one which precedes has so very greatly affected us. It would show that the one which followed did not, in itself, sufficiently affect our feelings. Still less motive would the poet have had to alter the coils of the serpents.

In the work of Art they occupy the hands and bind the feet. So pleasing to the eye is this distribution, so lively is the picture which remains of it in the imagination. It is so distinct and clear that it can be represented by words not much more feebly than by natural signs:

> Micat alter, et ipsum
> Laocoonta petit, totumque infraque supraque
> Implicat et rapido tandem ferit ilia morsu
> At serpens lapsu crebro redeunte subintrat
> Lubricus, intortoque ligat genua infima nodo

These are the lines of Sadolet, which would doubtless have been produced with yet more picturesqueness by Virgil if a visible model had kindled his fancy, and which would then certainly have been better than what he now gives us in their place:

> Bis medium amplexi, bis collo squamea circum
> Terga dati, superant capite et cervicibus altis

These traits entirely fill our imagination; but our imagination must not tarry there, it must not seek to analyse them, it must at one time see only the serpents, at another time only the Laocoon; it must not represent to us the effect which both together create. So far as it attempts to do this the Virgilian picture begins to be displeasing, and to be highly unpicturesque.

If, however, the alterations which Virgil would have made in the model presented to him would have been happy, they would still have been purely arbitrary. We imitate in order to produce resemblance; can we produce resemblance when we make alterations beyond the necessity of the case? Rather when this is done it is clear that we did not intend to produce a resemblance because we have not imitated. It may be replied, No, not the whole, but this or that part. Good. Still, what are then these individual parts which, in the description of the poet and in the work of the artist, so closely harmonize as to make the poet appear to have borrowed the former from the latter? The father, the children, the serpents were all furnished by history to the poet, as well as to the artist. Apart from history they agree in nothing but in this, that the children and the father were entwined in one serpent knot. But their harmony in this respect sprang from the altered version, that the very same misfortune which had smitten the father smote the children. But this alteration, as has been already said, Virgil appears to have made, for the Greek tradition is quite different. It follows that if in regard to this common fact of entwining there has been an imitation on the one side or the other, it may be presumed with greater probability to be on the side of the artist than of the poet. In all other respects the one differs from the other, only with this distinction, that if it is the artist that has made the deviation, his intention to imitate the poet may still be maintained, inasmuch as the vocation and the limits of his art constrained him to make this deviation; if, on the other hand, the poet be thought to have imitated the artist, then all the deviations which have been mentioned disprove this supposed imitation, and those who notwithstanding maintain it, can only mean that the work of Art is older than the poem.

II The Picture of Dorian Gray

(Excerpt)

Oscar Wilde (1854–1900)

The studio was filled with the rich odour of roses, and when the light summer wind stirred amidst the trees of the garden there came through the open door the heavy scent of the lilac, or the more delicate perfume of the pink-flowering thorn.

From the corner of the divan of Persian saddle-bags on which he was lying, smoking, as was his custom, innumerable cigarettes, Lord Henry Wotton could just catch the gleam of the honey-sweet and honey-coloured blossoms of a laburnum, whose tremulous branches seemed hardly able to bear the burden of a beauty so flamelike as theirs; and now and then the fantastic shadows of birds in flight flitted across the long tussore-silk curtains that were stretched in front of the huge window, producing a kind of momentary Japanese effect, and making him think of those pallid jade-faced painters of Tokyo who, through the medium of an art that is necessarily immobile, seek to convey the sense of swiftness and motion. The sullen murmur of the bees shouldering their way through the long unmown grass, or circling with monotonous insistence round the dusty gilt horns of the straggling woodbine, seemed to make the stillness more oppressive. The dim roar of London was like the bourdon note of a distant organ.

In the centre of the room, clamped to an upright easel, stood the full-length portrait of a young man of extraordinary personal beauty, and in front of it, some little distance away, was sitting the artist himself, Basil Hallward, whose sudden disappearance some years ago caused, at the time, such public excitement, and gave rise to so many strange conjectures.

As the painter looked at the gracious and comely form he had so skilfully mirrored in his art, a smile of pleasure passed across his face, and seemed about to linger there. But he suddenly started up, and, closing his eyes, placed his fingers upon the lids, as though he sought to imprison within his brain some curious dream from which he feared he might awake.

"It is your best work, Basil, the best thing you have ever done," said Lord Henry, languidly. "You must certainly send it next year to the Grosvenor. The Academy is too large and too vulgar. Whenever I have gone there, there have been either so many people that I have not been able to see the pictures, which was dreadful, or so many pictures that I have not been able to see the people, which was worse. The Grosvenor is really the only place."

"I don't think I shall send it anywhere," he answered, tossing his head back in that odd way that used to make his friends laugh at him at Oxford. "No: I won't send it anywhere."

Lord Henry elevated his eyebrows, and looked at him in amazement through the thin blue wreaths of smoke that curled up in such fanciful whorls from his heavy opium-tainted cigarette. "Not send it anywhere? My dear fellow, why? Have you any reason? What odd chaps you painters are! You do anything in the world to gain a reputation. As soon as you have one, you seem to want to throw it away. It is silly of you, for there is only one thing in the world worse than being talked about, and that is not being talked about. A portrait like this would set you far above all the young men in England, and make the old men quite jealous, if old men are ever capable of any emotion."

"I know you will laugh at me," he replied, "but I really can't exhibit it. I have put too much of myself into it."

Lord Henry stretched himself out on the divan and laughed.

"Yes, I knew you would; but it is quite true, all the same."

"Too much of yourself in it! Upon my word, Basil, I didn't know you were so vain; and I really can't see any resemblance between you, with your rugged strong face and your coal-black hair, and this young Adonis, who looks as if he was made out of ivory and rose-leaves. Why, my dear Basil, he is a Narcissus, and you—well, of course you have an intellectual expression, and all that. But beauty, real beauty, ends where an intellectual expression begins. Intellect is in itself a mode of exaggeration, and destroys the harmony of any face. The moment one sits down to think, one becomes all nose, or all forehead, or something horrid. Look at the successful men in any of the learned professions. How perfectly hideous they are! Except, of course, in the Church. But then in the Church they don't think. A bishop keeps on saying at the age of eighty what he was told to say when he was a boy of eighteen, and as a natural consequence he always looks absolutely delightful. Your mysterious young friend, whose name you have never told me, but whose picture really fascinates me, never thinks. I feel quite sure of that. He is some brainless, beautiful creature, who should be always here in winter when we have no flowers to look at, and always here in summer when we want something to chill our intelligence. Don't flatter yourself, Basil: you are not in the least like him."

"You don't understand me, Harry," answered the artist. "Of course I am not like him. I know that perfectly well. Indeed, I should be sorry to look like him. You shrug your shoulders? I am telling you the truth. There is a fatality about all physical and intellectual distinction, the sort of fatality that seems to dog through history the faltering steps of kings. It is better not to be different from one's fellows. The ugly and the stupid have the best of it in this world. They can sit at their ease and gape at the play. If they know nothing of victory, they are at least spared the knowledge of defeat. They live as we all should live—undisturbed, indifferent, and without disquiet. They neither bring ruin upon others, nor ever receive it from alien hands. Your rank and wealth, Harry; my brains, such as they are—my art, whatever it may be worth; Dorian Gray's good looks—we shall all suffer for what the gods have given us, suffer terribly."

"Dorian Gray? Is that his name?" asked Lord Henry, walking across the studio towards Basil Hallward.

"Yes, that is his name. I didn't intend to tell it to you."

"But why not?"

"Oh, I can't explain. When I like people immensely I never tell their names to any one. It is like surrendering a part of them. I have grown to love secrecy. It seems to be the one thing that can make modern life mysterious or marvellous to us. The commonest thing is delightful if one only hides it. When I leave town now I never tell my people where I am going. If I did, I would lose all my pleasure. It is a silly habit, I dare say, but somehow it seems to bring a great deal of romance into one's life. I suppose you think me awfully foolish about it?"

"Not at all," answered Lord Henry, "not at all, my dear Basil. You seem to forget that I am married, and the one charm of marriage is that it makes a life of deception absolutely necessary for both parties. I never know where my wife is, and my wife never knows what I am doing. When we meet—we do meet occasionally, when we dine out together, or go down to the Duke's—we tell each other the most absurd stories with the most serious faces. My wife is very good at it—much better, in fact, than I am. She never gets confused over her dates, and I always do. But when she does find me out, she makes no row at all. I sometimes wish she would; but she merely laughs at me."

"I hate the way you talk about your married life, Harry," said Basil Hallward, strolling towards the door that led into the garden. "I believe that you are really a very good husband, but that you are thoroughly ashamed of your own virtues. You are an extraordinary fellow. You never say a moral thing, and you never do a wrong thing. Your cynicism is simply a pose."

"Being natural is simply a pose, and the most irritating pose I know," cried Lord Henry, laughing; and the two young men went out into the garden together, and ensconced themselves on a long bamboo seat that stood in the shade of a tall laurel bush. The sunlight slipped over the polished leaves. In the grass, white daisies were tremulous.

After a pause, Lord Henry pulled out his watch. "I am afraid I must be going, Basil," he murmured, "and before I go, I insist on your answering a question I put to you some time ago."

"What is that?" said the painter, keeping his eyes fixed on the ground.

"You know quite well."

"I do not, Harry."

"Well, I will tell you what it is. I want you to explain to me why you won't exhibit Dorian Gray's picture. I want the real reason."

"I told you the real reason."

"No, you did not. You said it was because there was too much of yourself in it.

Now, that is childish."

"Harry," said Basil Hallward, looking him straight in the face, "every portrait that is painted with feeling is a portrait of the artist, not of the sitter. The sitter is merely the accident, the occasion. It is not he who is revealed by the painter; it is rather the painter who, on the coloured canvas, reveals himself. The reason I will not exhibit this picture is that I am afraid that I have shown in it the secret of my own soul."

Lord Henry laughed. "And what is that?" he asked.

"I will tell you," said Hallward; but an expression of perplexity came over his face.

"I am all expectation, Basil," continued his companion, glancing at him.

"Oh, there is really very little to tell, Harry," answered the painter; "and I am afraid you will hardly understand it. Perhaps you will hardly believe it."

Lord Henry smiled, and, leaning down, plucked a pink-petalled daisy from the grass, and examined it. "I am quite sure I shall understand it," he replied, gazing intently at the little golden white-feathered disk, "and as for believing things, I can believe anything, provided that it is quite incredible."

The wind shook some blossoms from the trees, and the heavy lilac-blooms, with their clustering stars, moved to and fro in the languid air. A grasshopper began to chirrup by the wall, and like a blue thread a long thin dragon-fly floated past on its brown gauze wings. Lord Henry felt as if he could hear Basil Hallward's heart beating, and wondered what was coming.

"The story is simply this," said the painter after some time. "Two months ago I went to a crush at Lady Brandon's. You know we poor artists have to show ourselves in society from time to time, just to remind the public that we are not savages. With an evening coat and a white tie, as you told me once, anybody, even a stock-broker, can gain a reputation for being civilized. Well, after I had been in the room about ten minutes, talking to huge overdressed dowagers and tedious academicians, I suddenly became conscious that some one was looking at me. I turned half-way round, and saw Dorian Gray for the first time. When our eyes met, I felt that I was growing pale. A curious sensation of terror came over me. I knew that I had come face to face with some one whose mere personality was so fascinating that, if I allowed it to do so, it would absorb my whole nature, my whole soul, my very art itself. I did not want any external influence in my life. You know yourself, Harry, how independent I am by nature. I have always been my own master; had at least always been so, till I met Dorian Gray. Then — but I don't know how to explain it to you. Something seemed to tell me that I was on the verge of a terrible crisis in my life. I had a strange feeling that Fate had in store for me exquisite joys and exquisite sorrows. I grew afraid, and turned to quit the room. It was not conscience that made me do so: it was a sort of cowardice. I take no credit to myself for trying to escape."

"Conscience and cowardice are really the same things, Basil. Conscience is the trade-name of the firm. That is all."

"I don't believe that, Harry, and I don't believe you do either. However, whatever was my motive—and it may have been pride, for I used to be very proud—I certainly struggled to the door. There, of course, I stumbled against Lady Brandon. 'You are not going to run away so soon, Mr. Hallward?' she screamed out. You know her curiously shrill voice?"

"Yes; she is a peacock in everything but beauty," said Lord Henry, pulling the daisy to bits with his long, nervous fingers.

"I could not get rid of her. She brought me up to royalties, and people with stars and garters, and elderly ladies with gigantic tiaras and parrot noses. She spoke of me as her dearest friend. I had only met her once before, but she took it into her head to lionize me. I believe some picture of mine had made a great success at the time, at least had been chattered about in the penny newspapers, which is the nineteenth-century standard of immortality. Suddenly I found myself face to face with the young man whose personality had so strangely stirred me. We were quite close, almost touching. Our eyes met again. It was reckless of me, but I asked Lady Brandon to introduce me to him. Perhaps it was not so reckless, after all. It was simply inevitable. We would have spoken to each other without any introduction. I am sure of that. Dorian told me so afterwards. He, too, felt that we were destined to know each other."

"And how did Lady Brandon describe this wonderful young man?" asked his companion. "I know she goes in for giving a rapid *précis* of all her guests. I remember her bringing me up to a truculent and redfaced old gentleman covered all over with orders and ribbons, and hissing into my ear, in a tragic whisper which must have been perfectly audible to everybody in the room, the most astounding details. I simply fled. I like to find out people for myself. But Lady Brandon treats her guests exactly as an auctioneer treats his goods. She either explains them entirely away, or tells one everything about them except what one wants to know."

"Poor Lady Brandon! You are hard on her, Harry!" said Hallward, listlessly.

"My dear fellow, she tried to found a *salon*, and only succeeded in opening a restaurant. How could I admire her? But tell me, what did she say about Mr. Dorian Gray?"

"Oh, something like, 'Charming boy—poor dear mother and I absolutely inseparable. Quite forget what he does—afraid he—doesn't do anything—oh, yes, plays the piano—or is it the violin, dear Mr. Gray?' Neither of us could help laughing, and we became friends at once."

"Laughter is not at all a bad beginning for a friendship, and it is far the best ending for one," said the young lord, plucking another daisy.

Hallward shook his head. "You don't understand what friendship is, Harry," he murmured—"or what enmity is, for that matter. You like every one; that is to say, you are indifferent to every one."

"How horribly unjust of you!" cried Lord Henry, tilting his hat back, and looking up at the little clouds that, like ravelled skeins of glossy white silk, were drifting across the hollowed turquoise of the summer sky. "Yes; horribly unjust of you. I make a great difference between people. I choose my friends for their good looks, my acquaintances for their good characters, and my enemies for their good intellects. A man cannot be too careful in the choice of his enemies. I have not got one who is a fool. They are all men of some intellectual power, and consequently they all appreciate me. Is that very vain of me? I think it is rather vain."

"I should think it was, Harry. But according to your category I must be merely an acquaintance."

"My dear old Basil, you are much more than an acquaintance."

"And much less than a friend. A sort of brother, I suppose?"

"Oh, brothers! I don't care for brothers. My elder brother won't die, and my younger brothers seem never to do anything else."

"Harry!" exclaimed Hallward, frowning.

"My dear fellow, I am not quite serious. But I can't help detesting my relations. I suppose it comes from the fact that none of us can stand other people having the same faults as ourselves. I quite sympathize with the rage of the English democracy against what they call the vices of the upper orders. The masses feel that drunkenness, stupidity, and immorality should be their own special property, and that if any one of us makes an ass of himself he is poaching on their preserves. When poor Southwark got into the divorce court, their indignation was quite magnificent. And yet I don't suppose that ten per cent. of the proletariat live correctly."

"I don't agree with a single word that you have said, and, what is more, Harry, I feel sure you don't either."

Lord Henry stroked his pointed brown beard, and tapped the toe of his patent-leather boot with a tasselled ebony cane. "How English you are, Basil! That is the second time you have made that observation. If one puts forward an idea to a true Englishman—always a rash thing to do—he never dreams of considering whether the idea is right or wrong. The only thing he considers of any importance is whether one believes it oneself. Now, the value of an idea has nothing whatsoever to do with the sincerity of the man who expresses it. Indeed, the probabilities are that the more insincere the man is, the more purely intellectual will the idea be, as in that case it will not be coloured by either his wants, his desires, or his prejudices. However, I don't propose to discuss politics, sociology, or metaphysics with you. I like persons better than principles, and I like persons with no principles better than anything else in the world. Tell me more about Mr. Dorian Gray. How often do you see him?"

"Every day. I couldn't be happy if I didn't see him every day. He is absolutely necessary to me."

"How extraordinary! I thought you would never care for anything but your art."

"He is all my art to me now," said the painter, gravely. "I sometimes think, Harry, that there are only two eras of any importance in the world's history. The first is the appearance of a new medium for art, and the second is the appearance of a new personality for art also. What the invention of oil-painting was to the Venetians, the face of Antinoüs was to late Greek sculpture, and the face of Dorian Gray will some day be to me. It is not merely that I paint from him, draw from him, sketch from him. Of course I have done all that. But he is much more to me than a model or a sitter. I won't tell you that I am dissatisfied with what I have done of him, or that his beauty is such that art cannot express it. There is nothing that art cannot express, and I know that the work I have done, since I met Dorian Gray, is good work, is the best work of my life. But in some curious way—I wonder will you understand me?—his personality has suggested to me an entirely new manner in art, an entirely new mode of style. I see things differently, I think of them differently. I can now recreate life in a way that was hidden from me before. 'A dream of form in days of thought' —who is it who says that? I forget; but it is what Dorian Gray has been to me. The merely visible presence of this lad—for he seems to me little more than a lad, though he is really over twenty—his merely visible presence—ah! I wonder can you realize all that that means? Unconsciously he defines for me the lines of a fresh school, a school that is to have in it all the passion of the romantic spirit, all the perfection of the spirit that is Greek. The harmony of soul and body—how much that is! We in our madness have separated the two, and have invented a realism that is vulgar, an ideality that is void. Harry! If you only knew what Dorian Gray is to me! You remember that landscape of mine, for which Agnew offered me such a huge price, but which I would not part with? It is one of the best things I have ever done. And why is it so? Because, while I was painting it, Dorian Gray sat beside me. Some subtle influence passed from him to me, and for the first time in my life I saw in the plain woodland the wonder I had always looked for, and always missed."

"Basil, this is extraordinary! I must see Dorian Gray."

Hallward got up from the seat, and walked up and down the garden. After some time he came back. "Harry," he said, "Dorian Gray is to me simply a motive in art. You might see nothing in him. I see everything in him. He is never more present in my work than when no image of him is there. He is a suggestion, as I have said, of a new manner. I find him in the curves of certain lines, in the loveliness and subtleties of certain colours. That is all."

"Then why won't you exhibit his portrait?" asked Lord Henry.

"Because, without intending it, I have put into it some expression of all this curious artistic idolatry, of which, of course, I have never cared to speak to him. He knows nothing about it. He shall never know anything about it. But the world might guess it; and I will not bare my soul to their shallow, prying eyes. My heart shall never be put under their microscope. There is too much of myself in the thing, Harry—too much of myself!"

"Poets are not so scrupulous as you are. They know how useful passion is for publication. Nowadays a broken heart will run to many editions."

"I hate them for it," cried Hallward. "An artist should create beautiful things, but should put nothing of his own life into them. We live in an age when men treat art as if it were meant to be a form of autobiography. We have lost the abstract sense of beauty. Some day I will show the world what it is; and for that reason the world shall never see my portrait of Dorian Gray."

"I think you are wrong, Basil, but I won't argue with you. It is only the intellectually lost who ever argue. Tell me, is Dorian Gray very fond of you?"

The painter considered for a few moments. "He likes me," he answered, after a pause; "I know he likes me. Of course I flatter him dreadfully. I find a strange pleasure in saying things to him that I know I shall be sorry for having said. As a rule, he is charming to me, and we sit in the studio and talk of a thousand things. Now and then, however, he is horribly thoughtless, and seems to take a real delight in giving me pain. Then I feel, Harry, that I have given away my whole soul to some one who treats it as if it were a flower to put in his coat, a bit of decoration to charm his vanity, an ornament for a summer's day."

"Days in summer, Basil, are apt to linger," murmured Lord Henry. "Perhaps you will tire sooner than he will. It is a sad thing to think of, but there is no doubt that Genius lasts longer than Beauty. That accounts for the fact that we all take such pains to over-educate ourselves. In the wild struggle for existence, we want to have something that endures, and so we fill our minds with rubbish and facts, in the silly hope of keeping our place. The thoroughly well-informed man—that is the modern ideal. And the mind of the thoroughly well-informed man is a dreadful thing. It is like a bric-à-brac shop, all monsters and dust, with everything priced above its proper value. I think you will tire first, all the same. Some day you will look at your friend, and he will seem to you to be a little out of drawing, or you won't like his tone of colour, or something. You will bitterly reproach him in your own heart, and seriously think that he has behaved very badly to you. The next time he calls, you will be perfectly cold and indifferent. It will be a great pity, for it will alter you. What you have told me is quite a romance, a romance of art one might call it, and the worst of having a romance of any kind is that it leaves one so unromantic."

"Harry, don't talk like that. As long as I live, the personality of Dorian Gray will dominate me. You can't feel what I feel. You change too often."

"Ah, my dear Basil, that is exactly why I can feel it. Those who are faithful know only the trivial side of love: it is the faithless who know love's tragedies." And Lord Henry struck a light on a dainty silver case, and began to smoke a cigarette with a self-conscious and satisfied air, as if he had summed up the world in a phrase. There was a rustle of chirruping sparrows in the green lacquer leaves of the ivy, and the blue cloud-shadows chased themselves across the grass like swallows. How pleasant it was in the garden! And how delightful other people's emotions were!—much more delightful than their ideas, it seemed to him. One's own soul, and the passions of one's friends—those were the fascinating things in life. He pictured to himself with silent amusement the tedious luncheon that he had missed by staying so long with Basil Hallward. Had he gone to his aunt's, he would have been sure to have met Lord Goodbody there, and the whole conversation would have been about the feeding of the poor, and the necessity for model lodging-houses. Each class would have preached the importance of those virtues, for whose exercise there was no necessity in their own lives. The rich would have spoken on the value of thrift, and the idle grown eloquent over the dignity of labour. It was charming to have escaped all that! As he thought of his aunt, an idea seemed to strike him. He turned to Hallward, and said, "My dear fellow, I have just remembered."

"Remembered what, Harry?"

"Where I heard the name of Dorian Gray."

"Where was it?" asked Hallward, with a slight frown.

"Don't look so angry, Basil. It was at my aunt, Lady Agatha's. She told me she had discovered a wonderful young man, who was going to help her in the East End, and that his name was Dorian Gray. I am bound to state that she never told me he was good-looking. Women have no appreciation of good looks; at least, good women have not. She said that he was very earnest, and had a beautiful nature. I at once pictured to myself a creature with spectacles and lank hair, horribly freckled, and tramping about on huge feet. I wish I had known it was your friend."

"I am very glad you didn't, Harry."

"Why?"

"I don't want you to meet him."

"You don't want me to meet him?"

"No."

"Mr. Dorian Gray is in the studio, sir," said the butler, coming into the garden.

"You must introduce me now," cried Lord Henry, laughing.

The painter turned to his servant, who stood blinking in the sunlight. "Ask Mr. Gray to wait, Parker: I shall be in in a few moments." The man bowed, and went up the walk.

Then he looked at Lord Henry. "Dorian Gray is my dearest friend," he said. "He has a simple and a beautiful nature. Your aunt was quite right in what she said of him. Don't spoil him. Don't try to influence him. Your influence would be bad. The world is wide, and has many marvellous people in it. Don't take away from me the one person who gives to my art whatever charm it possesses: my life as an artist depends on him. Mind, Harry, I trust you." He spoke very slowly, and the words seemed wrung out of him almost against his will.

"What nonsense you talk!" said Lord Henry, smiling, and, taking Hallward by the arm, he almost led him into the house.

As they entered they saw Dorian Gray. He was seated at the piano, with his back to them, turning over the pages of a volume of Schumann's "Forest Scenes." "You must lend me these, Basil," he cried. "I want to learn them. They are perfectly charming."

"That entirely depends on how you sit to-day, Dorian."

"Oh, I am tired of sitting, and I don't want a life-sized portrait of myself," answered the lad, swinging round on the music-stool, in a wilful, petulant manner. When he caught sight of Lord Henry, a faint blush coloured his cheeks for a moment, and he started up.

"I beg your pardon, Basil, but I didn't know you had any one with you."

"This is Lord Henry Wotton, Dorian, an old Oxford friend of mine. I have just been telling him what a capital sitter you were, and now you have spoiled everything."

"You have not spoiled my pleasure in meeting you, Mr. Gray," said Lord

Henry, stepping forward and extending his hand. "My aunt has often spoken to me about you. You are one of her favourites, and, I am afraid, one of her victims also."

"I am in Lady Agatha's black books at present," answered Dorian, with a funny look of penitence. "I promised to go to a club in Whitechapel with her last Tuesday, and I really forgot all about it. We were to have played a duet together—three duets, I believe. I don't know what she will say to me. I am far too frightened to call."

"Oh, I will make your peace with my aunt. She is quite devoted to you. And I don't think it really matters about your not being there. The audience probably thought it was a duet. When Aunt Agatha sits down to the piano she makes quite enough noise for two people."

"That is very horrid to her, and not very nice to me," answered Dorian, laughing.

Lord Henry looked at him. Yes, he was certainly wonderfully handsome, with his finely-curved scarlet lips, his frank blue eyes, his crisp gold hair. There was something in his face that made one trust him at once. All the candour of youth was there, as well as all youth's passionate purity. One felt that he had kept himself unspotted from the world. No wonder Basil Hallward worshipped him.

"You are too charming to go in for philanthropy, Mr. Gray—far too charming." And Lord Henry flung himself down on the divan, and opened his cigarette-case.

The painter had been busy mixing his colours and getting his brushes ready. He was looking worried, and when he heard Lord Henry's last remark he glanced at him, hesitated for a moment, and then said, "Harry, I want to finish this picture to-day. Would you think it awfully rude of me if I asked you to go away?"

Lord Henry smiled, and looked at Dorian Gray. "Am I to go, Mr. Gray?" he asked.

"Oh, please don't, Lord Henry. I see that Basil is in one of his sulky moods; and I can't bear him when he sulks. Besides, I want you to tell me why I should not go in for philanthropy."

"I don't know that I shall tell you that, Mr. Gray. It is so tedious a subject that one would have to talk seriously about it. But I certainly shall not run away, now that you have asked me to stop. You don't really mind, Basil, do you? You have often told me that you liked your sitters to have some one to chat to."

Hallward bit his lip. "If Dorian wishes it, of course you must stay. Dorian's whims are laws to everybody, except himself."

Lord Henry took up his hat and gloves. "You are very pressing, Basil, but I am afraid I must go. I have promised to meet a man at the Orleans. Good-bye, Mr. Gray. Come and see me some afternoon in Curzon Street. I am nearly always at home at five o'clock. Write to me when you are coming. I should be sorry to miss you."

"Basil," cried Dorian Gray, "if Lord Henry Wotton goes I shall go too. You never open your lips while you are painting, and it is horribly dull standing on a platform and trying to look pleasant. Ask him to stay. I insist upon it."

"Stay, Harry, to oblige Dorian, and to oblige me," said Hallward, gazing intently at his picture. "It is quite true, I never talk when I am working, and never listen either, and it must be dreadfully tedious for my unfortunate sitters. I beg you to stay."

"But what about my man at the Orleans?"

The painter laughed. "I don't think there will be any difficulty about that. Sit down again, Harry. And now, Dorian, get up on the platform, and don't move about too much, or pay any attention to what Lord Henry says. He has a very bad influence over all his friends, with the single exception of myself."

Dorian Gray stepped up on the dais, with the air of a young Greek martyr, and made a little *moue* of discontent to Lord Henry, to whom he had rather taken a fancy. He was so unlike Basil. They made a delightful contrast. And he had such a beautiful voice. After a few moments he said to him, "Have you really a very bad influence, Lord Henry? As bad as Basil says?"

"There is no such thing as a good influence, Mr. Gray. All influence is immoral—immoral from the scientific point of view."

"Why?"

"Because to influence a person is to give him one's own soul. He does not think his natural thoughts, or burn with his natural passions. His virtues are not real to him. His sins, if there are such things as sins, are borrowed. He becomes an echo of some one else's music, an actor of a part that has not been written for him. The aim of life is self-development. To realize one's nature perfectly—that is what each of us is here for. People are afraid of themselves, nowadays. They have forgotten the highest of all duties, the duty that one owes to one's self. Of course they are charitable. They feed the hungry, and clothe the beggar. But their own souls starve, and are naked. Courage has gone out of our race. Perhaps we never really had it. The terror of society, which is the basis of morals, the terror of God, which is the secret of religion—these are the two things that govern us. And yet—"

"Just turn your head a little more to the right, Dorian, like a good boy," said the painter, deep in his work, and conscious only that a look had come into the lad's face that he had never seen there before.

"And yet," continued Lord Henry, in his low, musical voice, and with that graceful wave of the hand that was always so characteristic of him, and that he had even in his Eton days, "I believe that if one man were to live out his life fully and completely, were to give form to every feeling, expression to every thought, reality to every dream—I believe that the world would gain such a fresh impulse of joy that we would forget all the maladies of medievalism, and return to the Hellenic ideal—to something finer, richer, than the Hellenic ideal, it may be. But the bravest man amongst us is afraid of himself. The mutilation of the savage has its tragic survival in the self-denial that mars our lives. We are punished for our refusals. Every impulse that we strive to strangle broods in the mind, and poisons us. The body sins once, and has done with its sin, for action is a mode of purification. Nothing remains then but the recollection of a pleasure, or the luxury of a regret. The only way to get rid of a temptation is to yield to it. Resist it, and your soul grows sick with longing for the things it has forbidden to itself, with desire for what its monstrous laws have made monstrous and unlawful. It has been said that the great events of the world take place in the brain. It is in the brain, and the brain only, that the great sins of the world take place also. You, Mr. Gray, you yourself, with your rose-red youth and your rose-white boyhood, you have had passions that have made you afraid, thoughts that have filled you with terror, day-dreams and sleeping dreams whose mere memory might stain your cheek with shame—"

"Stop!" faltered Dorian Gray, "Stop! You bewilder me. I don't know what to say. There is some answer to you, but I cannot find it. Don't speak. Let me think. Or, rather, let me try not to think."

For nearly ten minutes he stood there, motionless, with parted lips, and eyes strangely bright. He was dimly conscious that entirely fresh influences were at work within him. Yet they seemed to him to have come really from himself. The few words that Basil's friend had said to him—words spoken by chance, no doubt, and with wilful paradox in them—had touched some secret chord that had never been touched before, but that he felt was now vibrating and throbbing to curious pulses.

Music had stirred him like that. Music had troubled him many times. But music was not articulate. It was not a new world, but rather another chaos, that it created in us. Words! Mere words! How terrible they were! How clear, and vivid, and cruel! One could not escape from them. And yet what a subtle magic there was in them! They seemed to be able to give a plastic form to formless things, and to have a music of their own as sweet as that of viol or of lute. Mere words! Was there anything so real as words?

Yes; there had been things in his boyhood that he had not understood. He understood them now. Life suddenly became fiery-coloured to him. It seemed to him that he had been walking in fire. Why had he not known it?

With his subtle smile, Lord Henry watched him. He knew the precise psychological moment when to say nothing. He felt intensely interested. He was amazed at the sudden impression that his words had produced, and, remembering a book that he had read when he was sixteen, a book which had revealed to him much that he had not known before, he wondered whether Dorian Gray was passing through a similar experience. He had merely shot an arrow into the air. Had it hit the mark? How fascinating the lad was!

Hallward painted away with that marvellous bold touch of his, that had the true refinement and perfect delicacy that in art, at any rate, comes only from strength. He was unconscious of the silence.

"Basil, I am tired of standing," cried Dorian Gray, suddenly. "I must go out and sit in the garden. The air is stifling here."

"My dear fellow, I am so sorry. When I am painting, I can't think of anything else. But you never sat better. You were perfectly still. And I have caught the effect I wanted—the half-parted lips, and the bright look in the eyes. I don't know what Harry has been saying to you, but he has certainly made you have the most wonderful expression. I suppose he has been paying you compliments. You mustn't believe a word that he says."

"He has certainly not been paying me compliments. Perhaps that is the reason that I don't believe anything he has told me."

"You know you believe it all," said Lord Henry, looking at him with his dreamy, languorous eyes. "I will go out to the garden with you. It is horribly hot in the studio. Basil, let us have something iced to drink, something with strawberries in it."

"Certainly, Harry. Just touch the bell, and when Parker comes I will tell him what you want. I have got to work up this background, so I will join you later on. Don't keep Dorian too long. I have never been in better form for painting than I am today. This is going to be my masterpiece. It is my masterpiece as it stands."

Lord Henry went out to the garden, and found Dorian Gray burying his face in the great cool lilac-blossoms, feverishly drinking in their perfume as if it had been wine. He came close to him, and put his hand upon his shoulder. "You are quite right to do that," he murmured. "Nothing can cure the soul but the senses, just as nothing can cure the senses but the soul."

The lad started and drew back. He was bare-headed, and the leaves had tossed his rebellious curls and tangled all their gilded threads. There was a look of fear in his eyes, such as people have when they are suddenly awakened. His finely-chiselled nostrils quivered, and some hidden nerve shook the scarlet of his lips and left them trembling.

"Yes," continued Lord Henry, "that is one of the great secrets of life—to cure the soul by means of the senses, and the senses by means of the soul. You are a wonderful creation. You know more than you think you know, just as you know less than you want to know."

Dorian Gray frowned and turned his head away. He could not help liking the tall, graceful young man who was standing by him. His romantic olive-coloured face and worn expression interested him. There was something in his low, languid voice that was absolutely fascinating. His cool, white, flower-like hands, even, had a curious charm. They moved, as he spoke, like music, and seemed to have a language of their own. But he felt afraid of him, and ashamed of being afraid. Why had it been left for a stranger to reveal him to himself? He had known Basil Hallward for months, but the friendship between them had never altered him. Suddenly there had come some one across his life who seemed to have disclosed to him life's mystery. And, yet, what was there to be afraid of? He was not a schoolboy or a girl. It was absurd to be frightened.

"Let us go and sit in the shade," said Lord Henry. "Parker has brought out the drinks, and if you stay any longer in this glare you will be quite spoiled, and Basil will never paint you again. You really must not allow yourself to become sunburnt. It would be unbecoming."

"What can it matter?" cried Dorian Gray, laughing, as he sat down on the seat at the end of the garden.

"It should matter everything to you, Mr. Gray."

"Why?"

"Because you have the most marvellous youth, and youth is the one thing worth having."

"I don't feel that, Lord Henry."

"No, you don't feel it now. Some day, when you are old and wrinkled and ugly, when thought has seared your forehead with its lines, and passion branded your lips with its hideous fires, you will feel it, you will feel it terribly. Now, wherever you go, you charm the world. Will it always be so? ... You have a wonderfully beautiful face, Mr. Gray. Don't frown. You have. And Beauty is a form of Genius—is higher, indeed, than Genius, as it needs no explanation. It is one of the great facts of the world, like sunlight, or spring-time, or the reflection in dark waters of that silver shell we call the moon. It cannot be questioned. It has its divine right of sovereignty. It makes princes of those who have it. You smile? Ah! when you have lost it you won't smile. ... People say sometimes that Beauty is only superficial. That may be so. But at least it is not so superficial as thought is. To me, Beauty is the wonder of wonders. It is only shallow people who do not judge by appearances. The true mystery of the world is the visible, not the invisible. ... Yes, Mr. Gray, the gods have been good to you. But what the gods give they quickly take away. You have only a few years in which to live really, perfectly, and fully. When your youth goes, your beauty will go with it, and then you will suddenly discover that there are no triumphs left for you, or have to content yourself with those mean triumphs that the memory of your past will make more bitter than defeats. Every month as it wanes brings you nearer to something dreadful. Time is jealous of you, and wars against your lilies and your roses. You will become sallow, and hollow-cheeked, and dull-eyed. You will suffer horribly. ... Ah! realize your youth while you have it. Don't squander the gold of your days, listening to the tedious, trying to improve the hopeless failure, or giving away your life to the ignorant, the common, and the vulgar. These are the sickly aims, the false ideals, of our age. Live! Live the wonderful life that is in you! Let nothing be lost upon you. Be always searching for new sensations. Be afraid of nothing. ... A new Hedonism—that is what our century wants. You might be its visible symbol. With your personality there is nothing you could not do. The world belongs to you for a season. ... The moment I met you I saw that you were quite unconscious of what you really are, of what you really might be. There was so much in you that charmed me that I felt I must tell you something about yourself. I thought how tragic it would be if you were wasted. For there is such a little time that your youth will last—such a little time. The common hill-flowers wither, but they blossom again. The laburnum will be as yellow next June as it is now. In a month there will be purple stars on the clematis, and year after year the green night of its leaves will hold its purple stars. But we never get back our youth. The pulse of joy that beats in us at twenty, becomes sluggish. Our limbs fail, our senses rot. We degenerate into hideous puppets, haunted by the memory of the passions of which we were too much afraid, and the exquisite temptations that we had not the courage to yield to. Youth! Youth! There is absolutely nothing in the world but youth!"

Dorian Gray listened, open-eyed and wondering. The spray of lilac fell from his hand upon the gravel. A furry bee came and buzzed round it for a moment. Then it began to scramble all over the oval stellated globe of the tiny blossoms. He watched it with that strange interest in trivial things that we try to develop when things of high import make us afraid, or when we are stirred by some new emotion for which we cannot find expression, or when some thought that terrifies us lays sudden siege to the brain and calls on us to yield. After a time the bee flew away. He saw it creeping into the stained trumpet of a Tyrian convolvulus. The flower seemed to quiver, and then swayed gently to and fro.

Suddenly the painter appeared at the door of the studio, and made staccato signs for them to come in. They turned to each other, and smiled.

"I am waiting," he cried. "Do come in. The light is quite perfect, and you can bring your drinks."

They rose up, and sauntered down the walk together. Two green-and-white butterflies fluttered past them, and in the pear-tree at the corner of the garden a thrush began to sing.

"You are glad you have met me, Mr. Gray," said Lord Henry, looking at him.

"Yes, I am glad now. I wonder shall I always be glad?"

"Always! That is a dreadful word. It makes me shudder when I hear it. Women are so fond of using it. They spoil every romance by trying to make it last for ever. It is a meaningless word, too. The only difference between a caprice and a life-long passion is that the caprice lasts a little longer."

As they entered the studio, Dorian Gray put his hand upon Lord Henry's arm. "In that case, let our friendship be a caprice," he murmured, flushing at his own boldness, then stepped up on the platform and resumed his pose.

Lord Henry flung himself into a large wicker arm-chair, and watched him. The sweep and dash of the brush on the canvas made the only sound that broke the stillness, except when, now and then, Hallward stepped back to look at his work from a distance. In the slanting beams that streamed through the open doorway the dust danced and was golden. The heavy scent of the roses seemed to brood over everything.

After about a quarter of an hour Hallward stopped painting, looked for a long time at Dorian Gray, and then for a long time at the picture, biting the end of one of his huge brushes, and frowning. "It is quite finished," he cried at last, and stooping down he wrote his name in long vermilion letters on the left-hand corner of the canvas.

Lord Henry came over and examined the picture. It was certainly a wonderful work of art, and a wonderful likeness as well.

"My dear fellow, I congratulate you most warmly," he said. "It is the finest portrait of modern times. Mr. Gray, come over and look at yourself."

The lad started, as if awakened from some dream. "Is it really finished?" he murmured, stepping down from the platform.

"Quite finished," said the painter. "And you have sat splendidly today. I am awfully obliged to you."

"That is entirely due to me," broke in Lord Henry. "Isn't it, Mr. Gray?"

Dorian made no answer, but passed listlessly in front of his picture and turned towards it. When he saw it he drew back, and his cheeks flushed for a moment with pleasure. A look of joy came into his eyes, as if he had recognized himself for the first time. He stood there motionless and in wonder, dimly conscious that

Hallward was speaking to him, but not catching the meaning of his words. The sense of his own beauty came on him like a revelation. He had never felt it before. Basil Hallward's compliments had seemed to him to be merely the charming exaggerations of friendship. He had listened to them, laughed at them, forgotten them. They had not influenced his nature. Then had come Lord Henry Wotton with his strange panegyric on youth, his terrible warning of its brevity. That had stirred him at the time, and now, as he stood gazing at the shadow of his own loveliness, the full reality of the description flashed across him. Yes, there would be a day when his face would be wrinkled and wizen, his eyes dim and colourless, the grace of his figure broken and deformed. The scarlet would pass away from his lips, and the gold steal from his hair. The life that was to make his soul would mar his body. He would become dreadful, hideous, and uncouth.

As he thought of it, a sharp pang of pain struck through him like a knife, and made each delicate fibre of his nature quiver. His eyes deepened into amethyst, and across them came a mist of tears. He felt as if a hand of ice had been laid upon his heart.

"Don't you like it?" cried Hallward at last, stung a little by the lad's silence, not understanding what it meant.

"Of course he likes it," said Lord Henry. "Who wouldn't like it? It is one of the greatest things in modern art. I will give you anything you like to ask for it. I must have it."

"It is not my property, Harry."

"Whose property is it?"

"Dorian's, of course," answered the painter.

"He is a very lucky fellow."

"How sad it is!" murmured Dorian Gray, with his eyes still fixed upon his own portrait. "How sad it is! I shall grow old, and horrible, and dreadful. But this picture will remain always young. It will never be older than this particular day of June... If it were only the other way! If it were I who was to be always young, and the picture that was to grow old! For that—for that—I would give everything! Yes, there is nothing in the whole world I would not give! I would give my soul for that!"

"You would hardly care for such an arrangement, Basil," cried Lord Henry, laughing. "It would be rather hard lines on your work."

"I should object very strongly, Harry," said Hallward.

Dorian Gray turned and looked at him. "I believe you would, Basil. You like your art better than your friends. I am no more to you than a green bronze figure. Hardly as much, I dare say."

The painter stared in amazement. It was so unlike Dorian to speak like that. What had happened? He seemed quite angry. His face was flushed and his cheeks burning.

"Yes," he continued, "I am less to you than your ivory Hermes or your silver Faun. You will like them always. How long will you like me? Till I have my first wrinkle, I suppose. I know, now, that when one loses one's good looks, whatever they may be, one loses everything. Your picture has taught me that. Lord Henry Wotton is perfectly right. Youth is the only thing worth having. When I find that I am growing old, I shall kill myself."

Hallward turned pale, and caught his hand. "Dorian! Dorian!" he cried, "don't talk like that. I have never had such a friend as you, and I shall never have such another. You are not jealous of material things, are you?—you who are finer than any of them!"

"I am jealous of everything whose beauty does not die. I am jealous of the portrait you have painted of me. Why should it keep what I must lose? Every moment that passes takes something from me, and gives something to it. Oh, if it were only the other way! If the picture could change, and I could be always what I am now! Why did you paint it? It will mock me some day—mock me horribly!" The hot tears welled into his eyes; he tore his hand away, and, flinging himself on the divan, he buried his face in the cushions, as though he was praying.

"This is your doing, Harry," said the painter, bitterly.

Lord Henry shrugged his shoulders. "It is the real Dorian Gray—that is all."

"It is not."

"If it is not, what have I to do with it?"

"You should have gone away when I asked you," he muttered.

"I stayed when you asked me," was Lord Henry's answer.

"Harry, I can't quarrel with my two best friends at once, but between you both you have made me hate the finest piece of work I have ever done, and I will destroy it. What is it but canvas and colour? I will not let it come across our three lives and mar them."

Dorian Gray lifted his golden head from the pillow, and with pallid face and tear-stained eyes looked at him, as he walked over to the deal painting-table that was set beneath the high curtained window. What was he doing there? His fingers were straying about among the litter of tin tubes and dry brushes, seeking for something. Yes, it was for the long palette-knife, with its thin blade of lithe steel. He had found it at last. He was going to rip up the canvas.

With a stifled sob the lad leaped from the couch, and, rushing over to Hallward, tore the knife out of his hand, and flung it to the end of the studio. "Don't, Basil, don't!" he cried. "It would be murder!"

"I am glad you appreciate my work at last, Dorian," said the painter, coldly, when he had recovered from his surprise. "I never thought you would."

"Appreciate it? I am in love with it, Basil. It is part of myself. I feel that."

"Well, as soon as you are dry, you shall be varnished, and framed, and sent home. Then you can do what you like with yourself." And he walked across the room and rang the bell for tea. "You will have tea, of course, Dorian? And so will you, Harry? Or do you object to such simple pleasures?"

"I adore simple pleasures," said Lord Henry. "They are the last refuge of the complex. But I don't like scenes, except on the stage. What absurd fellows you are, both of you! I wonder who it was defined man as a rational animal. It was the most premature definition ever given. Man is many things, but he is not rational. I am glad he is not, after all: though I wish you chaps would not squabble over the picture. You had much better let me have it, Basil. This silly boy doesn't really want it, and I really do."

"If you let any one have it but me, Basil, I shall never forgive you!" cried Dorian Gray; "And I don't allow people to call me a silly boy."

"You know the picture is yours, Dorian. I gave it to you before it existed."

"And you know you have been a little silly, Mr. Gray, and that you don't really object to being reminded that you are extremely young."

"I should have objected very strongly this morning, Lord Henry."

"Ah! this morning! You have lived since then."

There came a knock at the door, and the butler entered with a laden tea-tray and set it down upon a small Japanese table. There was a rattle of cups and saucers and the hissing of a fluted Georgian urn. Two globe-shaped china dishes were brought in by a page. Dorian Gray went over and poured out the tea. The two men sauntered languidly to the table, and examined what was under the covers.

"Let us go to the theatre tonight," said Lord Henry. "There is sure to be something on, somewhere. I have promised to dine at White's, but it is only with an old friend, so I can send him a wire to say that I am ill, or that I am prevented from coming in consequence of a subsequent engagement. I think that would be a rather nice excuse: it would have all the surprise of candour."

"It is such a bore putting on one's dress-clothes," muttered Hallward. "And, when one has them on, they are so horrid."

"Yes," answered Lord Henry, dreamily, "the costume of the nineteenth century is detestable. It is so sombre, so depressing. Sin is the only real colour-element left in modern life."

"You really must not say things like that before Dorian, Harry."

"Before which Dorian? The one who is pouring out tea for us, or the one in the picture?"

"Before either."

"I should like to come to the theatre with you, Lord Henry," said the lad.

"Then you shall come; and you will come too, Basil, won't you?"

"I can't, really. I would sooner not. I have a lot of work to do."

"Well, then, you and I will go alone, Mr. Gray."

"I should like that awfully."

The painter bit his lip and walked over, cup in hand, to the picture. "I shall stay with the real Dorian," he said, sadly.

"Is it the real Dorian?" cried the original of the portrait, strolling across to him. "Am I really like that?"

"Yes; you are just like that."

"How wonderful, Basil!"

"At least you are like it in appearance. But it will never alter," sighed Hallward. "That is something."

"What a fuss people make about fidelity!" exclaimed Lord Henry. "Why, even in love it is purely a question for physiology. It has nothing to do with our own will. Young men want to be faithful, and are not; old men want to be faithless, and cannot: that is all one can say."

"Don't go to the theatre to-night, Dorian," said Hallward. "Stop and dine with me."

"I can't, Basil."

"Why?"

"Because I have promised Lord Henry Wotton to go with him."

"He won't like you the better for keeping your promises. He always breaks his own. I beg you not to go."

Dorian Gray laughed and shook his head.

"I entreat you."

The lad hesitated, and looked over at Lord Henry, who was watching them from the tea-table with an amused smile.

"I must go, Basil," he answered.

"Very well," said Hallward; and he went over and laid down his cup on the tray. “It is rather late, and, as you have to dress, you had better lose no time. Goodbye, Harry. Goodbye, Dorian. Come and see me soon. Come tomorrow.”

“Certainly.”

“You won’t forget?”

“No, of course not,” cried Dorian.

“And... Harry!”

“Yes, Basil?”

“Remember what I asked you, when we were in the garden this morning.”

“I have forgotten it.”

“I trust you.”

“I wish I could trust myself,” said Lord Henry, laughing. “Come, Mr. Gray, my hansom is outside, and I can drop you at your own place. Goodbye, Basil. It has been a most interesting afternoon.”

As the door closed behind them, the painter flung himself down on a sofa, and a look of pain came into his face.

Topics for Discussion

1. What might be Lessing’s view concerning the image of Laocoon in Virgil’s poem and the sculpture—the Laocoon group?
2. How does Lessing distinguish poetry from sculpture?
3. What role does the art of painting play in *The Picture of Dorian Gray*?
4. Interpret the relationship between Dorian Gray and his portrait.
5. Interpret the relationship between Basil Hallward the painter, Dorian Gray and Oscar Wilde.
6. Give more examples of intertextuality between literature and arts.

Monograph Six Literature and Science

I Salomon's House

(Excerpt from *The New Atlantis*)

Francis Bacon (1561–1626)

We sailed from Peru, (where we had continued for the space of one whole year) for China and Japan, by the South Sea; taking with us victuals for twelve months; and had good winds from the east, though soft and weak, for five months space, and more. But the wind came about, and settled in the west for many days, so as we could make little or no way, and were sometime in purpose to turn back. But then again there arose strong and great winds from the south, with a point east, which carried us up (for all that we could do) towards the north; by which time our victuals failed us, though we had made good spare of them. So that finding ourselves, in the midst of the greatest wilderness of waters in the world, without victuals, we gave ourselves for lost men and prepared for death. Yet we did lift up our hearts and voices to God above, who showeth his wonders in the deep, beseeching him of his mercy, that as in the beginning he discovered the face of the deep, and brought forth dry land, so he would now discover land to us, that we might not perish.

And it came to pass that the next day about evening we saw within a kenning before us, towards the north, as it were thick clouds, which did put us in some hope of land; knowing how that part of the South Sea was utterly unknown; and might have islands, or continents, that hitherto were not come to light. Wherefore we bent our course thither, where we saw the appearance of land, all that night; and in the dawning of the next day, we might plainly discern that it was a land; flat to our sight, and full of boscage; which made it show the more dark. And after an hour and a half's sailing, we entered into a good haven, being the port of a fair city; not great indeed, but well built, and that gave a pleasant view from the sea: and we thinking every minute long, till we were on land, came close to the shore, and offered to land. But straightways we saw divers of the people, with bastons in their hands (as it were) forbidding us to land; yet without any cries of fierceness, but only as warning us off, by signs that they made. Whereupon being not a little discomforted, we were advising with ourselves, what we should do.

During which time, there made forth to us a small boat, with about eight persons in it; whereof one of them had in his hand a tipstaff of a yellow cane, tipped at both ends with blue, who came aboard our ship, without any show of distrust at all. And when he saw one of our number, present himself somewhat before the rest, he drew forth a little scroll of parchment (somewhat yellower than our parchment, and shining like the leaves of writing tables, but otherwise soft and flexible,) and delivered it to our foremost man. In which scroll were written in ancient Hebrew, and in ancient Greek, and in good Latin of the school, and in Spanish, these words: Land ye not, none of you; and provide to be gone from this coast, within sixteen days, except you have further time given you. Meanwhile, if you want fresh water or victuals, or help for your sick, or that your ship needeth repairs, write down your wants, and you shall have that, which belongeth to mercy. This scroll was signed with a stamp of cherubim: wings, not spread, but hanging downwards; and by them a cross. This being delivered, the officer returned, and left only a servant with us to receive our answer.

Consulting hereupon amongst ourselves, we were much perplexed. The denial of landing and hasty warning us away troubled us much; on the other side, to find that the people had languages, and were so full of humanity, did comfort us not a little. And above all, the sign of the cross to that instrument was to us a great rejoicing, and as it were a certain presage of good. Our answer was in the Spanish tongue; that for our ship, it was well; for we had rather met with calms and contrary winds than any tempests. For our sick, they were many, and in very ill case; so that if they were not permitted to land, they ran danger of their lives. Our other wants we set down in particular; adding, that we had some little store of merchandise, which if it pleased them to deal for, it might supply our wants, without being chargeable unto them. We offered some reward in pistols unto the servant, and a piece of crimson velvet to be presented to the officer; but the servant took them not, nor would scarce look upon them; and so left us, and went back in another little boat, which was sent for him.

About three hours after we had dispatched our answer, there came towards us a person (as it seemed) of place. He had on him a gown with wide sleeves, of a kind of water chamolet, of an excellent azure colour, fair more glossy than ours; his under apparel was green; and so was his hat, being in the form of a turban, daintily made, and not so huge as the Turkish turbans; and the locks of his hair came down below the brims of it. A reverend man was he to behold. He came in a boat, gilt in some part of it, with four persons more only in that boat; and was followed by another boat, wherein were some twenty. When he was come within a flightshot of our ship, signs were made to us, that we should send forth some to meet him upon the water; which we presently did in our ship-boat, sending the principal man amongst us save one, and four of our number with him.

When we were come within six yards of their boat, they called to us to stay, and not to approach farther; which we did. And thereupon the man, whom I before described, stood up, and with a loud voice, in Spanish, asked, "Are ye Christians?"We answered, "We were;"fearing the less, because of the cross we had seen in the subscription. At which answer the said person lifted up his right hand towards Heaven, and drew it softly to his mouth (which is the gesture they use, when they thank God;) and then said, "If ye will swear (all of you) by the merits of the Saviour, that ye are no pirates, nor have shed blood, lawfully, nor unlawfully within forty days past, you may have licence to come on land."We said, "We were all ready to take that oath."Whereupon one of those that were with him, being (as it seemed) a notary, made an entry of this act. Which done, another of the attendants of the great person which was with him in the same boat, after his Lord had spoken a little to him, said aloud, "My Lord would have you know, that it is not of pride, or greatness, that he cometh not aboard your ship; but for that in your answer you declare that you have many sick amongst you, he was warned by the Conservator of Health of the city that he should keep a distance."We bowed ourselves towards him, and answered, "We were his humble servants; and accounted for great honour, and singular humanity towards us, that which was already done; but hoped well, that the nature of the sickness of our men was not infectious."So he returned; and a while after came the Notary to us aboard our ship; holding in his hand a fruit of that country, like an orange, but of color between orange-tawney and scarlet; which cast a most excellent odour. He used it (as it seemeth) for a preservative against infection. He gave us our oath:"By the name of Jesus, and his merits," and after told us, that the next day, by six of the Clock, in the Morning, we should be sent to, and brought to the Strangers' House, (so he called it,) where we should be accommodated of things, both for our whole, and for our sick. So he left us; and when we offered him some pistolets, he smiling said, "He must not be twice paid for one labour;" meaning (as I take it) that he had salary sufficient of the State for his service. For (as I after learned) they call an officer that taketh rewards, "twice paid."

...

The next day about ten of the clock, the Governor came to us again, and after salutations, said familiarly, "That he was come to visit us," and called for a chair, and sat him down; and we, being some ten of us, (the rest were of the meaner sort, or else gone abroad,) sat down with him. And when we were set, he began thus: "We of this island of Bensalem," (for so they call it in their language,) "have this; that by means of our solitary situation; and of the laws of secrecy, which we have for our travellers, and our rare admission of strangers; we know well most part of the habitable world, and are ourselves unknown. Therefore because he that knoweth least is fittest to ask questions, it is more reason, for the entertainment of the time, that ye ask me questions, than that I ask you."

We answered, "That we humbly thanked him that he would give us leave so to do: and that we conceived by the taste we had already, that there was no worldly thing on earth, more worthy to be known than the state of that happy land. But above all," (we said,) "since that we were met from the several ends of the world, and hoped assuredly that we should meet one day in the kingdom of Heaven, (for that we were both parts Christians,) we desired to know, (in respect that land was so remote, and so divided by vast and unknown seas, from the land where our Saviour walked on earth,) who was the apostle of that nation, and how it was converted to the faith?"It appeared in his face that he took great contentment in this our question: he said, "Ye knit my heart to you, by asking this question in the first place; for it sheweth that you *first seek the kingdom of heaven*; and I shall gladly, and briefly, satisfy your demand.

"About twenty years after the ascension of our Saviour, it came to pass, that there was seen by the people of Renfusa, (a city upon the eastern coast of our island,) within night, (the night was cloudy, and calm,) as it might be some mile into the sea, a great pillar of light; not sharp, but in form of a column, or cylinder, rising from the sea a great way up towards heaven; and on the top of it was seen a large cross of light, more bright and resplendent than the body of the pillar. Upon which so strange a spectacle, the people of the city gathered apace together upon the sands, to wonder; and so after put themselves into a number of small boats, to go nearer to this marvellous sight. But when the boats were come within (about) sixty yards of the pillar, they found themselves all bound, and could go no further; yet so as they might move to go about, but might not approach nearer: so as the boats stood all as in a theatre, beholding this light as an heavenly sign. It so fell out, that there was in one of the boats one of the wise men, of the society of Salomon's House; which house, or college (my good brethren) is the very eye of this kingdom; who having awhile attentively and devoutly viewed and contemplated this pillar and cross, fell down upon his face; and then raised himself upon his knees, and lifting up his hands to heaven, made his prayers in this manner.

> "'*Lord God of heaven and earth, thou hast vouchsafed of thy grace to those of our order, to know thy works of Creation, and the secrets of them: and to discern (as far as appertaineth to the generations of men) between divine miracles, works of nature, works of art, and impostures and illusions of all sorts. I do here acknowledge and testify before this people, that the thing which we now see before our eyes is thy Finger and a true Miracle. And forasmuch as we learn in our books that thou never workest miracles, but to divine and excellent end, (for the laws of nature are thine own laws, and thou exceedest them not but upon great cause,) we most humbly beseech thee to prosper this great sign, and to give us the interpretation and use of it in mercy; which thou dost in some part secretly promise by sending it unto us*.'

"When he had made his prayer, he presently found the boat he was in, moveable and unbound; whereas all the rest remained still fast; and taking that for an assurance of leave to approach, he caused the boat to be softly and with silence rowed towards the pillar. But ere he came near it, the pillar and cross of light brake up, and cast itself abroad, as it were, into a firmament of many stars; which also vanished soon after, and there was nothing left to be seen, but a small ark, or chest of cedar, dry, and not wet at all with water, though it swam. And in the fore-end of it, which was towards him, grew a small green branch of palm; and when the wise man had taken it, with all reverence, into his boat, it opened of itself, and there were found in it a Book and a Letter; both written in fine parchment, and wrapped in sindons of linen. The Book contained all the canonical books of *the Old and New Testament*, according as you have them; (for we know well what the churches with you receive); and the *Apocalypse* itself, and some other books of the *New Testament*, which were not at that time written, were nevertheless in the Book. And for the

Letter, it was in these words:

"'*I, Bartholomew, a servant of the Highest, and Apostle of Jesus Christ, was warned by an angel that appeareth to me, in a vision of glory, that I should commit this ark to the floods of the sea. Therefore I do testify and declare unto that people where God shall ordain this ark to come to land, that in the same day is come unto them salvation and peace and good-will, from the Father, and from the Lord Jesus.*'

"There was also in both these writings, as well the Book, as the Letter, wrought a great miracle, conform to that of the Apostles, in the original Gift of Tongues. For there being at that time in this land Hebrews, Persians, and Indians, besides the natives, every one read upon the Book, and Letter, as if they had been written in his own language. And thus was this land saved from infidelity (as the remainder of the old world was from water) by an ark, through the apostolical and miraculous evangelism of Saint Bartholomew."And here he paused, and a messenger came, and called him from us. So this was all that passed in that conference.

...

And as we were thus in conference, there came one that seemed to be a messenger, in a rich huke, that spake with the Jew: whereupon he turned to me and said, "You will pardon me, for I am commanded away in haste."The next morning he came to me again, joyful as it seemed, and said, "There is word come to the Governor of the city, that one of the Fathers of Salomon's House will be here this day seven-night: we have seen none of them this dozen years. His coming is in state; but the cause of his coming is secret. I will provide you and your fellows of a good standing to see his entry."I thanked him, and told him, I was most glad of the news.

The day being come, he made his entry. He was a man of middle stature and age, comely of person, and had an aspect as if he pitied men. He was clothed in a robe of fine black cloth, with wide sleeves and a cape. His under garment was of excellent white linen down to the foot, girt with a girdle of the same; and a sindon or tippet of the same about his neck. He had gloves, that were curious, and set with stone; and shoes of peach-coloured velvet. His neck was bare to the shoulders. His hat was like a helmet, or Spanish montera; and his locks curled below it decently: they were of colour brown. His beard was cut round, and of the same colour with his hair, somewhat lighter. He was carried in a rich chariot without wheels, litter-wise; with two horses at either end, richly trapped in blue velvet embroidered; and two footmen on each side in the like attire. The chariot was all of cedar, gilt, and adorned with crystal; save that the fore-end had panels of sapphires, set in borders of gold; and the hinder-end the like of emeralds of the Peru colour. There was also a sun of gold, radiant, upon the top, in the midst; and on the top before, a small cherub of gold, with wings displayed. The chariot was covered with cloth of gold tissued upon blue. He had before him fifty attendants, young men all, in white satin loose coats to the mid leg; and stockings of white silk; and shoes of blue velvet; and hats of blue velvet; with fine plumes of diverse colours, set round like hat-bands. Next before the chariot, went two men, bare-headed, in linen garments down the foot, girt, and shoes of blue velvet; who carried, the one a crosier, the other a pastoral staff like a sheep-hook; neither of them of metal, but the crosier of balm-wood, the pastoral staff of cedar. Horsemen he had none, neither before nor behind his chariot: as it seemeth, to avoid all tumult and trouble. Behind his chariot went all the officers and principals of the companies of the city. He sat alone, upon cushions of a kind of excellent plush, blue; and under his foot curious carpets of silk of diverse colours, like the Persian, but far finer. He held up his bare hand as he went, as blessing the people, but in silence. The street was wonderfully well kept: so that there was never any army had their men stand in better battle-array than the people stood. The windows likewise were not crowded, but every one stood in them as if they had been placed.

When the shew was past, the Jew said to me, “I shall not be able to attend you as I would, in regard of some charge the city hath laid upon me, for the entertaining of this great person.”Three days after the Jew came to me again, and said, “Ye are happy men; for the Father of Salomon's House taketh knowledge of your being here, and commanded me to tell you that he will admit all your company to his presence, and have private conference with one of you, that ye shall choose: and for this hath appointed the next day after to-morrow. And because he meaneth to give you his blessing, he hath appointed it in the forenoon."

We came at our day and hour, and I was chosen by my fellows for the private access. We found him in a fair chamber, richly hanged, and carpeted under foot without any degrees to the state. He was set upon a low Throne richly adorned, and a rich cloth of state over his head, of blue satin embroidered. He was alone, save that he had two pages of honour, on either hand one, finely attired in white. His under garments were the like that we saw him wear in the chariot; but instead of his gown, he had on him a mantle with a cape, of the same fine black, fastened about him. When we came in, as we were taught, we bowed low at our first entrance; and when we were come near his chair, he stood up, holding forth his hand ungloved, and in posture of blessing; and we every one of us stooped down, and kissed the hem of his tippet. That done, the rest departed, and I remained. Then he warned the pages forth of the room, and caused me to sit down beside him, and spake to me thus in the Spanish tongue.

"God bless thee, my son; I will give thee the greatest jewel I have. For I will impart unto thee, for the love of God and men, a relation of the true state of Salomon's House. Son, to make you know the true state of Salomon's House, I will keep this order. Firstly, I will set forth unto you the end of our foundation. Secondly, the preparations and instruments we have for our works. Thirdly, the several employments and functions whereto our fellows are assigned. And fourthly, the ordinances and rites which we observe.

"The end of our foundation is the knowledge of causes, and secret motions of things; and the enlarging of the bounds of human empire, to the effecting of all things possible.

"The Preparations and Instruments are these. We have large and deep caves of several depths: the deepest are sunk six hundred fathom: and some of them are digged and made under great hills and mountains: so that if you reckon together the depth of the hill and the depth of the cave, they are (some of them) above three miles deep. For we find, that the depth of a hill, and the depth of a cave from the flat, is the same thing; both remote alike, from the sun and heaven's beams, and from the open air. These caves we call the Lower Region; and we use them for all coagulations, indurations, refrigerations, and conservations of bodies. We use them likewise for the imitation of natural mines; and the producing also of new artificial metals, by compositions and materials which we use, and lay there for many years. We use them also sometimes, (which may seem strange,) for curing of some diseases, and for prolongation of life in some hermits that choose to live there, well accommodated of all things necessary, and indeed live very long; by whom also we learn many things.

"We have burials in several earths, where we put diverse cements, as the Chineses do their porcellain. But we have them in greater variety, and some of them more fine. We have also great variety of composts and soils, for the making of the earth fruitful.

"We have high towers; the highest about half a mile in height; and some of them likewise set upon high mountains; so that the vantage of the hill with the tower is in the highest of them three miles at least. And these places we call the Upper Region; accounting the air between the high places and the low, as a Middle Region. We use these towers, according to their several heights, and situations, for insolation, refrigeration, conservation; and for the view of divers meteors; as winds, rain, snow, hail; and some of the fiery meteors also. And upon them, in some places, are dwellings of hermits, whom we visit sometimes, and instruct what to observe.

"We have great lakes, both salt, and fresh; whereof we have use for the fish and fowl. We use them also for burials of some natural bodies: for we find a difference in things buried in earth or in air below the earth, and things buried in water. We have also pools, of which some do strain fresh water out of salt; and others by art do turn fresh water into salt. We have also some rocks in the midst of the sea, and some bays upon the shore for some works, wherein is required the air and vapor of the sea. We have likewise violent streams and cataracts, which serve us for many motions: and likewise engines for multiplying and enforcing of winds, to set also on going diverse motions.

"We have also a number of artificial wells and fountains, made in imitation of the natural sources and baths; as tincted upon vitriol, sulphur, steel, brass, lead, nitre, and other minerals. And again we have little wells for infusions of many things, where the waters take the virtue quicker and better, than in vessels or basins. And amongst them we have a water which we call Water of Paradise, being, by that we do to it made very sovereign for health, and prolongation of life.

"We have also great and spacious houses where we imitate and demonstrate meteors; as snow, hail, rain, some artificial rains of bodies and not of water, thunders, lightnings; also generations of bodies in air; as frogs, flies, and divers others.

"We have also certain chambers, which we call Chambers of Health, where we qualify the air as we think good and proper for the cure of divers diseases, and preservation of health.

"We have also fair and large baths, of several mixtures, for the cure of diseases, and the restoring of man's body from arefaction: and others for the confirming of it in strength of sinewes, vital parts, and the very juice and substance of the body.

"We have also large and various orchards and gardens; wherein we do not so much respect beauty, as variety of ground and soil, proper for divers trees and herbs: and some very spacious, where trees and berries are set whereof we make divers kinds of drinks, besides the vineyards. In these we practise likewise all conclusions of grafting, and inoculating as well of wild-trees as fruit-trees, which produceth many effects. And we make (by art) in the same orchards and gardens, trees and flowers to come earlier or later than their seasons; and to come up and bear more speedily than by their natural course they do. We make them also by art greater much than their nature; and their fruit greater and sweeter and of differing taste, smell, colour, and figure, from their nature. And many of them we so order, as they become of medicinal use.

"We have also means to make divers plants rise by mixtures of earths without seeds; and likewise to make divers new plants, differing from the vulgar; and to make one tree or plant turn into another.

"We have also parks and enclosures of all sorts of beasts and birds which we use not only for view or rareness, but likewise for dissections and trials; that thereby we may take light what may be wrought upon the body of man. Wherein we find many strange effects; as continuing life in them, though divers parts, which you account vital, be perished and taken forth; resuscitating of some that seem dead in appearance; and the like. We try also all poisons and other medicines upon them, as well of chirurgery, as physic. By art likewise, we make them greater or taller than their kind is; and contrariwise dwarf them, and stay their growth: we make them more fruitful and bearing than their kind is; and contrariwise barren and not generative. Also we make them differ in colour, shape, activity, many ways. We find means to make commixtures and copulations of different kinds; which have produced many new kinds, and them not barren, as the general opinion is. We make a number of kinds of serpents, worms, flies, fishes, of putrefaction; whereof some are advanced (in effect) to be perfect creatures, like bests or birds; and have sexes, and do propagate. Neither do we this by chance, but we know beforehand, of what matter and commixture what kind of those creatures will arise.

"We have also particular pools, where we make trials upon fishes, as we have said before of beasts and birds.

"We have also places for breed and generation of those kinds of worms and flies which are of special use; such as are with you your silk-worms and bees.

"I will not hold you long with recounting of our brewhouses, bake-houses, and kitchens, where are made divers drinks, breads, and meats, rare and of special effects. Wines we have of grapes; and drinks of other juice of fruits, of grains, and of roots; and of mixtures with honey, sugar, manna, and fruits dried, and decocted; also of the tears or woundings of trees; and of the pulp of canes. And these drinks are of several ages, some to the age or last of forty years. We have drinks also brewed with several herbs, and roots, and spices; yea with several fleshes, and white-meats; whereof some of the drinks are such, as they are in effect meat and drink both: so that divers, especially in age, do desire to live with them, with little or no meat or bread. And above all, we strive to have drink of extreme thin parts, to insinuate into the body, and yet without all biting, sharpness, or fretting; insomuch as some of them put upon the back of your hand will, with a little stay, pass through to the palm, and yet taste mild to the mouth. We have also waters which we ripen in that fashion, as they become nourishing; so that they are indeed excellent drink; and many will use no other. Breads we have of several grains, roots, and kernels; yea and some of flesh and fish dried; with divers kinds of leavenings and seasonings: so that some do extremely move appetites; some do nourish so, as divers do live of them, without any other meat; who live very long. So for meats, we have some of them so beaten and made tender and mortified, yet without all corrupting, as a weak heat of the stomach will turn them into good chylus; as well as a strong heat would meat otherwise prepared. We have some meats also and breads and drinks, which taken by men enable them to fast long after; and some other, that used make the very flesh of men's bodies sensibly' more hard and tough and their strength far greater than otherwise it would be.

"We have dispensatories, or shops of medicines. Wherein you may easily think, if we have such variety of plants and living creatures more than you have in Europe, (for we know what you have,) the simples, drugs, and ingredients of medicines, must likewise be in so much the greater variety. We have them likewise of divers ages, and long fermentations. And for their preparations, we have not only all manner of exquisite distillations and separations, and especially by gentle heats and percolations through divers strainers, yea and substances; but also exact forms of composition, whereby they incorporate almost, as they were natural simples.

"We have also divers mechanical arts, which you have not; and stuffs made by them; as papers, linen, silks, tissues; dainty works of feathers of wonderful lustre; excellent dies, and many others; and shops likewise, as well for such as are not brought into vulgar use amongst us as for those that are. For you must know that of the things before recited, many of them are grown into use throughout the kingdom; but yet, if they did flow from our invention, we have of them also for patterns and principals.

"We have also furnaces of great diversities, and that keep great diversity of heats; fierce and quick; strong and constant; soft and mild; blown, quiet; dry, moist; and the like. But above all, we have heats, in imitation of the Sun's and heavenly bodies' heats, that pass divers inequalities, and (as it were) orbs, progresses, and returns, whereby we produce admirable effects. Besides, we have heats of dungs; and of bellies and maws of living creatures, and of their bloods and bodies; and of hays and herbs laid up moist; of lime unquenched; and such like. Instruments also which generate heat only by motion. And farther, places for strong insulations; and again, places under the earth, which by nature, or art, yield heat. These divers heats we use, as the nature of the operation, which we intend, requireth.

"We have also perspective-houses, where we make demonstrations of all lights and radiations; and of all colours: and out of things uncoloured and transparent, we can represent unto you all several colours; not in rain-bows, (as it is in gems, and prisms,) but of themselves single. We represent also all multiplications of light, which we carry to great distance, and make so sharp as to discern small points and lines. Also all colourations of light; all delusions and deceits of the sight, in figures, magnitudes, motions, colours all demonstrations of shadows. We find also divers means, yet unknown to you, of producing of light originally from divers bodies. We procure means of seeing objects afar off; as in the heaven and remote places; and represent things near as afar off; and things afar off as near; making feigned distances. We have also helps for the sight, far above spectacles and glasses in use. We have also glasses and means to see small and minute bodies perfectly and distinctly; as the shapes and colours of small flies and worms, grains and flaws in gems, which cannot otherwise be seen, observations in urine and blood not otherwise to be seen. We make artificial rain-bows, halo's, and circles about light. We represent also all manner of reflexions, refractions, and multiplications of visual beams of objects.

"We have also precious stones of all kinds, many of them of great beauty, and to you unknown; crystals likewise; and glasses of divers kinds; and amongst them some of metals vitrificated, and other materials besides those of which you make glass. Also a number of fossils, and imperfect minerals, which you have not. Likewise loadstones of prodigious virtue; and other rare stones, both natural and artificial.

"We have also sound-houses, where we practise and demonstrate all sounds, and their generation. We have harmonies which you have not, of quarter-sounds, and lesser slides of sounds. Divers instruments of music likewise to you unknown, some sweeter than any you have, together with bells and rings that are dainty and sweet. We represent small sounds as great and deep; likewise great sounds extenuate and sharp; we make divers tremblings and warblings of sounds, which in their original are entire. We represent and imitate all articulate sounds and letters, and the voices and notes of beasts and birds. We have certain helps which set to the ear do further the hearing greatly. We have also divers strange and artificial echoes, reflecting the voice many times, and as it were tossing it: and some that give back the voice louder than it came, some shriller, and some deeper; yea, some rendering the voice differing in the letters or articulate sound from that they receive. We have also means to convey sounds in trunks and pipes, in strange lines and distances.

"We have also perfume-houses; wherewith we join also practices of taste. We multiply smells, which may seem strange. We imitate smells, making all smells to breathe outs of other mixtures than those that give them. We make divers imitations of taste likewise, so that they will deceive any man's taste. And in this house we contain also a confiture-house; where we make all sweet-meats, dry and moist; and divers pleasant wines, milks, broths, and sallets; in far greater variety than you have.

"We have also engine-houses, where are prepared engines and instruments for all sorts of motions. There we imitate and practise to make swifter motions than any you have, either out of your muskets or any engine that you have: and to make them and multiply them more easily, and with small force, by wheels and other means: and to make them stronger and more violent than yours are; exceeding your greatest cannons and basilisks. We represent also ordnance and instruments of war, and engines of all kinds: and likewise new mixtures and compositions of gun-powder, wild-fires burning in water, and unquenchable. Also fireworks of all variety both for pleasure and use. We imitate also flights of birds; we have some degrees of flying in the air. We have ships and boats for going under water, and brooking of seas; also swimming-girdles and supporters. We have divers curious clocks, and other like motions of return: and some perpetual motions. We imitate also motions of living creatures, by images, of men, beasts, birds, fishes, and serpents. We have also a great number of other various motions, strange for equality, fineness, and subtilty.

"We have also a mathematical house, where are represented all instruments, as well of geometry as astronomy, exquisitely made.

"We have also houses of deceits of the senses; where we represent all manner of feats of juggling, false apparitions, impostures, and illusions; and their fallacies. And surely you will easily believe that we that have so many things truly natural which induce admiration, could in a world of particulars deceive the senses, if we would disguise those things and labour to make them seem more miraculous. But we do hate all impostures, and lies; insomuch as we have severely forbidden it to all our fellows, under pain of ignominy and fines, that they do not show any natural work or thing, adorned or swelling; but only pure as it is, and without all affectation of strangeness.

"These are (my son) the riches of Salomon's House.

"For the several employments and offices of our fellows; we have twelve that sail into foreign countries, under the names of other nations, (for our own we conceal); who bring us the books, and abstracts, and patterns of experiments of all other parts. These we call Merchants of Light.

"We have three that collect the experiments which are in all books. These we call Depredators.

"We have three that collect the experiments of all mechanical arts; and also of liberal sciences; and also of practices which are not brought into arts. These we call Mystery-men.

"We have three that try new experiments, such as themselves think good. These we call Pioneers or Miners.

"We have three that draw the experiments of the former four into titles and tables, to give the better light for the drawing of observations and axioms out of them. These we call Compilers.

"We have three that bend themselves, looking into the experiments of their fellows, and cast about how to draw out of them things of use and practise for man's life, and knowledge, as well for works as for plain demonstration of causes, means of natural divinations, and the easy and clear discovery of the virtues and parts of bodies. These we call Dowry-men or Benefactors.

"Then after divers meetings and consults of our whole number, to consider of the former labours and collections, we have three that take care, out of them, to direct new experiments, of a higher light, more penetrating into nature than the former. These we call Lamps.

"We have three others that do execute the experiments so directed, and report them. These we call Inoculators.

"Lastly, we have three that raise the former discoveries by experiments into greater observations, axioms, and aphorisms. These we call Interpreters of Nature.

"We have also, as you must think, novices and apprentices, that the succession of the former employed men do not fail; besides, a great number of servants and attendants, men and women. And this we do also; we have consultations, which of the inventions and experiences which we have discovered shall be published, and which not; and take all an oath of secrecy, for the concealing of those which we think fit to keep secret; though some of those we do reveal sometimes to the state and some not.

"For our ordinances and rites; we have two very long and fair galleries; in one of these we place patterns and samples of all manner of the more rare and excellent inventions in the other we place the statues of all principal inventors. There we have the statue of your Columbus, that discovered the West Indies; also the inventor of ships; your monk that was the inventor of ordnance and of gunpowder; the inventor of music; the inventor of letters; the inventor of printing; the inventor of observations of astronomy; the inventor of works in metal: the inventor of glass; the inventor of silk of the worm; the inventor of wine: the inventor of corn and bread; the inventor of sugars; and all these, by more certain tradition than you have. Then have we divers inventors of our own, of excellent works; which since you have not seen, it were too long to make descriptions of them; and besides, in the right understanding of those descriptions you might easily err. For upon every invention of value, we erect a statue to the inventor, and give him a liberal and honourable reward. These statues are some of brass; some of marble and touch-stone; some of cedar and other special woods gilt and adorned; some of iron; some of silver; some of gold.

"We have certain hymns and services, which we say daily, of Lord and thanks to God for his marvellous works: and forms of prayers, imploring his aid and blessing for the illumination of our labours, and the turning of them into good and holy uses.

"Lastly, we have circuits or visits of divers principal cities of the kingdom; where, as it cometh to pass, we do publish such new profitable inventions as we think good. And we do also declare natural divinations of diseases, plagues, swarms-of hurtful creatures, scarcity, tempests, earthquakes, great inundations, comets, temperature of the year, and divers other things; and we give counsel thereupon, what the people shall do for the prevention and remedy of them."

And when he had said this, he stood up; and I, as I had been taught, kneeled down, and he laid his right hand upon my head, and said, "God bless thee, my son; and God bless this relation, which I have made. I give thee leave to publish it for the good of other nations; for we here are in God's bosom, a land unknown."And so he left me; having assigned a value of about two thousand ducats, for a bounty to me and my fellows. For they give great largesses where they come upon all occasions.

II The Flying Island

(Excerpt from *Gulliver's Travels*)

Jonathan Swift (1667–1745)

The flying or floating island is exactly circular, its diameter 7837 yards, or about four miles and a half, and consequently contains ten thousand acres. It is three hundred yards thick. The bottom, or under surface, which appears to those who view it below, is one even regular plate of adamant, shooting up to the height of about two hundred yards. Above it lie the several minerals in their usual order, and over all is a coat of rich mould, ten or twelve feet deep. The declivity of the upper surface, from the circumference to the centre, is the natural cause why all the dews and rains, which fall upon the island, are conveyed in small rivulets toward the middle, where they are emptied into four large basins, each of about half a mile in circuit, and two hundred yards distant from the centre. From these basins the water is continually exhaled by the sun in the daytime, which effectually prevents their overflowing. Besides, as it is in the power of the monarch to raise the island above the region of clouds and vapours, he can prevent the falling of dews and rain whenever he pleases. For the highest clouds cannot rise above two miles, as naturalists agree, at least they were never known to do so in that country.

At the centre of the island there is a chasm about fifty yards in diameter, whence the astronomers descend into a large dome, which is therefore called flandona gagnole, or the astronomer's cave, situated at the depth of a hundred yards beneath the upper surface of the adamant. In this cave are twenty lamps continually burning, which, from the reflection of the adamant, cast a strong light into every part. The place is stored with great variety of sextants, quadrants, telescopes, astrolabes, and other astronomical instruments. But the greatest curiosity, upon which the fate of the island depends, is a loadstone of a prodigious size, in shape resembling a weaver's shuttle. It is in length six yards, and in the thickest part at least three yards over. This magnet is sustained by a very strong axle of adamant passing through its middle, upon which it plays, and is poised so exactly that the weakest hand can turn it. It is hooped round with a hollow cylinder of adamant, four feet yards in diameter, placed horizontally, and supported by eight adamantine feet, each six yards high. In the middle of the concave side, there is a groove twelve inches deep, in which the extremities of the axle are lodged, and turned round as there is occasion.

The stone cannot be removed from its place by any force, because the hoop and its feet are one continued piece with that body of adamant which constitutes the bottom of the island.

By means of this loadstone, the island is made to rise and fall, and move from one place to another. For, with respect to that part of the earth over which the monarch presides, the stone is endued at one of its sides with an attractive power, and at the other with a repulsive. Upon placing the magnet erect, with its attracting end towards the earth, the island descends; but when the repelling extremity points downwards, the island mounts directly upwards. When the position of the stone is oblique, the motion of the island is so too: for in this magnet, the forces always act in lines parallel to its direction.

By this oblique motion, the island is conveyed to different parts of the monarch's dominions. To explain the manner of its progress, let A B represent a line drawn across the dominions of Balnibarbi, let the line C D represent the loadstone, of which let D be the repelling end, and C the attracting end, the island being over C: let the stone be placed in position C D, with its repelling end downwards; then the island will be driven upwards obliquely towards D. When it is arrived at D, let the stone be turned upon its axle, till its attracting end points towards E, and then the island will be carried obliquely towards E; where, if the stone be again turned upon its axle till it stands in the position E F, with its repelling point downwards, the island will rise obliquely towards F, where, by directing the attracting end towards G, the island may be carried to G, and from G to H, by turning the stone, so as to make its repelling extremity to point directly downward. And thus, by changing the situation of the stone, as often as there is occasion, the island is made to rise and fall by turns in an oblique direction, and by those alternate risings and fallings (the obliquity being not considerable) is conveyed from one part of the dominions to the other.

But it must be observed, that this island cannot move beyond the extent of the dominions below, nor can it rise above the height of four miles. For which the astronomers (who have written large systems concerning the stone) assign the following reason: that the magnetic virtue does not extend beyond the distance of four miles, and that the mineral, which acts upon the stone in the bowels of the earth, and in the sea about six leagues distant from the shore, is not diffused through the whole globe, but terminated with the limits of the king's dominions; and it was easy, from the great advantage of such a superior situation, for a prince to bring under his obedience whatever country lay within the attraction of that magnet.

When the stone is put parallel to the plane of the horizon, the island stands still; for in that case the extremities of it, being at equal distance from the earth, act with equal force, the one in drawing downwards, the other in pushing upwards, and consequently no motion can ensue.

This loadstone is under the care of certain astronomers, who, from time to time, give it such positions as the monarch directs. They spend the greatest part of their lives in observing the celestial bodies, which they do by the assistance of glasses, far excelling ours in goodness. For, although their largest telescopes do not exceed three feet, they magnify much more than those of a hundred with us, and show the stars with greater clearness. This advantage has enabled them to extend their discoveries much further than our astronomers in Europe; for they have made a catalogue of ten thousand fixed stars, whereas the largest of ours do not contain above one third part of that number. They have likewise discovered two lesser stars, or satellites, which revolve about Mars; whereof the innermost is distant from the centre of the primary planet exactly three of his diameters, and the outermost, five; the former revolves in the space of ten hours, and the latter in twenty-one and a half; so that the squares of their periodical times are very near in the same proportion with the cubes of their distance from the centre of Mars; which evidently shows them to be governed by the same law of gravitation that influences the other heavenly bodies.

They have observed ninety-three different comets, and settled their periods with great exactness. If this be true (and they affirm it with great confidence) it is much to be wished, that their observations were made public, whereby the theory of comets, which at present is very lame and defective, might be brought to the same perfection with other arts of astronomy.

The king would be the most absolute prince in the universe, if he could but prevail on a ministry to join with him; but these having their estates below on the continent, and considering that the office of a favourite has a very uncertain tenure, would never consent to the enslaving of their country.

If any town should engage in rebellion or mutiny, fall into violent factions, or refuse to pay the usual tribute, the king has two methods of reducing them to obedience. The first and the mildest course is, by keeping the island hovering over such a town, and the lands about it, whereby he can deprive them of the benefit of the sun and the rain, and consequently afflict the inhabitants with dearth and diseases: and if the crime deserve it, they are at the same time pelted from above with great stones, against which they have no defence but by creeping into cellars or caves, while the roofs of their houses are beaten to pieces. But if they still continue obstinate, or offer to raise insurrections, he proceeds to the last remedy, by letting the island drop directly upon their heads, which makes a universal destruction both of houses and men. However, this is an extremity to which the prince is seldom driven, neither indeed is he willing to put it in execution; nor dare his ministers advise him to an action, which, as it would render them odious to the people, so it would be a great damage to their own estates, which all lie below; for the island is the king's demesne.

But there is still indeed a more weighty reason, why the kings of this country have been always averse from executing so terrible an action, unless upon the utmost necessity. For, if the town intended to be destroyed should have in it any tall rocks, as it generally falls out in the larger cities, a situation probably chosen at first with a view to prevent such a catastrophe; or if it abound in high spires, or pillars of stone, a sudden fall might endanger the bottom or under surface of the island, which, although it consist, as I have said, of one entire adamant, two hundred yards thick, might happen to crack by too great a shock, or burst by approaching too near the fires from the houses below, as the backs, both of iron and stone, will often do in our chimneys. Of all this the people are well apprised, and understand how far to carry their obstinacy, where their liberty or property is concerned. And the king, when he is highest provoked, and most determined to press a city to rubbish, orders the island to descend with great gentleness, out of a pretence of tenderness to his people, but, indeed for fear of breaking the adamantine bottom; in which case, it is the opinion of all their philosophers, that the loadstone could no longer hold it up, and the whole mass would fall to the ground.

By a fundamental law of this realm, neither the king, nor either of his two eldest sons, are permitted to leave the island; nor the queen, till she is past child-bearing.

Although I cannot say that I was ill treated in this island, yet I must confess I thought myself too much neglected, not without some degree of contempt; for neither prince nor people appeared to be curious in any part of knowledge, except mathematics and music, wherein I was far their inferior, and upon that account very little regarded.

On the other side, after having seen all the curiosities of the island, I was very desirous to leave it, being heartily weary of those people. They were indeed excellent in two sciences for which I have great esteem, and wherein I am not unversed; but, at the same time, so abstracted and involved in speculation, that I never met with such disagreeable companions. I conversed only with women, tradesmen, flappers, and court-pages, during two months of my abode there; by which, at last, I rendered myself extremely contemptible; yet these were the only people from whom I could ever receive a reasonable answer.

I had obtained, by hard study, a good degree of knowledge in their language: I was weary of being confined to an island where I received so little countenance, and resolved to leave it with the first opportunity.

There was a great lord at court, nearly related to the king, and for that reason alone used with respect. He was universally reckoned the most ignorant and stupid person among them. He had performed many eminent services for the crown, had great natural and acquired parts, adorned with integrity and honour; but so ill an ear for music, that his detractors reported, "he had been often known to beat time in the wrong place;" neither could his tutors, without extreme difficulty, teach him to demonstrate the most easy proposition in the mathematics. He was pleased to show me many marks of favour, often did me the honour of a visit, desired to be informed in the affairs of Europe, the laws and customs, the manners and learning of the several countries where I had travelled. He listened to me with great attention, and made very wise observations on all I spoke. He had two flappers attending him for state, but never made use of them, except at court and in visits of ceremony, and would always command them to withdraw, when we were alone together.

I entreated this illustrious person, to intercede in my behalf with his majesty, for leave to depart; which he accordingly did, as he was pleased to tell me, with regret: for indeed he had made me several offers very advantageous, which, however, I refused, with expressions of the highest acknowledgment.

On the 16th of February I took leave of his majesty and the court. The king made me a present to the value of about two hundred pounds English, and my protector, his kinsman, as much more, together with a letter of recommendation to a friend of his in Lagado, the metropolis. The island being then hovering over a mountain about two miles from it, I was let down from the lowest gallery, in the same manner as I had been taken up.

The continent, as far as it is subject to the monarch of the flying island, passes under the general name of Balnibarbi; and the metropolis, as I said before, is called Lagado. I felt some little satisfaction in finding myself on firm ground. I walked to the city without any concern, being clad like one of the natives, and sufficiently instructed to converse with them. I soon found out the person's house to whom I was recommended, presented my letter from his friend the grandee in the island, and was received with much kindness. This great lord, whose name was Munodi, ordered me an apartment in his own house, where I continued during my stay, and was entertained in a most hospitable manner.

The next morning after my arrival, he took me in his chariot to see the town, which is about half the bigness of London; but the housesvery strangely built, and most of them out of repair. The people in the streets walked fast, looked wild, their eyes fixed, and were generally in rags. We passed through one of the town gates, and went about three miles into the country, where I saw many labourers working with several sorts of tools in the ground, but was not able to conjecture what they were about: neither did observe any expectation either of corn or grass, although the soil appeared to be excellent. I could not forbear admiring at these odd appearances, both in town and country; and I made bold to desire my conductor, that he would be pleased to explain to me, what could be meant by so many busy heads, hands, and faces, both in the streets and the fields, because I did not discover any good effects they produced; but, on the contrary, I never knew a soil so unhappily cultivated, houses so ill contrived and so ruinous, or a people whose countenances and habit expressed so much misery and want.

This lord Munodi was a person of the first rank, and had been some years governor of Lagado; but, by a cabal of ministers, was discharged for insufficiency. However, the king treated him with tenderness, as a well-meaning man, but of a low contemptible understanding.

When I gave that free censure of the country and its inhabitants, he made no further answer than by telling me, "that I had not been long enough among them to form a judgment; and that the different nations of the world had different customs;" with other common topics to the same purpose. But, when we returned to his palace, he asked me, "how I liked the building, what absurdities I observed, and what quarrel I had with the dress or looks of his domestics?" This he might safely do; because every thing about him was magnificent, regular, and polite. I answered, "that his excellency's prudence, quality, and fortune, had exempted him from those defects, which folly and beggary had produced in others." He said, "if I would go with him to his country-house, about twenty miles distant, where his estate lay, there would be more leisure for this kind of conversation." I told his excellency "that I was entirely at his disposal;" and accordingly we set out next morning.

During our journey he made me observe the several methods used by farmers in managing their lands, which to me were wholly unaccountable; for, except in some very few places, I could not discover one ear of corn or blade of grass. But, in three hours travelling, the scene was wholly altered; we came into a most beautiful country; farmers' houses, at small distances, neatly built; the fields enclosed, containing vineyards, corn-grounds, and meadows. Neither do I remember to have seen a more delightful prospect. His excellency observed my countenance to clear up; he told me, with a sigh, "that there his estate began, and would continue the same, till we should come to his house: that his countrymen ridiculed and despised him, for managing his affairs no better, and for setting so ill an example to the kingdom; which, however, was followed by very few, such as were old, and wilful, and weak like himself."

We came at length to the house, which was indeed a noble structure, built according to the best rules of ancient architecture. The fountains, gardens, walks, avenues, and groves, were all disposed with exact judgment and taste. I gave due praises to every thing I saw, whereof his excellency took not the least notice till after supper; when, there being no third companion, he told me with a very melancholy air "that he doubted he must throw down his houses in town and country, to rebuild them after the present mode; destroy all his plantations, and cast others into such a form as modern usage required, and give the same directions to all his tenants, unless he would submit to incur the censure of pride, singularity, affectation, ignorance, caprice, and perhaps increase his majesty's displeasure; that the admiration I appeared to be under would cease or diminish, when he had informed me of some particulars which, probably, I never heard of at court, the people there being too much taken up in their own speculations, to have regard to what passed here below."

The sum of his discourse was to this effect: "That about forty years ago, certain persons went up to Laputa, either upon business or diversion, and, after five months continuance, came back with a very little smattering in mathematics, but full of volatile spirits acquired in that airy region: that these persons, upon their return, began to dislike the management of every thing below, and fell into schemes of putting all arts, sciences, languages, and mechanics, upon a new foot. To this end, they procured a royal patent for erecting an academy of projectors in Lagado; and the humour prevailed so strongly among the people, that there is not a town of any consequence in the kingdom without such an academy. In these colleges the professors contrive new rules and methods of agriculture and building, and new instruments, and tools for all trades and manufactures; whereby, as they undertake, one man shall do the work of ten; a palace may be built in a week, of materials so durable as to last for ever without repairing. All the fruits of the earth shall come to maturity at whatever season we think fit to choose, and increase a hundred fold more than they do at present; with innumerable other happy proposals. The only inconvenience is, that none of these projects are yet brought to perfection; and in the mean time, the whole country lies miserably waste, the houses in ruins, and the people without food or clothes. By all which, instead of being discouraged, they are fifty times more violently bent upon prosecuting their schemes, driven equally on by hope and despair: that as for himself, being not of an enterprising spirit, he was content to go on in the old forms, to live in the houses his ancestors had built, and act as they did, in every part of life, without innovation: that some few other persons of quality and gentry had done the same, but were looked on with an eye of contempt and ill-will, as enemies to art, ignorant, and ill common-wealth's men, preferring their own ease and sloth before the general improvement of their country."

His lordship added, "That he would not, by any further particulars, prevent the pleasure I should certainly take in viewing the grand academy, whither he was resolved I should go." He only desired me to observe a ruined building, upon the side of a mountain about three miles distant, of which he gave me this account:"That he had a very convenient mill within half a mile of his house, turned by a current from a large river, and sufficient for his own family, as well as a great number of his tenants; that about seven years ago, a club of those projectors came to him with proposals to destroy this mill, and build another on the side of that mountain, on the long ridge whereof a long canal must be cut, for a repository of water, to be conveyed up by pipes and engines to supply the mill, because the wind and air upon a height agitated the water, and thereby made it fitter for motion, and because the water, descending down a declivity, would turn the mill with half the current of a river whose course is more upon a level." He said, "that being then not very well with the court, and pressed by many of his friends, he complied with the proposal; and after employing a hundred men for two years, the work miscarried, the projectors went off, laying the blame entirely upon him, railing at him ever since, and putting others upon the same experiment, with equal assurance of success, as well as equal disappointment."

In a few days we came back to town; and his excellency, considering the bad character he had in the academy, would not go with me himself, but recommended me to a friend of his, to bear me company thither. My lord was pleased to represent me as a great admirer of projects, and a person of much curiosity and easy belief; which, indeed, was not without truth; for I had myself been a sort of projector in my younger days.

This academy is not an entire single building, but a continuation of several houses on both sides of a street, which growing waste, was purchased and applied to that use.

I was received very kindly by the warden, and went for many days to the academy. Every room has in it one or more projectors; and I believe I could not be in fewer than five hundred rooms.

The first man I saw was of a meagre aspect, with sooty hands and face, his hair and beard long, ragged, and singed in several places. His clothes, shirt, and skin, were all of the same colour. He has been eight years upon a project for extracting sunbeams out of cucumbers, which were to be put in phials hermetically sealed, and let out to warm the air in raw inclement summers. He told me, he did not doubt, that, in eight years more, he should be able to supply the governor's gardens with sunshine, at a reasonable rate: but he complained that his stock was low, and entreated me "to give him something as an encouragement to ingenuity, especially since this had been a very dear season for cucumbers." I made him a small present, for my lord had furnished me with money on purpose, because he knew their practice of begging from all who go to see them.

I went into another chamber, but was ready to hasten back, being almost overcome with a horrible stink. My conductor pressed me forward, conjuring me in a whisper "to give no offence, which would be highly resented;" and therefore I durst not so much as stop my nose. The projector of this cell was the most ancient student of the academy; his face and beard were of a pale yellow; his hands and clothes daubed over with filth. When I was presented to him, he gave me a close embrace, a compliment I could well have excused. His employment, from his first coming into the academy, was an operation to reduce human excrement to its original food, by separating the several parts, removing the tincture which it receives from the gall, making the odour exhale, and scumming off the saliva. He had a weekly allowance, from the society, of a vessel filled with human ordure, about the bigness of a Bristol barrel.

I saw another at work to calcine ice into gunpowder; who likewise showed me a treatise he had written concerning the malleability of fire, which he intended to publish.

There was a most ingenious architect, who had contrived a new method for building houses, by beginning at the roof, and working downward to the foundation; which he justified to me, by the like practice of those two prudent insects, the bee and the spider.

There was a man born blind, who had several apprentices in his own condition: their employment was to mix colours for painters, which their master taught them to distinguish by feeling and smelling. It was indeed my misfortune to find them at that time not very perfect in their lessons, and the professor himself happened to be generally mistaken. This artist is much encouraged and esteemed by the whole fraternity.

In another apartment I was highly pleased with a projector who had found a device of ploughing the ground with hogs, to save the charges of ploughs, cattle, and labour. The method is this: in an acre of ground you bury, at six inches distance and eight deep, a quantity of acorns, dates, chestnuts, and other mast or vegetables, whereof these animals are fondest; then you drive six hundred or more of them into the field, where, in a few days, they will root up the whole ground in search of their food, and make it fit for sowing, at the same time manuring it with their dung: it is true, upon experiment, they found the charge and trouble very great, and they had little or no crop. However it is not doubted, that this invention may be capable of great improvement.

I went into another room, where the walls and ceiling were all hung round with cobwebs, except a narrow passage for the artist to go in and out. At my entrance, he called aloud to me, "not to disturb his webs." He lamented "the fatal mistake the world had been so long in, of using silkworms, while we had such plenty of domestic insects who infinitely excelled the former, because they understood how to weave, as well as spin." And he proposed further, "that by employing spiders, the charge of dyeing silks should be wholly saved;" whereof I was fully convinced, when he showed me a vast number of flies most beautifully coloured, wherewith he fed his spiders, assuring us "that the webs would take a tincture from them; and as he had them of all hues, he hoped to fit everybody's fancy, as soon as he could find proper food for the flies, of certain gums, oils, and other glutinous matter, to give a strength and consistence to the threads."

There was an astronomer, who had undertaken to place a sun-dial upon the great weathercock on the town-house, by adjusting the annual and diurnal motions of the earth and sun, so as to answer and coincide with all accidental turnings of the wind.

I was complaining of a small fit of the colic, upon which my conductor led me into a room where a great physician resided, who was famous for curing that disease, by contrary operations from the same instrument. He had a large pair of bellows, with a long slender muzzle of ivory: this he conveyed eight inches up the anus, and drawing in the wind, he affirmed he could make the guts as lank as a dried bladder. But when the disease was more stubborn and violent, he let in the muzzle while the bellows were full of wind, which he discharged into the body of the patient; then withdrew the instrument to replenish it, clapping his thumb strongly against the orifice of then fundament; and this being repeated three or four times, the adventitious wind would rush out, bringing the noxious along with it, (like water put into a pump), and the patient recovered. I saw him try both experiments upon a dog, but could not discern any effect from the former. After the latter the animal was ready to burst, and made so violent a discharge as was very offensive to me and my companion. The dog died on the spot, and we left the doctor endeavouring to recover him, by the same operation.

I visited many other apartments, but shall not trouble my reader with all the curiosities I observed, being studious of brevity.

I had hitherto seen only one side of the academy, the other being appropriated to the advancers of speculative learning, of whom I shall say something, when I have mentioned one illustrious person more, who is called among them "the universal artist." He told us "he had been thirty years employing his thoughts for the improvement of human life." He had two large rooms full of wonderful curiosities, and fifty men at work. Some were condensing air into a dry tangible substance, by extracting the nitre, and letting the aqueous or fluid particles percolate; others softening marble, for pillows and pin-cushions; others petrifying the hoofs of a living horse, to preserve them from foundering. The artist himself was at that time busy upon two great designs; the first, to sow land with chaff, wherein he affirmed the true seminal virtue to be contained, as he demonstrated by several experiments, which I was not skilful enough to comprehend. The other was, by a certain composition of gums, minerals, and vegetables, outwardly applied, to prevent the growth of wool upon two young lambs; and he hoped, in a reasonable time to propagate the breed of naked sheep, all over the kingdom.

We crossed a walk to the other part of the academy, where, as I have already said, the projectors in speculative learning resided.

The first professor I saw, was in a very large room, with forty pupils about him. After salutation, observing me to look earnestly upon a frame, which took up the greatest part of both the length and breadth of the room, he said, "Perhaps I might wonder to see him employed in a project for improving speculative knowledge, by practical and mechanical operations. But the world would soon be sensible of its usefulness; and he flattered himself, that a more noble, exalted thought never sprang in any other man's head. Every one knew how laborious the usual method is of attaining to arts and sciences; whereas, by his contrivance, the most ignorant person, at a reasonable charge, and with a little bodily labour, might write books in philosophy, poetry, politics, laws, mathematics, and theology, without the least assistance from genius or study." He then led me to the frame, about the sides, whereof all his pupils stood in ranks. It was twenty feet square, placed in the middle of the room. The superfices was composed of several bits of wood, about the bigness of a die, but some larger than others. They were all linked together by slender wires. These bits of wood were covered, on every square, with paper pasted on them; and on these papers were written all the words of their language, in their several moods, tenses, and declensions; but without any order. The professor then desired me "to observe; for he was going to set his engine at work." The pupils, at his command, took each of them hold of an iron handle, whereof there were forty fixed round the edges of the frame; and giving them a sudden turn, the whole disposition of the words was entirely changed. He then commanded six-and-thirty of the lads, to read the several lines softly, as they appeared upon the frame; and where they found three or four words together that might make part of a sentence, they dictated to the four remaining boys, who were scribes. This work was repeated three or four times, and at every turn, the engine was so contrived, that the words shifted into new places, as the square bits of wood moved upside down.

Six hours a day the young students were employed in this labour; and the professor showed me several volumes in large folio, already collected, of broken sentences, which he intended to piece together, and out of those rich materials, to give the world a complete body of all arts and sciences; which, however, might be still improved, and much expedited, if the public would raise a fund for making and employing five hundred such frames in Lagado, and oblige the managers to contribute in common their several collections.

He assured me "that this invention had employed all his thoughts from his youth; that he had emptied the whole vocabulary into his frame, and made the strictest computation of the general proportion there is in books between the numbers of particles, nouns, and verbs, and other parts of speech."

I made my humblest acknowledgment to this illustrious person, for his great communicativeness; and promised, "if ever I had the good fortune to return to my native country, that I would do him justice, as the sole inventor of this wonderful machine;" the form and contrivance of which I desired leave to delineate on paper, as in the figure here annexed. I told him, "although it were the custom of our learned in Europe to steal inventions from each other, who had thereby at least this advantage, that it became a controversy which was the right owner; yet I would take such caution, that he should have the honour entire, without a rival."

We next went to the school of languages, where three professors sat in consultation upon improving that of their own country.

The first project was, to shorten discourse, by cutting polysyllables into one, and leaving out verbs and participles, because, in reality, all things imaginable are but norms.

The other project was, a scheme for entirely abolishing all words whatsoever; and this was urged as a great advantage in point of health, as well as brevity. For it is plain, that every word we speak is, in some degree, a diminution of our lunge by corrosion, and, consequently, contributes to the shortening of our lives. An expedient was therefore offered, "that since words are only names for things, it would be more convenient for all men to carry about them such things as were necessary to express a particular business they are to discourse on." And this invention would certainly have taken place, to the great ease as well as health of the subject, if the women, in conjunction with the vulgar and illiterate, had not threatened to raise a rebellion unless they might be allowed the liberty to speak with their tongues, after the manner of their forefathers; such constant irreconcilable enemies to science are the common people. However, many of the most learned and wise adhere to the new scheme of expressing themselves by things; which has only this inconvenience attending it, that if a man's business be very great, and of various kinds, he must be obliged, in proportion, to carry a greater bundle of things upon his back, unless he can afford one or two strong servants to attend him. I have often beheld two of those sages almost sinking under the weight of their packs, like pedlars among us, who, when they met in the street, would lay down their loads, open their sacks, and hold conversation for an hour together; then put up their implements, help each other to resume their burdens, and take their leave.

But for short conversations, a man may carry implements in his pockets, and under his arms, enough to supply him; and in his house, he cannot be at a loss. Therefore the room where company meet who practise this art, is full of all things, ready at hand, requisite to furnish matter for this kind of artificial converse.

Another great advantage proposed by this invention was, that it would serve as a universal language, to be understood in all civilised nations, whose goods and utensils are generally of the same kind, or nearly resembling, so that their uses might easily be comprehended. And thus ambassadors would be qualified to treat with foreign princes, or ministers of state, to whose tongues they were utter strangers.

I was at the mathematical school, where the master taught his pupils after a method scarce imaginable to us in Europe. The proposition, and demonstration, were fairly written on a thin wafer, with ink composed of a cephalic tincture. This, the student was to swallow upon a fasting stomach, and for three days following, eat nothing but bread and water. As the wafer digested, the tincture mounted to his brain, bearing the proposition along with it. But the success has not hitherto been answerable, partly by some error in the quantum or composition, and partly by the perverseness of lads, to whom this bolus is so nauseous, that they generally steal aside, and discharge it upwards, before it can operate; neither have they been yet persuaded to use so long an abstinence, as the prescription requires.

Topics for Discussion

1. Interpret *The New Atlantis* against the rise of modern science in the West.
2. How are Francis Bacon's double roles—scientist and fiction writer embodied in *The New Atlantis*?
3. What kind of scientific invention is the Flying Island?
4. Interpret the academy in Lagado in association with the Royal Society.
5. Compare Bacon's and Swift's attitudes toward science based on your reading of their fiction.
6. Give more literary examples concerning the role of science in human life.

Monograph Seven Literature and Nature

I The Three Strangers

Thomas Hardy (1840–1928)

Among the few features of agricultural England which retain an appearance but little modified by the lapse of centuries, may be reckoned the high, grassy and furzy downs, coombs, or ewe-leases, as they are indifferently called, that fill a large area of certain counties in the south and south-west. If any mark of human occupation is met with hereon, it usually takes the form of the solitary cottage of some shepherd.

Fifty years ago such a lonely cottage stood on such a down, and may possibly be standing there now. In spite of its loneliness, however, the spot, by actual measurement, was not more than five miles from a county-town. Yet that affected it little. Five miles of irregular upland, during the long inimical seasons, with their sleets, snows, rains, and mists, afford withdrawing space enough to isolate a Timon or a Nebuchadnezzar; much less, in fair weather, to please that less repellent tribe, the poets, philosophers, artists, and others who "conceive and meditate of pleasant things."

Some old earthen camp or barrow, some clump of trees, at least some starved fragment of ancient hedge is usually taken advantage of in the erection of these forlorn dwellings. But, in the present case, such a kind of shelter had been disregarded. Higher Crowstairs, as the house was called, stood quite detached and undefended. The only reason for its precise situation seemed to be the crossing of two footpaths at right angles hard by, which may have crossed there and thus for a good five hundred years. Hence the house was exposed to the elements on all sides. But, though the wind up here blew unmistakably when it did blow, and the rain hit hard whenever it fell, the various weathers of the winter season were not quite so formidable on the coomb as they were imagined to be by dwellers on low ground. The raw rimes were not so pernicious as in the hollows, and the frosts were scarcely so severe. When the shepherd and his family who tenanted the house were pitied for their sufferings from the exposure, they said that upon the whole they were less inconvenienced by "wuzzes and flames" (hoarses and phlegms) than when they had lived by the stream of a snug neighbouring valley.

The night of March 28, 182-, was precisely one of the nights that were wont to call forth these expressions of commiseration. The level rainstorm smote walls, slopes, and hedges like the clothyard shafts of Senlac and Crecy. Such sheep and outdoor animals as had no shelter stood with their buttocks to the winds; while the tails of little birds trying to roost on some scraggy thorn were blown inside-out like umbrellas. The gable-end of the cottage was stained with wet, and the eaves droppings flapped against the wall. Yet never was commiseration for the shepherd more misplaced. For that cheerful rustic was entertaining a large party in glorification of the christening of his second girl.

The guests had arrived before the rain began to fall, and they were all now assembled in the chief or living room of the dwelling. A glance into the apartment at eight o'clock on this eventful evening would have resulted in the opinion that it was as cosy and comfortable a nook as could be wished for in boisterous weather. The calling of its inhabitant was proclaimed by a number of highly-polished sheep-crooks without stems that were hung ornamentally over the fireplace, the curl of each shining crook varying from the antiquated type engraved in the patriarchal pictures of old family Bibles to the most approved fashion of the last local sheep-fair. The room was lighted by half-a-dozen candles, having wicks only a trifle smaller than the grease which enveloped them, in candlesticks that were never used but at high-days, holy-days, and family feasts. The lights were scattered about the room, two of them standing on the chimney-piece. This position of candles was in itself significant. Candles on the chimney-piece always meant a party.

On the hearth, in front of a back-brand to give substance, blazed a fire of thorns, that crackled "like the laughter of the fool."

Nineteen persons were gathered here. Of these, five women, wearing gowns of various bright hues, sat in chairs along the wall; girls shy and not shy filled the window-bench; four men, including Charley Jake the hedge-carpenter, Elijah New the parish-clerk, and John Pitcher, a neighbouring dairyman, the shepherd's father-in-law, lolled in the settle; a young man and maid, who were blushing over tentative pourparlers on a life-companionship, sat beneath the corner-cupboard; and an elderly engaged man of fifty or upward moved restlessly about from spots where his betrothed was not to the spot where she was. Enjoyment was pretty general, and so much the more prevailed in being unhampered by conventional restrictions. Absolute confidence in each other's good opinion begat perfect ease, while the finishing stroke of manner, amounting to a truly princely serenity, was lent to the majority by the absence of any expression or trait denoting that they wished to get on in the world, enlarge their minds, or do any eclipsing thing whatever—which nowadays so generally nips the bloom and bonhomie of all except the two extremes of the social scale.

Shepherd Fennel had married well, his wife being a dairyman's daughter from a vale at a distance, who brought fifty guineas in her pocket—and kept them there, till they should be required for ministering to the needs of a coming family. This frugal woman had been somewhat exercised as to the character that should be given to the gathering. A sit-still party had its advantages; but an undisturbed position of ease in chairs and settles was apt to lead on the men to such an unconscionable deal of toping that they would sometimes fairly drink the house dry. A dancing-party was the alternative; but this, while avoiding the foregoing objection on the score of good drink, had a counterbalancing disadvantage in the matter of good victuals, the ravenous appetites engendered by the exercise causing immense havoc in the buttery. Shepherdess Fennel fell back upon the intermediate plan of mingling short dances with short periods of talk and singing, so as to hinder any ungovernable rage in either. But this scheme was entirely confined to her own gentle mind: the shepherd himself was in the mood to exhibit the most reckless phases of hospitality.

The fiddler was a boy of those parts, about twelve years of age, who had a wonderful dexterity in jigs and reels, though his fingers were so small and short as to necessitate a constant shifting for the high notes, from which he scrambled back to the first position with sounds not of unmixed purity of tone. At seven the shrill tweedle-dee of this youngster had begun, accompanied by a booming ground-bass from Elijah New, the parish-clerk, who had thoughtfully brought with him his favourite musical instrument, the serpent. Dancing was instantaneous, Mrs. Fennel privately enjoining the players on no account to let the dance exceed the length of a quarter of an hour.

But Elijah and the boy, in the excitement of their position, quite forgot the injunction. Moreover, Oliver Giles, a man of seventeen, one of the dancers, who was enamoured of his partner, a fair girl of thirty-three rolling years, had recklessly handed a new crown-piece to the musicians, as a bribe to keep going as long as they had muscle and wind. Mrs. Fennel, seeing the steam begin to generate on the countenances of her guests, crossed over and touched the fiddler's elbow and put her hand on the serpent's mouth. But they took no notice, and fearing she might lose her character of genial hostess if she were to interfere too markedly, she retired and sat down helpless. And so the dance whizzed on with cumulative fury, the performers moving in their planet-like courses, direct and retrograde, from apogee to perigee, till the hand of the well-kicked clock at the bottom of the room had travelled over the circumference of an hour.

While these cheerful events were in course of enactment within Fennel's pastoral dwelling, an incident having considerable bearing on the party had occurred in the gloomy night without. Mrs. Fennel's concern about the growing fierceness of the dance corresponded in point of time with the ascent of a human figure to the solitary hill of Higher Crowstairs from the direction of the distant town. This personage strode on through the rain without a pause, following the little-worn path which, further on in its course, skirted the shepherd's cottage.

It was nearly the time of full moon, and on this account, though the sky was lined with a uniform sheet of dripping cloud, ordinary objects out of doors were readily visible. The sad wan light revealed the lonely pedestrian to be a man of supple frame; his gait suggested that he had somewhat passed the period of perfect and instinctive agility, though not so far as to be otherwise than rapid of motion when occasion required. At a rough guess, he might have been about forty years of age. He appeared tall, but a recruiting sergeant, or other person accustomed to the judging of men's heights by the eye, would have discerned that this was chiefly owing to his gauntness, and that he was not more than five-feet-eight or nine.

Notwithstanding the regularity of his tread, there was caution in it, as in that of one who mentally feels his way; and despite the fact that it was not a black coat nor a dark garment of any sort that he wore, there was something about him which suggested that he naturally belonged to the black-coated tribes of men. His clothes were of fustian, and his boots hobnailed, yet in his progress he showed not the mud-accustomed bearing of hobnailed and fustianed peasantry.

By the time that he had arrived abreast of the shepherd's premises the rain came down, or rather came along, with yet more determined violence. The outskirts of the little settlement partially broke the force of wind and rain, and this induced him to stand still. The most salient of the shepherd's domestic erections was an empty sty at the forward corner of his hedgeless garden, for in these latitudes the principle of masking the homelier features of your establishment by a conventional frontage was unknown. The traveller's eye was attracted to this small building by the pallid shine of the wet slates that covered it. He turned aside, and, finding it empty, stood under the pent-roof for shelter.

While he stood, the boom of the serpent within the adjacent house, and the lesser strains of the fiddler, reached the spot as an accompaniment to the surging hiss of the flying rain on the sod, its louder beating on the cabbage-leaves of the garden, on the eight or ten beehives just discernible by the path, and its dripping from the eaves into a row of buckets and pans that had been placed under the walls of the cottage. For at Higher Crowstairs, as at all such elevated domiciles, the grand difficulty of housekeeping was an insufficiency of water; and a casual rainfall was utilized by turning out, as catchers, every utensil that the house contained. Some queer stories might be told of the contrivances for economy in suds and dish-waters that are absolutely necessitated in upland habitations during the droughts of summer. But at this season there were no such exigencies; a mere acceptance of what the skies bestowed was sufficient for an abundant store.

At last the notes of the serpent ceased and the house was silent. This cessation of activity aroused the solitary pedestrian from the reverie into which he had lapsed, and, emerging from the shed, with an apparently new intention, he walked up the path to the house-door. Arrived here, his first act was to kneel down on a large stone beside the row of vessels, and to drink a copious draught from one of them. Having quenched his thirst he rose and lifted his hand to knock, but paused with his eye upon the panel. Since the dark surface of the wood revealed absolutely nothing, it was evident that he must be mentally looking through the door, as if he wished to measure thereby all the possibilities that a house of this sort might include, and how they might bear upon the question of his entry.

In his indecision he turned and surveyed the scene around. Not a soul was anywhere visible. The garden-path stretched downward from his feet, gleaming like the track of a snail the roof of the little well (mostly dry), the well-cover, the top rail of the garden-gate, were varnished with the same dull liquid glaze; while, far away in the vale, a faint whiteness of more than usual extent showed that the rivers were high in the meads. Beyond all this winked a few bleared lamplights through the beating drops—lights that denoted the situation of the county-town from which he had appeared to come. The absence of all notes of life in that direction seemed to clinch his intentions, and he knocked at the door.

Within, a desultory chat had taken the place of movement and musical sound. The hedge-carpenter was suggesting a song to the company, which nobody just then was inclined to undertake, so that the knock afforded a not unwelcome diversion.

"Walk in!" said the shepherd promptly.

The latch clicked upward, and out of the night our pedestrian appeared upon the door-mat. The shepherd arose, snuffed two of the nearest candles, and turned to look at him.

Their light disclosed that the stranger was dark in complexion and not unprepossessing as to feature. His hat, which for a moment he did not remove, hung low over his eyes, without concealing that they were large, open, and determined, moving with a flash rather than a glance round the room. He seemed pleased with his survey, and, baring his shaggy head, said, in a rich deep voice, "The rain is so heavy, friends, that I ask leave to come in and rest awhile."

"To be sure, stranger," said the shepherd. "And faith, you've been lucky in choosing your time, for we are having a bit of a fling for a glad cause—though, to be sure, a man could hardly wish that glad cause to happen more than once a year."

"Nor less," spoke up a woman. "For'tis best to get your family over and done with, as soon as you can, so as to be all the earlier out of the fag o't."

"And what may be this glad cause?" asked the stranger.

"A birth and christening," said the shepherd.

The stranger hoped his host might not be made unhappy either by too many or too few of such episodes, and being invited by a gesture to a pull at the mug, he readily acquiesced. His manner, which, before entering, had been so dubious, was now altogether that of a careless and candid man.

"Late to be traipsing athwart this coomb—hey?" said the engaged man of fifty.

"Late it is, master, as you say.—I'll take a seat in the chimney-corner, if you have nothing to urge against it, ma'am; for I am a little moist on the side that was next the rain."

Mrs. Shepherd Fennel assented, and made room for the self-invited comer, who, having got completely inside the chimney-corner, stretched out his legs and his arms with the expansiveness of a person quite at home.

"Yes, I am rather cracked in the vamp," he said freely, seeing that the eyes of the shepherd's wife fell upon his boots, "and I am not well fitted either. I have had some rough times lately, and have been forced to pick up what I can get in the way of wearing, but I must find a suit better fit for working-days when I reach home."

"One of hereabouts?" she inquired.

"Not quite that—further up the country."

"I thought so. And so be I; and by your tongue you come from my neighbourhood."

"But you would hardly have heard of me," he said quickly. "My time would be long before yours, ma'am, you see."

This testimony to the youthfulness of his hostess had the effect of stopping her cross-examination.

"There is only one thing more wanted to make me happy," continued the new-comer. "And that is a little baccy, which I am sorry to say I am out of."

"I'll fill your pipe," said the shepherd.

"I must ask you to lend me a pipe likewise."

"A smoker, and no pipe about' ee?"

"I have dropped it somewhere on the road."

The shepherd filled and handed him a new clay pipe, saying, as he did so, "Hand me your baccy-box—I'll fill that too, now I am about it."

The man went through the movement of searching his pockets.

"Lost that too?" said his entertainer, with some surprise.

"I am afraid so," said the man with some confusion. "Give it to me in a screw of paper." Lighting his pipe at the candle with a suction that drew the whole flame into the bowl, he resettled himself in the corner and bent his looks upon the faint steam from his damp legs, as if he wished to say no more.

Meanwhile the general body of guests had been taking little notice of this visitor by reason of an absorbing discussion in which they were engaged with the band about a tune for the next dance. The matter being settled, they were about to stand up when an interruption came in the shape of another knock at the door.

At sound of the same the man in the chimney-corner took up the poker and began stirring the brands as if doing it thoroughly were the one aim of his existence; and a second time the shepherd said, "Walk in!" In a moment another man stood upon the straw-woven door-mat. He too was a stranger.

This individual was one of a type radically different from the first. There was more of the commonplace in his manner, and a certain jovial cosmopolitanism sat upon his features. He was several years older than the first arrival, his hair being slightly frosted, his eyebrows bristly, and his whiskers cut back from his cheeks. His face was rather full and flabby, and yet it was not altogether a face without power. A few grog-blossoms marked the neighbourhood of his nose. He flung back his long drab greatcoat, revealing that beneath it he wore a suit of cinder-gray shade throughout, large heavy seals, of some metal or other that would take a polish, dangling from his fob as his only personal ornament. Shaking the water-drops from his low-crowned glazed hat, he said, "I must ask for a few minutes' shelter, comrades, or I shall be wetted to my skin before I get to Casterbridge."

"Make yourself at home, master," said the shepherd, perhaps a trifle less heartily than on the first occasion. Not that Fennel had the least tinge of niggardliness in his composition; but the room was far from large, spare chairs were not numerous, and damp companions were not altogether desirable at close quarters for the women and girls in their bright-coloured gowns.

However, the second comer, after taking off his greatcoat, and hanging his hat on a nail in one of the ceiling-beams as if he had been specially invited to put it there, advanced and sat down at the table. This had been pushed so closely into the chimney-corner, to give all available room to the dancers, that its inner edge grazed the elbow of the man who had ensconced himself by the fire; and thus the two strangers were brought into close companionship. They nodded to each other by way of breaking the ice of unacquaintance, and the first stranger handed his neighbour the family mug—a huge vessel of brown ware, having its upper edge worn away like a threshold by the rub of whole generations of thirsty lips that had gone the way of all flesh, and bearing the following inscription burnt upon its rotund side in yellow letters: —

THERE IS NO FUN UNTILL i CUM.

The other man, nothing loth, raised the mug to his lips, and drank on, and on, and on—till a curious blueness overspread the countenance of the shepherd's wife, who had regarded with no little surprise the first stranger's free offer to the second of what did not belong to him to dispense.

"I knew it!" said the toper to the shepherd with much satisfaction. "When I walked up your garden before coming in, and saw the hives all of a row, I said to myself, 'Where there's bees there's honey, and where there's honey there's mead.' But mead of such a truly comfortable sort as this I really didn't expect to meet in my older days." He took yet another pull at the mug, till it assumed an ominous elevation. "Glad you enjoy it!" I said the shepherd warmly.

"It is goodish mead," assented Mrs. Fennel, with an absence of enthusiasm which seemed to say that it was possible to buy praise for one's cellar at too heavy a price. "It is trouble enough to make—and really I hardly think we shall make any more. For honey sells well, and we ourselves can make shift with a drop o'small mead and metheglin for common use from the comb-washings."

"O, but you'll never have the heart!" reproachfully cried the stranger in cinder-gray, after taking up the mug a third time and setting it down empty. "I love mead, when 'tis old like this, as I love to go to church o' Sundays, or to relieve the needy any day of the week."

"Ha, ha, ha!" said the man in the chimney-corner, who, in spite of the taciturnity induced by the pipe of tobacco, could not or would not refrain from this slight testimony to his comrade's humour.

Now the old mead of those days, brewed of the purest first-year or maiden honey, four pounds to the gallon—with its due complement of white of eggs, cinnamon, ginger, cloves, mace, rosemary, yeast, and processes of working, bottling, and cellaring—tasted remarkably strong; but it did not taste so strong as it actually was. Hence, presently, the stranger in cinder-gray at the table, moved by its creeping influence, unbuttoned his waistcoat, threw himself back in his chair, spread his legs, and made his presence felt in various ways.

"Well, well, as I say," he resumed, "I am going to Casterbridge, and to Casterbridge I must go. I should have been almost there by this time; but the rain drove me into your dwelling, and I'm not sorry for it."

"You don't live in Casterbridge?" said the shepherd.

"Not as yet; though I shortly mean to move there."

"Going to set up in trade, perhaps?"

"No, no," said the shepherd's wife. "It is easy to see that the gentleman is rich, and don't want to work at anything."

The cinder-gray stranger paused, as if to consider whether he would accept that definition of himself. He presently rejected it by answering, "Rich is not quite the word for me, dame. I do work, and I must work. And even if I only get to Casterbridge by midnight I must begin work there at eight to-morrow morning. Yes, het or wet, blow or snow, famine or sword, my day's work to-morrow must be done."

"Poor man! Then, in spite o'seeming, you be worse off than we?" replied the shepherd's wife.

"'Tis the nature of my trade, men and maidens. 'Tis the nature of my trade more than my poverty... But really and truly I must up and off, or I shan't get a lodging in the town." However, the speaker did not move, and directly added,

"There's time for one more draught of friendship before I go; and I'd perform it at once if the mug were not dry."

"Here's a mug o'small," said Mrs. Fennel. "Small, we call it, though to be sure'tis only the first wash o' the combs."

"No," said the stranger disdainfully. "I won't spoil your first kindness by partaking o'your second."

"Certainly not," broke in Fennel. "We don't increase and multiply every day, and I'll fill the mug again." He went away to the dark place under the stairs where the barrel stood. The shepherdess followed him.

"Why should you do this?" she said reproachfully, as soon as they were alone. "He's emptied it once, though it held enough for ten people; and now he's not contented wi' the small, but must needs call for more o' the strong! And a stranger unbeknown to any of us. For my part, I don't like the look o' the man at all."

"But he's in the house, my honey; and 'tis a wet night, and a christening. Daze it, what's a cup of mead more or less? There'll be plenty more next bee-burning."

"Very well—this time, then," she answered, looking wistfully at the barrel. "But what is the man's calling, and where is he one of, that he should come in and join us like this?"

"I don't know. I'll ask him again."

The catastrophe of having the mug drained dry at one pull by the stranger in cinder-gray was effectually guarded against this time by Mrs. Fennel. She poured out his allowance in a small cup, keeping the large one at a discreet distance from him. When he had tossed off his portion the shepherd renewed his inquiry about the stranger's occupation.

The latter did not immediately reply, and the man in the chimney-corner, with sudden demonstrativeness, said, "Anybody may know my trade—I'm a wheel-wright."

"A very good trade for these parts," said the shepherd.

"And anybody may know mine—if they've the sense to find it out," said the stranger in cinder-gray.

"You may generally tell what a man is by his claws," observed the hedge-carpenter, looking at his own hands. "My fingers be as full of thorns as an old pin-cushion is of pins."

The hands of the man in the chimney-corner instinctively sought the shade, and he gazed into the fire as he resumed his pipe. The man at the table took up the hedge-carpenter's remark, and added smartly, "True; but the oddity of my trade is that, instead of setting a mark upon me, it sets a mark upon my customers."

No observation being offered by anybody in elucidation of this enigma, the shepherd's wife once more called for a song. The same obstacles presented themselves as at the former time—one had no voice, another had forgotten the first verse. The stranger at the table, whose soul had now risen to a good working temperature, relieved the difficulty by exclaiming that, to start the company, he would sing himself. Thrusting one thumb into the arm-hole of his waistcoat, he waved the other hand in the air, and, with an extemporizing gaze at the shining sheep-crooks above the mantelpiece, began: —

"O my trade it is the rarest one, Simple shepherds all—My trade is a sight to see; For my customers I tie, and take them up on high, And waft'em to a far countree!"

The room was silent when he had finished the verse—with one exception, that of the man in the chimney-corner, who, at the singer's word, "Chorus!" joined him in a deep bass voice of musical relish—

"And waft 'em to a far countree!"

Oliver Giles, John Pitcher the dairyman, the parish-clerk, the engaged man of fifty, the row of young women against the wall, seemed lost in thought not of the gayest kind. The shepherd looked meditatively on the ground, the shepherdess gazed keenly at the singer, and with some suspicion; she was doubting whether this stranger were merely singing an old song from recollection, or was composing one there and then for the occasion. All were as perplexed at the obscure revelation as the guests at Belshazzar's Feast, except the man in the chimney-corner, who quietly said, "Second verse, stranger," and smoked on.

The singer thoroughly moistened himself from his lips inwards, and went on with the next stanza as requested: —

"My tools are but common ones, Simple shepherds all— My tools are no sight to see: A little hempen string, and a post whereon to swing Are implements enough for me!"

Shepherd Fennel glanced round. There was no longer any doubt that the stranger was answering his question rhythmically. The guests one and all started back with suppressed exclamations. The young woman engaged to the man of fifty fainted half-way, and would have proceeded, but finding him wanting in alacrity for catching her she sat down trembling.

"O, he's the—!" whispered the people in the background, mentioning the name of an ominous public officer. "He's come to do it!" Tis to be at Casterbridge jail to-morrow—the man for sheep-stealing—the poor clock-maker we heard of, who used to live away at Shottsford and had no work to do—Timothy Summers, whose family were a-starving, and so he went out of Shottsford by the high-road, and took a sheep in open daylight, defying the farmer and the farmer's wife and the farmer's lad, and every man jack among 'em. He (and they nodded towards the stranger of the deadly trade) "is come from up the country to do it because there's not enough to do in his own county-town, and he's got the place here now our own county man's dead; he's going to live in the same cottage under the prison wall."

The stranger in cinder-gray took no notice of this whispered string of observations, but again wetted his lips. Seeing that his friend in the chimney-corner was the only one who reciprocated his joviality in any way, he held out his cup towards that appreciative comrade, who also held out his own. They clinked together, the eyes of the rest of the room hanging upon the singer's actions. He parted his lips for the third verse; but at that moment another knock was audible upon the door. This time the knock was faint and hesitating.

The company seemed scared; the shepherd looked with consternation towards the entrance, and it was with some effort that he resisted his alarmed wife's deprecatory glance, and uttered for the third time the welcoming words, "Walk in!"

The door was gently opened, and another man stood upon the mat. He, like those who had preceded him, was a stranger. This time it was a short, small personage, of fair complexion, and dressed in a decent suit of dark clothes.

"Can you tell me the way to—?" he began: when, gazing round the room to observe the nature of the company amongst whom he had fallen, his eyes lighted on the stranger in cinder-gray. It was just at the instant when the latter, who had thrown his mind into his song with such a will that he scarcely heeded the interruption, silenced all whispers and inquiries by bursting into his third verse: —

"To-morrow is my working day, Simple shepherds all— To-morrow is a working day for me: For the farmer's sheep is slain, and the lad who did it ta'en, And on his soul may God ha' merc-y!"

The stranger in the chimney-corner, waving cups with the singer so heartily that his mead splashed over on the hearth, repeated in his bass voice as before: —

"And on his soul may God ha' merc-y!"

All this time the third stranger had been standing in the doorway. Finding now that he did not come forward or go on speaking, the guests particularly regarded him. They noticed to their surprise that he stood before them the picture of abject terror—his knees trembling, his hand shaking so violently that the door-latch by which he supported himself rattled audibly: his white lips were parted, and his eyes fixed on the merry officer of justice in the middle of the room. A moment more and he had turned, closed the door, and fled.

"What a man can it be?" said the shepherd.

The rest, between the awfulness of their late discovery and the odd conduct of this third visitor, looked as if they knew not what to think, and said nothing. Instinctively they withdrew further and further from the grim gentleman in their midst, whom some of them seemed to take for the Prince of Darkness himself, till they formed a remote circle, an empty space of floor being left between them and him—

"... circulus, cujus centrum diabolus."

The room was so silent—though there were more than twenty people in it—that nothing could be heard but the patter of the rain against the window-shutters, accompanied by the occasional hiss of a stray drop that fell down the chimney into the fire, and the steady puffing of the man in the corner, who had now resumed his pipe of long clay.

The stillness was unexpectedly broken. The distant sound of a gun reverberated through the air—apparently from the direction of the county-town.

"Be jiggered!" cried the stranger who had sung the song, jumping up.

"What does that mean?" asked several.

"A prisoner has escaped from the jail—that's what it means."

All listened. The sound was repeated, and none of them spoke but the man in the chimney-corner, who said quietly, "I've often been told that in this county they fire a gun at such times; but I never heard it till now."

"I wonder if it is my man?" murmured the personage in cinder-gray.

"Surely it is!" said the shepherd involuntarily. "And surely we've zeed him! That little man who looked in at the door by now, and quivered like a leaf when he zeed ye and heard your song!"

"His teeth chattered, and the breath went out of his body," said the dairyman.

"And his heart seemed to sink within him like a stone," said Oliver Giles.

"And he bolted as if he'd been shot at," said the hedge-carpenter.

"True—his teeth chattered, and his heart seemed to sink; and he bolted as if he'd been shot at," slowly summed up the man in the chimney-corner.

"I didn't notice it," remarked the hangman.

"We were all a-wondering what made him run off in such a fright," faltered one of the women against the wall, "and now 'tis explained!"

The firing of the alarm-gun went on at intervals, low and sullenly, and their suspicions became a certainty. The sinister gentleman in cinder-gray roused himself. "Is there a constable here?" he asked, in thick tones. "If so, let him step forward."

The engaged man of fifty stepped quavering out from the wall, his betrothed beginning to sob on the back of the chair.

"You are a sworn constable?"

"I be, sir."

"Then, pursue the criminal at once, with assistance, and bring him back here. He can't have gone far."

"I will sir, I will—when I've got my staff. I'll go home and get it, and come sharp here, and start in a body."

"Staff!—never mind your staff; the man'll be gone!"

"But I can't do nothing without my staff—can I, William, and John, and Charles Jake? No; for there's the king's royal crown a painted on en in yaller and gold, and the lion and the unicorn, so as when I raise en up and hit my prisoner, 'tis made a lawful blow thereby. I wouldn't 'tempt to take up a man without my staff—no, not I. If I hadn't the law to gie me courage, why, instead o' my taking up him he might take up me!"

"Now, I'm a king's man myself, and can give you authority enough for this," said the formidable officer in gray. "Now then, all of ye, be ready. Have ye any lanterns?"

"Yes—have ye any lanterns?—I demand it!" said the constable.

"And the rest of you able-bodied—"

"Able-bodied men—yes—the rest of ye!" said the constable.

"Have you some good stout staves and pitch-forks—"

"Staves and pitchforks—in the name o'the law! And take 'em in yer hands and go in quest, and do as we in authority tell ye!"

Thus aroused, the men prepared to give chase. The evidence was, indeed, though circumstantial, so convincing, that but little argument was needed to show the shepherd's guests that after what they had seen it would look very much like connivance if they did not instantly pursue the unhappy third stranger, who could not as yet have gone more than a few hundred yards over such uneven country.

A shepherd is always well provided with lanterns; and, lighting these hastily, and with hurdle-staves in their hands, they poured out of the door, taking a direction along the crest of the hill, away from the town, the rain having fortunately a little abated.

Disturbed by the noise, or possibly by unpleasant dreams of her baptism, the child who had been christened began to cry heart-brokenly in the room overhead. These notes of grief came down through the chinks of the floor to the ears of the women below, who jumped up one by one, and seemed glad of the excuse to ascend and comfort the baby, for the incidents of the last half-hour greatly oppressed them. Thus in the space of two or three minutes the room on the ground-floor was deserted quite.

But it was not for long. Hardly had the sound of footsteps died away when a man returned round the corner of the house from the direction the pursuers had taken. Peeping in at the door, and seeing nobody there, he entered leisurely. It was the stranger of the chimney-corner, who had gone out with the rest. The motive of his return was shown by his helping himself to a cut piece of skimmer-cake that lay on a ledge beside where he had sat, and which he had apparently forgotten to take with him. He also poured out half a cup more mead from the quantity that remained, ravenously eating and drinking these as he stood. He had not finished when another figure came in just as quietly—his friend in cinder-gray.

"O—you here?" said the latter, smiling. "I thought you had gone to help in the capture." And this speaker also revealed the object of his return by looking solicitously round for the fascinating mug of old mead.

"And I thought you had gone," said the other, continuing his skimmer-cake with some effort.

"Well, on second thoughts, I felt there were enough without me," said the first confidentially, "and such a night as it is, too. Besides, 'tis the business o' the Government to take care of its criminals—not mine."

"True; so it is. And I felt as you did, that there were enough without me."

"I don't want to break my limbs running over the humps and hollows of this wild country."

"Nor I neither, between you and me."

"These shepherd-people are used to it—simple-minded souls, you know, stirred up to anything in a moment. They'll have him ready for me before the morning, and no trouble to me at all."

"They'll have him, and we shall have saved ourselves all labour in the matter."

"True, true. Well, my way is to Casterbridge; and 'tis as much as my legs will do to take me that far. Going the same way?"

"No, I am sorry to say! I have to get home over there" (he nodded indefinitely to the right), "and I feel as you do, that it is quite enough for my legs to do before bedtime."

The other had by this time finished the mead in the mug, after which, shaking hands heartily at the door, and wishing each other well, they went their several ways.

In the meantime the company of pursuers had reached the end of the hog's-back elevation which dominated this part of the down. They had decided on no particular plan of action; and, finding that the man of the baleful trade was no longer in their company, they seemed quite unable to form any such plan now. They descended in all directions down the hill, and straightway several of the party fell into the snare set by Nature for all misguided midnight ramblers over this part of the cretaceous formation. The "lanchets," or flint slopes, which belted the escarpment at intervals of a dozen yards, took the less cautious ones unawares, and losing their footing on the rubbly steep they slid sharply downwards, the lanterns rolling from their hands to the bottom, and there lying on their sides till the horn was scorched through.

When they had again gathered themselves together, the shepherd, as the man who knew the country best, took the lead, and guided them round these treacherous inclines. The lanterns, which seemed rather to dazzle their eyes and warn the fugitive than to assist them in the exploration, were extinguished, due silence was observed; and in this more rational order they plunged into the vale. It was a grassy, briery, moist defile, affording some shelter to any person who had sought it; but the party perambulated it in vain, and ascended on the other side. Here they wandered apart, and after an interval closed together again to report progress. At the second time of closing in they found themselves near a lonely ash, the single tree on this part of the coomb, probably sown there by a passing bird some fifty years before. And here, standing a little to one side of the trunk, as motionless as the trunk itself, appeared the man they were in quest of, his outline being well defined against the sky beyond. The band noiselessly drew up and faced him.

"Your money or your life!" said the constable sternly to the still figure.

"No, no," whispered John Pitcher. "Tisn't our side ought to say that. That's the doctrine of vagabonds like him, and we be on the side of the law."

"Well, well," replied the constable impatiently; "I must say something, mustn't I? and if you had all the weight o' this undertaking upon your mind, perhaps you'd say the wrong thing too!—Prisoner at the bar, surrender, in the name of the Father—the Crown, I mane!"

The man under the tree seemed now to notice them for the first time, and, giving them no opportunity whatever for exhibiting their courage, he strolled slowly towards them. He was, indeed, the little man, the third stranger; but his trepidation had in a great measure gone.

"Well, travellers," he said, "did I hear ye speak to me?"

"You did: you've got to come and be our prisoner at once!" said the constable. "We arrest 'ee on the charge of not biding in Casterbridge jail in a decent proper manner to be hung to-morrow morning. Neighbours, do your duty, and seize the culpet!"

On hearing the charge, the man seemed enlightened, and, saying not another word, resigned himself with preternatural civility to the search-party, who, with their staves in their hands, surrounded him on all sides, and marched him back towards the shepherd's cottage.

It was eleven o'clock by the time they arrived. The light shining from the open door, a sound of men's voices within, proclaimed to them as they approached the house that some new events had arisen in their absence. On entering they discovered the shepherd's living room to be invaded by two officers from Casterbridge jail, and a well-known magistrate who lived at the nearest country-seat, intelligence of the escape having become generally circulated.

"Gentlemen," said the constable, "I have brought back your man—not without risk and danger; but every one must do his duty! He is inside this circle of able-bodied persons, who have lent me useful aid, considering their ignorance of Crown work. Men, bring forward your prisoner!" And the third stranger was led to the light.

"Who is this?" said one of the officials.

"The man," said the constable.

"Certainly not," said the turnkey; and the first corroborated his statement.

"But how can it be otherwise?" asked the constable. "or why was he so terrified at sight o' the singing instrument of the law who sat there?" Here he related the strange behaviour of the third stranger on entering the house during the hangman's song.

"Can't understand it," said the officer coolly. "All I know is that it is not the condemned man. He's quite a different character from this one; a gauntish fellow, with dark hair and eyes, rather good-looking, and with a musical bass voice that if you heard it once you'd never mistake as long as you lived."

"Why, souls—'twas the man in the chimney-corner!"

"Hey—what?" said the magistrate, coming forward after inquiring particulars from the shepherd in the background. "Haven't you got the man after all?"

"Well, sir," said the constable, "he's the man we were in search of, that's true; and yet he's not the man we were in search of. For the man we were in search of was not the man we wanted, sir, if you understand my every-day way; for 'twas the man in the chimney-corner!"

"A pretty kettle of fish altogether!" said the magistrate. "You had better start for the other man at once."

The prisoner now spoke for the first time. The mention of the man in the chimney-corner seemed to have moved him as nothing else could do. "Sir," he said, stepping forward to the magistrate, "take no more trouble about me. The time is come when I may as well speak. I have done nothing; my crime is that the condemned man is my brother. Early this afternoon I left home at Shottsford to tramp it all the way to Casterbridge jail to bid him farewell. I was benighted, and called here to rest and ask the way. When I opened the door I saw before me the very man, my brother, that I thought to see in the condemned cell at Casterbridge. He was in this chimney-corner; and jammed close to him, so that he could not have got out if he had tried, was the executioner who'd come to take his life, singing a song about it and not knowing that it was his victim who was close by, joining in to save appearances. My brother looked a glance of agony at me, and I knew he meant, 'Don't reveal what you see; my life depends on it.' I was so terror-struck that I could hardly stand, and, not knowing what I did, I turned and hurried away."

The narrator's manner and tone had the stamp of truth, and his story made a great impression on all around. "And do you know where your brother is at the present time?" asked the magistrate.

"I do not. I have never seen him since I closed this door."

"I can testify to that, for we've been between ye ever since," said the constable.

"Where does he think to fly to?—what is his occupation?"

"He's a watch-and-clock-maker, sir."

"A said a was a wheelwright—a wicked rogue," said the constable.

"The wheels of clocks and watches he meant, no doubt," said Shepherd Fennel. "I thought his hands were palish for's trade."

"Well, it appears to me that nothing can be gained by retaining this poor man in custody," said the magistrate; "your business lies with the other, unquestionably."

And so the little man was released off-hand; but he looked nothing the less sad on that account, it being beyond the power of magistrate or constable to raze out the written troubles in his brain, for they concerned another whom he regarded with more solicitude than himself. When this was done, and the man had gone his way, the night was found to be so far advanced that it was deemed useless to renew the search before the next morning.

Next day, accordingly, the quest for the clever sheep-stealer became general and keen, to all appearance at least. But the intended punishment was cruelly disproportioned to the transgression, and the sympathy of a great many country-folk in that district was strongly on the side of the fugitive. Moreover, his marvellous coolness and daring in hob-and-nobbing with the hangman, under the unprecedented circumstances of the shepherd's party, won their admiration. So that it may be questioned if all those who ostensibly made themselves so busy in exploring woods and fields and lanes were quite so thorough when it came to the private examination of their own lofts and outhouses. Stories were afloat of a mysterious figure being occasionally seen in some old overgrown trackway or other, remote from turnpike roads; but when a search was instituted in any of these suspected quarters nobody was found. Thus the days and weeks passed without tidings.

In brief, the bass-voiced man of the chimney-corner was never recaptured. Some said that he went across the sea, others that he did not, but buried himself in the depths of a populous city. At any rate, the gentleman in cinder-gray never did his morning's work at Casterbridge, nor met anywhere at all, for business purposes, the genial comrade with whom he had passed an hour of relaxation in the lonely house on the coomb.

The grass has long been green on the graves of Shepherd Fennel and his frugal wife; the guests who made up the christening party have mainly followed their entertainers to the tomb; the baby in whose honour they all had met is a matron in the sere and yellow leaf. But the arrival of the three strangers at the shepherd's that night, and the details connected therewith, is a story as well known as ever in the country about Higher Crowstairs.

II Moby Dick and His Whiteness

(Excerpt from *Moby Dick*)

Herman Melville (1819–1891)

I, Ishmael, was one of that crew; my shouts had gone up with the rest; my oath had been welded with theirs; and stronger I shouted, and more did I hammer and clinch my oath, because of the dread in my soul. A wild, mystical, sympathetical feeling was in me; Ahab's quenchless feud seemed mine. With greedy ears I learned the history of that murderous monster against whom I and all the others had taken our oaths of violence and revenge.

For some time past, though at intervals only, the unaccompanied, secluded White Whale had haunted those uncivilized seas mostly frequented by the Sperm Whale fishermen. But not all of them knew of his existence; only a few of them, comparatively, had knowingly seen him; while the number who as yet had actually and knowingly given battle to him, was small indeed. For, owing to the large number of whale-cruisers; the disorderly way they were sprinkled over the entire watery circumference, many of them adventurously pushing their quest along solitary latitudes, so as seldom or never for a whole twelvemonth or more on a stretch, to encounter a single news-telling sail of any sort; the inordinate length of each separate voyage; the irregularity of the times of sailing from home; all these, with other circumstances, direct and indirect, long obstructed the spread through the whole world-wide whaling-fleet of the special individualizing tidings concerning Moby Dick. It was hardly to be doubted, that several vessels reported to have encountered, at such or such a time, or on such or such a meridian, a Sperm Whale of uncommon magnitude and malignity, which whale, after doing great mischief to his assailants, had completely escaped them; to some minds it was not an unfair presumption, I say, that the whale in question must have been no other than Moby Dick. Yet as of late the Sperm Whale fishery had been marked by various and not unfrequent instances of great ferocity, cunning, and malice in the monster attacked; therefore it was, that those who by accident ignorantly gave battle to Moby Dick; such hunters, perhaps, for the most part, were content to ascribe the peculiar terror he bred, more, as it were, to the perils of the Sperm Whale fishery at large, than to the individual cause. In that way, mostly, the disastrous encounter between Ahab and the whale had hitherto been popularly regarded.

And as for those who, previously hearing of the White Whale, by chance caught sight of him; in the beginning of the thing they had every one of them, almost, as boldly and fearlessly lowered for him, as for any other whale of that species. But at length, such calamities did ensue in these assaults—not restricted to sprained wrists and ankles, broken limbs, or devouring amputations—but fatal to the last degree of fatality; those repeated disastrous repulses, all accumulating and piling their terrors upon Moby Dick; those things had gone far to shake the fortitude of many brave hunters, to whom the story of the White Whale had eventually come.

Nor did wild rumors of all sorts fail to exaggerate, and still the more horrify the true histories of these deadly encounters. For not only do fabulous rumors naturally grow out of the very body of all surprising terrible events, —as the smitten tree gives birth to its fungi; but, in maritime life, far more than in that of terra firma, wild rumors abound, wherever there is any adequate reality for them to cling to. And as the sea surpasses the land in this matter, so the whale fishery surpasses every other sort of maritime life, in the wonderfulness and fearfulness of the rumors which sometimes circulate there. For not only are whalemen as a body unexempt from that ignorance and superstitiousness hereditary to all sailors; but of all sailors, they are by all odds the most directly brought into contact with whatever is appallingly astonishing in the sea; face to face they not only eye its greatest marvels, but, hand to jaw, give battle to them. Alone, in such remotest waters, that though you sailed a thousand miles, and passed a thousand shores, you would not come to any chiseled hearth-stone, or aught hospitable beneath that part of the sun; in such latitudes and longitudes, pursuing too such a calling as he does, the whaleman is wrapped by influences all tending to make his fancy pregnant with many a mighty birth.

No wonder, then, that ever gathering volume from the mere transit over the widest watery spaces, the outblown rumors of the White Whale did in the end incorporate with themselves all manner of morbid hints, and half-formed foetal suggestions of supernatural agencies, which eventually invested Moby Dick with new terrors unborrowed from anything that visibly appears. So that in many cases such a panic did he finally strike, that few who by those rumors, at least, had heard of the White Whale, few of those hunters were willing to encounter the perils of his jaw.

But there were still other and more vital practical influences at work. Not even at the present day has the original prestige of the Sperm Whale, as fearfully distinguished from all other species of the leviathan, died out of the minds of the whalemen as a body. There are those this day among them, who, though intelligent and courageous enough in offering battle to the Greenland or Right whale, would perhaps—either from professional inexperience, or incompetency, or timidity, decline a contest with the Sperm Whale; at any rate, there are plenty of whalemen, especially among those whaling nations not sailing under the American flag, who have never hostilely encountered the Sperm Whale, but whose sole knowledge of the leviathan is restricted to the ignoble monster primitively pursued in the North; seated on their hatches, these men will hearken with a childish fireside interest and awe, to the wild, strange tales of Southern whaling. Nor is the pre-eminent tremendousness of the great Sperm Whale anywhere more feelingly comprehended, than on board of those prows which stem him.

And as if the now tested reality of his might had in former legendary times thrown its shadow before it; we find some book naturalists—Olassen and Povelson—declaring the Sperm Whale not only to be a consternation to every other creature in the sea, but also to be so incredibly ferocious as continually to be athirst for human blood. Nor even down to so late a time as Cuvier's, were these or almost similar impressions effaced. For in his Natural History, the Baron himself affirms that at sight of the Sperm Whale, all fish (sharks included) are "struck with the most lively terrors," and "often in the precipitancy of their flight dash themselves against the rocks with such violence as to cause instantaneous death." And however the general experiences in the fishery may amend such reports as these; yet in their full terribleness, even to the bloodthirsty item of Povelson, the superstitious belief in them is, in some vicissitudes of their vocation, revived in the minds of the hunters.

So that overawed by the rumors and portents concerning him, not a few of the fishermen recalled, in reference to Moby Dick, the earlier days of the Sperm Whale fishery, when it was oftentimes hard to induce long practised Right whalemen to embark in the perils of this new and daring warfare; such men protesting that although other leviathans might be hopefully pursued, yet to chase and point lance at such an apparition as the Sperm Whale was not for mortal man. That to attempt it, would be inevitably to be torn into a quick eternity. On this head, there are some remarkable documents that may be consulted.

Nevertheless, some there were, who even in the face of these things were ready to give chase to Moby Dick; and a still greater number who, chancing only to hear of him distantly and vaguely, without the specific details of any certain calamity, and without superstitious accompaniments, were sufficiently hardy not to flee from the battle if offered.

One of the wild suggestions referred to, as at last coming to be linked with the White Whale in the minds of the superstitiously inclined, was the unearthly conceit that Moby Dick was ubiquitous; that he had actually been encountered in opposite latitudes at one and the same instant of time.

Nor, credulous as such minds must have been, was this conceit altogether without some faint show of superstitious probability. For as the secrets of the currents in the seas have never yet been divulged, even to the most erudite research; so the hidden ways of the Sperm Whale when beneath the surface remain, in great part, unaccountable to his pursuers; and from time to time have originated the most curious and contradictory speculations regarding them, especially concerning the mystic modes whereby, after sounding to a great depth, he transports himself with such vast swiftness to the most widely distant points.

It is a thing well known to both American and English whale-ships, and as well a thing placed upon authoritative record years ago by Scoresby, that some whales have been captured far north in the Pacific, in whose bodies have been found the barbs of harpoons darted in the Greenland seas. Nor is it to be gainsaid, that in some of these instances it has been declared that the interval of time between the two assaults could not have exceeded very many days. Hence, by inference, it has been believed by some whalemen, that the Nor' West Passage, so long a problem to man, was never a problem to the whale. So that here, in the real living experience of living men, the prodigies related in old times of the inland Strello mountain in Portugal (near whose top there was said to be a lake in which the wrecks of ships floated up to the surface); and that still more wonderful story of the Arethusa fountain near Syracuse (whose waters were believed to have come from the Holy Land by an underground passage); these fabulous narrations are almost fully equalled by the realities of the whalemen.

Forced into familiarity, then, with such prodigies as these; and knowing that after repeated, intrepid assaults, the White Whale had escaped alive; it cannot be much matter of surprise that some whalemen should go still further in their superstitions; declaring Moby Dick not only ubiquitous, but immortal (for immortality is but ubiquity in time); that though groves of spears should be planted in his flanks, he would still swim away unharmed; or if indeed he should ever be made to spout thick blood, such a sight would be but a ghastly deception; for again in unensanguined billows hundreds of leagues away, his unsullied jet would once more be seen.

But even stripped of these supernatural surmisings, there was enough in the earthly make and incontestable character of the monster to strike the imagination with unwonted power. For, it was not so much his uncommon bulk that so much distinguished him from other sperm whales, but, as was elsewhere thrown out—a peculiar snow-white wrinkled forehead, and a high, pyramidical white hump. These were his prominent features; the tokens whereby, even in the limitless, uncharted seas, he revealed his identity, at a long distance, to those who knew him.

The rest of his body was so streaked, and spotted, and marbled with the same shrouded hue, that, in the end, he had gained his distinctive appellation of the White Whale; a name, indeed, literally justified by his vivid aspect, when seen gliding at high noon through a dark blue sea, leaving a milky-way wake of creamy foam, all spangled with golden gleamings.

Nor was it his unwonted magnitude, nor his remarkable hue, nor yet his deformed lower jaw, that so much invested the whale with natural terror, as that unexampled, intelligent malignity which, according to specific accounts, he had over and over again evinced in his assaults. More than all, his treacherous retreats struck more of dismay than perhaps aught else. For, when swimming before his exulting pursuers, with every apparent symptom of alarm, he had several times been known to turn round suddenly, and, bearing down upon them, either stave their boats to splinters, or drive them back in consternation to their ship.

Already several fatalities had attended his chase. But though similar disasters, however little bruited ashore, were by no means unusual in the fishery; yet, in most instances, such seemed the White Whale's infernal aforethought of ferocity, that every dismembering or death that he caused, was not wholly regarded as having been inflicted by an unintelligent agent.

Judge, then, to what pitches of inflamed, distracted fury the minds of his more desperate hunters were impelled, when amid the chips of chewed boats, and the sinking limbs of torn comrades, they swam out of the white curds of the whale's direful wrath into the serene, exasperating sunlight, that smiled on, as if at a birth or a bridal.

His three boats stove around him, and oars and men both whirling in the eddies; one captain, seizing the line-knife from his broken prow, had dashed at the whale, as an Arkansas duellist at his foe, blindly seeking with a six inch blade to reach the fathom-deep life of the whale. That captain was Ahab. And then it was, that suddenly sweeping his sickle-shaped lower jaw beneath him, Moby Dick had reaped away Ahab's leg, as a mower a blade of grass in the field. No turbaned Turk, no hired Venetian or Malay, could have smote him with more seeming malice. Small reason was there to doubt, then, that ever since that almost fatal encounter, Ahab had cherished a wild vindictiveness against the whale, all the more fell for that in his frantic morbidness he at last came to identify with him, not only all his bodily woes, but all his intellectual and spiritual exasperations. The White Whale swam before him as the monomaniac incarnation of all those malicious agencies which some deep men feel eating in them, till they are left living on with half a heart and half a lung. That intangible malignity which has been from the beginning; to whose dominion even the modern Christians ascribe one-half of the worlds; which the ancient Ophites of the east reverenced in their statue devil;—Ahab did not fall down and worship it like them; but deliriously transferring its idea to the abhorred white whale, he pitted himself, all mutilated, against it. All that most maddens and torments; all that stirs up the lees of things; all truth with malice in it; all that cracks the sinews and cakes the brain; all the subtle demonisms of life and thought; all evil, to crazy Ahab, were visibly personified, and made practically assailable in Moby Dick. He piled upon the whale's white hump the sum of all the general rage and hate felt by his whole race from Adam down; and then, as if his chest had been a mortar, he burst his hot heart's shell upon it.

It is not probable that this monomania in him took its instant rise at the precise time of his bodily dismemberment. Then, in darting at the monster, knife in hand, he had but given loose to a sudden, passionate, corporal animosity; and when he received the stroke that tore him, he probably but felt the agonizing bodily laceration, but nothing more. Yet, when by this collision forced to turn towards home, and for long months of days and weeks, Ahab and anguish lay stretched together in one hammock, rounding in mid winter that dreary, howling Patagonian Cape; then it was, that his torn body and gashed soul bled into one another; and so interfusing, made him mad. That it was only then, on the homeward voyage, after the encounter, that the final monomania seized him, seems all but certain from the fact that, at intervals during the passage, he was a raving lunatic; and, though unlimbed of a leg, yet such vital strength yet lurked in his Egyptian chest, and was moreover intensified by his delirium, that his mates were forced to lace him fast, even there, as he sailed, raving in his hammock. In a strait-jacket, he swung to the mad rockings of the gales. And, when running into more sufferable latitudes, the ship, with mild stun'sails spread, floated across the tranquil tropics, and, to all appearances, the old man's delirium seemed left behind him with the Cape Horn swells, and he came forth from his dark den into the blessed light and air; even then, when he bore that firm, collected front, however pale, and issued his calm orders once again; and his mates thanked God the direful madness was now gone; even then, Ahab, in his hidden self, raved on. Human madness is oftentimes a cunning and most feline thing. When you think it fled, it may have but become transfigured into some still subtler form. Ahab's full lunacy subsided not, but deepeningly contracted; like the unabated Hudson, when that noble Northman flows narrowly, but unfathomably through the Highland gorge. But, as in his narrow-flowing monomania, not one jot of Ahab's broad madness had been left behind; so in that broad madness, not one jot of his great natural intellect had perished. That before living agent, now became the living instrument. If such a furious trope may stand, his special lunacy stormed his general sanity, and carried it, and turned all its concentred cannon upon its own mad mark; so that far from having lost his strength, Ahab, to that one end, did now possess a thousand fold more potency than ever he had sanely brought to bear upon any one reasonable object.

This is much; yet Ahab's larger, darker, deeper part remains unhinted. But vain to popularize profundities, and all truth is profound. Winding far down from within the very heart of this spiked Hotel de Cluny where we here stand—however grand and wonderful, now quit it;—and take your way, ye nobler, sadder souls, to those vast Roman halls of Thermes; where far beneath the fantastic towers of man's upper earth, his root of grandeur, his whole awful essence sits in bearded state; an antique buried beneath antiquities, and throned on torsoes! So with a broken throne, the great gods mock that captive king; so like a Caryatid, he patient sits, upholding on his frozen brow the piled entablatures of ages. Wind ye down there, ye prouder, sadder souls! question that proud, sad king! A family likeness! aye, he did beget ye, ye young exiled royalties; and from your grim sire only will the old State-secret come.

Now, in his heart, Ahab had some glimpse of this, namely: all my means are sane, my motive and my object mad. Yet without power to kill, or change, or shun the fact; he likewise knew that to mankind he did long dissemble; in some sort, did still. But that thing of his dissembling was only subject to his perceptibility, not to his will determinate. Nevertheless, so well did he succeed in that dissembling, that when with ivory leg he stepped ashore at last, no Nantucketer thought him otherwise than but naturally grieved, and that to the quick, with the terrible casualty which had overtaken him.

The report of his undeniable delirium at sea was likewise popularly ascribed to a kindred cause. And so too, all the added moodiness which always afterwards, to the very day of sailing in the Pequod on the present voyage, sat brooding on his brow. Nor is it so very unlikely, that far from distrusting his fitness for another whaling voyage, on account of such dark symptoms, the calculating people of that prudent isle were inclined to harbor the conceit, that for those very reasons he was all the better qualified and set on edge, for a pursuit so full of rage and wildness as the bloody hunt of whales. Gnawed within and scorched without, with the infixed, unrelenting fangs of some incurable idea; such an one, could he be found, would seem the very man to dart his iron and lift his lance against the most appalling of all brutes. Or, if for any reason thought to be corporeally incapacitated for that, yet such an one would seem superlatively competent to cheer and howl on his underlings to the attack. But be all this as it may, certain it is, that with the mad secret of his unabated rage bolted up and keyed in him, Ahab had purposely sailed upon the present voyage with the one only and all-engrossing object of hunting the White Whale. Had any one of his old acquaintances on shore but half dreamed of what was lurking in him then, how soon would their aghast and righteous souls have wrenched the ship from such a fiendish man! They were bent on profitable cruises, the profit to be counted down in dollars from the mint. He was intent on an audacious, immitigable, and supernatural revenge.

Here, then, was this grey-headed, ungodly old man, chasing with curses a Job's whale round the world, at the head of a crew, too, chiefly made up of mongrel renegades, and castaways, and cannibals—morally enfeebled also, by the incompetence of mere unaided virtue or right-mindedness in Starbuck, the invunerable jollity of indifference and recklessness in Stubb, and the pervading mediocrity in Flask. Such a crew, so officered, seemed specially picked and packed by some infernal fatality to help him to his monomaniac revenge. How it was that they so aboundingly responded to the old man's ire—by what evil magic their souls were possessed, that at times his hate seemed almost theirs; the White Whale as much their insufferable foe as his; how all this came to be—what the White Whale was to them, or how to their unconscious understandings, also, in some dim, unsuspected way, he might have seemed the gliding great demon of the seas of life,—all this to explain, would be to dive deeper than Ishmael can go. The subterranean miner that works in us all, how can one tell whither leads his shaft by the ever shifting, muffled sound of his pick? Who does not feel the irresistible arm drag? What skiff in tow of a seventy-four can stand still? For one, I gave myself up to the abandonment of the time and the place; but while yet all a-rush to encounter the whale, could see naught in that brute but the deadliest ill.

What the white whale was to Ahab, has been hinted; what, at times, he was to me, as yet remains unsaid. Aside from those more obvious considerations touching Moby Dick, which could not but occasionally awaken in any man's soul some alarm, there was another thought, or rather vague, nameless horror concerning him, which at times by its intensity completely overpowered all the rest; and yet so mystical and well nigh ineffable was it, that I almost despair of putting it in a comprehensible form. It was the whiteness of the whale that above all things appalled me. But how can I hope to explain myself here; and yet, in some dim, random way, explain myself I must, else all these chapters might be naught.

Though in many natural objects, whiteness refiningly enhances beauty, as if imparting some special virtue of its own, as in marbles, japonicas, and pearls; and though various nations have in some way recognised a certain royal preeminence in this hue; even the barbaric, grand old kings of Pegu placing the title "Lord of the White Elephants" above all their other magniloquent ascriptions of dominion; and the modern kings of Siam unfurling the same snow-white quadruped in the royal standard; and the Hanoverian flag bearing the one figure of a snow-white charger; and the great Austrian Empire, Caesarian, heir to overlording Rome, having for the imperial colour the same imperial hue; and though this pre-eminence in it applies to the human race itself, giving the white man ideal mastership over every dusky tribe; and though, besides, all this, whiteness has been even made significant of gladness, for among the Romans a white stone marked a joyful day; and though in other mortal sympathies and symbolizings, this same hue is made the emblem of many touching, noble things—the innocence of brides, the benignity of age; though among the Red Men of America the giving of the white belt of wampum was the deepest pledge of honour; though in many climes, whiteness typifies the majesty of Justice in the ermine of the Judge, and contributes to the daily state of kings and queens drawn by milk-white steeds; though even in the higher mysteries of the most august religions it has been made the symbol of the divine spotlessness and power; by the Persian fire worshippers, the white forked flame being held the holiest on the altar; and in the Greek mythologies, Great Jove himself being made incarnate in a snow-white bull; and though to the noble Iroquois, the midwinter sacrifice of the sacred White Dog was by far the holiest festival of their theology, that spotless, faithful creature being held the purest envoy they could send to the Great Spirit with the annual tidings of their own fidelity; and though directly from the Latin word for white, all Christian priests derive the name of one part of their sacred vesture, the alb or tunic, worn beneath the cassock; and though among the holy pomps of the Romish faith, white is specially employed in the celebration of the Passion of our Lord; though in the Vision of St. John, white robes are given to the redeemed, and the four-and-twenty elders stand clothed in white before the great-white throne, and the Holy One that sitteth there white like wool; yet for all these accumulated associations, with whatever is sweet, and honourable, and sublime, there yet lurks an elusive something in the innermost idea of this hue, which strikes more of panic to the soul than that redness which affrights in blood.

This elusive quality it is, which causes the thought of whiteness, when divorced from more kindly associations, and coupled with any object terrible in itself, to heighten that terror to the furthest bounds. Witness the white bear of the poles, and the white shark of the tropics; what but their smooth, flaky whiteness makes them the transcendent horrors they are? That ghastly whiteness it is which imparts such an abhorrent mildness, even more loathsome than terrific, to the dumb gloating of their aspect. So that not the fierce-fanged tiger in his heraldic coat can so stagger courage as the white-shrouded bear or shark.

With reference to the Polar bear, it may possibly be urged by him who would fain go still deeper into this matter, that it is not the whiteness, separately regarded, which heightens the intolerable hideousness of that brute; for, analysed, that heightened hideousness, it might be said, only rises from the circumstance, that the irresponsible ferociousness of the creature stands invested in the fleece of celestial innocence and love; and hence, by bringing together two such opposite emotions in our minds, the Polar bear frightens us with so unnatural a contrast. But even assuming all this to be true; yet, were it not for the whiteness, you would not have that intensified terror.

As for the white shark, the white gliding ghostliness of repose in that creature, when beheld in his ordinary moods, strangely tallies with the same quality in the Polar quadruped. This peculiarity is most vividly hit by the French in the name they bestow upon that fish. The Romish mass for the dead begins with "Requiem eternam" (eternal rest), whence REQUIEM denominating the mass itself, and any other funeral music. Now, in allusion to the white, silent stillness of death in this shark, and the mild deadliness of his habits, the French call him REQUIEN.

Bethink thee of the albatross, whence come those clouds of spiritual wonderment and pale dread, in which that white phantom sails in all imaginations? Not Coleridge first threw that spell; but God's great, unflattering laureate, Nature.

I remember the first albatross I ever saw. It was during a prolonged gale, in waters hard upon the Antarctic seas. From my forenoon watch below, I ascended to the overclouded deck; and there, dashed upon the main hatches, I saw a regal, feathery thing of unspotted whiteness, and with a hooked, Roman bill sublime. At intervals, it arched forth its vast archangel wings, as if to embrace some holy ark. Wondrous flutterings and throbbings shook it. Though bodily unharmed, it uttered cries, as some king's ghost in supernatural distress. Through its inexpressible, strange eyes, methought I peeped to secrets which took hold of God. As Abraham before the angels, I bowed myself; the white thing was so white, its wings so wide, and in those for ever exiled waters, I had lost the miserable warping memories of traditions and of towns. Long I gazed at that prodigy of plumage. I cannot tell, can only hint, the things that darted through me then. But at last I awoke; and turning, asked a sailor what bird was this. A goney, he replied. Goney! Never had heard that name before; is it conceivable that this glorious thing is utterly unknown to men ashore! Never! But some time after, I learned that goney was some seaman's name for albatross. So that by no possibility could Coleridge's wild Rhyme have had aught to do with those mystical impressions which were mine, when I saw that bird upon our deck. For neither had I then read the Rhyme, nor knew the bird to be an albatross. Yet, in saying this, I do but indirectly burnish a little brighter the noble merit of the poem and the poet.

I assert, then, that in the wondrous bodily whiteness of the bird chiefly lurks the secret of the spell; a truth the more evinced in this, that by a solecism of terms there are birds called grey albatrosses; and these I have frequently seen, but never with such emotions as when I beheld the Antarctic fowl.

But how had the mystic thing been caught? Whisper it not, and I will tell; with a treacherous hook and line, as the fowl floated on the sea. At last the Captain made a postman of it; tying a lettered, leathern tally round its neck, with the ship's time and place; and then letting it escape. But I doubt not, that leathern tally, meant for man, was taken off in Heaven, when the white fowl flew to join the wing-folding, the invoking, and adoring cherubim!

Most famous in our Western annals and Indian traditions is that of the White Steed of the Prairies; a magnificent milk-white charger, large-eyed, small-headed, bluff-chested, and with the dignity of a thousand monarchs in his lofty, overscorning carriage. He was the elected Xerxes of vast herds of wild horses, whose pastures in those days were only fenced by the Rocky Mountains and the Alleghanies. At their flaming head he westward trooped it like that chosen star which every evening leads on the hosts of light. The flashing cascade of his mane, the curving comet of his tail, invested him with housings more resplendent than gold and silver-beaters could have furnished him. A most imperial and archangelical apparition of that unfallen, western world, which to the eyes of the old trappers and hunters revived the glories of those primeval times when Adam walked majestic as a god, bluff-browed and fearless as this mighty steed. Whether marching amid his aides and marshals in the van of countless cohorts that endlessly streamed it over the plains, like an Ohio; or whether with his circumambient subjects browsing all around at the horizon, the White Steed gallopingly reviewed them with warm nostrils reddening through his cool milkiness; in whatever aspect he presented himself, always to the bravest Indians he was the object of trembling reverence and awe. Nor can it be questioned from what stands on legendary record of this noble horse, that it was his spiritual whiteness chiefly, which so clothed him with divineness; and that this divineness had that in it which, though commanding worship, at the same time enforced a certain nameless terror.

But there are other instances where this whiteness loses all that accessory and strange glory which invests it in the White Steed and Albatross.

What is it that in the Albino man so peculiarly repels and often shocks the eye, as that sometimes he is loathed by his own kith and kin! It is that whiteness which invests him, a thing expressed by the name he bears. The Albino is as well made as other men—has no substantive deformity—and yet this mere aspect of all-pervading whiteness makes him more strangely hideous than the ugliest abortion. Why should this be so?

Nor, in quite other aspects, does Nature in her least palpable but not the less malicious agencies, fail to enlist among her forces this crowning attribute of the terrible. From its snowy aspect, the gauntleted ghost of the Southern Seas has been denominated the White Squall. Nor, in some historic instances, has the art of human malice omitted so potent an auxiliary. How wildly it heightens the effect of that passage in Froissart, when, masked in the snowy symbol of their faction, the desperate White Hoods of Ghent murder their bailiff in the market-place!

Nor, in some things, does the common, hereditary experience of all mankind fail to bear witness to the supernaturalism of this hue. It cannot well be doubted, that the one visible quality in the aspect of the dead which most indeed that pallor were as much like the badge of consternation in the other world, as of mortal trepidation here. And from that pallor of the dead, we borrow the expressive hue of the shroud in which we wrap them. Nor even in our superstitions do we fail to throw the same snowy mantle round our phantoms; all ghosts rising in a milk-white fog—Yea, while these terrors seize us, let us add, that even the king of terrors, when personified by the evangelist, rides on his pallid horse.

Therefore, in his other moods, symbolize whatever grand or gracious thing he will by whiteness, no man can deny that in its profoundest idealized significance it calls up a peculiar apparition to the soul.

But though without dissent this point be fixed, how is mortal man to account for it? To analyse it, would seem impossible. Can we, then, by the citation of some of those instances wherein this thing of whiteness—though for the time either wholly or in great part stripped of all direct associations calculated to impart to it aught fearful, but nevertheless, is found to exert over us the same sorcery, however modified;—can we thus hope to light upon some chance clue to conduct us to the hidden cause we seek?

Let us try. But in a matter like this, subtlety appeals to subtlety, and without imagination no man can follow another into these halls. And though, doubtless, some at least of the imaginative impressions about to be presented may have been shared by most men, yet few perhaps were entirely conscious of them at the time, and therefore may not be able to recall them now.

Why to the man of untutored ideality, who happens to be but loosely acquainted with the peculiar character of the day, does the bare mention of Whitsuntide marshal in the fancy such long, dreary, speechless processions of slow-pacing pilgrims, down-cast and hooded with new-fallen snow? Or, to the unread, unsophisticated Protestant of the Middle American States, why does the passing mention of a White Friar or a White Nun, evoke such an eyeless statue in the soul?

Or what is there apart from the traditions of dungeoned warriors and kings (which will not wholly account for it) that makes the White Tower of London tell so much more strongly on the imagination of an untravelled American, than those other storied structures, its neighbors—the Byward Tower, or even the Bloody? And those sublimer towers, the White Mountains of New Hampshire, whence, in peculiar moods, comes that gigantic ghostliness over the soul at the bare mention of that name, while the thought of Virginia's Blue Ridge is full of a soft, dewy, distant dreaminess? Or why, irrespective of all latitudes and longitudes, does the name of the White Sea exert such a spectralness over the fancy, while that of the Yellow Sea lulls us with mortal thoughts of long lacquered mild afternoons on the waves, followed by the gaudiest and yet sleepiest of sunsets? Or, to choose a wholly unsubstantial instance, purely addressed to the fancy, why, in reading the old fairy tales of Central Europe, does "the tall pale man" of the Hartz forests, whose changeless pallor unrustlingly glides through the green of the groves—why is this phantom more terrible than all the whooping imps of the Blocksburg?

Nor is it, altogether, the remembrance of her cathedral-toppling earthquakes; nor the stampedoes of her frantic seas; nor the tearlessness of arid skies that never rain; nor the sight of her wide field of leaning spires, wrenched cope-stones, and crosses all adroop (like canted yards of anchored fleets); and her suburban avenues of house-walls lying over upon each other, as a tossed pack of cards;—it is not these things alone which make tearless Lima, the strangest, saddest city thou can'st see. For Lima has taken the white veil; and there is a higher horror in this whiteness of her woe. Old as Pizarro, this whiteness keeps her ruins for ever new; admits not the cheerful greenness of complete decay; spreads over her broken ramparts the rigid pallor of an apoplexy that fixes its own distortions.

I know that, to the common apprehension, this phenomenon of whiteness is not confessed to be the prime agent in exaggerating the terror of objects otherwise terrible; nor to the unimaginative mind is there aught of terror in those appearances whose awfulness to another mind almost solely consists in this one phenomenon, especially when exhibited under any form at all approaching to muteness or universality. What I mean by these two statements may perhaps be respectively elucidated by the following examples.

First: The mariner, when drawing nigh the coasts of foreign lands, if by night he hear the roar of breakers, starts to vigilance, and feels just enough of trepidation to sharpen all his faculties; but under precisely similar circumstances, let him be called from his hammock to view his ship sailing through a midnight sea of milky whiteness—as if from encircling headlands shoals of combed white bears were swimming round him, then he feels a silent, superstitious dread; the shrouded phantom of the whitened waters is horrible to him as a real ghost; in vain the lead assures him he is still off soundings; heart and helm they both go down; he never rests till blue water is under him again. Yet where is the mariner who will tell thee, "Sir, it was not so much the fear of striking hidden rocks, as the fear of that hideous whiteness that so stirred me?"

Second: To the native Indian of Peru, the continual sight of the snowhowdahed Andes conveys naught of dread, except, perhaps, in the mere fancying of the eternal frosted desolateness reigning at such vast altitudes, and the natural conceit of what a fearfulness it would be to lose oneself in such inhuman solitudes. Much the same is it with the backwoodsman of the West, who with comparative indifference views an unbounded prairie sheeted with driven snow, no shadow of tree or twig to break the fixed trance of whiteness. Not so the sailor, beholding the scenery of the Antarctic seas; where at times, by some infernal trick of legerdemain in the powers of frost and air, he, shivering and half shipwrecked, instead of rainbows speaking hope and solace to his misery, views what seems a boundless churchyard grinning upon him with its lean ice monuments and splintered crosses.

But thou sayest, methinks that white-lead chapter about whiteness is but a white flag hung out from a craven soul; thou surrenderest to a hypo, Ishmael.

Tell me, why this strong young colt, foaled in some peaceful valley of Vermont, far removed from all beasts of prey—why is it that upon the sunniest day, if you but shake a fresh buffalo robe behind him, so that he cannot even see it, but only smells its wild animal muskiness—why will he start, snort, and with bursting eyes paw the ground in phrensies of affright? There is no remembrance in him of any gorings of wild creatures in his green northern home, so that the strange muskiness he smells cannot recall to him anything associated with the experience of former perils; for what knows he, this New England colt, of the black bisons of distant Oregon?

No; but here thou beholdest even in a dumb brute, the instinct of the knowledge of the demonism in the world. Though thousands of miles from Oregon, still when he smells that savage musk, the rending, goring bison herds are as present as to the deserted wild foal of the prairies, which this instant they may be trampling into dust.

Thus, then, the muffled rollings of a milky sea; the bleak rustlings of the festooned frosts of mountains; the desolate shiftings of the windrowed snows of prairies; all these, to Ishmael, are as the shaking of that buffalo robe to the frightened colt!

Though neither knows where lie the nameless things of which the mystic sign gives forth such hints; yet with me, as with the colt, somewhere those things must exist. Though in many of its aspects this visible world seems formed in love, the invisible spheres were formed in fright.

But not yet have we solved the incantation of this whiteness, and learned why it appeals with such power to the soul; and more strange and far more portentous—why, as we have seen, it is at once the most meaning symbol of spiritual things, nay, the very veil of the Christian's Deity; and yet should be as it is, the intensifying agent in things the most appalling to mankind.

Is it that by its indefiniteness it shadows forth the heartless voids and immensities of the universe, and thus stabs us from behind with the thought of annihilation, when beholding the white depths of the milky way? Or is it, that as in essence whiteness is not so much a colour as the visible absence of colour; and at the same time the concrete of all colours; is it for these reasons that there is such a dumb blankness, full of meaning, in a wide landscape of snows—a colourless, all-colour of atheism from which we shrink? And when we consider that other theory of the natural philosophers, that all other earthly hues—every stately or lovely emblazoning—the sweet tinges of sunset skies and woods; yea, and the gilded velvets of butterflies, and the butterfly cheeks of young girls; all these are but subtile deceits, not actually inherent in substances, but only laid on from without; so that all deified Nature absolutely paints like the harlot, whose allurements cover nothing but the charnel-house within; and when we proceed further, and consider that the mystical cosmetic which produces every one of her hues, the great principle of light, for ever remains white or colourless in itself, and if operating without medium upon matter, would touch all objects, even tulips and roses, with its own blank tinge—pondering all this, the palsied universe lies before us a leper; and like wilful travellers in Lapland, who refuse to wear coloured and colouring glasses upon their eyes, so the wretched infidel gazes himself blind at the monumental white shroud that wraps all the prospect around him. And of all these things the Albino whale was the symbol. Wonder ye then at the fiery hunt?

Topics for Discussion

1. Why does Thomas Hardy sandwich the story of the three strangers with descriptions of nature?
2. Interpret the spatial and temporal dimensions in Hardy's descriptions of nature.
3. What kind of man-nature relationship is depicted in *Moby Dick*?
4. Is nature in *Moby Dick* a pure spatial background? Why or why not?
5. How to judge the aesthetic value of nature in Hardy's and Melville's fictions?
6. Give more literary examples with contemplations on man-nature relationship.

Monograph Eight   Literature and the Self

I Walden, or Life in the Woods

(Excerpt)

Henry David Thoreau (1817-1862)

At a certain season of our life we are accustomed to consider every spot as the possible site of a house. I have thus surveyed the country on every side within a dozen miles of where I live. In imagination I have bought all the farms in succession, for all were to be bought, and I knew their price. I walked over each farmer's premises, tasted his wild apples, discoursed on husbandry with him, took his farm at his price, at any price, mortgaging it to him in my mind; even put a higher price on it—took everything but a deed of it—took his word for his deed, for I dearly love to talk—cultivated it, and him too to some extent, I trust, and withdrew when I had enjoyed it long enough, leaving him to carry it on. This experience entitled me to be regarded as a sort of real-estate broker by my friends. Wherever I sat, there I might live, and the landscape radiated from me accordingly. What is a house but a sedes, a seat?—better if a country seat. I discovered many a site for a house not likely to be soon improved, which some might have thought too far from the village, but to my eyes the village was too far from it. Well, there I might live, I said; and there I did live, for an hour, a summer and a winter life; saw how I could let the years run off, buffet the winter through, and see the spring come in.

The future inhabitants of this region, wherever they may place their houses, may be sure that they have been anticipated. An afternoon sufficed to lay out the land into orchard, wood-lot, and pasture, and to decide what fine oaks or pines should be left to stand before the door, and whence each blasted tree could be seen to the best advantage; and then I let it lie, fallow, perchance, for a man is rich in proportion to the number of things which he can afford to let alone.

My imagination carried me so far that I even had the refusal of several farms—the refusal was all I wanted—but I never got my fingers burned by actual possession. The nearest that I came to actual possession was when I bought the Hollowell place, and had begun to sort my seeds, and collected materials with which to make a wheelbarrow to carry it on or off with; but before the owner gave me a deed of it, his wife— every man has such a wife— changed her mind and wished to keep it, and he offered me ten dollars to release him. Now, to speak the truth, I had but ten cents in the world, and it surpassed my arithmetic to tell, if I was that man who had ten cents, or who had a farm, or ten dollars, or all together. However, I let him keep the ten dollars and the farm too, for I had carried it far enough; or rather, to be generous, I sold him the farm for just what I gave for it, and, as he was not a rich man, made him a present of ten dollars, and still had my ten cents, and seeds, and materials for a wheelbarrow left. I found thus that I had been a rich man without any damage to my poverty. But I retained the landscape, and I have since annually carried off what it yielded without a wheelbarrow. With respect to landscapes.

"I am monarch of all I survey,
My right there is none to dispute."

I have frequently seen a poet withdraw, having enjoyed the most valuable part of a farm, while the crusty farmer supposed that he had got a few wild apples only. Why, the owner does not know it for many years when a poet has put his farm in rhyme, the most admirable kind of invisible fence, has fairly impounded it, milked it, skimmed it, and got all the cream, and left the farmer only the skimmed milk.

The real attractions of the Hollowell farm, to me, were: its complete retirement, being, about two miles from the village, half a mile from the nearest neighbor, and separated from the highway by a broad field; its bounding on the river, which the owner said protected it by its fogs from frosts in the spring, though that was nothing to me; the gray color and ruinous state of the house and barn, and the dilapidated fences, which put such an interval between me and the last occupant; the hollow and lichen-covered apple trees, nawed by rabbits, showing what kind of neighbors I should have; but above all, the recollection I had of it from my earliest voyages up the river, when the house was concealed behind a dense grove of red maples, through which I heard the house-dog bark. I was in haste to buy it, before the proprietor finished getting out some rocks, cutting down the hollow apple trees, and grubbing up some young birches which had sprung up in the pasture, or, in short, had made any more of his improvements. To enjoy these advantages I was ready to carry it on; like Atlas, to take the world on my shoulders- I never heard what compensation he received for that- and do all those things which had no other motive or excuse but that I might pay for it and be unmolested in my possession of it; for I knew all the while that it would yield the most abundant crop of the kind I wanted, if I could only afford to let it alone. But it turned out as I have said.

All that I could say, then, with respect to farming on a large scale—I have always cultivated a garden—was, that I had had my seeds ready. Many think that seeds improve with age. I have no doubt that time discriminates between the good and the bad; and when at last I shall plant, I shall be less likely to be disappointed. But I would say to my fellows, once for all, As long as possible live free and uncommitted. It makes but little difference whether you are committed to a farm or the county jail.

Old Cato, whose "*De Re Rustica*"is my "*Cultivator*," says—and the only translation I have seen makes sheer nonsense of the passage—"When you think of getting a farm turn it thus in your mind, not to buy greedily; nor spare your pains to look at it, and do not think it enough to go round it once. The oftener you go there the more it will please you, if it is good."I think I shall not buy greedily, but go round and round it as long as I live, and be buried in it first, that it may please me the more at last.

The present was my next experiment of this kind, which I purpose to describe more at length, for convenience putting the experience of two years into one. As I have said, I do not propose to write an ode to dejection, but to brag as lustily as chanticleer in the morning, standing on his roost, if only to wake my neighbors up.

When first I took up my abode in the woods, that is, began to spend my nights as well as days there, which, by accident, was on Independence Day, or the Fourth of July, 1845, my house was not finished for winter, but was merely a defence against the rain, without plastering or chimney, the walls being of rough, weather-stained boards, with wide chinks, which made it cool at night. The upright white hewn studs and freshly planed door and window casings gave it a clean and airy look, especially in the morning, when its timbers were saturated with dew, so that I fancied that by noon some sweet gum would exude from them. To my imagination it retained throughout the day more or less of this auroral character, reminding me of a certain house on a mountain which I had visited a year before. This was an airy and unplastered cabin, fit to entertain a travelling god, and where a goddess might trail her garments. The winds which passed over my dwelling were such as sweep over the ridges of mountains, bearing the broken strains, or celestial parts only, of terrestrial music. The morning wind forever blows, the poem of creation is uninterrupted; but few are the ears that hear it. Olympus is but the outside of the earth everywhere.

The only house I had been the owner of before, if I except a boat, was a tent, which I used occasionally when making excursions in the summer, and this is still rolled up in my garret; but the boat, after passing from hand to hand, has gone down the stream of time. With this more substantial shelter about me, I had made some progress toward settling in the world. This frame, so slightly clad, was a sort of crystallization around me, and reacted on the builder. It was suggestive somewhat as a picture in outlines. I did not need to go outdoors to take the air, for the atmosphere within had lost none of its freshness. It was not so much within doors as behind a door where I sat, even in the rainiest weather. The Harivansa says, "An abode without birds is like a meat without seasoning."Such was not my abode, for I found myself suddenly neighbor to the birds; not by having imprisoned one, but having caged myself near them. I was not only nearer to some of those which commonly frequent the garden and the orchard, but to those smaller and more thrilling songsters of the forest which never, or rarely, serenade a villager—the wood thrush, the veery, the scarlet tanager, the field sparrow, the whip-poor-will, and many others.

I was seated by the shore of a small pond, about a mile and a half south of the village of Concord and somewhat higher than it, in the midst of an extensive wood between that town and Lincoln, and about two miles south of that our only field known to fame, Concord Battle Ground; but I was so low in the woods that the opposite shore, half a mile off, like the rest, covered with wood, was my most distant horizon. For the first week, whenever I looked out on the pond it impressed me like a tarn high up on the side of a mountain, its bottom far above the surface of other lakes, and, as the sun arose, I saw it throwing off its nightly clothing of mist, and here and there, by degrees, its soft ripples or its smooth reflecting surface was revealed, while the mists, like ghosts, were stealthily withdrawing in every direction into the woods, as at the breaking up of some nocturnal conventicle. The very dew seemed to hang upon the trees later into the day than usual, as on the sides of mountains.

This small lake was of most value as a neighbor in the intervals of a gentle rain-storm in August, when, both air and water being perfectly still, but the sky overcast, mid-afternoon had all the serenity of evening, and the wood thrush sang around, and was heard from shore to shore. A lake like this is never smoother than at such a time; and the clear portion of the air above it being, shallow and darkened by clouds, the water, full of light and reflections, becomes a lower heaven itself so much the more important. From a hill-top near by, where the wood had been recently cut off, there was a pleasing vista southward across the pond, through a wide indentation in the hills which form the shore there, where their opposite sides sloping toward each other suggested a stream flowing out in that direction through a wooded valley, but stream there was none. That way I looked between and over the near green hills to some distant and higher ones in the horizon, tinged with blue. Indeed, by standing on tiptoe I could catch a glimpse of some of the peaks of the still bluer and more distant mountain ranges in the northwest, those true-blue coins from heaven's own mint, and also of some portion of the village. But in other directions, even from this point, I could not see over or beyond the woods which surrounded me. It is well to have some water in your neighborhood, to give buoyancy to and float the earth. One value even of the smallest well is, that when you look into it you see that earth is not continent but insular. This is as important as that it keeps butter cool. When I looked across the pond from this peak toward the Sudbury meadows, which in time of flood I distinguished elevated perhaps by a mirage in their seething valley, like a coin in a basin, all the earth beyond the pond appeared like a thin crust insulated and floated even by this small sheet of interverting water, and I was reminded that this on which I dwelt was but dry land.

Though the view from my door was still more contracted, I did not feel crowded or confined in the least. There was pasture enough for my imagination. The low shrub oak plateau to which the opposite shore arose stretched away toward the prairies of the West and the steppes of Tartary, affording ample room for all the roving families of men. "There are none happy in the world but beings who enjoy freely a vast horizon"— said Damodara, when his herds required new and larger pastures.

Both place and time were changed, and I dwelt nearer to those parts of the universe and to those eras in history which had most attracted me. Where I lived was as far off as many a region viewed nightly by astronomers. We are wont to imagine rare and delectable places in some remote and more celestial corner of the system, behind the constellation of Cassiopeia's Chair, far from noise and disturbance. I discovered that my house actually had its site in such a withdrawn, but forever new and unprofaned, part of the universe. If it were worth the while to settle in those parts near to the Pleiades or the Hyades, to Aldebaran or Altair, then I was really there, or at an equal remoteness from the life which I had left behind, dwindled and twinkling with as fine a ray to my nearest neighbor, and to be seen only in moonless nights by him. Such was that part of creation where I had squatted;

"There was a shepherd that did live
And held his thoughts as high
As were the mounts whereon his flocks
Did hourly feed him by."

What should we think of the shepherd's life if his flocks always wandered to higher pastures than his thoughts?

Every morning was a cheerful invitation to make my life of equal simplicity, and I may say innocence, with Nature herself. I have been as sincere a worshipper of Aurora as the Greeks. I got up early and bathed in the pond; that was a religious exercise, and one of the best things which I did. They say that characters were engraven on the bathing tub of King Tching-thang to this effect: "Renew thyself completely each day; do it again, and again, and forever again."I can understand that. Morning brings back the heroic ages. I was as much affected by the faint burn of a mosquito making its invisible and unimaginable tour through my apartment at earliest dawn, when I was sitting with door and windows open, as I could be by any trumpet that ever sang of fame. It was Homer's requiem; itself an Iliad and Odyssey in the air, singing its own wrath and wanderings. There was something cosmical about it; a standing advertisement, till forbidden, of the everlasting vigor and fertility of the world. The morning, which is the most memorable season of the day, is the awakening hour. Then there is least somnolence in us; and for an hour, at least, some part of us awakes which slumbers all the rest of the day and night. Little is to be expected of that day, if it can be called a day, to which we are not awakened by our Genius, but by the mechanical nudgings of some servitor, are not awakened by our own newly acquired force and aspirations from within, accompanied by the undulations of celestial music, instead of factory bells, and a fragrance filling the air- to a higher life than we fell asleep from; and thus thc darkness bear its fruit, and prove itself to be good, no less than the light. That man who does not believe that each day contains an earlier, more sacred, and auroral hour than he has yet profaned, has despaired of life, and is pursuing a descending and darkening way. After a partial cessation of his sensuous life, the soul of man, or its organs rather, are reinvigorated each day, and his Genius tries again what noble life it can make. All memorable events, I should say, transpire in morning time and in a morning atmosphere. The Vedas say, "All intelligences awake with the morning."Poetry and art, and the fairest and most memorable of the actions of men, date from such an hour. All poets and heroes, like Memnon, are the children of Aurora, and emit their music at sunrise. To him whose elastic and vigorous thought keeps pace with the sun, the day is a perpetual morning. It matters not what the clocks say or the attitudes and labors of men. Morning is when I am awake and there is a dawn in me. Moral reform is the effort to throw off sleep. Why is it that men give so poor an account of their day if they have not been slumbering? They are not such poor calculators. If they had not been overcome with drowsiness, they would have performed something. The millions are awake enough for physical labor; but only one in a million is awake enough for effective intellectual exertion, only one in a hundred millions to a poetic or divine life. To be awake is to be alive. I have never yet met a man who was quite awake. How could I have looked him in the face?

We must learn to reawaken and keep ourselves awake, not by mechanical aids, but by an infinite expectation of the dawn, which does not forsake us in our soundest sleep. I know of no more encouraging fact than the unquestionable ability of man to elevate his life by a conscious endeavor. It is something to be able to paint a particular picture, or to carve a statue, and so to make a few objects beautiful; but it is far more glorious to carve and paint the very atmosphere and medium through which we look, which morally we can do. To affect the quality of the day, that is the highest of arts. Every man is tasked to make his life, even in its details, worthy of the contemplation of his most elevated and critical hour. If we refused, or rather used up, such paltry information as we get, the oracles would distinctly inform us how this might be done.

I went to the woods because I wished to live deliberately, to front only the essential facts of life, and see if I could not learn what it had to teach, and not, when I came to die, discover that I had not lived. I did not wish to live what was not life, living is so dear; nor did I wish to practise resignation, unless it was quite necessary. I wanted to live deep and suck out all the marrow of life, to live so sturdily and Spartan-like as to put to rout all that was not life, to cut a broad swath and shave close, to drive life into a corner, and reduce it to its lowest terms, and, if it proved to be mean, why then to get the whole and genuine meanness of it, and publish its meanness to the world; or if it were sublime, to know it by experience, and be able to give a true account of it in my next excursion. For most men, it appears to me, are in a strange certainty about it, whether it is of the devil or of God, and have somewhat hastily concluded that it is the chief end of man here to "glorify God and enjoy him forever."

Still we live meanly, like ants; though the fable tells us that we were long ago changed into men; like pygmies we fight with cranes; it is error upon error, and clout upon clout, and our best virtue has for its occasion a superfluous and evitable wretchedness. Our life is frittered away by detail. An honest man has hardly need to count more than his ten fingers, or in extreme cases he may add his ten toes, and lump the rest. Simplicity, simplicity, simplicity! I say, let your affairs be as two or three, and not a hundred or a thousand; instead of a million count half a dozen, and keep your accounts on your thumb-nail. In the midst of this chopping sea of civilized life, such are the clouds and storms and quicksands and thousand-and-one items to be allowed for, that a man has to live, if he would not founder and go to the bottom and not make his port at all, by dead reckoning, and he must be a great calculator indeed who succeeds. Simplify, simplify. Instead of three meals a day, if it be necessary eat but one; instead of a hundred dishes, five; and reduce other things in proportion. Our life is like a German Confederacy, made up of petty states, with its boundary forever fluctuating, so that even a German cannot tell you how it is bounded at any moment. The nation itself, with all its so- called internal improvements, which, by the way are all external and superficial, is just such an unwieldy and overgrown establishment, cluttered with furniture and tripped up by its own traps, ruined by luxury and heedless expense, by want of calculation and a worthy aim, as the million households in the land; and the only cure for it, as for them, is in a rigid economy, a stern and more than Spartan simplicity of life and elevation of purpose. It lives too fast. Men think that it is essential that the Nation have commerce, and export ice, and talk through a telegraph, and ride thirty miles an hour, without a doubt, whether they do or not; but whether we should live like baboons or like men, is a little uncertain. If we do not get out sleepers, and forge rails, and devote days and nights to the work, but go to tinkering upon our lives to improve them, who will build railroads? And if railroads are not built, how shall we get to heaven in season? But if we stay at home and mind our business, who will want railroads? We do not ride on the railroad; it rides upon us. Did you ever think what those sleepers are that underlie the railroad? Each one is a man, an Irishman, or a Yankee man. The rails are laid on them, and they are covered with sand, and the cars run smoothly over them. They are sound sleepers, I assure you. And every few years a new lot is laid down and run over; so that, if some have the pleasure of riding on a rail, others have the misfortune to be ridden upon. And when they run over a man that is walking in his sleep, a supernumerary sleeper in the wrong position, and wake him up, they suddenly stop the cars, and make a hue and cry about it, as if this were an exception. I am glad to know that it takes a gang of men for every five miles to keep the sleepers down and level in their beds as it is, for this is a sign that they may sometime get up again.

Why should we live with such hurry and waste of life? We are determined to be starved before we are hungry. Men say that a stitch in time saves nine, and so they take a thousand stitches today to save nine tomorrow. As for work, we haven't any of any consequence. We have Saint Vitus' dance, and cannot possibly keep our heads still. If I should only give a few pulls at the parish bell-rope, as for a fire, that is, without setting the bell, there is hardly a man on his farm in the outskirts of Concord, notwithstanding that press of engagements which was his excuse so many times this morning, nor a boy, nor a woman, I might almost say, but would forsake all and follow that sound, not mainly to save property from the flames, but, if we will confess the truth, much more to see it burn, since burn it must, and we, be it known, did not set it on fire- or to see it put out, and have a hand in it, if that is done as handsomely; yes, even if it were the parish church itself. Hardly a man takes a half-hour's nap after dinner, but when he wakes he holds up his head and asks, "What's the news?"as if the rest of mankind had stood his sentinels. Some give directions to be waked every half-hour, doubtless for no other purpose; and then, to pay for it, they tell what they have dreamed. After a night's sleep the news is as indispensable as the breakfast. "Pray tell me anything new that has happened to a man anywhere on this globe"—and he reads it over his coffee and rolls, that a man has had his eyes gouged out this morning on the Wachito River; never dreaming the while that he lives in the dark unfathomed mammoth cave of this world, and has but the rudiment of an eye himself.

For my part, I could easily do without the post-office. I think that there are very few important communications made through it. To speak critically, I never received more than one or two letters in my life—I wrote this some years ago— that were worth the postage. The penny-post is, commonly, an institution through which you seriously offer a man that penny for his thoughts which is so often safely offered in jest. And I am sure that I never read any memorable news in a newspaper. If we read of one man robbed, or murdered, or killed by accident, or one house burned, or one vessel wrecked, or one steamboat blown up, or one cow run over on the Western Railroad, or one mad dog killed, or one lot of grasshoppers in the winter—we never need read of another. One is enough. If you are acquainted with the principle, what do you care for a myriad instances and applications? To a philosopher all news, as it is called, is gossip, and they who edit and read it are old women over their tea. Yet not a few are greedy after this gossip. There was such a rush, as I hear, the other day at one of the offices to learn the foreign news by the last arrival, that several large squares of plate glass belonging to the establishment were broken by the pressure—news which I seriously think a ready wit might write a twelve-month, or twelve years, beforehand with sufficient accuracy. As for Spain, for instance, if you know how to throw in Don Carlos and the Infanta, and Don Pedro and Seville and Granada, from time to time in the right proportions—they may have changed the names a little since I saw the papers—and serve up a bull-fight when other entertainments fail, it will be true to the letter, and give us as good an idea of the exact state or ruin of things in Spain as the most succinct and lucid reports under this head in the newspapers: and as for England, almost the last significant scrap of news from that quarter was the revolution of 1649; and if you have learned the history of her crops for an average year, you never need attend to that thing again, unless your speculations are of a merely pecuniary character. If one may judge who rarely looks into the newspapers, nothing new does ever happen in foreign parts, a French revolution not excepted.

What news! how much more important to know what that is which was never old! "Kieou-he-yu (great dignitary of the state of Wei) sent a man to Khoung-tseu to know his news. Khoung-tseu caused the messenger to be seated near him, and questioned him in these terms: What is your master doing? The messenger answered with respect: My master desires to diminish the number of his faults, but he cannot come to the end of them. The messenger being gone, the philosopher remarked: What a worthy messenger! "What a worthy messenger!"The preacher, instead of vexing the ears of drowsy farmers on their day of rest at the end of the week—for Sunday is the fit conclusion of an ill-spent week, and not the fresh and brave beginning of a new one—with this one other draggle-tail of a sermon, should shout with thundering voice, "Pause! Avast! Why so seeming fast, but deadly slow?"

Shams and delusions are esteemed for soundest truths, while reality is fabulous. If men would steadily observe realities only, and not allow themselves to be deluded, life, to compare it with such things as we know, would be like a fairy tale and the Arabian Nights' Entertainments. If we respected only what is inevitable and has a right to be, music and poetry would resound along the streets. When we are unhurried and wise, we perceive that only great and worthy things have any permanent and absolute existence, that petty fears and petty pleasures are but the shadow of the reality. This is always exhilarating and sublime. By closing the eyes and slumbering, and consenting to be deceived by shows, men establish and confirm their daily life of routine and habit everywhere, which still is built on purely illusory foundations. Children, who play life, discern its true law and relations more clearly than men, who fail to live it worthily, but who think that they are wiser by experience, that is, by failure. I have read in a Hindoo book, that "there was a king's son, who, being expelled in infancy from his native city, was brought up by a forester, and, growing up to maturity in that state, imagined himself to belong to the barbarous race with which he lived. One of his father's ministers having discovered him, revealed to him what he was, and the misconception of his character was removed, and he knew himself to be a prince. So soul," continues the Hindoo philosopher, "from the circumstances in which it is placed, mistakes its own character, until the truth is revealed to it by some holy teacher, and then it knows itself to be Brahme."I perceive that we inhabitants of New England live this mean life that we do because our vision does not penetrate the surface of things. We think that that is which appears to be. If a man should walk through this town and see only the reality, where, think you, would the "Mill-dam"go to? If he should give us an account of the realities he beheld there, we should not recognize the place in his description. Look at a meeting-house, or a court-house, or a jail, or a shop, or a dwelling-house, and say what that thing really is before a true gaze, and they would all go to pieces in your account of them. Men esteem truth remote, in the outskirts of the system, behind the farthest star, before Adam and after the last man. In eternity there is indeed something true and sublime. But all these times and places and occasions are now and here. God himself culminates in the present moment, and will never be more divine in the lapse of all the ages. And we are enabled to apprehend at all what is sublime and noble only by the perpetual instilling and drenching of the reality that surrounds us. The universe constantly and obediently answers to our conceptions; whether we travel fast or slow, the track is laid for us. Let us spend our lives in conceiving then. The poet or the artist never yet had so fair and noble a design but some of his posterity at least could accomplish it.

Let us spend one day as deliberately as Nature, and not be thrown off the track by every nutshell and mosquito's wing that falls on the rails. Let us rise early and fast, or break fast, gently and without perturbation; let company come and let company go, let the bells ring and the children cry—determined to make a day of it. Why should we knock under and go with the stream? Let us not be upset and overwhelmed in that terrible rapid and whirlpool called a dinner, situated in the meridian shallows. Weather this danger and you are safe, for the rest of the way is down hill. With unrelaxed nerves, with morning vigor, sail by it, looking another way, tied to the mast like Ulysses. If the engine whistles, let it whistle till it is hoarse for its pains. If the bell rings, why should we run? We will consider what kind of music they are like. Let us settle ourselves, and work and wedge our feet downward through the mud and slush of opinion, and prejudice, and tradition, and delusion, and appearance, that alluvion which covers the globe, through Paris and London, through New York and Boston and Concord, through Church and State, through poetry and philosophy and religion, till we come to a hard bottom and rocks in place, which we can call reality, and say, This is, and no mistake; and then begin, having a point d'appui, below freshet and frost and fire, a place where you might found a wall or a state, or set a lamp-post safely, or perhaps a gauge, not a Nilometer, but a Realometer, that future ages might know how deep a freshet of shams and appearances had gathered from time to time. If you stand right fronting and face to face to a fact, you will see the sun glimmer on both its surfaces, as if it were a cimeter, and feel its sweet edge dividing you through the heart and marrow, and so you will happily conclude your mortal career. Be it life or death, we crave only reality. If we are really dying, let us hear the rattle in our throats and feel cold in the extremities; if we are alive, let us go about our business.

Time is but the stream I go a-fishing in. I drink at it; but while I drink I see the sandy bottom and detect how shallow it is. Its thin current slides away, but eternity remains. I would drink deeper; fish in the sky, whose bottom is pebbly with stars. I cannot count one. I know not the first letter of the alphabet. I have always been regretting that I was not as wise as the day I was born. The intellect is a cleaver; it discerns and rifts its way into the secret of things. I do not wish to be any more busy with my hands than is necessary. My head is hands and feet. I feel all my best faculties concentrated in it. My instinct tells me that my head is an organ for burrowing, as some creatures use their snout and fore paws, and with it I would mine and burrow my way through these hills. I think that the richest vein is somewhere hereabouts; so by the divining-rod and thin rising vapors I judge; and here I will begin to mine.

With a little more deliberation in the choice of their pursuits, all men would perhaps become essentially students and observers, for certainly their nature and destiny are interesting to all alike. In accumulating property for ourselves or our posterity, in founding a family or a state, or acquiring fame even, we are mortal; but in dealing with truth we are immortal, and need fear no change nor accident. The oldest Egyptian or Hindoo philosopher raised a corner of the veil from the statue of the divinity; and still the trembling robe remains raised, and I gaze upon as fresh a glory as he did, since it was I in him that was then so bold, and it is he in me that now reviews the vision. No dust has settled on that robe; no time has elapsed since that divinity was revealed. That time which we really improve, or which is improvable, is neither past, present, nor future.

My residence was more favorable, not only to thought, but to serious reading, than a university; and though I was beyond the range of the ordinary circulating library, I had more than ever come within the influence of those books which circulate round the world, whose sentences were first written on bark, and are now merely copied from time to time on to linen paper. Says the poet Mir Camar Uddin Mast, "Being seated, to run through the region of the spiritual world; I have had this advantage in books. To be intoxicated by a single glass of wine; I have experienced this pleasure when I have drunk the liquor of the esoteric doctrines."I kept Homer's *Iliad* on my table through the summer, though I looked at his page only now and then. Incessant labor with my hands, at first, for I had my house to finish and my beans to hoe at the same time, made more study impossible. Yet I sustained myself by the prospect of such reading in future. I read one or two shallow books of travel in the intervals of my work, till that employment made me ashamed of myself, and I asked where it was then that I lived.

The student may read Homer or Aeschylus in the Greek without danger of dissipation or luxuriousness, for it implies that he in some measure emulate their heroes, and consecrate morning hours to their pages. The heroic books, even if printed in the character of our mother tongue, will always be in a language dead to degenerate times; and we must laboriously seek the meaning of each word and line, conjecturing a larger sense than common use permits out of what wisdom and valor and generosity we have. The modern cheap and fertile press, with all its translations, has done little to bring us nearer to the heroic writers of antiquity. They seem as solitary, and the letter in which they are printed as rare and curious, as ever. It is worth the expense of youthful days and costly hours, if you learn only some words of an ancient language, which are raised out of the trivialness of the street, to be perpetual suggestions and provocations. It is not in vain that the farmer remembers and repeats the few Latin words which he has heard. Men sometimes speak as if the study of the classics would at length make way for more modern and practical studies; but the adventurous student will always study classics, in whatever language they may be written and however ancient they may be. For what are the classics but the noblest recorded thoughts of man? They are the only oracles which are not decayed, and there are such answers to the most modern inquiry in them as Delphi and Dodona never gave. We might as well omit to study Nature because she is old. To read well, that is, to read true books in a true spirit, is a noble exercise, and one that will task the reader more than any exercise which the customs of the day esteem. It requires a training such as the athletes underwent, the steady intention almost of the whole life to this object. Books must be read as deliberately and reservedly as they were written. It is not enough even to be able to speak the language of that nation by which they are written, for there is a memorable interval between the spoken and the written language, the language heard and the language read. The one is commonly transitory, a sound, a tongue, a dialect merely, almost brutish, and we learn it unconsciously, like the brutes, of our mothers. The other is the maturity and experience of that; if that is our mother tongue, this is our father tongue, a reserved and select expression, too significant to be heard by the ear, which we must be born again in order to speak. The crowds of men who merely spoke the Greek and Latin tongues in the Middle Ages were not entitled by the accident of birth to read the works of genius written in those languages; for these were not written in that Greek or Latin which they knew, but in the select language of literature. They had not learned the nobler dialects of Greece and Rome, but the very materials on which they were written were waste paper to them, and they prized instead a cheap contemporary literature. But when the several nations of Europe had acquired distinct though rude written languages of their own, sufficient for the purposes of their rising literatures, then first learning revived, and scholars were enabled to discern from that remoteness the treasures of antiquity. What the Roman and Grecian multitude could not hear, after the lapse of ages a few scholars read, and a few scholars only are still reading it.

However much we may admire the orator's occasional bursts of eloquence, the noblest written words are commonly as far behind or above the fleeting spoken language as the firmament with its stars is behind the clouds. There are the stars, and they who can may read them. The astronomers forever comment on and observe them. They are not exhalations like our daily colloquies and vaporous breath. What is called eloquence in the forum is commonly found to be rhetoric in the study. The orator yields to the inspiration of a transient occasion, and speaks to the mob before him, to those who can hear him; but the writer, whose more equable life is his occasion, and who would be distracted by the event and the crowd which inspire the orator, speaks to the intellect and health of mankind, to all in any age who can understand him.

No wonder that Alexander carried the *Iliad* with him on his expeditions in a precious casket. A written word is the choicest of relics. It is something at once more intimate with us and more universal than any other work of art. It is the work of art nearest to life itself. It may be translated into every language, and not only be read but actually breathed from all human lips;—not be represented on canvas or in marble only, but be carved out of the breath of life itself. The symbol of an ancient man's thought becomes a modern man's speech. Two thousand summers have imparted to the monuments of Grecian literature, as to her marbles, only a maturer golden and autumnal tint, for they have carried their own serene and celestial atmosphere into all lands to protect them against the corrosion of time. Books are the treasured wealth of the world and the fit inheritance of generations and nations. Books, the oldest and the best, stand naturally and rightfully on the shelves of every cottage. They have no cause of their own to plead, but while they enlighten and sustain the reader his common sense will not refuse them. Their authors are a natural and irresistible aristocracy in every society, and, more than kings or emperors, exert an influence on mankind. When the illiterate and perhaps scornful trader has earned by enterprise and industry his coveted leisure and independence, and is admitted to the circles of wealth and fashion, he turns inevitably at last to those still higher but yet inaccessible circles of intellect and genius, and is sensible only of the imperfection of his culture and the vanity and insufficiency of all his riches, and further proves his good sense by the pains which be takes to secure for his children that intellectual culture whose want he so keenly feels; and thus it is that he becomes the founder of a family.

Those who have not learned to read the ancient classics in the language in which they were written must have a very imperfect knowledge of the history of the human race; for it is remarkable that no transcript of them has ever been made into any modern tongue, unless our civilization itself may be regarded as such a transcript. Homer has never yet been printed in English, nor Aeschylus, nor Virgil even— works as refined, as solidly done, and as beautiful almost as the morning itself; for later writers, say what we will of their genius, have rarely, if ever, equalled the elaborate beauty and finish and the lifelong and heroic literary labors of the ancients. They only talk of forgetting them who never knew them. It will be soon enough to forget them when we have the learning and the genius which will enable us to attend to and appreciate them. That age will be rich indeed when those relics which we call Classics, and the still older and more than classic but even less known Scriptures of the nations, shall have still further accumulated, when the Vaticans shall be filled with Vedas and Zendavestas and Bibles, with Homers and Dantes and Shakespeares, and all the centuries to come shall have successively deposited their trophies in the forum of the world. By such a pile we may hope to scale heaven at last.

The works of the great poets have never yet been read by mankind, for only great poets can read them. They have only been read as the multitude read the stars, at most astrologically, not astronomically. Most men have learned to read to serve a paltry convenience, as they have learned to cipher in order to keep accounts and not be cheated in trade; but of reading as a noble intellectual exercise they know little or nothing; yet this only is reading, in a high sense, not that which lulls us as a luxury and suffers the nobler faculties to sleep the while, but what we have to stand on tiptoe to read and devote our most alert and wakeful hours to.

I think that having learned our letters we should read the best that is in literature, and not be forever repeating our a-b-abs, and words of one syllable, in the fourth or fifth classes, sitting on the lowest and foremost form all our lives. Most men are satisfied if they read or hear read, and perchance have been convicted by the wisdom of one good book, the Bible, and for the rest of their lives vegetate and dissipate their faculties in what is called easy reading. There is a work in several volumes in our Circulating Library entitled "Little Reading," which I thought referred to a town of that name which I had not been to. There are those who, like cormorants and ostriches, can digest all sorts of this, even after the fullest dinner of meats and vegetables, for they suffer nothing to be wasted. If others are the machines to provide this provender, they are the machines to read it. They read the nine thousandth tale about Zebulon and Sophronia, and how they loved as none had ever loved before, and neither did the course of their true love run smooth- at any rate, how it did run and stumble, and get up again and go on! how some poor unfortunate got up on to a steeple, who had better never have gone up as far as the belfry; and then, having needlessly got him up there, the happy novelist rings the bell for all the world to come together and hear, O dear! how he did get down again! For my part, I think that they had better metamorphose all such aspiring heroes of universal noveldom into man weather-cocks, as they used to put heroes among the constellations, and let them swing round there till they are rusty, and not come down at all to bother honest men with their pranks. The next time the novelist rings the bell I will not stir though the meeting-house burn down. "The Skip of the Tip-Toe-Hop, a Romance of the Middle Ages, by the celebrated author of 'Tittle-Tol-Tan,' to appear in monthly parts; a great rush; don't all come together."All this they read with saucer eyes, and erect and primitive curiosity, and with unwearied gizzard, whose corrugations even yet need no sharpening, just as some little four-year-old bencher his two-cent gilt-covered edition of Cinderella—without any improvement, that I can see, in the pronunciation, or accent, or emphasis, or any more skill in extracting or inserting the moral. The result is dulness of sight, a stagnation of the vital circulations, and a general deliquium and sloughing off of all the intellectual faculties. This sort of gingerbread is baked daily and more sedulously than pure wheat or rye-and-Indian in almost every oven, and finds a surer market.

The best books are not read even by those who are called good readers. What does our Concord culture amount to? There is in this town, with a very few exceptions, no taste for the best or for very good books even in English literature, whose words all can read and spell. Even the college-bred and so-called liberally educated men here and elsewhere have really little or no acquaintance with the English classics; and as for the recorded wisdom of mankind, the ancient classics and Bibles, which are accessible to all who will know of them, there are the feeblest efforts anywhere made to become acquainted with them. I know a woodchopper, of middle age, who takes a French paper, not for news as he says, for he is above that, but to "keep himself in practice," he being a Canadian by birth; and when I ask him what he considers the best thing he can do in this world, he says, beside this, to keep up and add to his English. This is about as much as the college-bred generally do or aspire to do, and they take an English paper for the purpose. One who has just come from reading perhaps one of the best English books will find how many with whom he can converse about it? Or suppose he comes from reading a Greek or Latin classic in the original, whose praises are familiar even to the so-called illiterate; he will find nobody at all to speak to, but must keep silence about it. Indeed, there is hardly the professor in our colleges, who, if he has mastered the difficulties of the language, has proportionally mastered the difficulties of the wit and poetry of a Greek poet, and has any sympathy to impart to the alert and heroic reader; and as for the sacred Scriptures, or Bibles of mankind, who in this town can tell me even their titles? Most men do not know that any nation but the Hebrews have had a scripture. A man, any man, will go considerably out of his way to pick up a silver dollar; but here are golden words, which the wisest men of antiquity have uttered, and whose worth the wise of every succeeding age have assured us of; —and yet we learn to read only as far as Easy Reading, the primers and class-books, and when we leave school, the "Little Reading," and story-books, which are for boys and beginners; and our reading, our conversation and thinking, are all on a very low level, worthy only of pygmies and manikins.

I aspire to be acquainted with wiser men than this our Concord soil has produced, whose names are hardly known here. Or shall I hear the name of Plato and never read his book? As if Plato were my townsman and I never saw him—my next neighbor and I never heard him speak or attended to the wisdom of his words. But how actually is it? His Dialogues, which contain what was immortal in him, lie on the next shelf, and yet I never read them. We are underbred and low-lived and illiterate; and in this respect I confess I do not make any very broad distinction between the illiterateness of my townsman who cannot read at all and the illiterateness of him who has learned to read only what is for children and feeble intellects. We should be as good as the worthies of antiquity, but partly by first knowing how good they were. We are a race of tit-men, and soar but little higher in our intellectual flights than the columns of the daily paper.

It is not all books that are as dull as their readers. There are probably words addressed to our condition exactly, which, if we could really bear and understand, would be more salutary than the morning or the spring to our lives, and possibly put a new aspect on the face of things for us. How many a man has dated a new era in his life from the reading of a book! The book exists for us, perchance, which will explain our miracles and reveal new ones. The at present unutterable things we may find somewhere uttered. These same questions that disturb and puzzle and confound us have in their turn occurred to all the wise men; not one has been omitted; and each has answered them, according to his ability, by his words and his life. Moreover, with wisdom we shall learn liberality. The solitary hired man on a farm in the outskirts of Concord, who has had his second birth and peculiar religious experience, and is driven as he believes into the silent gravity and exclusiveness by his faith, may think it is not true; but Zoroaster, thousands of years ago, travelled the same road and had the same experience; but he, being wise, knew it to be universal, and treated his neighbors accordingly, and is even said to have invented and established worship among men. Let him humbly commune with Zoroaster then, and through the liberalizing influence of all the worthies, with Jesus Christ himself, and let "our church"go by the board.

We boast that we belong to the Nineteenth Century and are making the most rapid strides of any nation. But consider how little this village does for its own culture. I do not wish to flatter my townsmen, nor to be flattered by them, for that will not advance either of us. We need to be provoked—goaded like oxen, as we are, into a trot. We have a comparatively decent system of common schools, schools for infants only; but excepting the half-starved Lyceum in the winter, and latterly the puny beginning of a library suggested by the State, no school for ourselves. We spend more on almost any article of bodily aliment or ailment than on our mental ailment. It is time that we had uncommon schools, that we did not leave off our education when we begin to be men and women. It is time that villages were universities, and their elder inhabitants the fellows of universities, with leisure—if they are, indeed, so well off- to pursue liberal studies the rest of their lives. Shall the world be confined to one Paris or one Oxford forever? Cannot students be boarded here and get a liberal education under the skies of Concord? Can we not hire some Abelard to lecture to us? Alas! what with foddering the cattle and tending the store, we are kept from school too long, and our education is sadly neglected. In this country, the village should in some respects take the place of the nobleman of Europe. It should be the patron of the fine arts. It is rich enough. It wants only the magnanimity and refinement. It can spend money enough on such things as farmers and traders value, but it is thought Utopian to propose spending money for things which more intelligent men know to be of far more worth. This town has spent seventeen thousand dollars on a town-house, thank fortune or politics, but probably it will not spend so much on living wit, the true meat to put into that shell, in a hundred years. The one hundred and twenty-five dollars annually subscribed for a

Lyceum in the winter is better spent than any other equal sum raised in the town. If we live in the Nineteenth Century, why should we not enjoy the advantages which the Nineteenth Century offers? Why should our life be in any respect provincial? If we will read newspapers, why not skip the gossip of Boston and take the best newspaper in the world at once?—not be sucking the pap of "neutral family"papers, or browsing "Olive Branches"here in New England. Let the reports of all the learned societies come to us, and we will see if they know anything. Why should we leave it to Harper & Brothers and Redding & Co. to select our reading? As the nobleman of cultivated taste surrounds himself with whatever conduces to his culture-genius-learning-wit-books-paintings-statuary-music-philosophical instruments, and the like; so let the village do—not stop short at a pedagogue, a parson, a sexton, a parish library, and three selectmen, because our Pilgrim forefathers got through a cold winter once on a bleak rock with these. To act collectively is according to the spirit of our institutions; and I am confident that, as our circumstances are more flourishing, our means are greater than the nobleman's. New England can hire all the wise men in the world to come and teach her, and board them round the while, and not be provincial at all. That is the uncommon school we want. Instead of noblemen, let us have noble villages of men. If it is necessary, omit one bridge over the river, go round a little there, and throw one arch at least over the darker gulf of ignorance which surrounds us.

But while we are confined to books, though the most select and classic, and read only particular written languages, which are themselves but dialects and provincial, we are in danger of forgetting the language which all things and events speak without metaphor, which alone is copious and standard. Much is published, but little printed. The rays which stream through the shutter will be no longer remembered when the shutter is wholly removed. No method nor discipline can supersede the necessity of being forever on the alert. What is a course of history or philosophy, or poetry, no matter how well selected, or the best society, or the most admirable routine of life, compared with the discipline of looking always at what is to be seen? Will you be a reader, a student merely, or a seer? Read your fate, see what is before you, and walk on into futurity.

I did not read books the first summer; I hoed beans. Nay, I often did better than this. There were times when I could not afford to sacrifice the bloom of the present moment to any work, whether of the head or hands. I love a broad margin to my life. Sometimes, in a summer morning, having taken my accustomed bath, I sat in my sunny doorway from sunrise till noon, rapt in a revery, amidst the pines and hickories and sumachs, in undisturbed solitude and stillness, while the birds sing around or flitted noiseless through the house, until by the sun falling in at my west window, or the noise of some traveller's wagon on the distant highway, I was reminded of the lapse of time. I grew in those seasons like corn in the night, and they were far better than any work of the hands would have been. They were not time subtracted from my life, but so much over and above my usual allowance. I realized what the Orientals mean by contemplation and the forsaking of works. For the most part, I minded not how the hours went. The day advanced as if to light some work of mine; it was morning, and lo, now it is evening, and nothing memorable is accomplished. Instead of singing like the birds, I silently smiled at my incessant good fortune. As the sparrow had its trill, sitting on the hickory before my door, so had I my chuckle or suppressed warble which he might hear out of my nest. My days were not days of the week, bearing the stamp of any heathen deity, nor were they minced into hours and fretted by the ticking of a clock; for I lived like the Puri Indians, of whom it is said that "for yesterday, today, and tomorrow they have only one word, and they express the variety of meaning by pointing backward for yesterday forward for tomorrow, and overhead for the passing day."This was sheer idleness to my fellow-townsmen, no doubt; but if the birds and flowers had tried me by their standard, I should not have been found wanting. A man must find his occasions in himself, it is true. The natural day is very calm, and will hardly reprove his indolence.

I had this advantage, at least, in my mode of life, over those who were obliged to look abroad for amusement, to society and the theatre, that my life itself was become my amusement and never ceased to be novel. It was a drama of many scenes and without an end. If we were always, indeed, getting our living, and regulating our lives according to the last and best mode we had learned, we should never be troubled with ennui. Follow your genius closely enough, and it will not fail to show you a fresh prospect every hour.

II A Little Cloud

James Joyce (1882–1941)

Eight years before he had seen his friend off at the North Wall and wished him godspeed. Gallaher had got on. You could tell that at once by his travelled air, his well-cut tweed suit, and fearless accent. Few fellows had talents like his and fewer still could remain unspoiled by such success. Gallaher's heart was in the right place and he had deserved to win. It was something to have a friend like that.

Little Chandler's thoughts ever since lunch-time had been of his meeting with Gallaher, of Gallaher's invitation and of the great city London where Gallaher lived. He was called Little Chandler because, though he was but slightly under the average stature, he gave one the idea of being a little man. His hands were white and small, his frame was fragile, his voice was quiet and his manners were refined. He took the greatest care of his fair silken hair and moustache and used perfume discreetly on his handkerchief. The half-moons of his nails were perfect and when he smiled you caught a glimpse of a row of childish white teeth.

As he sat at his desk in the King's Inns he thought what changes those eight years had brought. The friend whom he had known under a shabby and necessitous guise had become a brilliant figure on the London Press. He turned often from his tiresome writing to gaze out of the office window. The glow of a late autumn sunset covered the grass plots and walks. It cast a shower of kindly golden dust on the untidy nurses and decrepit old men who drowsed on the benches; it flickered upon all the moving figures—on the children who ran screaming along the gravel paths and on everyone who passed through the gardens. He watched the scene and thought of life; and (as always happened when he thought of life) he became sad. A gentle melancholy took possession of him. He felt how useless it was to struggle against fortune, this being the burden of wisdom which the ages had bequeathed to him.

He remembered the books of poetry upon his shelves at home. He had bought them in his bachelor days and many an evening, as he sat in the little room off the hall, he had been tempted to take one down from the bookshelf and read out something to his wife. But shyness had always held him back; and so the books had remained on their shelves. At times he repeated lines to himself and this consoled him.

When his hour had struck he stood up and took leave of his desk and of his fellow-clerks punctiliously. He emerged from under the feudal arch of the King's Inns, a neat modest figure, and walked swiftly down Henrietta Street. The golden sunset was waning and the air had grown sharp. A horde of grimy children populated the street. They stood or ran in the roadway or crawled up the steps before the gaping doors or squatted like mice upon the thresholds. Little Chandler gave them no thought. He picked his way deftly through all that minute vermin-like life and under the shadow of the gaunt spectral mansions in which the old nobility of Dublin had roystered. No memory of the past touched him, for his mind was full of a present joy.

He had never been in Corless's but he knew the value of the name. He knew that people went there after the theatre to eat oysters and drink liqueurs; and he had heard that the waiters there spoke French and German. Walking swiftly by at night he had seen cabs drawn up before the door and richly dressed ladies, escorted by cavaliers, alight and enter quickly. They wore noisy dresses and many wraps. Their faces were powdered and they caught up their dresses, when they touched earth, like alarmed Atalantas. He had always passed without turning his head to look. It was his habit to walk swiftly in the street even by day and whenever he found himself in the city late at night he hurried on his way apprehensively and excitedly. Sometimes, however, he courted the causes of his fear. He chose the darkest and narrowest streets and, as he walked boldly forward, the silence that was spread about his footsteps troubled him, the wandering, silent figures troubled him; and at times a sound of low fugitive laughter made him tremble like a leaf.

He turned to the right towards Capel Street. Ignatius Gallaher on the London Press! Who would have thought it possible eight years before? Still, now that he reviewed the past, Little Chandler could remember many signs of future greatness in his friend. People used to say that Ignatius Gallaher was wild. Of course, he did mix with a rakish set of fellows at that time, drank freely and borrowed money on all sides. In the end he had got mixed up in some shady affair, some money transaction: at least, that was one version of his flight. But nobody denied him talent. There was always a certain... something in Ignatius Gallaher that impressed you in spite of yourself. Even when he was out at elbows and at his wits' end for money he kept up a bold face. Little Chandler remembered (and the remembrance brought a slight flush of pride to his cheek) one of Ignatius Gallaher's sayings when he was in a tight corner:

"Half time now, boys," he used to say light-heartedly. "Where's my considering cap?"

That was Ignatius Gallaher all out; and, damn it, you couldn't but admire him for it.

Little Chandler quickened his pace. For the first time in his life he felt himself superior to the people he passed. For the first time his soul revolted against the dull inelegance of Capel Street. There was no doubt about it: if you wanted to succeed you had to go away. You could do nothing in Dublin. As he crossed Grattan Bridge he looked down the river towards the lower quays and pitied the poor stunted houses. They seemed to him a band of tramps, huddled together along the riverbanks, their old coats covered with dust and soot, stupefied by the panorama of sunset and waiting for the first chill of night bid them arise, shake themselves and begone. He wondered whether he could write a poem to express his idea. Perhaps Gallaher might be able to get it into some London paper for him. Could he write something original? He was not sure what idea he wished to express but the thought that a poetic moment had touched him took life within him like an infant hope. He stepped onward bravely.

Every step brought him nearer to London, farther from his own sober inartistic life. A light began to tremble on the horizon of his mind. He was not so old—thirty-two. His temperament might be said to be just at the point of maturity. There were so many different moods and impressions that he wished to express in verse. He felt them within him. He tried to weigh his soul to see if it was a poet's soul. Melancholy was the dominant note of his temperament, he thought, but it was a melancholy tempered by recurrences of faith and resignation and simple joy. If he could give expression to it in a book of poems perhaps men would listen. He would never be popular: he saw that. He could not sway the crowd but he might appeal to a little circle of kindred minds. The English critics, perhaps, would recognise him as one of the Celtic school by reason of the melancholy tone of his poems; besides that, he would put in allusions. He began to invent sentences and phrases from the notice which his book would get. "Mr. Chandler has the gift of easy and graceful verse."... "wistful sadness pervades these poems."... "The Celtic note."It was a pity his name was not more Irish-looking. Perhaps it would be better to insert his mother's name before the surname: Thomas Malone Chandler, or better still: T. Malone Chandler. He would speak to Gallaher about it.

He pursued his revery so ardently that he passed his street and had to turn back. As he came near Corless's his former agitation began to overmaster him and he halted before the door in indecision. Finally he opened the door and entered.

The light and noise of the bar held him at the doorways for a few moments. He looked about him, but his sight was confused by the shining of many red and green wine-glasses The bar seemed to him to be full of people and he felt that the people were observing him curiously. He glanced quickly to right and left (frowning slightly to make his errand appear serious), but when his sight cleared a little he saw that nobody had turned to look at him: and there, sure enough, was Ignatius Gallaher leaning with his back against the counter and his feet planted far apart.

"Hallo, Tommy, old hero, here you are! What is it to be? What will you have? I'm taking whisky: better stuff than we get across the water. Soda? Lithia? No mineral? I'm the same. Spoils the flavour.... Here, garcon, bring us two halves of malt whisky, like a good fellow.... Well, and how have you been pulling along since I saw you last? Dear God, how old we're getting! Do you see any signs of aging in me—eh, what? A little grey and thin on the top—what?"

Ignatius Gallaher took off his hat and displayed a large closely cropped head. His face was heavy, pale and cleanshaven. His eyes, which were of bluish slate-colour, relieved his unhealthy pallor and shone out plainly above the vivid orange tie he wore. Between these rival features the lips appeared very long and shapeless and colourless. He bent his head and felt with two sympathetic fingers the thin hair at the crown. Little Chandler shook his head as a denial. Ignatius Galaher put on his hat again.

"It pulls you down," he said. "Press life. Always hurry and scurry, looking for copy and sometimes not finding it: and then, always to have something new in your stuff. Damn proofs and printers, I say, for a few days. I'm deuced glad, I can tell you, to get back to the old country. Does a fellow good, a bit of a holiday. I feel a ton better since I landed again in dear dirty Dublin.... Here you are, Tommy. Water? Say when."

Little Chandler allowed his whisky to be very much diluted.

"You don't know what's good for you, my boy," said Ignatius Gallaher. "I drink mine neat."

"I drink very little as a rule," said Little Chandler modestly. "An odd half-one or so when I meet any of the old crowd: that's all."

"Ah well," said Ignatius Gallaher, cheerfully, "here's to us and to old times and old acquaintance."

They clinked glasses and drank the toast.

"I met some of the old gang today," said Ignatius Gallaher. "O'Hara seems to be in a bad way. What's he doing?"

"Nothing," said Little Chandler. "He's gone to the dogs."

"But Hogan has a good sit, hasn't he?"

"Yes; he's in the Land Commission."

"I met him one night in London and he seemed to be very flush.... Poor O'Hara! Boose, I suppose?"

"Other things, too," said Little Chandler shortly.

Ignatius Gallaher laughed.

"Tommy," he said, "I see you haven't changed an atom. You're the very same serious person that used to lecture me on Sunday mornings when I had a sore head and a fur on my tongue. You'd want to knock about a bit in the world. Have you never been anywhere even for a trip?"

"I've been to the Isle of Man," said Little Chandler.

Ignatius Gallaher laughed.

"The Isle of Man!"he said. "Go to London or Paris: Paris, for choice. That'd do you good."

"Have you seen Paris?"

"I should think I have! I've knocked about there a little."

"And is it really so beautiful as they say?"asked Little Chandler.

He sipped a little of his drink while Ignatius Gallaher finished his boldly.

"Beautiful?"said Ignatius Gallaher, pausing on the word and on the flavour of his drink. "It's not so beautiful, you know. Of course, it is beautiful... But it's the life of Paris; that's the thing. Ah, there's no city like Paris for gaiety, movement, excitement..."

Little Chandler finished his whisky and, after some trouble, succeeded in catching the barman's eye. He ordered the same again.

"I've been to the Moulin Rouge," Ignatius Gallaher continued when the barman had removed their glasses, "and I've been to all the Bohemian cafes. Hot stuff! Not for a pious chap like you, Tommy."

Little Chandler said nothing until the barman returned with two glasses: then he touched his friend's glass lightly and reciprocated the former toast. He was beginning to feel somewhat disillusioned. Gallaher's accent and way of expressing himself did not please him. There was something vulgar in his friend which he had not observed before. But perhaps it was only the result of living in London amid the bustle and competition of the Press. The old personal charm was still there under this new gaudy manner. And, after all, Gallaher had lived, he had seen the world. Little Chandler looked at his friend enviously.

"Everything in Paris is gay," said Ignatius Gallaher. "They believe in enjoying life—and don't you think they're right? If you want to enjoy yourself properly you must go to Paris. And, mind you, they've a great feeling for the Irish there. When they heard I was from Ireland they were ready to eat me, man."

Little Chandler took four or five sips from his glass.

"Tell me," he said, "is it true that Paris is so... immoral as they say?"

Ignatius Gallaher made a catholic gesture with his right arm.

"Every place is immoral," he said. "Of course you do find spicy bits in Paris. Go to one of the students' balls, for instance. That's lively, if you like, when the cocottes begin to let themselves loose. You know what they are, I suppose?"

"I've heard of them," said Little Chandler.

Ignatius Gallaher drank off his whisky and shook his head.

"Ah," he said, "you may say what you like. There's no woman like the Parisienne—for style, for go."

"Then it is an immoral city," said Little Chandler, with timid insistence—"I mean, compared with London or Dublin?"

"London!"said Ignatius Gallaher. "It's six of one and half-a-dozen of the other. You ask Hogan, my boy. I showed him a bit about London when he was over there. He'd open your eye... I say, Tommy, don't make punch of that whisky: liquor up."

"No, really..."

"O, come on, another one won't do you any harm. What is it? The same again, I suppose?"

"Well... all right."

"Francois, the same again... Will you smoke, Tommy?"

Ignatius Gallaher produced his cigar-case. The two friends lit their cigars and puffed at them in silence until their drinks were served.

"I'll tell you my opinion," said Ignatius Gallaher, emerging after some time from the clouds of smoke in which he had taken refuge, "it's a rum world. Talk of immorality! I've heard of cases—what am I saying?—I've known them: cases of... immorality..."

Ignatius Gallaher puffed thoughtfully at his cigar and then, in a calm historian's tone, he proceeded to sketch for his friend some pictures of the corruption which was rife abroad. He summarised the vices of many capitals and seemed inclined to award the palm to Berlin. Some things he could not vouch for (his friends had told him), but of others he had had personal experience. He spared neither rank nor caste. He revealed many of the secrets of religious houses on the Continent and described some of the practices which were fashionable in high society and ended by telling, with details, a story about an English duchess—a story which he knew to be true. Little Chandler was astonished.

"Ah, well," said Ignatius Gallaher, "here we are in old jog-along Dublin where nothing is known of such things."

"How dull you must find it," said Little Chandler, "after all the other places you've seen!"

"Well," said Ignatius Gallaher, "it's a relaxation to come over here, you know. And, after all, it's the old country, as they say, isn't it? You can't help having a certain feeling for it. That's human nature... But tell me something about yourself. Hogan told me you had... tasted the joys of connubial bliss. Two years ago, wasn't it?"

Little Chandler blushed and smiled.

"Yes," he said. "I was married last May twelve months."

"I hope it's not too late in the day to offer my best wishes," said Ignatius Gallaher. "I didn't know your address or I'd have done so at the time."

He extended his hand, which Little Chandler took.

"Well, Tommy," he said, "I wish you and yours every joy in life, old chap, and tons of money, and may you never die till I shoot you. And that's the wish of a sincere friend, an old friend. You know that?"

"I know that," said Little Chandler.

"Any youngsters?" said Ignatius Gallaher.

Little Chandler blushed again.

"We have one child," he said.

"Son or daughter?"

"A little boy."

Ignatius Gallaher slapped his friend sonorously on the back.

"Bravo," he said, "I wouldn't doubt you, Tommy."

Little Chandler smiled, looked confusedly at his glass and bit his lower lip with three childishly white front teeth.

"I hope you'll spend an evening with us," he said, "before you go back. My wife will be delighted to meet you. We can have a little music and——"

"Thanks awfully, old chap," said Ignatius Gallaher, "I'm sorry we didn't meet earlier. But I must leave tomorrow night."

"Tonight, perhaps...?"

"I'm awfully sorry, old man. You see I'm over here with another fellow, clever young chap he is too, and we arranged to go to a little card-party. Only for that..."

"O, in that case ..."

"But who knows?" said Ignatius Gallaher considerately. "Next year I may take a little skip over here now that I've broken the ice. It's only a pleasure deferred."

"Very well," said Little Chandler, "the next time you come we must have an evening together. That's agreed now, isn't it?"

"Yes, that's agreed," said Ignatius Gallaher. "Next year if I come, parole d'honneur."

"And to clinch the bargain," said Little Chandler, "we'll just have one more now."

Ignatius Gallaher took out a large gold watch and looked at it.

"Is it to be the last?" he said. "Because you know, I have an a.p."

"O, yes, positively," said Little Chandler.

"Very well, then," said Ignatius Gallaher, "let us have another one as a deoc an doruis—that's good vernacular for a small whisky, I believe."

Little Chandler ordered the drinks. The blush which had risen to his face a few moments before was establishing itself. A trifle made him blush at any time: and now he felt warm and excited. Three small whiskies had gone to his head and Gallaher's strong cigar had confused his mind, for he was a delicate and abstinent person. The adventure of meeting Gallaher after eight years, of finding himself with Gallaher in Corless's surrounded by lights and noise, of listening to Gallaher's stories and of sharing for a brief space Gallaher's vagrant and triumphant life, upset the equipoise of his sensitive nature. He felt acutely the contrast between his own life and his friend's and it seemed to him unjust. Gallaher was his inferior in birth and education. He was sure that he could do something better than his friend had ever done, or could ever do, something higher than mere tawdry journalism if he only got the chance. What was it that stood in his way? His unfortunate timidity! He wished to vindicate himself in some way, to assert his manhood. He saw behind Gallaher's refusal of his invitation. Gallaher was only patronising him by his friendliness just as he was patronising Ireland by his visit.

The barman brought their drinks. Little Chandler pushed one glass towards his friend and took up the other boldly.

"Who knows?" he said, as they lifted their glasses. "When you come next year I may have the pleasure of wishing long life and happiness to Mr. and Mrs. Ignatius Gallaher."

Ignatius Gallaher in the act of drinking closed one eye expressively over the rim of his glass. When he had drunk he smacked his lips decisivcly, set down his glass and said, "No blooming fear of that, my boy. I'm going to have my fling first and see a bit of life and the world before I put my head in the sack—if I ever do."

"Some day you will," said Little Chandler calmly.

Ignatius Gallaher turned his orange tie and slate-blue eyes full upon his friend.

"You think so?" he said.

"You'll put your head in the sack," repeated Little Chandler stoutly, "like everyone else if you can find the girl."

He had slightly emphasised his tone and he was aware that he had betrayed himself; but, though the colour had heightened in his cheek, he did not flinch from his friend's gaze. Ignatius Gallaher watched him for a few moments and then said:

"If ever it occurs, you may bet your bottom dollar there'll be no mooning and spooning about it. I mean to marry money. She'll have a good fat account at the bank or she won't do for me."

Little Chandler shook his head.

"Why, man alive," said Ignatius Gallaher, vehemently, "do you know what it is? I've only to say the word and tomorrow I can have the woman and the cash. You don't believe it? Well, I know it. There are hundreds—what am I saying?—thousands of rich Germans and Jews, rotten with money, that'd only be too glad... You wait a while my boy. See if I don't play my cards properly. When I go about a thing I mean business, I tell you. You just wait."

He tossed his glass to his mouth, finished his drink and laughed loudly. Then he looked thoughtfully before him and said in a calmer tone: "But I'm in no hurry. They can wait. I don't fancy tying myself up to one woman, you know."

He imitated with his mouth the act of tasting and made a wry face.

"Must get a bit stale, I should think, " he said.

Little Chandler sat in the room off the hall, holding a child in his arms. To save money they kept no servant but Annie's young sister Monica came for an hour or so in the morning and an hour or so in the evening to help. But Monica had gone home long ago. It was a quarter to nine. Little Chandler had come home late for tea and, moreover, he had forgotten to bring Annie home the parcel of coffee from Bewley's. Of course she was in a bad humour and gave him short answers. She said she would do without any tea but when it came near the time at which the shop at the corner closed she decided to go out herself for a quarter of a pound of tea and two pounds of sugar. She put the sleeping child deftly in his arms and said, "Here. Don't waken him."

A little lamp with a white china shade stood upon the table and its light fell over a photograph which was enclosed in a frame of crumpled horn. It was Annie's photograph. Little Chandler looked at it, pausing at the thin tight lips. She wore the pale blue summer blouse which he had brought her home as a present one Saturday. It had cost him ten and elevenpence; but what an agony of nervousness it had cost him! How he had suffered that day, waiting at the shop door until the shop was empty, standing at the counter and trying to appear at his ease while the girl piled ladies' blouses before him, paying at the desk and forgetting to take up the odd penny of his change, being called back by the cashier, and finally, striving to hide his blushes as he left the shop by examining the parcel to see if it was securely tied. When he brought the blouse home Annie kissed him and said it was very pretty and stylish; but when she heard the price she threw the blouse on the table and said it was a regular swindle to charge ten and elevenpence for it. At first she wanted to take it back but when she tried it on she was delighted with it, especially with the make of the sleeves, and kissed him and said he was very good to think of her.

Hm!...

He looked coldly into the eyes of the photograph and they answered coldly. Certainly they were pretty and the face itself was pretty. But he found something mean in it. Why was it so unconscious and ladylike? The composure of the eyes irritated him. They repelled him and defied him: there was no passion in them, no rapture. He thought of what Gallaher had said about rich Jewesses. Those dark Oriental eyes, he thought, how full they are of passion, of voluptuous longing!... Why had he married the eyes in the photograph?

He caught himself up at the question and glanced nervously round the room. He found something mean in the pretty furniture which he had bought for his house on the hire system. Annie had chosen it herself and it reminded him of her. It too was prim and pretty. A dull resentment against his life awoke within him. Could he not escape from his little house? Was it too late for him to try to live bravely like Gallaher? Could he go to London? There was the furniture still to be paid for. If he could only write a book and get it published, that might open the way for him.

A volume of Byron's poems lay before him on the table. He opened it cautiously with his left hand lest he should waken the child and began to read the first poem in the book:

> Hushed are the winds and still the evening gloom,
> Not e'en a Zephyr wanders through the grove,
> Whilst I return to view my Margaret's tomb
> And scatter flowers on the dust I love.

He paused. He felt the rhythm of the verse about him in the room. How melancholy it was! Could he, too, write like that, express the melancholy of his soul in verse? There were so many things he wanted to describe: his sensation of a few hours before on Grattan Bridge, for example. If he could get back again into that mood...

The child awoke and began to cry. He turned from the page and tried to hush it: but it would not be hushed. He began to rock it to and fro in his arms but its wailing cry grew keener. He rocked it faster while his eyes began to read the second stanza:

Within this narrow cell reclines her clay,
That clay where once...

It was useless. He couldn't read. He couldn't do anything. The wailing of the child pierced the drum of his ear. It was useless, useless! He was a prisoner for life. His arms trembled with anger and suddenly bending to the child's face he shouted, "Stop!"

The child stopped for an instant, had a spasm of fright and began to scream. He jumped up from his chair and walked hastily up and down the room with the child in his arms. It began to sob piteously, losing its breath for four or five seconds, and then bursting out anew. The thin walls of the room echoed the sound. He tried to soothe it but it sobbed more convulsively. He looked at the contracted and quivering face of the child and began to be alarmed. He counted seven sobs without a break between them and caught the child to his breast in fright. If it died!...

The door was burst open and a young woman ran in, panting.

"What is it? What is it?" she cried.

The child, hearing its mother's voice, broke out into a paroxysm of sobbing.

"It's nothing, Annie... it's nothing... He began to cry..."

She flung her parcels on the floor and snatched the child from him.

"What have you done to him?"she cried, glaring into his face.

Little Chandler sustained for one moment the gaze of her eyes and his heart closed together as he met the hatred in them. He began to stammer:

"It's nothing... He... he began to cry... I couldn't... I didn't do anything... What?"

Giving no heed to him she began to walk up and down the room, clasping the child tightly in her arms and murmuring:

"My little man! My little mannie! Was 'ou frightened, love?... There now, love! There now!... Lambabaun! Mamma's little lamb of the world!... There now!"

Little Chandler felt his cheeks suffused with shame and he stood back out of the lamplight. He listened while the paroxysm of the child's sobbing grew less and less; and tears of remorse started to his eyes.

Topics for Discussion

1. Is *Walden* a book of Thoreau's self-reflection? Why?
2. How do you judge Thoreau's self-image in *Walden*?
3. How does Joyce depict Little Chandler's journey toward self-discovery in "A Little Cloud"?
4. What role does Ignatius Gallaher play in Little Chandler's self-discovery?
5. Are the self-images in *Walden* and "A Little Cloud" purely of Thoreau and Little Chandler as individuals?
6. Give more literary examples with contemplations on the Self.